O9-BSU-186

PAPER STAR

ALSO BY MARY-ROSE HAYES

The Neighbors

The Caller

The Yacht People

The Winter Women

Amethyst

PAPER STAR

by

Mary-Rose Hayes

A DUTTON BOOK

For Ellen Levine, my agent, with thanks as always.

DUTTON
Published by the Penguin Group
Penguin Books USA Inc., 375 Hudson Street,
New York, New York 10014, U.S.A.
Penguin Books Ltd, 27 Wrights Lane,
London W8 5TZ, England
Penguin Books Australia Ltd, Ringwood,
Victoria, Australia
Penguin Books Canada Ltd, 2801 John Street,
Markham, Ontario, Canada L3R 1B4
Penguin Books (N.Z.) Ltd, 182–190 Wairau Road,
Auckland 10, New Zealand

Penguin Books Ltd, Registered Offices:
Harmondsworth, Middlesex, England

First published by Dutton, an imprint of New American Library, a
division of Penguin Books USA Inc.
Distributed in Canada by McClelland & Stewart Inc.

First Printing, May, 1991
10 9 8 7 6 5 4 3 2 1

Copyright © Mary-Rose Hayes, 1991
All rights reserved

 REGISTERED TRADEMARK—MARCA REGISTRADA

LIBRARY OF CONGRESS CATALOGING IN PUBLICATION DATA:
Hayes, Mary-Rose.
    Paper star / Mary-Rose Hayes.
      p.   cm.
    I. Title.
    ISBN : 0-5 25-2 4975-3
  PR6058.A982P37   1991
823'.914—dc20   90–19682
                                                  CIP

Printed in the United States of America

PUBLISHER'S NOTE
This is a work of fiction. Names, characters, places, and incidents either are the products of the
author's imagination or are used fictitiously, and any resemblance to actual persons, living or
dead, events, or locales is entirely coincidental.

Without limiting the rights under copyright reserved above, no part of this publication may be
reproduced, stored in or introduced into a retrieval system, or transmitted, in any form, or by
any means (electronic, mechanical, photocopying, recording, or otherwise), without the prior
written permission of both the copyright owner and the above publisher of this book.

Prologue

1989

The bay was a perfect horseshoe, its sides steeply forested, the small fishing village of La Playita nestling behind the golden sandbar at the mouth of the Río Verde.

It was an idyllic place, tropical and languid and untainted by the world, an Eden on the west coast of Mexico.

The bay was discovered for the first time in the seventeenth century by Spaniards who officially named it Bahía Herradura in recognition of its shape, found it disappointingly exposed to the strong northwest swells, and soon abandoned it.

The next time wasn't until 1972, when a Venezuelan oil billionaire, captivated by the wild beauty of the place, visualized La Playita as the site for the ultimate chic resort.

The village had not changed much in three hundred years, the population had increased relatively little and continued to live in a state of cheerfully corrupt anarchy, catching fish and farming the steep volcanic soil.

Only the cantina and the grocery store had electricity, which was provided by two private generators. The water supply was murky in color and arrived intermittently through a tortuous network of rusted galvanized piping, requiring twenty minutes' boiling before it was safe to drink. There were no telephones, no cars, no streets, no drains.

The village was still cut off from the outside world by twenty-five kilometers of mountain and jungle, the terrain pleated by precipitous barrancas and bisected by the turbulent waters of the Río Verde, and although a fierce Catholicism had arrived long ago with the Spaniards, the inhabitants had merely grafted Jesus Christ and the Virgin Mary onto their own gallery of deities and demons. These included Xichamorro, a huge legless dog which screamed like a woman, and Chirihuatetl, pale-haired witch-goddess from the sea. Those unfortunate enough to see or hear Xichamorro would die before morning; the man who bedded Chirihuatetl would be forever sexually insatiable and grow an organ like a stallion. Or so it was said.

The only minor difference in three hundred years was a certain new prosperity: in addition to fruit and wild rice, the farmers grew a high-grade marijuana in hidden plots in the hills, which they sold to the tourists who arrived twice weekly on a little cruise boat from Puerto Vallarta.

In 1972, however, a bone-jarring corkscrew of a road was laid and for several years the barrancas reverberated with the rumble of trucks carrying gravel, lumber, pipe, sheet metal, spools of telephone wire, bathroom fixtures, refrigerators, and furniture to La Playita.

The hotel began to take shape, its adobe guest cottages rambling up the hillside connected by a maze of terraces and stairways overhung with flowering shrubbery. A swimming pool was excavated from living rock. The restaurant, under the direction of a master chef, was a romantic haven commanding a spectacular view of jungle, cliff, and ocean.

La Playita opened in 1976 and became an overnight sensation, the grand-opening party making headlines around the world. La Playita was the "in" spot, the ultimate in secluded luxury. It lasted most of one season, by which time the dream had become a nightmare.

The water ran out in March and the electric generator gave up the unequal struggle against insuperable demands. The laundry went unwashed. The food spoiled. Most of the imported staff, including the chef, deserted the sinking ship.

During the summer, heavy rains washed out a section of the road and a raging windstorm knocked out the telephone lines.

The resort, battered and patched up, reopened at Thanksgiving but was closed again before Christmas.

The following May a hurricane demolished the new bridge. The villagers once again waded across the Río Verde at low tide and crossed at high tide by dugout canoe.

The hotel went on the market. There were no offers.

The untended swimming pool cracked and drained. The palapa roofs of the cottages blew away or rotted. A mysterious fire destroyed the restaurant. The jungle, enhanced by all the newly planted and well-nourished shrubbery, grew in a riotous tangle over the steps, paths, and walls until the buildings were almost completely lost, their new tenants snakes, rodents, insects, and, occasionally, Royal Gutiérrez, a yellow-eyed mestizo who grew marijuana upriver.

The villagers were afraid of Royal, never without a razor-sharp machete swinging at his hip, who suffered bouts of madness each full moon.

Nobody went up those crumbling steps anymore, or braved the littered, ruined rooms, although some sheltered their animals behind the charred walls of the restaurant. The road over the mountain to the main highway eroded more each year and La Playita returned to its normal torpor until its discovery by Victor Diamond, who had heard of it and came on a boat from Puerto Vallarta to see it.

He was captivated, as he had suspected he might be, by the ruined grandeur of the place, visualizing it as a perfect location for his film *Starfire II*.

The road was repaired and resurfaced in record time, once again trucks thundered over the mountains, the bridge was rebuilt over the Río Verde, and various extraordinary edifices in the jungle too, including a pre-Columbian ruin built entirely of Styrofoam blocks, which looked more authentic than the real ruin upriver.

Electric generators arrived on flatbed trucks, and trailers with satellite dishes on their roofs. Seaplanes roared in and out in the mornings before the afternoon thunderstorms; large yachts bobbed in the bay in the uneasy swell. There was work for everybody who wanted it, and the marijuana growers upriver did a roaring trade.

It was boomtime all over again. La Playita was once again briefly connected to the rest of the world. The gringos were back, and what excitement, what a spectacle! There would be gossip for decades; new legends would be born:

About Vera, the artist who drew the children's portraits, whom they liked.

About Arnie, the movie star, so famous and so troubled, whom they pitied.

The writer known as Saint, the hero who had survived torture in the infamous Santa Paula prison, whom they admired.

Starfire, the strangest woman they had ever seen, who arrived riding a bird from the sea, so pale, so beautiful, whom many thought to be an incarnation of Chirihuatetl herself.

And then there was Victor Diamond, the kingly Hollywood producer, who—so said Father Ignacio, who was ninety-two and whose Catholicism had become inextricably tangled with pagan influences, along with everybody else's—was clearly possessed of the evil eye. Diamond they feared. He must have such power, they argued, to keep Chirihuatetl his prisoner.

PART ONE

Part One

Chapter

I

1979

Vera Brown sat at her desk blocking out Sunday's cartoon strip. The strip was called *The Adventures of Diana Starr*. Diana was a London party girl. Vera didn't exactly know what a London party girl was, but it sounded exciting, glamorous, and headstrong—everything which Vera herself was not.

Diana was seventeen, Vera's age, but that was all they had in common. Diana was tall, slender, with a tiny waist and high breasts. Her hair was a tumbling blond mane. She was quite beautiful; or she would be when Vera finally settled on a face for her, and she was a very trendy dresser, always wearing a different outfit, today's a black leather miniskirt, high-heeled boots, and a satin blouse with a daringly low-cut neckline; the kind of clothes which Vera herself would love to own, would not be allowed to buy, and would never in any case dare wear.

In the fourth and final panel Diana stood with hand on hip, innocently provocative, outside a huge mansion with pillars and cupolas, gables and tiers of glittering windows. A few deft pen strokes and Vera suggested a line of opulent cars drawn up in the driveway—Rolls-Royce and Jaguar were the easiest to profile. Diana was planning to crash the twenty-first birthday party given by Lord Adolphus Kreesos, magnate and billionaire, for his handsome son Alexander.

Vera had been developing *The Adventures of Diana Starr* for a month and was proud of the strip; it seemed very professional, with just the right balance between light and dark, close-up, long shot, and silhouette. A little more work and surely it would be good enough to submit to the *Daily Mirror* or the *Express*. If only she could get Diana's face *right*.

Vera had tried again and again, but now, as always, Diana's real features eluded her, although she knew that somewhere the real Diana was waiting; she could almost see her. Meantime, Vera's own face stubbornly emerged, which was wrong. Even glamorized, her own face would never do for Diana.

Diana was rich, stylish, and beautiful. She lived alone in the Mayfair flat which had been left her when her dashing, handsome parents were killed in a plane crash over the Atlas Mountains. She certainly didn't live with an aging Mum and Dad in a painfully genteel little suburban house in Orpington, Kent.

Everything Diana did was glamorous. She rose late and drank black coffee for breakfast. She spent the afternoon shopping at Harrods or Fortnum and Mason, browsing through art galleries, attending high-price auctions at Sotheby's, or being photographed for the social pages in the papers. In the evening she drank champagne at the Ritz Hotel and went to beautiful parties with a sequence of dashing men. She made impromptu flights to the south of France or drove her Aston Martin at breakneck speed on the motorway. The only thing Diana never appeared to do was eat, which was why she was so slim.

Not like Vera, who was overweight. Very overweight.

Teenage appetite, Mum said; but, "Vera should be on a diet," Dr. Wheeler said.

Dr. Wheeler was half-American and Mum mistrusted Americans on principle. Conveniently ignoring the fact that his father had been English, and also a doctor: "Dieting's an *obsession* with Americans!" And to Dr. Wheeler himself: "She'll fine down. It's just puppy fat."

Vera liked Dr. Wheeler. She liked his friendliness, his informality, his easy laugh. She especially liked the way he thought of her as a whole person, how she thought and felt, not just as an unfortunately overweight body.

"What's the book?" he'd asked one afternoon, finding her quietly engrossed in the waiting room.

Vera showed him. *Under the Volcano*, by Malcolm Lowry. "Good Lord,"

Dr. Wheeler said, and studied her with new interest. "What do think of it?"

"I don't really understand it," Vera said, "but it doesn't matter much. I like it, and it's so . . . " She groped for the right word and settled for ". . . so different from *here*."

After that they talked about books much more than the routine teenage problems Mum thought so important. He asked if she ever thought of being a writer herself. Vera shook her head. Perhaps, Dr. Wheeler suggested, she might think about it. Did she keep a diary? That was a good beginning.

"Not in writing. I draw my diary," Vera said, which was the first time she confided in anyone about her cartoons.

Mum increasingly loathed Dr. Wheeler and what she considered his growing influence over Vera. "You watch out, young lady—that man has designs. They're all the same, Americans." With sinister implication: "He's not only American, he comes from *California*," for in Mum's mind California was synonymous with Hollywood, which might as well be a combination of Sodom and Gomorrah. Thank goodness he wouldn't be here much longer; within two years, three, surely five at the very most, he would be returning where he came from, and good riddance.

Now, as if on cue, Mum's voice called, "Tea's ready, dear."

"Oh, hell!" cried Vera, and flung down her pen in despair. She dreaded teatime. Each day she would swear to herself she would just nibble on a water biscuit; each day she gave in. Dad, who was an invalid, got up for tea, and Mum made a little ceremony of it.

There she would sit, changed into her best brown-and-white wool and the gray cable-knit cardigan, pouring out Earl Grey from the silver teapot that had belonged to Grandmother, endlessly passing buttered crumpets, sandwiches, rich cookies, and cake to Vera on her left and to Dad on her right.

Vera would eat and eat. Concentrating on food helped her not listen to Dad describe his day and to Mum's little cries of sympathy. Dad suffered from high blood pressure, insomnia, lung congestion, a spastic colon, and various traveling aches and pains. Except for teatimes he lived in a hospital bed in the downstairs back room surrounded by medical paraphernalia.

Vera couldn't share Mum's preoccupation with Dad's health, to her shame and guilt found herself increasingly revolted by the parade of ailments, and sought comfort in food. Today, as always, she ate with a hopeless insatiability.

After tea Dad returned to his room as usual to take his temperature and blood pressure and record the results in his diary. He would phone Dr. Wheeler's office in the morning to report. The nurse would receive the news politely but without marked enthusiasm. In Mum's opinion she was as callous as Dr. Wheeler himself.

Vera helped Mum wash the dishes and begin to prepare for supper. Then she went to her room too. She had an hour of free time before helping Dad prepare for his bath and remaking his bed with clean sheets.

She glanced at the artwork on her desk, at Diana Starr strutting gaily in front of Lord Adolphus' mansion and gazing at the world through Vera's own eyes.

She began to take off her clothes, pausing once to turn the artwork upside down, suddenly painfully self-conscious. What would Diana think of her?

Then she stared at her naked reflection with despair. At the young breasts buried in swaths of fat; the layers of stomach; the thick marbled thighs. She began to cry. How Diana would despise her. But what was she to do?

Vera didn't understand, herself, why she was driven to eat—even when she wasn't hungry.

Miserably she opened her bureau drawer where she kept emergency supplies hidden under her neat pile of cotton blouses. She tore the wrapper off a Mars bar and ate it all, cramming it into her mouth, staring at herself in the mirror the whole time, watching the chocolate smear on her lips, blur with the tears, and trickle in small brown rivulets down her chin.

She didn't like herself. She didn't want to be Vera Brown. If only, only she could be Diana. Vera knew she'd give her soul to spend one day as Diana Starr.

The Treadwell Communications Network occupied a forty-story black marble building on Madison Avenue.

The twenty-foot-high main entrance, doors of bronze and two-inch-thick glass topped with a neoclassical pediment, led into a lofty marble lobby frantic with people in motion between the banks of elevators and the doors.

Reception for the executive suites was on the thirty-ninth floor, a plush upholstered arena of pearl gray where the phones and the elevators chimed on different notes in concert with soothing piped music.

At three o'clock that afternoon the elevator doors hushed open to release a teenage boy with shoulder-length black hair. He was a handsome boy, with finely chiseled features and intense dark eyes. His deep tan stood out like an accusation among the pallid winter New York faces.

He sauntered with a graceful stride up to the reception desk, a freeform slab of Lucite and gray Formica. The receptionist, a woman in her thirties, was lacquered, frosted, and enameled and might, he thought, have been delivered along with the desk as part of the set.

He told her, "I'd like to see Mr. Treadwell, please." And, as though she might not be familiar with the name of the president of her company, "Mr. Sloane St. John Treadwell."

The receptionist smiled a professional red-lipped smile. "Yes, sir. I'll see if he's in. What name should I give?"

"Tell him his son."

"Take a seat, please." She picked up a white phone and tapped in a number. "Mr. Treadwell's son is here."

The boy did not take a seat as ordered but loomed over her impatiently, shifting his weight from foot to foot.

The receptionist replaced the receiver. "I'm sorry. He's in conference right now. Miss Gerrity said . . ." Same story. He had heard it many times before. The president of Treadwell Communications was interrupted by nobody when in conference, especially by family members for their inevitably trivial reasons. But this time was different. It was shatteringly important. His father would find out soon enough.

The boy tugged a well-worn envelope from the tight pocket of his jeans. "I don't want Miss Gerrity. I need to see my father personally."

"No, sir." The receptionist flung out a restraining hand. "She said to wait here. She'll be down in just a minute."

"Never mind. I know the way."

He marched toward the closed door which led to a passage, a private elevator, and his father's penthouse office on the fortieth floor.

He wrenched at the handle, which did not give.

"Hey," the boy cried, "it's locked."

"Yes, Mr. Treadwell."

He made himself say politely, "Can you please open it for me?"

"I'm sorry, Mr. Treadwell. I can't do that." The receptionist made a smile shape on her mouth and suggested, "Perhaps you'd like to read a magazine while you wait," adding placatingly, "we have *Rolling Stone* . . ."

He felt an angry flush rise up his neck. They wouldn't let him in. He couldn't believe it, not today of all days. Didn't they understand what had happened?

"Miss Gerrity will be down directly." And again, "Please sit down."

The boy opened his mouth to make furious rebuttal, then with visible effort calmed himself. Okay, cool it. He'd behave himself—for now. He knew Gerrity disliked him and regarded him as a troublemaker, but she was his father's private secretary and punctilious in her duties. She would have to show his father the letter. And then Sloane St. John Treadwell Sr. would understand everything.

He walked stiffly across reception to the seating area and flung himself into one of the gray velvet armchairs placed around a circular glass table. Upon the table was a white ceramic pot of white cyclamens bedded in moss. Around the pot, industry and general-interest magazines were arranged in neat rows with precisely aligned corners.

He sighed ostentatiously, crossed one leg over the other, leaned his head against the soft chair back, and stared fixedly up at the recessed ceiling lights; a moment later he hunched forward, poised on the edge of the seat, hands dangling between his knees. He didn't look at *Rolling Stone* magazine but took the letter out of its soiled envelope and read it intently yet again.

Miss Gerrity arrived five minutes later, a middle-aged, trim woman wearing a neat navy suit over a white blouse with floppy bow. "My goodness, Junior! What a surprise."

The boy stood up precipitately. His nostrils flared with irritation. He hated to be called Junior. He made himself say politely, "Good afternoon, Miss Gerrity."

She veered at once to the attack. "What are you doing in New York?"

"I want to see my father."

"Your father's a busy man. And he wasn't expecting you. Why aren't you in school?"

"Because I quit."

"Oh, *Junior*. Not again. How could you?"

"It was a waste of time. I told him it would be." He knew he was sounding like a sulky teenager, and mentally cursed himself; but he couldn't help it. Miss Gerrity brought out the worst in him.

He knew exactly what she would say now, and braced himself to survive the litany of reproach he had heard several times before. This was the third prep school he had walked out of—how utterly inconsiderate . . . how *inexcusable* when his father went to such trouble to get him in. He knew how Miss Gerrity's mind worked. You've had the best of everything all your life, she might have cried. The best schools, camps, excursions, treats, and toys—such a devoted father, and you just fling his love back in his face. While: How can he say he loves me if he never sees me? the boy might have protested in turn; I don't want to be sent away, further and further away each time, until now, finally, to Santa Barbara, about as far away as I can get and still be in the same country. He never gives me a chance to show what I can do.

But perhaps that was all over now. Now his father would be surprised and pleased. He thought: He'll *have* to take me seriously, he'll have to find the time . . .

. . . because the Treadwell network had a new series in development, *Nightwatch*, and he would fit right in. He had exulted in hearing about that series, and the very next day the letter came. It was a sign.

"I don't need school anymore," he insisted. "I want to work for him, here. And I have something to show him." He held out the letter.

Miss Gerrity didn't take it. "Junior, be reasonable. He can't see anyone right now. He's in an important meeting, and he's flying to Japan at five-thirty."

"I won't take much of his time. I could ride out to the airport with him."

"He has a meeting scheduled during the ride."

"But this is important *too*!" He thrust the letter into her reluctant hands so she could see it came from an editor at a magazine called *Terror Tales*.

He watched her eyes flick down the page. "See?" In the letter the editor thanked him for his submission, apologized for not being able to use the story at this time, but asked him to send anything else he might have written. The boy jabbed a finger at the paragraph which he had memorized by now. "*Anything* else. They like my work."

"But they didn't buy it."

"Not yet. But," with certainty, "they will."

Miss Gerrity said with unconscious cruelty, "You came all the way from Santa Barbara just for this?" Then, resignedly, "All right. I'll show it to him. Wait here."

Another ten minutes passed. The boy roamed the perimeter of reception, scanning the framed photographs of stars and celebrities on the gray grasscloth walls. Finally he waited, expectantly, outside the closed door for the inevitable summons to go in.

The music tinkled through a selection from *My Fair Lady* and began *West Side Story*.

Eventually Miss Gerrity returned. She still held the letter in her hand, and now a thick envelope in addition.

"Well? What did he say?"

"You're to go back to California at once. He called the principal. They're prepared to take you back . . ."

The boy stared at her, shocked. "But doesn't he understand? I can't." And, impatiently: "What did he say about the letter?"

"Nothing."

"You mean he didn't even read it?"

"I warned you, Junior. He doesn't have time. He's running late." Now Miss Gerrity offered the envelope. "This is for your expenses. It ought to be enough."

The boy took out the money and counted it carefully. Ten brand-new one-hundred-dollar bills.

"A thousand bucks," he said carefully. "Yeah, that should be enough, all right."

"Very generous," agreed Miss Gerrity.

The boy replaced the money in the envelope. He was breathing harshly now, and a small white patch showed on each cheek. He said in a hard, tight voice, "Tell my father that I just wanted five seconds of his valuable time, not his fucking money." Then he tore the envelope in two neat halves and dropped them on the floor, to land just in front of the toes of Miss Gerrity's well-polished black pumps.

In a parting shot: "And don't call me Junior."

The fury and disbelief carried him safely into the elevator and down to the lobby. It wasn't until he fought his way toward the door through the seething indifferent people who brushed past him as though he wasn't there that he felt the tightness swell unbearably in his chest and the angry lonely tears forcing into his eyes. He felt humiliated by the tears, but need not have worried, for nobody noticed. He might as well have been invisible.

Phil's Sandwich Shop, the diner where Jo-Beth Feeney worked five days a week after school and all day Saturday, faced onto Corsica's main and only street, which was three blocks of gas stations, fast-food franchises, convenience stores, and the meeting hall of the Gospel Bearers, where Jo-Beth's mother spent most of her time when she wasn't working as a maid at the Motel 6 just off the interstate. Out back, beyond the dusty yard and sagging Cyclone fence, there was nothing for thirty miles but dwarf mesquite, scrubby cottonwoods, and the tumbleweed which rolled over and over, back and forth, in the perpetual wind.

Jo-Beth was seventeen, five-foot-ten with blond, sun-streaked hair. To the casual onlooker she was definitely a pretty girl; anybody looking close enough to notice her eyes, a luminous pale gray ringed with indigo, would find her beautiful. Jo-Beth wouldn't agree. All her life she had been compared with Melody Rose, her older sister, and Melody Rose, as everyone knew, really *was* beautiful.

Jo-Beth Feeney had always lived in Corsica, Texas. Amarillo, thirty-five miles away, was the Big City. Dallas, hundreds of miles away, was exotic almost beyond the powers of imagination—but Melody Rose had gone even further, to New York. She was a famous model now, with her pictures in *Vogue* and *Harper's Bazaar*.

This afternoon Jo-Beth, in her pink nylon waitress uniform, spread the clipped-out magazine photographs on the counter and stared excitedly at the beautiful redhead wearing all those stunning clothes.

Charlene, six years older than Jo-Beth, and growing heavy, tugged absently at the pink uniform bow clipped to the front of her hairdo and said cautiously, "It's real nice, but . . . she sure don't *look* like Melody Rose."

"Does too," Jo-Beth contradicted. "It's Mel, all right."

Of course it was Melody, her very own sister, the top model of Exotica Inc., a world-famous high-fashion agency.

Charlene objected, "But this gal has red hair."

"So what?" Jo-Beth said airily. "She dyed it. Or it's a wig."

Melody Rose didn't write much, but when she did, it was always to the diner. She didn't dare send a letter home in case Floyd saw it. And even if he didn't, Momma might see, and then she'd tell him anyway and he'd know where Mel was. Momma always told Floyd everything. Maybe she thought if she did, Floyd would reward her by not hitting her.

No one was allowed to talk about Melody Rose. She had run off last year after a fight with Floyd.

The only one who knew any details was the Martinez kid from the trailer next door. He had listened to sounds like brawling animals. He told Jo-Beth, "They were yellin' and screamin' at each other something terrible. Then he musta socked her a good one and she started in to cryin'. Soon's he left for work, she packed her bag and lit out of there. I seen her."

That night, finding Melody gone, Floyd got so mad Jo-Beth thought he'd have a heart attack. His face went white, then dark red and mottled with rage. "After all I done for that girl, and she not even my own kin."

He accused Momma of helping Melody run away and then lying to him. He slapped her across the face.

Jo-Beth yelled, "You leave her alone. She didn't know nothing."

He swore at her. "You shut your mouth. Don't you talk to your pa that way."

"You're not my pa. You're nothing to do with me. And don't you touch Momma again, you son of a bitch!"

Afterward Momma put salve on her black eye and talked through split lips about the will of Jesus and how Floyd was her cross to bear.

Jo-Beth worried desperately about Melody Rose for the next three months.

Where had she run to? She had been talking since she was fourteen of being a high-paid model in New York City.

Was that where she had gone, all that way? How had she found the money? Was she all right?

Eventually a postcard came. Melody was safe, had an apartment, and was working. Jo-Beth sighed with relief. Two more cards arrived over the next few months, a view of the Empire State Building and one showing the Manhattan skyline at sunset. Melody was a model now, with that famous agency, Exotica Inc. She loved New York.

Three cards in nine months, however, weren't much to go on. Jo-Beth wished that Melody was better at writing. She longed to know more, where her sister lived, how a model spent her day, who Melody's friends were.

But at last, with today's package, there was something tangible to see, to admire. There was Melody, wearing beautiful clothes, looking glamorous and rich.

She absolutely refused to believe the girl in the pictures wasn't Melody. "Char, don't be dumb. Why'd she send them if they aren't her?"

Receiving the pictures of Melody Rose, which proved it could all be done, Jo-Beth was spurred to action.

As soon as she graduated from high school she would get away from Corsica, away from Floyd, and go to New York City to live with Melody. There were grand, expensive restaurants there where she could earn a lot of money waitressing; enough to make a home for Momma.

Poor Momma; she'd been pretty once; there was an old photo of her, wearing a flowered housedress and a happy smile, holding two little girls by the hand. The thin, coltish child with the serious face was Jo-Beth. Melody Rose, all corkscrew curls and ribbons, clung to Momma's dress and smiled winningly up at the camera. Melody Rose was already the beauty of the family. Momma spent hours brushing her hair and dressing her up in pretty clothes and telling her how she looked just like Shirley Temple.

Pa must have taken the picture not long before he left them. One morning he had climbed into the cab of his blue-and-silver Kenwood and driven away down the interstate and out of their lives. Jo-Beth, five, then six, and then seven, had persisted, "Why'd he go, Momma? Why'd he up and leave us? When's he coming back?" There were no photos of Pa, and Momma never talked about him. Jo-Beth couldn't remember how he looked but she could remember the hurt. It still hurt, that Pa had walked away; it ached inside her sometimes, especially at Christmas and birthdays, like an open wound.

Then Ma married Floyd, who hit her when he got mean drunk and sometimes when he was just plain mean.

Jo-Beth demanded, "Why'd you marry him?"

"A woman got to have a man, honey." But Momma didn't smile much anymore and Jo-Beth couldn't see the sense in it. Surely they could get on just fine without Floyd.

Jo-Beth longed to see Momma smile. She vowed to make her happy, living in New York. Momma wouldn't have to work anymore and she could have nice things.

But oh, how painfully slowly Jo-Beth's savings mounted. Floyd knew exactly how much she earned and made her turn most of her money over—" 'Bout time you earned your keep around here"—but of course he didn't know about the tips. Thank God for tips, although, "You'd make a whole lot more if you acted more friendly," Charlene advised.

Jo-Beth grimaced. "Like let some guy pat me on the ass? Thanks a lot."

Charlene tossed her head. "You don't have to act like the Queen of Sheba. Anyone'd think you were a virgin."

"Well, so I am. Is that a crime?"

Charlene stared at her. "No kidding?" And, with a giggle, "Kinda hard, thinking of you and Mel being sisters!"

As time went by, the size of her tips increased even though Jo-Beth didn't "act more friendly." The men were starting to watch her. Charlene said matter-of-factly, "Why, sure they are, honey. You're getting yourself some figure. Don't tell me you didn't notice."

Jo-Beth colored. Yes, she had noticed. During the past year she had filled out dramatically and suddenly. She was nervous of her new breasts, so round, high, and firm; they didn't seem to fit right; she felt sure they had been intended for someone else, and compensated for the mistake by wearing oversize baggy clothes and walking with her arms crossed in front of her to try to hide them.

"But it don't do no good. They got eyes. Hell, they got radar vision." Charlene sighed. "You can't fool the boys, honey."

"I guess not," Jo-Beth said reluctantly, mistrusting and even fearing her newly voluptuous body, for the man who watched her most was Floyd, her stepfather, who had beaten her and Melody Rose once, along with Momma. Now, in retrospect, the beatings seemed infinitely preferable to his newly insinuating voice and crawling hands.

Jo-Beth avoided him as much as possible. She worked extra shifts on weekends and saved all she could. Charlene shook her head. "Listen, J.B. Whyncha go out sometimes and have some fun? There's more to life than this dump."

"Yeah," Jo-Beth agreed. "I know." And thought: New York.

For added incentive, she took a risk and pinned one of the pictures of Melody Rose on the wall above her bunk bed.

Melody Rose was wearing a stunning navy jacket with brass buttons and elegant white slacks, and posed, gracefully windblown, in the cockpit of a yacht. She was smiling at a handsome man whose royal-blue alligator shirt matched his eyes. Jo-Beth would lie in bed and look at the picture and imagine herself wearing a pretty white outfit like Melody's, in a beautiful boat. Why, she'd think, I've never even seen the sea. . . .

Noticing it for the first time, Momma demanded, "What's that there?"

"Just a picture from a magazine. I kinda liked it."

Momma pursed her lips, looked from Jo-Beth to the picture, and back again. After a moment of disapproving silence: "Those pretty boys in the magazines are all hommo-sexuals."

She said nothing about the girl, how she looked just like Melody Rose.

Jo-Beth reckoned she could stop worrying. If Momma didn't recognize her own daughter, there was no reason to worry that Floyd would.

Chapter
2

It was a strange day, that January Wednesday when Vera's life changed forever. It was a restless day, unseasonably springlike. A gusty wind was blowing while long dark clouds raced overhead, flinging desultory splatters of rain as warm as April.

Dr. Wheeler was leaving his office to make his rounds just as Vera came in to pick up Dad's latest prescription from the desk. He was coatless, wearing beige twill slacks and an Aran Island fisherman's sweater, the informal garb which Mum disapproved of so strongly. He wasn't her idea of a doctor at all; he looked as if he'd rather be playing soccer, or farming, or sailing a boat.

Dr. Wheeler was quite good-looking, Vera supposed, with reddish curling hair, fox-colored eyes, and of course that quirky, warm smile. It was a pity he was so old; he was probably at least thirty-five, although of course there was no point in Vera thinking of him that way. She wondered whether Diana would find him physically attractive but decided no—he wasn't nearly dashing enough for Diana; she'd only be interested in a Harley Street specialist, never a mere suburban G.P., even if he was born in America.

He smiled at her. "Hi, Vera." And then he turned, opened his office door again, and impulsively pushed her inside. "I'm glad you showed up—I need to talk with you."

It wasn't until the middle of the afternoon, Dad settled down for his nap and Mum gone out to the shops, that Vera had a chance to think about what he had said.

She sat at her desk, the latest drawings spread out in front of her. Diana was attending a party at the Soviet embassy. She wore a black sheath dress and today her abundant hair was drawn back into a French braid. She had attracted the attention and suspicion of Yuri Andreyev, KGB, a hard-faced man in his thirties . . . But Vera's mind, for the first time, kept drifting.

Dr. Wheeler had asked abruptly, "What are your plans, Vera?"

"Plans?" Vera blinked at him in surprise.

"For your future. You're almost eighteen. What are you going to do with yourself?"

She stammered, "What do you mean?"

He drummed restless fingers on the desktop. "Like a career. If you're not going to college, how about getting a job?"

"I . . . hadn't thought about it."

"Why not?"

"They need me at home." *"I don't know what I'd do without you, Vera." Mum was always saying that. "We depend on you, dear."* Vera said slowly, "Anyway, I can't do anything." Which was true. She knew it. She couldn't even type. Just draw, and that was only a hobby. She was told so often enough.

Dr. Wheeler said, "Do they really need you?" Then, curiously, "Do you ever get away from home? Do you go out on dates? Do you have a boyfriend?"

Vera blushed crimson. "Of course not." She decided she hated Dr. Wheeler. What a horrible, cruel thing to say.

He sighed. "Vera Brown, you're your own worst enemy." And then, "Don't blush and look away; look at me."

She raised her eyes defiantly. She felt hot and angry and jostled about inside. Dr. Wheeler's eyes met hers. They were flecked with green and amber and fringed with thick, pale lashes. He was watching her very steadily, without blinking. "You could have a boyfriend. You could have a job too. You could have a lot of things, everything you should have as a right." And then, shockingly, "Your dad's not all that sick, you know. He'll outlive all of us, probably."

Vera demanded, "What do you mean? He's an invalid."

Dr. Wheeler didn't answer. Instead he asked, "Are you happy at home?"

"Happy?" Vera shrugged. She had never thought about it. "I suppose so."

"Why don't you stay on the diet I gave you?"

Vehemently: "I do!"

"Don't give me that crap," Dr. Wheeler said rudely. "You've gained at least eight pounds this month."

"But it's puppy fat. Mum says——"

"I'm going to stick my neck out," Dr. Wheeler said then, "and say something perhaps I shouldn't. But, Vera, did you ever wonder whether your Mum *wants* you to stay fat?" He leaned forward, tucked his hand under her chin, and tilted up her face. He looked at her very seriously. "You have good features, Vera Brown, good bones, and lovely eyes. Inside you there's an attractive young girl trying to get out. A very bright one, too. That girl deserves better from you." He added, "No one can let her out except you."

Now Vera absentmindedly gave the Soviet ambassador a distinguished little beard and rows of medals while in her mind Dr. Wheeler told her, "Your world is too cramped, Vera, and it'll get more so as your father gets older. You need to live life firsthand, not just read about it or draw it." And he'd gone on to say an extraordinary thing. "Have you thought of working abroad, as an au pair? You don't really need any training. And once you'd stretched your wings a little, who knows? I could help you there, if you wanted . . . I have contacts . . . think about it."

Andreyev, the KGB man, had heavy eyebrows, a slash of a mouth, and deeply grooved cheeks. She wanted him to be sinister, but not without sex appeal, and gave him a fuller, more sensuous lower lip.

There was too much to think about. Too much altogether. It was confusing and disturbing. First she wondered: Why would Mum want me to be fat?

And a cold little voice inside her replied: So you don't have a boyfriend, so you're ashamed to go out, you stay home and never get a job, and take care of them when they're old.

At lunch, "Shepherd's pie," Mum said brightly. "Your favorite. For being such a good sweet girl and such a help to your mum."

Vera ate the stewed grayish hamburger and left the mashed potato on the side of her plate.

Mum looked insulted and then hurt. "I made it especially for you."

"Dr. Wheeler says I shouldn't eat so much starch."

"That Dr. Wheeler. What does he know? He doesn't have any children. He's not even married. And why's he paying you all this attention? I don't like it. It's not natural."

"He's a doctor, Mum."

"Well, I'm your mother."

"But I want to lose weight."

"You'll fine down when you're older."

"Mum, I'm nearly eighteen." And other girls wore pretty clothes and went to movies and dances with boys.

"He shouldn't interfere. I know what's best. Clean up your plate."

"No, Mum. Sorry."

"Vera!" Mum's face went pink and shiny. She said with a small sniff, when Vera sat there woodenly and showed no signs of giving in, "One day I hope you'll be unappreciated, like me. *Then* you'll be sorry."

But for the first time Vera wasn't brought to her knees in spasms of guilt.

Now, paying little attention to what she was doing, working automatically, embellishing, shading, she wondered whether Dr. Wheeler meant what he said. That he really could help her find a job as an au pair. Somewhere abroad. France or Italy. Perhaps, Vera thought daringly, even America. But how it frightened her, thinking of leaving home. She had hardly ever been away from home except once, years ago, to stay with Aunt Cynthia in Yorkshire.

Diana stared directly up at her, surely sneering at her weakness. Diana would go anywhere. She was afraid of nothing.

Vera altered the angle of Diana's eyes. Now she was smiling at Andreyev, telling him good night and good-bye . . .

America.

An uncouth country full of hippies, drug addicts, and gangsters, Mum said, where no one had respect for anything and nobody dressed properly.

A place where, Vera thought, anything could happen. Anything at all.

What would it be like, being an au pair? Vera knew how to take care of old people; a job in a household with children had to be a lot more fun that that . . .

MEDIUM SHOT: *Diana climbs from her sports car, low perspective of long legs and elegant shoes. A limousine with darkened windows in the background.*

TWO-SHOT: *Diana and Andreyev in silhouette.*

Diana: What do you want?

Andreyev: You're coming with me.

CLOSE-UP: *Diana (eyes wide): No. You can't make me.*

CLOSE-UP: *Andreyev (with a sinister smile): Yes, I can. Get in the car.*

But Diana does not get in the car. Instead . . .

What? Suddenly Vera felt she had no control over her hand. She watched her pencil fly across the paper as though driven by someone else's fingers, as though someone else had taken over entirely. Whatever was happening?

She drew faster and faster:

LONG SHOT: *Diana and Andreyev, in silhouette, are thrust apart by blinding light. A voice speaks from the light source:*

Voice: Diana Starr?

CLOSE-UP: *Diana (lips parted in surprise): Yes?*

Voice: I am an energy force from the system of Rigel, many light-years away. I need to take physical form, and have chosen to inhabit your body.

Diana: No! You can't do that.

Voice: Don't be afraid. You'll have great power of mind and spirit, and you'll be stronger than you can imagine. Your name will be Starfire.

Diana: But why? What do you want from me?

Voice: You will be told, all in good time.

Vera drew wild zigzags, stars, exclamation points, and question marks.

FULL SHOT: *Diana, no longer a mere fun-loving party girl, but a force. She is taller, stronger, commanding. Her hair flies in a wild halo around her head. Her eyes flash. She has become Starfire.*

MEDIUM SHOT: *Andreyev and Starfire. He holds her forcefully by the arm.*

Andreyev: In the car, now. Don't give me any trouble.

CLOSE-UP: *Starfire: Leave me alone. (Her eyes are wide; symbols like lightning bolts radiate from her head.)*

FULL SHOT: *Andreyev (reacts as if to an electric shock; mouth wide, hair bristling): What the—*

FULL SHOT: *Starfire (points a commanding finger): Go back where you belong!*

LONG SHOT: *Red Square, Moscow. The onion domes of St. Basil's Cathedral, the bristling wall of the Kremlin. A winter blizzard. Andreyev stares wildly through a curtain of falling snow.*

CLOSE-UP: *Andreyev (crossing himself): My God, oh, my God. What happened to me?*

CLOSE-UP: *Starfire: I don't know my own strength. I have a lot to learn. . . .*

Exhausted, Vera put her pen down and stared at the three strips she had drawn so incredibly fast and well.

In unconscious echo of the bewildered Andreyev: "What happened to me?" For Starfire was a new character and the story an entirely new concept. Where had she come from, this beautiful supergirl who could propel a man through thousands of miles with her mind?

Vera answered herself. From me, she thought; from inside my own head. She felt not only tired and bewildered but also a little frightened.

She stared down at Starfire, who gazed calmly back at her—through my own eyes, thought Vera.

In her mind Dr. Wheeler's voice said: "There's an attractive girl inside you. No one can let her out but you."

Silently Vera asked Starfire: Are you me? Inside, do I look like you? Could I, truly, look like you? And the excitement flared through her body.

Sloane St. John Treadwell Jr. strode up Fifth Avenue toward Central Park.

His misery had hardened into anger. He was so angry he wanted to smash something, to exhaust his rage in bodily violence. Then, without warning, the anger shifted into disappointment so intense and bitter he felt he could hardly breathe.

He had wanted so badly to show his father that if he was not already a success, then he would be soon. Five minutes, it would have taken. Just five minutes. Not even that much; enough to read the letter and understand and perhaps even offer praise: "Good for you, Sloane. I didn't know you had it in you." Not much to ask, and he would have walked on air.

He crunched the letter up in a ball and flung it viciously into a wire trash basket on the corner of Fifty-second Street. A half-block further he turned and ran back for it, knowing he couldn't bear to lose it. He extracted the letter, his heart thumping; smoothed out the creases and put it back in his pocket.

Damn his father. And then Sloane damned himself. Why did he do this to himself, over and over again? Why knock himself out trying to make his father understand what he was trying to do? For whatever reason, his father didn't care about him and never had. Nothing was going to change.

Sloane Jr. told himself fiercely: So grow up, asshole!

His eyes were watering from cold and the tears froze on his incongruously tanned cheeks. He had forgotten how cold it could be in New York.

He thrust his freezing hands deep into the pockets of his thin jacket and lowered his head against the cutting edge of the wind, feeling the flurries of dry snow burn his ears.

He had felt so excited on the plane from California, so mesmerized by the rushing shapes of clouds, the Duran Duran tape singing in his ears, and the dreams of a new life unrolling as a writer for *Nightwatch*, that he hadn't felt hungry. He had probably believed he would never want to eat again.

That had been a mistake, he thought, for he hadn't eaten since five that morning, and although his mind and soul were wasted and burned out, his body was ravenous. Now, in retrospect, that mystery meat and watery broccoli would look pretty good.

He was even regretting not accepting his father's money, for he had exactly $3.75 left in his pocket. Of course, he could go back to the office and Miss Gerrity would give it back to him—but no, he thought with a resurgence of violence, he'd rather starve and freeze.

He turned up the collar of the jacket and walked faster and faster to try to keep warm. It occurred to him this was stupid; he would burn up the calories faster, and he had no place to go anyway.

He came to an abrupt stop beside a vendor's cart on Fifty-ninth Street just across the street from the park. "Bernie's Polish Franks" the flaking letters said across a red-striped awning. Bernie was heavyset and wore a cap with earflaps. The rubber soles of his boots squeaked on the dry snow as he stamped his feet up and down for warmth.

Sloane bought a hot dog with everything on it—mustard, relish, and pickle—and gulped it down.

Bernie eyed his cotton jacket and grunted, "Snowin'. Aincha noticed?"

"Yeah," Sloane agreed. "I noticed, all right." For exactly a minute and a half, standing beside the steaming cart and wolfing his frankfurter, he felt warm and comforted. Then, as the satisfaction faded into memory and he knew he would be hungry again in half an hour or so, he decided he was being ridiculous. This whole scene was ridiculous.

So he was alone in New York in winter with now just $1.25 in his wallet. Well, he also had a California driver's license in there with his photograph and name on it; he had a checkbook, and so far as he knew, there was money in the account; he also had a telephone-company credit card. He could call somebody.

So cool it with the drama, Sloane told himself, with this whining-orphan-in-the-storm bit. It's all wasted. Nobody gives a shit anyway. Stop being an asshole.

For a brief moment he thought about calling his mother, but he had never spent much time with his famous mother, he hadn't seen her for months, and these days, unless he caught her in full makeup, costumed for her TV series, he doubted he would even recognize her.

All his friends were in school.

Except for Arnie Blessing, who had graduated at sixteen and then . . .

Arnie! The wheels in his head clicked and meshed. Arnie Blessing! Christ, yes.

He and Arnie had briefly been in pre-prep school together at the St. Regius Academy in Vermont.

Arnie had been stout, nearsighted, too intelligent for his own good, Californian, and Jewish. He had also sported a horrible crop of vivid zits. Under the circumstances he had fallen a natural victim to the sadism of his upper-middle-class Wasp classmates. In those days Sloane St. John Treadwell Jr. had been his only friend.

"How can you stand that fat creep?" demanded the twelve-year-old son of a prominent Boston judge. "Greasy bastard; makes me wanna barf."

At first Sloane had only stood up for Arnie because he hated to see mindless, cowardly cruelty. Seeing the defenseless fat boy the butt of endless mean and spiteful taunts and practical jokes made his blood boil with rage. Soon, however, the support became genuine friendship. Sloane *liked* Arnie. He looked beyond the blubber and saw the wit, the brains, and the numb courage to go on from day to day through hell. Arnie was also the only person who had never called him either Sloane, Treadwell, or Junior.

Mere association with Arnie Blessing, let alone friendship, should have made an instant social outcast of Sloane as well, but Sloane had not only the social weapons of background, wealth, looks, and athletic prowess in his armory but also the ultimate weapon of indifference. Sloane was cool. He could not be hurt because he wouldn't care even if he *was* an outcast.

The other boys had to accept the fact that for some weird reason, Arnie Blessing was under Treadwell's protection, so the little fat fuck had better be left alone. At least while Treadwell was around.

That had been six years ago, but they had kept in touch. And things were very different now for Arnie.

He was still Californian, Jewish, and bright, but he had thinned down, his face had cleared up, he wore emerald-green tinted contact lenses, and had somehow metamorphosed into a very handsome boy.

Then his mother, who knew a talent agent, had sent him up for an audition for a soft-drink commercial. Arnie had landed the part on his own merit—and as though life were trying to make up for the raw deal he had originally been dealt, Arnie Blessing became, in very short order, a Hollywood phenomenon.

The camera and Arnie were soul mates. Within two years he was a teenage heartthrob to rival Shaun Cassidy.

He was called Arnold Blaize now, and received ten thousand letters every week from fans around the world.

He owned a million-dollar beach house in Malibu and a penthouse apartment on Park Avenue. He drove a Ferrari for fun and rode in a chauffeured Lincoln for business.

He also had an insidiously growing cocaine habit, although Sloane, who hadn't seen Arnie for two years, didn't know that yet.

Arnie loved the cocaine; it made him feel as if he really was as handsome and popular as people said he was, and while it lasted he would forget that other Arnie, timid, wretched, and fat, and feel part of the action, with a million friends.

When the downside came, fat Arnie would take over. Fat Arnie had no friends at all.

Except for one. . . .

Sloane made his call from the Plaza Hotel.

The secretary checked Arnie's list of acceptable callers and found Sloane St. John Treadwell's name heading it. She gave out some highly privileged information. "He's in New York," she said. "He's shooting *Disco Dream*. You can reach him at this number."

Arnie in New York. Holy shit! Sloane told himself it was a sign. From now on things were going to be different.

He dialed the local number, was rerouted three times, and listened to an endless succession of clicks, whistles, and buzzes until an exhausted-sounding male voice said, "Yeah, they just wrapped, Mr. Blaize's here now . . ." and then Arnie's voice. Sloane hadn't yet become used to hearing Arnie's new, grown-up voice, for it hadn't deepened until Arnie had been fifteen, and yet there was still the same desperate eagerness, the childish need to be liked, the vulnerability.

"Saint!" Arnie cried now. "Is this you? Is this really fucking you? It's been so *long*! Where are you, man? I don't believe this! Jesus, it's been an awful day; it's better now, you believe it! Get your ass on over to the suite"—he gave an address on Park and Seventy-first—"and I'll see you there soon's I can get outta here. I'll call ahead, tell the gorillas to expect you 'n if they don't let you in they're dog meat . . ."

He gave a huge sigh of contentment. "Jesus, Saint! It's fucking great to hear you!"

Jo-Beth got up as usual that February morning and dressed for school, pretending she didn't feel terrible, that her head didn't throb and her throat didn't ache. However, peering at her throat in the mirror, seeing the dark swollen redness covered in little white dots, she felt even worse. It hurt to talk.

Shit, sighed Jo-Beth. She didn't mind missing school, but the job was something else. She thought of the money she wouldn't make this afternoon and evening.

Outside, the wind keened, rolling the bundles of tumbleweed over and over. The sky was gray and hazy. It was cold.

Jo-Beth returned to her bunk bed. When Mel left, she had moved from the top berth into the lower one. She kept on everything but her jeans, telling herself that if she didn't completely give in she would feel better later.

Jo-Beth was very seldom alone with nothing to do. If she wasn't in school or working, she was doing her homework or asleep. Being alone with nothing to do meant time to think, and her thoughts were not comforting.

First, Floyd and the way he watched her now, casting sidelong glances which made her feel dirty inside. Then Momma, a meek wraith accepting abuse and humiliation as her just deserts.

It was much better to fantasize about the three of them, she, Melody Rose, and Momma, living in a luxury apartment in New York. How happy they'd be.

Jo-Beth gazed up at the picture of Melody in the boat. Perhaps she, Momma, and Melody Rose could go out in a sailboat someday. After all, New York was on the Atlantic Ocean. She found herself craving beauty, space, water, freedom. . . .

She slipped into a waking dream where the three of them soared like gulls across sun-dazzled water before a freshening wind, the waves hissing and slapping against the white hull. Somehow Jo-Beth knew exactly how the waves would sound. She sat in the helmsman's seat, her flying hair damp with spray, the wheel firm under her hands, the boat responding to her lightest touch.

Then suddenly, shockingly, a rasping screech tore through the delicate fabric of the dream.

White sails, sky, water, and smiling faces shivered and faded.

Jo-Beth's eyes flicked open on a dirty green Formica wall where a magazine photo was stuck with Scotch tape.

She knew what the sound was at once. The screen door.

She felt the trailer tremble under heavy footsteps. In the living area, where the kitchenette was, the refrigerator door squealed open and slammed violently. There were sounds of someone gulping liquid; the rattle of an empty can flung into the sink; the bathroom door opening; someone urinating long and noisily into the toilet before clumping the few feet down the passage and stopping at her door.

It was Floyd, who was working a swing shift this week and got off at noon.

He shouldered his way into her room.

Floyd Feeney was a heavyset man. His blue denim overalls were stained with grease across the protruding belly where he generally wiped his hands. "What're you doing home, Jo-Beth?"

"I'm sick. I've got the flu or something." She didn't look at his face, but fixed her eyes on the red-and-blue Texaco logo stitched on his right breast pocket.

"Well, how 'bout that." With ingratiating heartiness, "Then you can be company for your old pa."

"It's real infectious. I wouldn't get too close if I was you." Jo-Beth squirmed away from him until her back pressed against the wall.

He stared fixedly at her, huddling in her quilt. "It don't bother me none." He moved forward until his thighs pressed against the edge of her bed. He filled the tiny room. She could smell the beer on his breath, the rank smell of his body.

"Floyd, now, you leave me be."

He reached out for her, big, hairy-fingered hands, oil-stained, grimy, broken nails. "Why, hell, honey, I was thinking you could be a good, kind girl to your pa. Ain't nobody been kind to your pa in quite a while."

With a sudden fast movement he pulled the quilt away and grabbed for her breasts.

Jo-Beth caught him by the wrists and tried to force him away from her. His wrists felt like thick steel bars. "Don't touch me there! Don't do that!"

"Jus' a li'l squeeze. Won't hurt." And with satisfaction: "Growin' a fine pair of tits at last."

She twisted sideways. "Floyd, you stop that right now. You hear?"

"C'mon, honey. It ain't like I'm your real pa." He reached down between her locked thighs. Jo-Beth tried to scream from her hurting throat and it was like a nightmare, when the loudest scream comes out as a mere croak.

He panted heavily, crushing her beneath him, his knee thrusting between her legs. She heard the rasp of his zipper. He'd torn her shirt open and fumbled with one hand at her breasts while with the other he wrestled his penis through the fly of his overalls. It was horrifying, disgusting, dark red and thickly straining.

Jesus Christ. Jo-Beth thought she'd be sick.

She tore her hands free and gouged her thumbs into his eyes while shoving hard against the wall. The free-standing bunk-bed structure tottered forward.

Floyd screeched, rocked backward, and cracked the back of his head on the wooden slats of the top bunk as Jo-Beth rolled into the narrow space beside the wall, writhed under the bed, and sprang for the door.

He caught her by the back of her torn blouse, swung her around, and belted her across the side of the head. His face was murderous and congested with blood; his breath wheezed in and out in loud sobs. A thin line of blood trickled down his forehead.

Jo-Beth watched the tiny room spin dizzily around her. She staggered and almost fell, knew she dared not fall, pivoted clumsily, raising her knee, and as Floyd flung himself onto her, drove her foot into his groin as hard as she possibly could.

It wasn't hard enough, but it stopped him long enough to get away. Maybe.

She dived down the narrow little aisle to the living area and the outside door, but he was right behind her and she knew she hadn't a chance. She heard herself shriek harshly, "Don't you touch me, I'll kill you, you son of a bitch."

He was right behind her. "Oh, honey, you made yourself one big old mistake . . ."

What happened next would repeat itself in her nightmares over and over again. In slow motion she'd watch herself snatch up Momma's china statuette of the Virgin Mary holding the baby Jesus.

She would hold it in both hands like a baseball bat and smash Floyd across the forehead.

She would watch him stagger toward her, a great bloody gash across his face, his huge oily hands still grasping. She would hear her breath sobbing in and out, then watch herself slam the statue down onto his head as hard as she possibly could. And again. And again, until Mary snapped in two across the waist, Floyd's eyes rolled up into his head, he folded up in sections like a carpenter's rule, and crashed onto the floor, stone dead.

Chapter

3

"Hello." Starfire, at the Dorchester Hotel for her interview, held out her hand and smiled with confidence at Spring Kentfield's London secretary. "My name's Veronica Brown but I'm usually called Vera. I'm very interested in working for Miss Kentfield in New York . . ."

Afterward, "They liked me," Vera told Dr. Wheeler incredulously. "They hired me. I can't believe it."

She couldn't have done it on her own, of course; she attributed her success entirely to Starfire, who was able to take in stride situations which would otherwise be entirely daunting.

It was Starfire who broke the news to Mum and Dad, explaining, "Spring Kentfield's a well-known actress. She's living in New York this summer, taping some television specials. She has a little boy called William. She advertised in the *Times* for a nanny's assistant, and they chose me!"

And it was Starfire who handled the dreadful scene which followed. "But, Vera, what are we supposed to do?"

"Dr. Wheeler is finding a home help for Dad, to come in every day."

"But Dad doesn't like strangers. I don't understand. How could you? Don't you love us anymore? After all we've done for you . . . And with Dad so ill . . . It'll kill him. You're killing your father, Vera."

"I'm sorry, Mum. I want to go."

Mum's voice began to tremble. She knotted her hands together and literally wrung them, like a Victorian heroine. "There's such a hard look in your eye these days. It frightens me." And with unwitting accuracy,

"This isn't *my* daughter saying these terrible things. This can't be my Vera."

Vera shut herself in her room for the whole afternoon. She stared down at last night's drawings of Starfire entering the forecourt of the Dorchester; shaking hands with the secretary, drawn more imposing than she had really been; a close-up of Starfire accepting the job.

Her changing life had become a daily strip, with Starfire playing the Vera role; each evening she would record the new developments.

Now Vera began to draw Starfire telling Mum and Dad she was leaving home, but this time the drawing didn't come out right. Vera felt too guilty. She bit her lip and tried not to cry. It was all very well for Starfire, but Mum and Dad were hers, Vera's, parents. She didn't want to hurt them. She leaned forward until her hot forehead was touching the paper. She felt so confused. She loved them, but she hated them too for making her feel guilty and so desperately needed. I don't want to be needed so much, Vera thought; there's nothing left over of *me*.

Spring Kentfield was forty-two years old and a household name as the glamorous star of an evening soap opera.

She had recently married a much younger man, a Beverly Hills real-estate broker, and her pregnancy had been carefully planned for maximum publicity value. Having a baby was what *young* people did, and by association Spring was sure she automatically shed ten years.

It seemed to work. Spring's popularity soared to an all-time high. Her fans were thrilled for her. The letters and gifts poured in. A baby was written into the story line of her series, and after the birth of little William, she was photographed endlessly in lots of floating muslin and *broderie anglaise* holding the baby in her arms and smiling mistily, a beautiful young mother.

Her Benedict Canyon home was equipped with a state-of-the-art nursery, the requisite English nanny hired to go with it.

However, good help, though easy to find, was hard to keep, especially since Spring was a difficult employer, erratic and demanding, contradicting her own orders and intolerant of the resulting confusion. She was also very tight with money unless it was spent on herself or was someone else's. The first nanny lasted for six months, the others for successively shorter periods. "He's a dear little boy," was the typical reaction, "but oh, what one has to put up with!"

Vera began work in late May; one week after her arrival, the senior nanny ran off with the Moonies. "You're a child of Satan," Nanny accused Spring, "and I'm leaving this hell house right now."

Spring did not attempt to replace her; William was no longer a tiny infant and Vera seemed efficient enough. She promoted Vera instead.

"She knows a good thing when she sees it." Geronia, the housekeeper, had been pounding dough back and forth on the marble pastry counter and tapping her foot in time to Otis Redding on the radio. Skinny and grape black, Geronia always wore brilliantly colored underwear that gleamed through her white uniform. She was married to a policeman and had three teenage sons. Vera, who had seldom had personal contact with a black person before, for there were very few in Orpington, Kent, found her excitingly exotic. "She paying you more money?"

Vera shook her head. Geronia nodded resignedly. "Thought as much. Miz Kentfield's tight with a buck wors'n anyone. You wanta raise, you better holler real loud."

Vera watched Geronia shape her dough in the pie pan, fill it with chopped strawberries, then baste it with honey glaze. Her mouth watered. She said hopelessly, "I can't. She'd fire me. And I only have a tourist visa. I'd have to go home."

"Taking advantage. She does that real good." Geronia pushed forward a platter of homemade shortbread. Vera took a piece with a sigh.

So her days fell into a routine of nursery chores, lonely evening television viewing, and guilty dreams of Mum and Dad.

She was often tired, for her nights were frequently interrupted by Spring returning in the small hours from some social event, tipsily maternal, demanding to see William.

"He's asleep, Miss Kentfield."

"Then wake him up, Vera. What do I pay you for? I simply have to see my Precious . . . I haven't seen him all day!"

Precious, yawning and complaining, would be duly presented to his mother, who would play with him strenuously for five minutes, until her maternal impulse was exhausted.

Then, "Put him back to bed now, Vera," and Spring would wander groggily off to her boudoir while the baby, wide-awake and by now ready to play all night, screamed in rage for an hour after being returned to his crib.

Mum wrote almost every day. "We're going on as best we can. Dad's had another bad turn. He's getting very frail now. I think of you so far away and start to cry inside. . . ."

Vera's only escape was through Starfire.

Starfire's mission to Earth was now defined: a feasibility study for the takeover of the planet through peaceful integration with suitable Earthlings like Diana Starr.

She must use her superpowers with discretion; her performance with Yuri Andreyev was too flamboyant for comfort and might attract the wrong kind of attention.

Infiltration was the key, preferably of a celebrity household such as that of Spring Kentfield, where Starfire would meet plenty of influential people.

However, it hadn't worked out that way, and wouldn't, unless things changed drastically. Starfire (through Vera), met no one but servants, doormen, elevator men, delivery people, and other baby-sitters in Central Park.

Vera had no other recourse but to create her own celebrities. She revenged herself on Spring by including her, in merciless caricature, in her new strip.

In the story line, Starfire thwarted Spring's marriage to charismatic young Senator Moore, presidential hopeful in the next election (who by coincidence looked exactly like Dr. Wheeler). Spring, portrayed with inch-long matted eyelashes, and an exaggerated bosom thrusting like twin cannon under her tight satin gown, nursed ambitions of political power and lusted after the senator's family fortune.

However, Starfire had plans of her own for the senator:

LONG SHOT: *The White House. Silhouettes of figures cast against brightly lit windows; an important reception in progress.*

CLOSE-UP: *Starfire. Background of smartly dressed people. Her eyes are wide and concentrated. Mind-probe symbols radiate from her head.*

Starfire (smiles): I'll show him what she really wants.

TWO-SHOT: *The senator and Spring. Spring gazes ardently up at him, but the pupils of her eyes are each replaced by minute images: the Presidential Seal and a dollar sign.*

Senator (recoils): You don't love me; you just want my money and my power.

TWO-SHOT: *Senator and Starfire, dancing.*

Senator: You're the most beautiful woman I've ever met.

CLOSE-UP: *Spring (rages): That bitch. I'll fix her; I'll turn her in to Immigration . . .*

But matters changed drastically one hot July afternoon.

Spring exploded into the apartment without warning, her personal maid panting at her heels. She was leaving for Kennedy at once. *Ladies' Home Journal* was doing a spread on Spring Kentfield, wife and mother, relaxing at home with her husband and child. Surely she had told Vera she was going to L.A. for a week of photo layouts. Had she not? Unthinkable. And why wasn't the baby ready? She needed William. Really, Vera was impossible. This couldn't go on. They'd speak as soon as Spring returned. Couldn't Vera remember *anything*? No, she would not be needed, Spring kept a permanent staff in California. She would have a week to enjoy New York on her own, not that she deserved it.

Spring tore, shouting, through her huge closet, flinging out shoes, sandals, blouses, bathing suits, and evening gowns while Barbara, her maid and dresser, who had somehow survived ten years of Spring's whims and tantrums, stood stoically by, caught each item, sometimes in midair, and stowed it in its appropriate piece of Gucci luggage while Vera feverishly gathered William's clothes, hats, bibs, diapers, lotions, bottles, and toys into a huge canvas bag.

Then they were gone. Vera couldn't quite believe it.

She leaned out the living-room window watching, twenty floors below, a bird's-eye view of Spring and her entourage climbing into a white stretch limo. When it pulled away and she knew she really was alone, she drew a deep breath of satisfaction. Feeling thoroughly emancipated for the first time, she fixed a gin and tonic with lots of ice and a slice of lime, then flung herself luxuriously into a living-room armchair upholstered in peach watered silk. She held up her glass, toasting herself, and drew happy little exclamation marks on its cold frosty side.

When the drink was finished she sought the drawing table set up in her bedroom. What a treat to know she wouldn't be disturbed.

TWO-SHOT: *Starfire and the senator, backseat of a chauffeur-driven limousine. The senator hands Starfire an envelope.*

Senator: Your green card, Diana. Congratulations. Now you're a permanent-resident alien!

Vera smiled at her own wit. She began to draw them kissing, but to her surprise, found her hand faltering.

It must be because she'd never kissed anyone. She didn't know what a young man's lips felt or tasted like, how to draw the expression in Starfire's eyes. She wondered whether she would ever know, and immediately felt very depressed.

She scrapped the episode, mentally dispatched the senator back to his home state of California, and brought Starfire to New York. She began again:

CLOSE-UP IN MIRROR. *Starfire studies herself appraisingly, lips slightly parted. She looks very beautiful, her pale hair styled in a French braid. She seems restless and eager for adventure.*

It was still no good. Vera couldn't continue. She laid her pen down in frustration. She felt restless too.

It wasn't enough just to send Starfire out there into the warm lavender twilight to seek paper adventures. Vera longed to go herself, but she was afraid to go alone.

She guessed she would spend the evening in the apartment as usual, more alone than ever, for even the baby had gone.

God, it was quiet!

As though sleepwalking, Vera wandered into the kitchen, an endless expanse of glistening tile and stainless steel, barren and silent without Geronia clattering pans and humming to her radio while the little Sony color TV burbled companionably in the corner.

Vera turned them both on before she opened the refrigerator.

She found half a chicken wrapped in foil and put it on a plate along with a large scoop of potato salad and a slab of garlic bread. There was a new chocolate cake. She cut herself a huge slice.

Despair and defiance raging in almost equal proportions, she returned to the living room, poured herself another gin and tonic, and switched on the TV.

She munched the chicken while watching a man drive a sports car at breakneck speed through a city street, shooting at a man in another fast car. She turned up the volume, needing to banish every cubic inch of silence. The big room resounded with screeching brakes, smashing glass, screams. Then a commercial. Vera popped a loaded forkful of potato salad into her mouth while a beautiful girl with a mane of marigold curls and a slinky black dress sprayed perfume onto her bosom, wrists, behind her ears, gazed meaningfully into Vera's eyes, and told her, "My husband puts in a long, hard day; don't you think he deserves a Feverbeat night? I do. . . ."

Vera started on the cake. She didn't think the model would eat cake; she was thin and gorgeous; she probably wore a size four.

When her plate was emptied of all but crumbs, she took her plates to the kitchen and put them in the dishwasher.

She ran the dishwasher, even though it was almost empty, because even with Geronia's radio and TV the room still seemed too large and too empty and cold-looking, and the rhythmic sloshing of the water was comforting.

She opened the refrigerator to look at the cake one more time. Then, with huge resolution, she made herself close it.

Instead she marched from room to room creating an illusion of gaiety and company with radio and stereo and each television set—there were at least five in the apartment—finally switching on the forty-eight-inch monster in the white-and-gold master bedroom.

It didn't help. She felt just as lonely. The only solution was—which would help was . . .

—inside the refrigerator, its creamy fudge frosting delicious, irresistible . . .

Dr. Wheeler had said, "Inside you there's an attractive young girl trying to get out."

And, "No!" Vera cried aloud. "I won't." She commanded herself to stop thinking about cake. She wouldn't give in. Not again.

She would Stay! Right! Here! in the room furthest from the kitchen.

She firmly closed the door, then glanced around for diversion. She wasn't often in Spring's room. It seemed to be walled entirely with mirrors. Wherever she looked, she saw herself, endless Vera Browns.

She stared very closely at her reflection. Surely she must have lost just a little weight over the past month, chasing after William and walking him in the park.

Vera began systematically to undress.

First the navy polyester blouse, then the too-long beige skirt, finally her bra and cotton panties.

Naked, she scrutinized herself from every angle. Despite the huge meal she had just eaten, surely she wasn't quite so heavy-looking as before?

Dr. Wheeler said, "You have good features, Vera Brown . . ."

Spring's bedroom contained a built-in makeup station. Vera sat down on the padded bench. Framed by an arch of blazing high-wattage bulbs, her face gazed anxiously back from every imaginable angle.

". . . good bones and lovely eyes." Dr. Wheeler had probably just said that to be kind, but—Vera sucked in her cheeks and pulled the flesh taut over her jawbones—but, well, maybe not. She wondered daringly: With some help, some makeup, and other things, could I actually look attractive?

She contemplated her reflection for a long minute. Then methodically sought among the lotions and bottles and pots and began to make up her face.

She patted on an all-over application of Elizabeth Arden base. Fluffed blush onto her cheekbones. Next the eyes: blue-gray shadow in the crease, with a dash of silver on the lids the way she thought Spring did it. Then plum-colored lipstick, and for the final challenge, a set of feathery eyelashes, which she finally stuck on slightly crooked.

She looked at herself expectantly. She didn't think the makeup made much difference, really—but what did it matter? Who would see?

Vera opened the door into Spring's thirty-by-fifteen-foot closet. Lights sprang on. Tiers of outfits for all occasions hung on rotating racks. There were hundreds of pairs of shoes, endless drawers of accessories, and . . . "Oh!" Vera recoiled with a small shriek from a row of smooth white faces, their sightless gaze somehow accusing, each wearing an immaculately coiffed head of hair.

For an instant her heart pounded in her ribs. Then she giggled at her stupidity.

Just wigs! Wigs on Styrofoam stands.

Deliberately she chose the finest wig, long and ash blond, and arranged it carefully on her own head to hide her own mouse-brown hair.

Much better!

Now she was starting to look like something!

Vera found a pair of silver Italian kid sandals and put them on. Spring took a larger size than she did, but her foot was narrower.

She posed carefully, hand on hip, knee flexed, toe pointed. Her reflection, naked but for wig and glittering shoes, gazed solemnly back at her. She giggled again.

Now she needed the perfect dress. She had hundreds from which to choose, and there it was—silver mesh, a sinuously flexible fabric, coated with abstract patterns of black and silver bugle beads. Of course Spring's dress size was many times smaller than Vera's, but since the dress wasn't designed to cling tightly to the figure, it might do.

Vera sucked in her stomach and tugged it over her hips.

She squirmed her arms through the straps and hauled it over her breasts. So far, so good. In fact, she thought she looked sensational. All I need now, she pondered dreamily, is for some devastatingly handsome man to appear and sweep me off into the night.

With a determined breath she pulled up the zipper at the back.

It jammed, of course. Vera wrenched and tugged, but the zipper was stuck fast. There was a frightening popping sound of overstrained beads.

Her romantic little fantasy died at once.

Oh, God, what now? What could she do? Who could help her? The elevator man? The doorman? She imagined their carefully impassive faces as they tried not to laugh at her, and cringed inside.

She wondered how much the dress had cost. Thousands of dollars, probably.

She tottered carefully back into the bedroom on her four-inch heels.

On the huge TV screen a young couple in formal evening dress dined al fresco on top of an Arizona mesa, a glossy silver automobile parked beside them. They were accompanied, from speakers around the apartment, by New Orleans jazz, a Mozart symphony, and the main title theme of *Hawaii Five-O*.

Vera turned back to the mirror with an anxious frown.

Engrossed, she never heard the door open behind her.

However, she did hear a man's rich chuckle, although it was another moment or two before Vera realized the sound did not come from the TV but from a living person. That someone else was in the room . . .

. . . and standing right behind her. There he was, in the mirror. Oh, God! She froze in terror. She couldn't even scream.

She watched her face turn absolutely white, the makeup glaring in weird colored blotches.

She couldn't move. She stood there waiting for him to kill her. He'd kill her, of course, she knew that . . . God!

Then he spoke. She saw white teeth laughing in a tanned face. "Hey, relax. It's okay. I didn't mean to scare you. I guess you didn't hear me yelling."

Vera began to shake. Someone's teeth were clattering; her own.

She made herself turn around, very, very slowly.

Face-to-face, he didn't look threatening at all; he was young, about the same age as she was, and really quite handsome in a wild kind of way. She took him in all at once, from the straight black hair worn a bit too long, to the rakish face with the dancing eyes, to the purple T-shirt, black jeans, and black canvas high-tops. She corrected herself. He was really very handsome. Even more than her fantasy lover. But . . .

He was still laughing. "What is this? What's with all the sound? Who *are* you?"

Vera managed, "I . . . I'm the nanny. The baby-sitter."

"Then where's the baby? And Spring?"

"In Los Angeles." The moment she said it, Vera knew she shouldn't have told him. Now he knew how truly alone she was—although the edge had gone off her alarm, and surely he wouldn't kill her if he was laughing.

He said, "It sounded like there were a thousand people in here."

At once Vera realized who he must be. He was from Maintenance. Of course. Someone complained about the noise and he came up to check. "I'm sorry. I'll turn it all off. I'll . . . Yes." She added, "You are from Building Maintenance, aren't you."

"No."

"*Ohhhh* . . ." Her fear returned. She whispered, "Then how did you get in?"

"With these." He dangled a pair of keys in front of her nose.

"You've got your own . . . But . . ." Fear shading to bewilderment: "Who are you?"

"I'm Sloane." He looked at her expectantly. When she didn't react: "Sloane St. John Treadwell Jr. Never heard of me?" Then he shrugged with resignation. "Oh, well. I guess I'm not surprised. I'm Mother's best-kept secret."

"Mother's——"

"And I've never liked the name anyway. You can call me Saint."

He moved away down the passage. Vera followed him, waiting while he crossed from room to room, extinguishing sound.

"Spring's your *mother?*"

"Yep."

"But why a secret?"

They reached the living room. Saint explained patiently, "Because she gets younger every year and I get older. Pretty soon we'll look the same age. I'm bad for her image." It was quiet in the apartment now. He said matter-of-factly, "I don't mind, though; I don't see her much anyway."

Vera asked curiously, "Do you live with your father, then?"

"Him? Are you joking? He's much too busy." It was said with an airy bravado which rang slightly false. Vera let it go. She said reasonably, "You must live somewhere."

"Well, sure I do. In boarding schools and summer camps. And with Aunt Gloria for anything in between. But I'm through all that now," he told her airily. "I'm a free man."

Vera couldn't help but wonder whether Saint really felt as cynical as he sounded. She didn't think so. She didn't know what to say. Finally, "Well," she ventured after a moment or two when they just stood looking at each other, "I'm sorry you missed your mother. Did you need to see her specially?"

"She wanted to see me. She said so. I guess she forgot."

"She had a photo session in L.A. for *Ladies' Home Journal.*" Vera added politely, "It was very sudden."

Saint nodded. He smiled wryly. "That'd do it. She'd never miss a photo opportunity. Well..." He turned back toward the hall. "It was nice meeting you. I'd better get moving."

Vera had known Saint for less than fifteen minutes, but felt crushed with disappointment that someone so attractive and so exciting had entered her life only to leave it at once. Inanely, like a polite hostess, she asked, "Oh. Must you really?" She trailed after him across golden oak parquet to the elevator. "Where are you going?"

"There's a party."

"Oh. Of course." Vera managed, "I mean, after all, it *is* Friday night . . ." Thinking about being all alone again in the huge, empty apartment, more lonely than ever now. She wondered whether she would ever see Saint again. Then she remembered her predicament, quite forgotten in the excitement. She asked anxiously, "Before you go, would you mind trying to unzip me?"

"Sure." He spun her around and leaned over to his task. She could feel his warm breath on her bare skin, his fingers fumbling, tugging. Then he sighed. "Sorry. No way. It's stuck. I mean *seriously*."

"Oh, Lord. What'll I do?"

"I could cut you out of it?"

"Oh, no! No, you can't do that—it's *hers*!"

"Yeah, I guess it is . . ." Then, for the first time, "Why?" Saint demanded. "Why are you wearing my mother's clothes?"

She couldn't tell him. She just couldn't—that she had wanted to see whether she might be beautiful, like Dr. Wheeler had said.

Vera swallowed. "Oh," she lied, "just for something to do. I was so bored. But," anxiously, "she simply mustn't know."

"You were bored?" It sounded as though he didn't know what the word meant. "Why don't you go out or something?"

"Because I . . ." She hung her head. "I was scared. I didn't want to go by myself."

"That's dumb. Tell you what . . ." Saint snapped his fingers, sounding pleased with himself. "Now you're all dressed up and can't get it off, you'd better come to the party with me!"

In the elevator he told her about the party. Arnie Blaize was the host. *The* Arnie Blaize. Vera made incoherent sounds of wonder. "You mean you *know* him?"

"Sure. For years. I stay with him sometimes. Now he's bought this place on the North Shore as a kind of retreat. This is his housewarming, I guess you'd call it."

Her wonder gave way to frozen terror. "Saint, I *can't* go to his party! I absolutely can't! Please, Saint, no."

"Why not?" The elevator doors opened at the lobby. Vera shrank back against the wall. "Come *on*!" People were waiting to enter, impatient people, a perspiring girl in sky-blue nylon jogging shorts and a fierce-looking woman wearing a Tyrolean hat with a feather, clutching two panting Yorkshire terriers. Saint ignored Vera and towed her across the lobby, through the doorway, and out into the street.

"You'll have a good time. Trust me."

A white Jaguar XK-E waited at the curb, illegally parked at a fire hydrant. Saint opened the door for her.

Vera sank helplessly into enfolding chocolate leather while Saint gave money to the doorman. She tried again to tell him she didn't want to come, that she was too shy, she didn't know what to say to wealthy, famous people.

"They're no different from anybody else."

"And I look *awful*." People would laugh at her. She'd die of humiliation.

"You look a hell of a lot better than Mother. Actually, you look great."

The engine started with a rich, rumbling purr. Vera felt the vibration under her thighs and feet and up her spine. Then they were pulling out into traffic and she thought she'd give anything to be back in Spring's apartment, safely watching television by herself.

Saint drove fast but skillfully. On the radio the Mamas and the Papas were singing how they were California dreaming on a winter's day. He hummed along.

Vera was glad he didn't talk to her. She would never have known what to say back to him.

She tried to tell herself that by some miracle her fantasy had come true, that just like Cinderella, Prince Charming had swept her off her feet and was even now driving her away in his fabulous coach to the ball at the palace. She consoled herself that Cinderella would have felt over-whelmed and scared too—but at least her dress would have fitted.

They were crossing the Fifty-ninth Street Bridge.

Vera turned backward in her seat, watching the Manhattan skyline diminish behind her. Above the jagged outline of towers lay a long smudgy finger of magenta cloud.

She supposed it was absolutely beautiful, but she couldn't appreciate it right now.

On Queens Boulevard she nervously stole a glance at Saint's profile, at his black hair whipping in the wind, at the smooth muscles of his bare arms, his fingers tapping lightly on the wheel in time to the music.

He turned briefly toward her and smiled. In the fading light she saw that his eyes were not black but a very dark blue. Then Vera felt something turn over inside her, something warm and delicious. Whatever happened tonight, however humiliating, there would still be this ride to remember.

And he said I looked great.

She thought about Starfire and Senator Moore in the limousine and how she'd been unable to draw them making love. Suddenly she wondered: Tomorrow, will I know more? Whether tonight she would learn what it was like to be held in someone's arms, to be touched, to be kissed. Might she and Saint even . . . ? And then she felt weak all over, thinking of Saint touching her, a warm heaviness centered between her thighs. She glanced at Saint's own thigh, lean and muscular under the tight fabric of his jeans, so close to hers. She wriggled surreptitiously on the seat and realized with shock: I'm wet down there. Oh, my God. Remembered she was wearing no underwear and hoped she hadn't left a telltale mark on Spring's dress.

Then she told herself not to be stupid, of course he wouldn't kiss her, why would anyone want to kiss Vera Brown; and once again passionately wished the drive would never end and the dream never be over. She knew, at that precise moment, that she was in love.

Chapter

4

"Okay, baby," the man said in a trembling voice, "let's see you shake them pom-poms."

"Sure, Coach." Jo-Beth Feeney bared her teeth in a frightening grin and went into her routine. Shaking the red-and-white cheerleader's pom-poms, kicking her legs high.

"Give me a W . . .

"Give me an I . . .

"Give me an L . . .

"Give me a D and a C . . ."

She wore her hair, deep auburn now, in bouncing braids; bright red lipstick on her mouth; a nylon mesh footballer's jersey cut off just below the rib cage, through which her full breasts were clearly visible, sneakers, and a pair of red-and-white-striped knee socks. She wore nothing at all between the tops of the socks and the bottom of the jersey.

". . . and an A-T-S . . ."

The man was middle-aged, wearing an expensive suit of lightweight wool. He was breathing heavily through his nose, the nostrils flared and white. "Go!" he said hoarsely. "Go, go, go." He sat straddle-legged, fly unzipped, pulling ferociously at the small pink organ between his fingers.

"W-I-L-D-C-A-T-S!"

"Wildcats! Goooooooo, Team!"

Jo-Beth leapt into the air, knees athletically flexed. The man leaned forward, forehead glistening with sweat, his eyes bulging at the fevered images of smooth young inner thigh, strip of golden fur, pouting moist lips which inside would be slick and hot, pink satin . . . Oh, Christ . . . and he tugged at himself ferociously, moaning now as she whirled, bent over to touch her toes, legs spread wide, beautiful firm young buttocks framing that heavenly target into which he wanted to hurl himself and drown . . .

"Oh, Jesus!" And at last it happened, something which happened so seldom these days: his limp penis stiffened and blurted a tiny little droplet into his cramped fingers.

She stood in front of him, strong dark brows drawn together in a scowl. Hands on hips. "Okay. That's it. How was it? Good enough for you?"

He raised his eyes, beseeching. "Would you . . . would you please . . . ?" He touched himself.

"Please what?" She stared at him coldly. "You want me to suck you?"

A whisper: "If you wouldn't mind . . ."

"Well, I *do* mind." Jo-Beth shuddered. "I mind very much. That's gross."

His lips wobbled tremulously. "Oh, yes, I know, I know."

"Forget it!"

Within seconds she had dressed in her street clothes, a short tan skirt, a khaki tank top, and a jungle-print scarf knotted around her hair, shaken loose from the braids Angelo had insisted she wear. She looked like a pretty high-school senior, which, until six months ago, was exactly what she had been.

In a shaking hand he held out a fifty-dollar bill.

She took it with reluctance, handling it between index finger and thumb as though it were slimy.

She slammed the door behind her as she left.

This evening the air was so thick you could slice it like cheese, Jo-Beth thought tiredly. It was five o'clock but the temperature was still in the high nineties, with matching humidity. Her whole body trembled in reaction. She had nerved herself up for that trick the whole afternoon. I'm not doing that again, Jo-Beth told herself, not again, never, never.

How he disgusted her, that pathetic man, that wealthy executive who could only get it up for very young girls. How could there be people like that in the world?

She had told him how much he disgusted her, too; how she despised him—which was just what he wanted to hear. Angelo had known that. Angelo knew everything there was to know about human weakness.

How could there be people like Angelo Primavera in the world?

What was she going to do?

She'd made three hundred and fifty bucks in half an hour.

She thought of the months in the diner—$2.50 an hour and ten-cent tips.

In some ways, if she could deaden herself, think of something else, meditate, whatever, it would be too easy . . . she could see how easy it would be just to go on, and that was simply frightening.

That was what had happened to Melody Rose. But Melody Rose had had a choice. She, Jo-Beth, had none.

A teenage boy walked past carrying an enormous radio. He was nodding his head in time to the rap music and didn't look at her. Behind him trudged a beaten-down middle-aged woman who reminded her of Momma.

Without warning, Jo-Beth's eyes filled with tears. It had torn her apart just leaving Momma like that, and she had never even called her or sent a note—but how could she, she was a wanted murderer now. What terrified her, she simply couldn't remember whether she had wiped her fingerprints off the statue. She remembered nothing between standing there frozen—Floyd lying there dead at her feet, Momma's religious statue clenched in her hand with blood and hair clotted all over Mary's blue-veiled head—and buying her bus ticket for New York in Amarillo.

The journey to New York had been a sixty-hour nightmare. At first she hadn't dared leave the bus, dreading each rest stop, where surely the police would be waiting for her. She spoke to no one and pretended to sleep most of the time, curled in her seat at the back, her hot forehead pressed against the window. Once the bus slowed and pulled over and a cop car went wailing by, red light flashing in blurring sweeps through the darkness and rain; but they didn't stop the bus, they were not after her, and by Saint Louis Jo-Beth's mind eased just a little, enough so she could be miserably aware of her aching body and burning throat.

Exhausted and feverish, she slid in and out of weird nightmares where Floyd chased her down an endless swaying corridor; each time, he'd trap her against the living-room wall and she'd see his head was smashed in and his face a sliding curtain of blood. Then she'd wake up with a crash, her heart booming inside her chest.

She'd try to stay awake and would count off the hours until they got to New York. Fifteen. Twelve. Ten. . . . She'd think about Melody. How she could fling herself into her sister's arms and it would be all right at last.

By the time they got in, late because of the weather, it was early evening, pitch dark, and snowing.

The West Side Terminal was an assault of noise and smells—of sweat, decades of stale popcorn, and dry heat gasped from miles of dusty air ducts. She had never seen so many people of all shapes, ages, and colors, who shoved past her or crashed right into her as she wandered, confused, looking for a phone. However, Jo-Beth felt comforted rather than afraid, for nobody, not one person, looked her in the face. She was anonymous. She might even be invisible.

Jo-Beth found the telephone number for Exotica Inc., although there was no street address.

A woman answered with a throaty purr, but didn't sound very friendly when Jo-Beth said who she was and asked for Melody Rose. She didn't even seem to have heard of Melody Rose, even though she was one of their top models. However, she grudgingly agreed to check around. Jo-Beth said she'd wait right here at the terminal. Then the operator broke in and demanded more money and Jo-Beth had none left.

She dozed fitfully on a bench, her empty purse clutched in her arms, shivering despite the heat. Toward midnight she fell into a heavy sleep, to be woken suddenly by someone shaking her shoulder.

"J.B. J.B., wake up!" It was Mel, at three o'clock in the morning. Mel, looking worn and tired and not particularly pleased to see her. "J.B., just what in hell are you doing here?"

A man stood beside Mel, small and beautifully dressed, with tender, thickly lashed brown eyes. He studied Jo-Beth with interest. That was the first time she saw Angelo.

The Respighi kids were playing with a garbage-can lid, rolling it back and forth and screaming. Old Mrs. Carlucci sat muttering on her steps, staring at her fluffy pink mules, an ancient kimono pulled tightly across her chest, as if she was cold. Yanni Spathis, wearing a bloodstained apron and his customary scowl, was dusting the grit off the metal chairs and tables chained outside his restaurant.

Jo-Beth waved to him. He waved perfunctorily back. "Hot enough for you?"

Just one more block and she would be home, if you could call it home, the apartment she shared with Melody Rose in a shabby three-story brownstone.

What a refuge it had been that first night. She remembered stumbling up the front steps, leaning against Melody while Angelo unlocked a metal gate, then a maroon-painted front door, inside stairs, dusty linoleum, one naked bulb burning in a narrow hallway, then more locks, three of them, and a tilted view of a pink room, everything pink and terribly warm, like walking inside her own throat. Angelo had poured something into a glass and made her drink it. It burned going down.

Then: "Looks like you've had a tough day." And he was putting her tenderly to bed, as if she was a baby, wrapped in blankets on a sofa in a tiny little room filled with racks of clothes, file cabinets, and boxes. Her last memories before dropping away into dark unconsciousness were of his light kiss on her forehead, the scent of his cologne, and the warm approval in his voice. "My, you're a pretty girl!"

Jo-Beth lay motionless in bed for more than a week, filled with antibiotics, antihistamines, and megavitamins. For another two weeks she crept about the apartment in a state of total lassitude and fatigue. She worried tearfully about her doctor's bills. Angelo told her not to worry, it was taken care of.

With returning health came a wave of terror and paranoia. She refused to leave the apartment, certain the cops would pick her up the moment she stepped outside. Angelo told her not to worry about that either, he would deal with it. No problem.

As soon as she was strong enough, he took her personally to the beauty parlor to have her hair color changed and her face made over.

Even she didn't recognize herself at first, her hair the same auburn shade as Mel's, her heavy eyebrows thinned, her brow higher, her whole face reshaped with the new shading and contouring. She felt safer at once. Angelo told her she was a natural beauty. Angelo was the first man who had treated her nice, who was kind and gentle and seemed to want nothing from her, who would never hit her, desert her, or try to force her to have sex. Jo-Beth could understand why Melody was in love with him. She was almost in love with him herself. "He's so generous," she told Melody. "I don't know how I can ever pay him back."

For a whole month, until the end of March, she had been too weak or too sick or too frightened to think straight.

It wasn't until early April that she began to see the whole picture.

That, yes, Melody Rose was certainly a model, but she didn't exactly pose for high-fashion photography. That those had not been her photos in *Vogue*; Charlene had been right.

Jo-Beth was mystified. "Why'd you send them, then?"

Melody looked evasive. "I guess I couldn't help it, seeing that girl who looked so like me; I wanted it so bad it hurt. I guess I kind of pretended she was me. It was kinda like bragging, you know, and I never thought you'd actually come here . . ." Her voice sank. "See, honey, I did try, but they laughed at me, the people at da Renza, Eileen Ford, and the others. They said I'd never be a model. They said I had the wrong kinda body." But Melody Rose's small, voluptuous body was perfect for Angelo's agency, Exotica Inc., whose models worked as escorts and convention hostesses and posed for raunchy magazines, fantasy underwear catalogs, and nude calendars. Jo-Beth thought about Melody's picture being on a calendar in the office at Floyd's Texaco station, and the men leering and whistling. "It's gross, Mel. How can you do it?"

"It's not so bad when you get used to it. And the money, Jo-Beth. Think about the money!" Money and possessions had always been important to Melody.

Jo-Beth told Angelo, "I don't want to get into this kind of stuff. No way."

He was very understanding. "Well, sure, baby. This isn't your kind of scene; you have real class. Just pay what you owe me and we'll call it quits."

Then he showed her an itemized bill that added to thousands of dollars.

Jo-Beth stared at it in shock. She had no idea doctors were paid so much. Then there'd been dental work, her new face and hair, her cosmetics and clothes. And her food and rent. "It'll take me *years* to pay you back."

Angelo smiled. "There ain't no free lunch, baby."

And then, at last, she had understood. Jo-Beth flushed, drew herself up to her full height, and glared down at him. "I'm not posing for dirty pictures. Forget it."

Angelo shook his head, tongue clicking gently. "No, baby, it's *you* who are forgetting . . . and you're not exactly in a position to forget, are you?"

She felt herself grow cold and hard inside and both ashamed and astonished at her naiveté. How could she have been so trusting? Angelo was not kind and gentle at all, he was a man—and the worst man she had ever met. Worst of all, she was completely in his power. If she didn't cooperate, he could turn her in to the cops. Just like that.

She went to Melody Rose. "What am I going to do, Mel?"

Melody had no idea. "I'd loan you the money if I had it, you know that, honey, but I'm flat broke."

Jo-Beth was shocked. Melody earned so much. How could she possibly be broke?

"Oh, this'n that, honey, you know how it is."

Jo-Beth didn't know—but she was learning. Melody's money was going straight up her nose.

"Now, you have more smarts than that," Angelo told Jo-Beth. "You just want to make a good living, have all the things you've ever dreamed of. Just think what you can do for your mother. You want to have your mother come live with you, don't you? . . . but dreams don't come cheap, baby."

Jo-Beth applied for a job as a waitress at a steakhouse on Broadway, but they wanted her social-security number and she panicked. The cops would trace her right away. For a month she worked for a coffeehouse that asked no questions, employed illegal aliens, and paid less than minimum wage. Angelo smiled and waited.

At the end of June he offered her a calendar job. She took it. She was beaten for now, and knew it.

At least the photographer and his two assistants were businesslike and in a hurry. They regarded her body with professional detachment, discussed her as though she wasn't even present, fluffed her all over with body makeup, and refused to allow her to sit down in case she got marks on her behind. She posed in several positions; in the one finally chosen, she half-knelt, her hair falling over one shoulder, arms crossed under her full, high breasts. She refused to smile. Those shots of Melody, pouting coyly, had made her cringe with humiliation. But it wasn't so bad. Afterward, "Bye, dear," the photographer called indifferently. "We'll be in touch if we need you again." No one hit on her; if they had, she'd probably have punched them out.

She was paid a hundred dollars, which was applied directly against Angelo's account.

Two weeks later came the date with Coach. Coach was a regular client, Angelo said. A piece of cake. He wouldn't even touch her, and if he did, he had a dick like a thimble.

Coach, president of a major electronics company, craved to be humiliated by high-school cheerleaders.

So she'd humiliated him and he was so grateful he'd given her three hundred bucks and a fifty-dollar tip.

Jo-Beth clashed the gate closed behind her and toiled up the stairs to the apartment she had at first thought so grand and which now looked frowzy and cluttered.

By now she hated the overstuffed chairs upholstered in pink rayon, the backs shawled with antimacassars; the little round tables with their pink skirts and lace cloths; especially the glass-fronted cabinet filled with imitation Dresden shepherds and shepherdesses. It was an awful room, a whore's room.

She unlocked the door and instantly knew she was walking in on a crisis. Melody Rose slumped in one of the pink chairs looking ill and shocked. Angelo lounged against the pink Formica bar holding a dark brown drink in his delicate fingers. They both stared at Jo-Beth.

Something had happened. Something was wrong.

Jo-Beth's stomach clenched with fear. Had the cops traced her at last?

Angelo thumped the glass down on the bar. "Thank Christ you got here in time."

Melody had been crying; her eyes were puffy. Jo-Beth felt her spine prickle. Mel was looking at her as if she hated her. God, what had happened?

She demanded, "Late for what?"

Angelo drew a deep breath and arranged his lips into a smile. "Go change right away. Put on something classy. Like you're a college coed."

Jo-Beth blinked in confusion. "A *what?*"

"You heard me. It's a fancy party out on Long Island. You're a gift for a kid movie star. This is big-time, baby. We're getting into heavy money." He sounded almost nervous.

Melody spoke for the first time. She snarled, "So what's wrong with me?"

"You crazy?" Angelo glanced at her dispassionately. "They want someone who looks like a sorority girl. Someone *young*."

"So I'm young. Christ, I'm only twenty."

"You shut your mouth." Angelo slapped her hard across the cheek.

Jo-Beth yelled, "Leave her alone, you bastard."

Angelo's eyes met hers over Melody's bent head. He said, "You got a big career ahead of you, babe." He checked his gold Rolex. "Go change. They'll be here in fifteen minutes."

Jo-Beth said through clenched teeth, "I won't. I won't do it."

Angelo said easily, "Sure you'll do it. You got a choice?"

As Jo-Beth slammed her bedroom door behind her, she heard Angelo tell Melody Rose: "And she's got something you probably forgot you ever had. She's a virgin."

Chapter

5

Blaine's Landing was a century-old, twenty-five-bedroom Gothic fantasy of terraces, cupolas, and high widow's walks. Its scores of windows commanded a majestic view of Long Island Sound. French doors opened from the living room onto a wide brick terrace and a swimming pool of Florentine tile. Beyond the terrace a luxurious lawn, soft and springy as foam, rolled in gentle undulations down to a weathered seawall.

Saint parked behind the house between a Rolls-Royce Silver Cloud and a Lamborghini. In the next row loomed a huge old-fashioned hearse. Between black-draped side windows the panels were decorated with grotesque designs and warped psychedelic lettering. The whole vehicle was splattered randomly with crimson, as though someone had upturned a pot of red paint over the roof.

"The Screaming Skulls." Saint nodded. "Arnie's pals."

The name meant nothing to Vera. "Who?"

"A rock band. Heavy metal."

Saint steered Vera between the cars, past a trio of tough-faced young men playing cards on the long hood of a Cadillac stretch limo. They wore sleeveless black T-shirts with the same gruesome logo emblazoned across the back as had been on the hearse. Down one brawny arm a tattooed snake coiled from shoulder to wrist. Vera asked, "Are they the Screaming Skulls?"

"Them?" Saint shook his head. "God, no. Much too clean and smooth. They're just roadies."

They paused in the baronial entrance to the mansion, where a heavy-shouldered man was checking names of arriving guests on a list.

Inside, a girl wearing a dazzling smile and little else offered champagne from a bottle decorated with white flowers. Saint took two glasses and gave one to Vera.

The champagne was very cold, sizzled on her palate, and made her feel more courageous. She reminded herself that Diana Starr drank champagne every day. And of course Starfire would feel perfectly at home in this conference of exotic earthlings. Vera drew a deep breath, held it a moment, and let it out slowly. She told herself: This is *it*. What you always wanted! Now's your chance to *really* live. And as Starfire, she knew it would be easy.

The main hall, where they stood beneath a multifaceted chandelier, was laid with black and white checkerboard tile. In front of them a wide staircase divided into a double sweep below a circular stained-glass window where emerald and turquoise peacocks strutted among magnolia petals.

"This must be the only part of it he hasn't fucked up," Saint told Vera as they moved further into the house.

He remembered Blaine's Landing from childhood; he had often been brought here while summering on the North Shore, farmed out with his Aunt Gloria in another great house down the coast. He would play on the lawn or in the rhododendron shrubbery—he wasn't allowed on the beach by himself—while Aunt Gloria drank iced tea on the terrace with cousin Betsey Blaine Wells and listened to Mantovani on the record player, which she still called a Victrola.

Saint remembered comfortably shabby furniture, worn rugs, bedroom wallpaper of faded roses, and damp-splotched watercolors of Venice painted by Great-Granny Blaine during her tour of Europe before World War I.

Now, as the playhouse of rich and famous Arnold Blaize, the old mansion had burst forth in a startling metamorphosis, like a dignified dowager wearing garish makeup and a miniskirt. The shabby family furniture was replaced by futuristic structures of stainless steel, leather, and glass; in the dining room, six-legged chairs in transparent green plastic surrounded a black glass triangle suspended from copper wires; abstract paintings in menacing colors hung in place of Granny Blaine's Venetian watercolors, and the house was now wired from attic to cellar for eight-track stereo, the Victrola long gone.

"He's very proud of it all," Saint told Vera. "Said it makes a statement."

"What kind of statement?"

" 'Fuck you,' I guess."

"Why?"

"Never mind, it's a long story. Let him enjoy it." He glanced at Vera, standing at his side sipping her champagne and staring at her surroundings with the astonished appraisal of one who had never before seen such a place or such people. Arriving, seeing this whole crazy setup through her innocent English-nanny eyes, he had had belated misgivings and wondered what the hell he'd been thinking about, bringing her. He had almost said, "Forget it, this will be a zoo," and taken her back to New York. He had not done so: first, because he had a bad feeling, a premonition almost, that Arnie was going to really need him; next, because, after her initial panic, Vera seemed to take things in stride. She even managed to project, in his mother's ill-fitting gown, a raffish, to-hell-with-it style.

Not that it actually mattered a damn what she wore.

Some guests, offspring of the old North Shore families, were studiedly casual in madras slacks and alligator shirts; Arnie's new people, hungry-eyed Hollywood types out from the Coast, sported the ultimate from Rodeo Avenue boutiques; the social- and art-circuit predators from Manhattan wore anything at all from Christian Dior to Salvation Army chic; a very drunk young man in a tuxedo lurched past, dragging a giggling girl in a pink satin formal and crushed gardenia corsage. Clearly they had escaped a debutante ball for a party with a louder band, more booze, and better drugs.

Saint turned abruptly as a heavy hand clasped his shoulder. "Hi, Saint. So you made it after all."

The man was muscular, prematurely balding, in his early thirties. He looked strangely out of place among the crowd, probably because he was sober. He was Frank Zelinsky, Arnie's bodyguard. He wore a vibrant plaid jacket which didn't fit well; Saint knew that beneath it he wore a Walther PPK .380 in a shoulder holster.

Saint asked, "So how's he doing?"

"How do you think?"

At once Saint was back there in that frigid afternoon last winter when, devastated by his father's rejection, he had called Arnie from the Plaza—only to find himself a front-line spectator for somebody else's hell.

After two days, having witnessed the full range of the mood swings and erratic behavior patterns, Saint was seriously disturbed about Arnie. He did drugs himself on a casual basis, everyone did—but this was different. This was serious, heavy stuff.

"Jesus, Saint," Arnie would cry, "don't be a drag. C'mon, man. Let's do some powder."

"No, Arn. I'm not into that."

He had thought that he might help, that he might bring Arnie back from the crumbling edge he was walking so blithely. What a mistake. Arnie didn't want help. Problem? What problem? There was nothing that couldn't be taken care of with vodka, 'ludes, or coke, and, furiously, "If you don't like it, then get your goddamn ass out of here. Who needs you?"

When Saint decided to return to California after all, Arnie had been hysterical with grief. "Saint! Don't go. Don't leave me—Saint, I can't handle it without you." Saint had felt like a coward and a traitor, but what else could he do?

School had seemed a refuge after that, and much to his surprise, Saint graduated. He wondered briefly whether his father would come. Standing on the platform receiving his diploma, he searched hopefully for his face among the rows of parents sitting on folding chairs in the shade of the oak trees, just in case he had come late. His father did not, of course, attend, but sent a sizable check and a summons back to New York to discuss his future.

Saint's first impulse had been to tear up the check; his roommate, a lawyer's son from San Francisco, had been appalled. "Are you out of your fucking mind?"

"I don't want his money."

"Then I'll take it. I'll do you a favor. I'm not proud."

After much thought, Saint decided to keep the money and spend it in a way his father would disapprove of. He found the Jaguar in a used-car showroom, an elegant automobile, totally and delightfully impractical. He spent the next month driving it across the country. He was not in a hurry, and the various catastrophes and breakdowns lent an air of exciting unpredictability to the journey.

Before broaching Manhattan, he paused for a breathing space with Aunt Gloria, somewhat of a recluse now, living frugally off her trust fund in a converted barn outside Stamford, Connecticut. Aunt Gloria had few interests beyond her garden, which was magnificent, and evening reruns of *Hogan's Heroes*, but in a distracted way she seemed glad to see him.

From Aunt Gloria's, Saint finally called his father, only to learn from Miss Gerrity that he was in London.

Then his mother: "Oh, it's you, Sloane. I was so sorry to miss graduation, dear, but I do have a gift for you. Maybe you could come over on Friday evening? Not too early, I'm terribly tied up—about nine or ten. Do you still have your key?"

Finally, anxiously, he called Arnie, who cried, "Jesus, Saint, where the fuck have you been? I've been calling all over. I've got this house, Saint, I bought it. Blaine's Landing. You remember it, where you used to go with Aunt Gloria when you were a kid . . . You've gotta see it." Urgently: "I'm having a party Friday. You've gotta come."

And now, here was Arnie himself, erupting with an audible crash through the double doors leading out to the terrace, Arnold Blaize, teenage superstar, in tight scarlet leather pants and matching vest, towing behind him the requisite dazzling model.

Arnie's face was ablaze with expectation and relief. "Saint! You made it! Thought you weren't coming, man."

And behind the glitz and the fancy outfit Saint still saw the fat boy of the eighth grade, with pleading eyes and something terrifying about his smile. He felt a moment of cold fear for Arnie. Then, recovering, he quipped, "Hey, man, if I didn't know better, I'd think you were a movie star."

Vera found her hands clasped and both cheeks kissed by the most famous teenager in the world. For an instant she was overwhelmed by the warmth of his welcome, his smile, his famous green eyes. Then he was tugging forward his girlfriend; she heard him say, "Saint and Vera, this is . . ." But the name was lost in a sudden surge of sound.

The girl was tall, wearing a short white dress of nubbly linen. Hair the color of autumn leaves was pinned behind her head in a heavy braid. Up close she was even more beautiful, or she would have been, with any animation or warmth in her face. She glanced first at Saint, then at Vera, from luminous gray eyes in which jewellike colors flared and danced. She gave a small mechanical smile.

"Hello," Vera said, staring.

The girl said "Hi" in a neutral voice. She was gazing over Vera's head at the stained-glass window. She wasn't happy. Vera knew this suddenly and completely, on a level of deep recognition which made the fine hairs bristle on the back of her neck. She knew at once the girl didn't want to be at the party. That she didn't want to talk to them. Wasn't pleased to be with Arnie. I *know* this girl, Vera realized. And not just casually. I know her well. I can almost read her mind.

She asked abruptly, "I've met you before. Where was it?"

The girl shook her head emphatically. "We've never met."

Arnie was telling Vera, ". . . he's my old, old buddy. One of the good guys. The only good guy. 'Cept he keeps going away." He gripped Saint by the arm. "Are you guys being taken care of? Gotta drink? Anything you want, let me know, it's all here—*anything*." He doubled up with hysteria and slapped himself hard on the thigh. "Skulls're playing . . ." He demanded of Vera, "Like the Skulls?" She tore her eyes from the red-haired girl and nodded: Oh, yes, of course she did.

"Yeah! Fuckin' A. Going on tour next month, world tour—England, Paris, Hamburg—but first a gig for old Arn." He dug Saint in the ribs. "Remember St. Regius? Huh? Things've changed. Huh?"

Saint nodded absently. "Yeah." He was staring at the red-haired girl too, Vera noticed, and with a similar dazed surprise.

"I do the ass-kicking now. Yeah . . ." For a second a film seemed to cover Arnie Blaize's bright green eyes. His face blanked out and his jaw sagged. Then he suddenly snapped to, like a slack-limbed marionette responding to a jerk on the strings. "Great to see you guys." He clung tight to their hands. "Old friends're the best. You know that? All this stuff—these people—they don't mean from shit. It's people like you guys—you're the best. I just *love* you guys." He hugged them both violently, his eyes brimming with sudden tears, then released them just as abruptly. "Hey, *fuck* . . ." He stared wildly around the room at his seething guests, then gave a delighted grin. "Check out the action! It's a *great* party. *Every*body's here! I gotta go circulate . . . see you later!"

Arnie plunged back into the crowd, dragging the girl after him.

At once Vera demanded, "What *was* her name? Saint, did you hear her name?"

He shook his head no.

"He told us. He must have." Vera said, puzzled, "I know her. I'm *sure* I do." She added wistfully, "She's beautiful, isn't she?"

Staring after her, Saint said, "She's more than that."

The boy in the tuxedo was vomiting behind a potted tree fern. Beside him, the girl in pink satin complained, "Brendan, you're such a fuckup."

Frank Zelinsky's voice told Tuxedo, "Better get outside, sir. You could use some fresh air."

The girl said, "He's a fuckup. Isn't he? A real fuckup."

"If you say so, miss."

Frank flagged a waiter. "Can you send someone out to deal with that?" He pointed behind the fern.

"Hey!" Saint caught Frank's arm. "Who's the girl with Arnie?"

The bodyguard said abstractedly, "Her? Who knows?"

"But don't you know her *name*?"

He shrugged. "Pick one. The name of the week. Tracy's in right now. Or Tiffany or Samantha . . ."

Saint's grip tightened on Frank's sleeve. "What are you saying?"

"That she's just a hooker, man. How the hell should I know her name?"

Saint's face was suddenly pale. He gave a small gasp. "You're kidding me."

"I kid you not. Studio rented her for the night. Paid top dollar."

"But she can't be. That's crazy."

A middle-aged maid, impassive face implying infinite downside experience with the leisured rich, appeared from the nether regions with a pail and mop.

From the terrace came a series of piercing screams.

"Oh, shit, now what? Gotta go." Frank shook himself free from Saint's grasp, shouldered his way through the partygoers, and disappeared.

Saint stared after him. "I don't care what he says. That girl's not a hooker."

Jo-Beth allowed Arnie to drag her right up beside the stage.

"You got a big career ahead of you, babe. . . . Better go change . . . There'll be a car here for you anytime . . .

"She's got what you've forgotten you ever had. She's a virgin."

"He won't give you any trouble." The driver had worn a lightweight black suit, white shirt, and striped tie. He had popped indigestion tablets all the way out on the expressway. "All he cares about is chemicals. He'll be a veggie by midnight; you got it made. Tomorrow just tell him how great he was. It's money for old rope."

She'd said nothing to the driver, not one word. He'd advised worriedly, "Hey, lighten up a bit, doll. You don't want to piss off the customers."

By tomorrow she would be a real pro.

Jesus.

Back in Corsica High, LuAnn Krebbs had had a photo of Arnie taped to the inside of her locker. "I'd just give my right arm to go on a date with that boy. I *would*."

You can have him, Jo-Beth thought, and welcome.

"You sure don't look like a hooker." Arnold Blaize had looked relieved, then doubtful. He asked with a glittering smile, "You gonna do everything I want? They paying you enough?" He had touched her bare arm; his skin felt hot and dry and . . . *He's never done this before.* In a sudden flash of intuition, Jo-Beth knew that Arnold Blaize was as virginal as she, technically, was. That, despite being an international teenage idol, he had never had sex with a girl. He looked very young and vulnerable. He was terrified. For a moment she felt tremendously sorry for him.

Since then, watching him become taut and brittle as an overwound watch while his party grew louder and wilder, she had grown steadily more nervous.

She had a bad feeling about this party, how it could turn weird really fast. One of the bartenders was openly dealing dope. Glass smashed with greater frequency. A destructive herd instinct was developing among the guests.

Anything might happen. An accident. A fight. Someone could O.D.

Then the cops would come and she'd be trapped, Arnold Blaize's "date," with no way out. They'd question her. Want to know who she was; they'd find out everything. . . .

Arnie was swaying to the beat of the music, pounding his bunched right fist into his left palm. His forehead was sleek with sweat, his face flashing crimson, magenta, and royal blue in sequence from the pulsing strobe lights above the stage. Beneath their emblem of a giant bloody-toothed steel skull shrieked four demons in black leather and ghoul makeup, led by lead singer Phil Zeitgeist, who, according to a press release, drank a quart of blood every day. He had also been known to urinate from his hotel window onto the massed heads of his ecstatic fans. He postured and howled, clutching the mike as though he would gnaw it in half, a necklace of animal teeth and bones bouncing rhythmically up and down on his bare chest.

Arnie had forgotten her. Jo-Beth retreated to the edge of the pool, which was filled with bobbing inflatable toys. She saw a Godzilla, an alligator, a yellow duck.

A girl in black lace underwear danced by herself, whipsawing her head back and forth, elbows thrusting like pistons. Jo-Beth saw her catch her foot on an uneven tile, stagger backward with windmilling arms, and fall with a piercing scream into the water. She surfaced a second later, head slick as a seal, and screamed again, louder. Two men roared with laughter and leapt in after her.

Arnie's bodyguard thrust his way through the horde to check out the noise, just as the Screaming Skulls brought their set to a close with a crashing satanic discord and loped offstage, where they would, she thought, slurp down Chivas from the bottle, pee, do a line or two or shoot up. She watched Arnie follow them.

Jo-Beth, alone for the first time in hours, wandered away down the lawn to stare out over the dark water. The comparative silence was blissful. She listened to the gentle slosh of the waves and to crickets chirping in the grass, thinking how she missed the huge silent emptiness of night, the wind and the stars. If only, by some stroke of magic, the house, the party, the Screaming Skulls, and Arnold Blaize would all disappear and leave her here alone.

A flicker of lightning revealed a long row of black, hanging cloud bellies. Moments later came a rolling grumble of thunder. Jo-Beth sighed with pleasure. She loved storms.

Now that her eyes were more adjusted, she could see the lighter shape of a dock reaching out on pilings into the inky water. There was a small boat, a dinghy, tied up at the end of the dock. Fifty yards further out, a sailboat bobbed at a mooring. It was long and sleek; its white hull gleamed through the darkness.

She stared longingly at the boat. She thought about running away down the dock, climbing into the boat, letting go the ropes, and sailing away into the gathering storm. Escape . . .

A hand touched her bare forearm. Jo-Beth leapt with fright.

"Sorry. I didn't mean to scare you." It was the English girl, Vera, the girl with the too-tight dress and the Farrah Fawcett wig. Arnie's friend, Saint, stood beside her.

"I was looking for you. I wanted to talk to you. Listen," Vera said, "what *is* your name?"

"Jo-Beth Feeney." She said it automatically, without thinking, and could have bitten off her tongue. Oh, what a fool, to give her real name. Hadn't she learned better than that?

Vera insisted, "I know we've met."

Jo-Beth shook her head with vehemence. "You're thinking of someone else."

A Y-shaped fork of lightning split the lowering clouds. The sailboat stood out in minute detail. Brilliant white mast and boom, stays, rigging, winches, wheel, and compass housing.

Jo-Beth said impulsively, "Isn't it beautiful!" In afterimage, the boat seemed printed black on a white sea. She said wistfully, "I'll bet you could go out on the ocean in that . . ."

"No," Vera said as though she hadn't spoken, "I'm sure it was you."

There was a long, ominous rumble of thunder.

Jo-Beth said, "It's coming closer." And wondered anxiously if Vera really *had* seen her before. If so, where?

In the paper? Or a "wanted" poster in the post office?

She felt cold with fright. Then told herself not to act crazy. Even if there had been a picture, Vera wouldn't have recognized her, not in a thousand years, with her different face and her red hair. . . . But Vera seemed so *sure*.

Jo-Beth decided she had better get away from Vera, but that meant returning to the pool, to the party.

She felt frightened and alone. If only, she thought, there was one person here whom she could trust. But there was no one. She knew nobody but Arnie, who was zapped out of his mind.

Vera announced abruptly, "Something's happening up there."

They turned in time to see Arnie Blaize leap with a maniacal howl onto the empty stage. He grabbed the mike. There was a vulgar sound like breaking wind, followed by a searing whistle. "Hey, everybody! You gotta have *fun*! This party's bor-*ring*!"

Arnie's face glared magenta, crimson, then royal blue, then blanched to a weird bone white as a lightning bolt sizzled across the sky.

"Hey!" Arnie yelled. "Do I put on a light show or do I?"

Thunder boomed. People screamed with laughter.

The metal skull swayed in a sudden gust of damp wind.

Arnie began to dance, the mike cradled close against his chest, and to sing in heavy rhythm. "*Where* the *fuck's* the *music*? *Where* the *fuck's* the *music*?"

A blond boy crash-dived into the pool and a wave flooded over the side across Italian shoes, sneakers, and bare feet.

Saint began to run across the grass toward the terrace. Jo-Beth and Vera followed.

Arnie sang in parody, "I'm gonna eat you up, I'm gonna eat your flesh . . ."

Then the rain began. Huge fat drops, plopping slowly one by one, picking up momentum.

The black-lace girl dragged herself out of the water and collapsed facedown on the tiles.

A bald man with a bristling black beard held up his arms as though administering a blessing. "Yea, I declare unto you—It's fucking raining!"

"Eat you up . . . eat you up . . ."

"Hey, Arnie! Way to go! Yay, Arnie!"

Saint shoved through the mob and climbed onstage just as Frank, ahead of him, grasped the star by the arm and shoulder. The amplified voices came over the mike in alternate booms and squeaks. "C'mon, man, that's enough. Cool it, now, you got company . . ."

"Bor-*ring*!"

Frank yelled at Saint. "You. Get down offa here. I've got him in control now."

"Don't shove him around like that. He'll freak out."

"Fuck off, Junior, and that means right now!"

"I wanna dance. Rain dance!" Arnie flung both arms around Frank's chest in a bear hug. They lurched awkwardly about the stage until Arnie shoved the bodyguard violently and angrily in the chest. "Leave me alone. These're my friends. I'm with my *friends* here . . ."

Frank lost his balance, tripped over an amplifier lead, and almost fell. He roared, "Hey, Arnie! What you think you're—?" and then, voice cracking with dismay, "*Jesus!* You give me that right now! You hear?"

"Shit, no." Arnold Blaize faced his audience, legs straddled to support his swaying body. He'd cut himself or bitten his lip; red blood trickled down his chin, black in the flash of the blue strobe.

From across the stage Saint said, "Arnie. It's me. It's Saint. Arnie, put it down."

Arnie laughed.

Frank yelled, "Everything's under control. You folks get inside. Right now."

A woman screamed. "Oh, my God he's got a—"

Thunder crashed.

Another scream: "—gun! Jesus fucking Christ, he's got a *gun*."

Arnie held the Walther 38 in his right hand, left hand clasping his wrist, just the way he'd been taught for his teenage cop movie. He moved in a slow half-crouch, aiming first at Frank's stomach, at Saint's head, finally taking careful aim at the living-room plate-glass window. A crash, and it disintegrated in a shower of glass.

Frank cried, "Don't panic! Don't nobody panic! Everyone keep down . . ."

"Hey! All *right!*" Arnie pivoted. "A one! A two! A three . . ."

More shattered windows; glass rain. Vera saw blood trickling down her arm.

Frank yelled at Saint, "I know what I'm doing here. Get the fuck outta the way."

Terrified guests jammed shrieking in the doorway.

Vera squeezed her eyes closed tight and opened them again. Starfire would be able to make him drop the gun with the force of her mind. She would—

Lightning flashed, a brilliant purple-white, and with the lightning Vera suddenly knew exactly where it was she had seen Jo-Beth before. Of course. No wonder she had recognized her.

The rain rattled on the tiles.

Arnie shot out another window.

"You're just pumping him up," Saint cried at Frank. "You're making it worse."

Arnie Blaize chortled, took aim at the blue spotlight. It exploded in smoke and a spray of sparks.

"C'mon," Jo-Beth ordered Vera, "get down." She dived behind a wrought-iron table and dragged Vera with her.

Arnie aimed for the red spot.

He fired. But the red spot did not die; instead, the grinning steel skull swung crazily from side to side and back and forth, and a second later they heard a hollow clang.

With a chuckle, Arnie faced the sign, sighted carefully, squeezed the trigger—but nothing happened. He frowned at the gun in irritation.

Jo-Beth sighed in relief. Clip's empty. They can get him . . ."

But now that he had his chance, the bodyguard did nothing.

From the edge of the stage he was staring at Arnie with an expression of pained surprise. Then he began to fall backward, thick limbs loose and ungainly, down through the rain, plowing into the gleaming turquoise water among the bright plastic toys.

Arnie peered dazedly down at him, the gun hanging loosely from his fingers. "Frank? Frankie? Hey, what's this shit, man?"

Arnie's guests crept back out through the shattered French doors and stood in a cluster around the pool, watching Frank float quietly on his face among frogs and rubber ducks, the blood fanning out around his head, black in the brilliant turquoise water.

Someone replied, "He's dead, man."

"Don't give me that shit," Arnie said into a ghastly silence. Then, his voice small and high-pitched, a very young, frightened voice, "Saint?" Arnie whispered, "Saint? Are you there? Help me. . . ."

Chapter
6

Vera heard Jo-Beth draw a deep, sobbing breath.

Then, without warning, she turned and plunged into the dense growth of rhododendrons that divided the lawn and pool area from the gravel driveway out front.

Vera followed, forcing her way through tearing branches and slashing, soaking leaves, knowing instinctively she mustn't let Jo-Beth run away. That it would be disastrous.

She caught up with her in the parking area.

Jo-Beth's face was scratched, her dress torn, her hair tumbling from its carefully groomed braid. She looked wild. Vera grabbed her by the wrist. "Wait."

"Let me go." Jo-Beth snatched her arm away. "I have to get *out* of here."

Vera almost panicked, then with intense relief caught sight of Saint. He was thrusting toward them through the crowd of people who streamed from the front door with the frenzy of a theater audience that has smelled smoke. He grabbed Jo-Beth by the shoulders. "It's all right," he said forcefully. "It's all *right*. Come on back inside."

She was trembling. "You must have a car. Get me out of this."

Saint cast one glance at the cars already jammed in the driveway. "No way. We're stuck. And I can't leave anyway. I have to stay with Arnie."

"But the cops will come. Any minute. Any *second*." She tore herself from Saint's grip. "You don't *understand*!"

"Hey! Cool it. Of course I understand."

"No, you don't. How could you?" Jo-Beth's voice rose raw and harsh and her face wore a look of trapped desperation. "You don't know *anything*. I can't let them get me."

"What happened back there had nothing to do with you."

"But I was with Arnie. I was his *date*."

"You were nowhere near him, and there's fifty, sixty people to tell them so."

"But they'll find out who I *am*!" And she stiffened, hearing above the struggle and racket of shouts and blaring horns the far-off, dreaded wail of sirens. She tried to lunge under Saint's arm. "They're coming. Right now!"

He caught her again and held her tight. "Listen! How are they going to *know* you're a hooker—unless you tell them yourself?"

Jo-Beth seemed to decide then that flight was useless. She drooped with despair. "It's much more than that. I said you didn't understand. She turned with sagging shoulders and allowed Saint to lead her back inside the house, explaining tonelessly, "They'll find me and I'll go to jail. I killed somebody, you see. I'm wanted for murder. . . ."

"Okay," Saint said gently, wiping the dirt from Jo-Beth's face with a cocktail napkin soaked in champagne, "you'd better tell us all about it. We'll get our stories straight and nobody'll find out. Tell us what happened, from the beginning."

Vera felt a flare of pride that Saint trusted her enough to include her in the conspiracy. It never occurred to her that she might automatically become an accessory to a crime. She listened intently, ready to help, as, in a shaking voice, Jo-Beth whispered, "It happened back home. I killed my stepfather. I killed him *dead*. He tried to . . . he was drunk and he . . . went after me. Tried to force me to . . ."

At first Vera didn't understand what Jo-Beth was trying to say. It was too appalling. Things like that didn't happen in her small secure world, at least not to anybody she knew. However, Saint seemed to understand at once, and Vera had never seen anyone so angry in her whole life. At that moment Saint looked wicked. Vera thought she would be very afraid of him if he was ever angry with her.

Later on she would try to draw that particular expression on Saint's face; she would fail and be glad—it was too violently personal and, for her, too painful. She would be reminded, each time she saw Saint's protective rage, that *that* was the moment he had fallen in love with Jo-Beth Feeney.

"All right," he said with effort, "all right, Jo-Beth, that's enough."

And Vera found herself saying, "Now, listen. When they ask you questions, this is what you say. . . ."

Hours passed.

The harsh overhead light spilled relentlessly on exhausted faces, the littered floor, and scattered glasses smeared with lipstick. The boy in the tuxedo lay flat on his back, unconscious; his date sat at his side, her pink dress soiled and crumpled. The girl in the black lace slip, now wearing a man's jacket, shivered in the corner with her head in her hands. Vera knew that she herself looked a terrible mess; her thick makeup had run, Spring's gown was missing a lot of sequins and was split under the arms, while the rain and clawing rhododendrons had wreaked havoc with the Farrah Fawcett wig.

Officials went about their business and left again: the county medical officer, a police photographer, the coroner. Vera and Jo-Beth sat side by side in the dining room on those ugly plastic chairs, which were actually more comfortable than they looked. Through the French doors they watched Frank's body, zipped into a black plastic bag, being carried past on a stretcher.

There were mingled sounds of vehicles arriving and departing, phones ringing, subdued weeping from behind a closed door, and the frustrated curses and mutterings of the Screaming Skulls, impatient to give interviews to the television newspeople.

More men arrived, wearing ordinary clothes. These were homicide investigators. They took Saint away with them to another room, where poor Arnie, shocked and incoherent, would say nothing unless his only friend was at his side.

Jo-Beth's face was stony, her knuckles white.

"It's all right," Vera reassured her, smoothing down Jo-Beth's tangled mane of hair and picking out an errant leaf. "It'll be all right. Just remember what I said."

The detective had light brown eyes with darker brown pouches under them. He was very quiet, very gentle. He looked like a tired basset hound.

His shirt was wrinkled and buttoned wrong, as though he had got dressed in too much of a hurry.

"My name's Diana Starr," Jo-Beth said. And gave Spring Kentfield's address on Central Park West. He didn't seem to find anything strange about it at all.

It was broad daylight when they got home at last. A cluster of waiting reporters streamed forward in a body and cameras flashed as Saint, Jo-Beth, and Vera tore through the doors into the lobby.

Upstairs, Jo-Beth began to cry. Even though she had hidden her face in her hands as she ran, her picture would be in all the papers and someone might still recognize her.

"They were after me, though," Saint tried to reassure her, "I'm Arnie's friend and Spring Kentfield's son. And don't worry, they'll give up and leave us alone if we just sit it out." But it didn't happen like that at all. Throughout the morning the numbers of patiently waiting newspeople swelled rather than diminished, until by ten o'clock there were three mobile TV news vans parked on the corner of Seventy-second Street.

Saint announced in heartfelt tones, "Thank God Mother's in L.A. She'd milk this one for all it's worth."

His first action on returning was to transfer all incoming calls to the answering service.

Next he made a series of outgoing calls. It seemed extraordinary to Vera that he could think so clearly, be so decisive. He appeared to have aged suddenly, to be far more mature than eighteen.

Saint's first call was to Mr. Friedman, his father's lawyer.

"Yes," Vera heard him say, "I'd be real glad if you'd come over. There're things I have to talk with you about. But I don't want a press conference. No way."

A fairly long pause, after which Saint said reluctantly, "Well, if you think it will get them off my back, I suppose . . ."

Another pause.

"Don't be dumb. Of course I'm not a hero."

Pause.

"Okay. I'll do like you say, but there's more. . . ." And here Saint gave a guarded account of Jo-Beth and her situation, not mentioning the killing of Floyd Feeney. "I brought her back with me. Said she was staying here.

I mean, why not? I'm Arnie's friend. I could've introduced them, couldn't I? . . . And one more thing. I'll explain when you get here. I'll need a rental car. Something real inconspicuous."

Next, Saint called Aunt Gloria.

Vera heard, "I need a favor, Aunt G. Are you home tonight? Can I come visit and bring a friend? For a couple of days? . . . Thanks a heap. We'll be over later. . . . No, it's a girl. . . . I'll tell you when we get there."

Finally, a call to Geronia, telling her to get over on the double, and pick up certain items from a drugstore on the way.

When Saint was through with the phone, Jo-Beth called Melody Rose. She talked for only a few seconds, and afterward sat crouched on Vera's bed, shivering with distress and anger. "She just asked about the money. She wanted to know had I got the money *first*, before the shooting. She didn't even ask was I all right."

Vera hadn't known what to do for her. In the end, deciding action was best, she put Jo-Beth to work helping her dry and fluff out Spring's wig.

Back on the Styrofoam stand, beside the other wigs, it looked disheveled and disorderly and had clearly had a rough time. Vera asked helplessly, "What'll I do?"

Jo-Beth said without much interest, "You'll have to take it to a salon and get it styled properly, I guess."

The dress, however, was beyond hope, especially since Jo-Beth had to cut her out of it. "You better dump that," Jo-Beth advised, "down the chute. She's got so many dresses she'll probably never notice it's gone." But somehow Vera guessed that when it came to her personal property, Spring would notice if so much as a pin were misplaced.

Geronia arrived at noon wearing her maid's uniform over a vibrant purple bra and half-slip. She carried a brown paper sack. No one had challenged her in the lobby, she told Saint cheerfully. Why should they? She was just a maid. No one noticed a maid.

Almost immediately afterward came Mr. Friedman, with whom Saint was closeted privately for half an hour. Then, looking considerably stressed, Friedman talked with Jo-Beth.

While Saint braved the reporters in the lobby, Friedman at his side, Geronia bustled Jo-Beth into the guest bathroom.

Vera perched on the edge of the tub while Geronia cut Jo-Beth's hair very short and dyed it a nondescript brown, ". . . though it seems a crying shame, pretty hair like this."

When she was done, Jo-Beth stared at herself in the mirror with an expression of dazed surprise. "I don't even know who that is anymore. It sure doesn't look like me."

"That's the idea, honey."

When Mr. Friedman and Geronia were both gone, the three of them—Saint, Vera, and Jo-Beth—clustered in the kitchen waiting for dark.

They spent a strange, sequestered afternoon eating chocolate cake and flipping channels on the television until Saint, restlessly prowling the apartment, found Vera's *Starfire* strips on the living-room table.

"Oh, Saint," Vera said, contrite, for they were not very kind to Spring and she was, after all, his mother, "I'm sorry. I shouldn't have done it."

However, to her relief, Saint found them hilarious. "Hey, this is too much. I didn't know you did this kind of stuff. You're really *talented*, Vera. This is *wicked*!"

Jo-Beth peered over his shoulder at Spring pouting up through beaded lashes at Senator Moore. She began to laugh too. It was an immense breaker of tension—a huge relief to scream, and scream again, with laughter. They spread the drawings on the living-room rug so they could see them better, and laughed so much they collapsed in an ungainly heap of limbs, hysterical.

When they'd recovered a little, Saint raided the refrigerator and returned with an armful of chicken, fruit, and garlic bread. He opened a bottle of champagne, very good stuff too, better than had been served at Arnie's party, and they drank together.

Vera raised her glass and said very solemnly, "I feel as if we've been through a war."

Jo-Beth looked solemnly from Saint to Vera. "Thank you. Both of you. I never thanked you before. I don't know why you're doing this for me."

"Because we're all in this together. We're the Starfire Trio. And if you end up in jail, Jo-Beth, we'll be right in there too. We've perjured ourselves," Saint said cheerfully. "Right?"

Vera asked, "But when will I see you both again?" With a sudden pang: "You're going away . . ."

Saint reassured her, "Only to Connecticut. We'll be back before you know it. Anyway, the three of us belong together, we're the Starfire Trio. Through thick and thin." He thought for a moment. "We'll make a pledge." He snapped his fingers commandingly. "On your feet, people. We'll do it the Russian way."

They drank the last of the champagne, solemnly clinked their glasses, then hurled them over their shoulders to crash into Spring Kentfield's onyx fireplace.

"There," Saint said with satisfaction. "Mother's Baccarat crystal. Now, *there's* a serious pledge."

Saint and Jo-Beth left after eight o'clock for Aunt Gloria's house in Connecticut. Vera said good-bye to them at the gate to the freight elevator, Jo-Beth almost unrecognizable with her short brown hair. They hugged each other, standing in a tight little circle. Vera said breathlessly, "The Starfire Trio, right? Through thick and thin."

The gate clashed shut. Vera leaned her face against the gate, watching the elevator roof descend the shaft until she couldn't see it anymore; then she watched the moving cables and counterweight until finally they were still and she knew the elevator had reached the bottom, that Saint and Jo-Beth were gone.

She closed the apartment door behind her, her eyes hot with unshed tears, shaking with delayed reaction to the shocks and emotions of that endless day.

She undressed and crept into bed, exhausted but knowing she would never sleep.

But she must have slept, and very deeply too, until her door crashed open, the overhead light glared into her shocked eyes, and a strident voice yelled, "All right, miss, out of that bed! Jesus *Christ*, do you have some explaining to do, you lousy, ungrateful little bitch!"

Vera gazed blankly up at Spring Kentfield, who surely was safely in Los Angeles.

She's not real, Vera started to tell herself; this is just another nightmare.

But it was no nightmare. Spring was completely real, eyes bulging with wrath, holding in one hand an empty champagne bottle, in the other a sheaf of drawings which, before Vera's eyes, she ceremoniously ripped into shreds and scattered on the floor. "After all I've done for you," Spring roared. "You can pack your bags and go back to England. And it can't be too soon."

So that was what happened.

The very next day, Vera found herself on a flight to London.

By the end of the week it all seemed like a dream, as though nothing had happened at all, as though she had never been to New York, never bathed little William, eaten Geronia's cookies, fallen in love, met a movie star, or attended a disastrous party on Long Island that had made national headlines.

She fell right back into her old routine.

Her first Sunday, at teatime: "Isn't it lovely," Mum said to Dad, "having our girl home? It seems she's never been away." She leaned over to pat Vera's plump knee. "Doesn't it, Dad?"

Vera sighed. She finished her muffin and wiped her buttery mouth.

Immediately, Mum passed the sponge cake. It was filled with cream and strawberry jam. "Here you are, dear. Jam sponge. I made it specially."

Vera cut a large piece. When she finished it, she cut another.

Mum watched her eat and looked very happy.

No, nothing had changed.

But that wasn't really true.

Sitting down at last at her desk to resume the *Starfire* drawings—she might as well do something, mightn't she?—she found that at least one problem was resolved.

Her heroine had a face at last.

Starfire now looked just like Jo-Beth Feeney, and it seemed absolutely and completely right, as though it had been meant that way from the first. She thought: Of course I knew Jo-Beth.

She *is* Starfire.

PART TWO

Chapter

7

Saint lay on his motel bed, the Indiana dawn red against his closed eyelids. It would be time to get up soon, find some coffee, get back on the road.

He was driving J.B. to San Francisco. He had started calling her J.B. She seemed to like it. And she wanted to go to San Francisco. She had no idea what she would do when she got there: "I just want to get as far away from here as I can, someplace nobody's ever heard of me." As though mere distance would help.

Saint had said at once, "Okay. When do you want to start? I'll drive you."

At once her eyes narrowed. Without Vera, her attitude toward him had changed. She was mistrustful and edgy. "Thanks. But no thanks."

"Why not? I can go to San Francisco too if I want."

"Sure. But I don't need your help." Hurriedly: "I don't want to seem rude, and I'm really and truly grateful to you, but you've done enough for me. I can make it on my own now."

"Don't be dumb. How? Listen, you go on a plane, or a bus or something, you can be traced. People will remember you. If you come with me, we can use back roads. We can camp. No one can find you. Anyway," Saint had said ruthlessly, "what are you going to do for money?"

Reluctantly she had to admit she didn't know. She'd looked down at her hands and sighed. "Okay," she agreed tonelessly. "I guess you're right. But I'll pay you back," she said through tight lips, obviously hating to be beholden. "I'll pay you back every cent. I promise."

"You don't need to do that."

"Yes I do."

"Okay. We'll talk about it later. When we get there." And in the meantime, Saint had thought with a lifting heart, there would be long days on the road with this strange, independent, troubled girl with whom he had fallen so precipitately in love. By San Francisco, they would know each other inside out. And surely by then she would trust him and love him too.

The moment she grudgingly agreed, he threw his entire energy into preparing for the trip. He felt a sudden immense urgency to leave, that they must leave *now*, and his instinct was right. Mr. Friedman called just as they finished packing the car. First it was merely a routine update, news of Arnie's court date, at which Saint must appear, details and logistics. Then, like a crack of doom: "About the girl, now. You'd better sit down, Sloane."

I knew it, Saint thought; I knew something would happen. Through the window he could see J.B. and Aunt Gloria securing the tent to the roof racks of the Ford.

"I called the county sheriff," Friedman said, "the Amarillo P.D., and the D.A.'s office there. Wait till you hear *this*! It changes everything."

Saint watched J.B. tugging on the end of a rope and tying it with businesslike knots, and as the significance of the news dawned on him, protested, "But that's impossible—"

"Well, it's not," Friedman said, "and you'd better tell her right away."

"Yeah," Saint agreed slowly. "Sure."

But he didn't tell her right away; he couldn't. Soon, of course—but not quite yet. Just a few more days, he told himself; when we get to Ohio, I'll tell her. But it was more difficult in Ohio than it had been in Pennsylvania. It was more difficult each day. He didn't know what to do, so he said nothing at all. If only they had left just a half-hour earlier.

Now he rolled onto his side and gazed at her in the other bed, a humped shape under the yellow chenille spread. He loved her more today than he had last night. He would love her more tonight than he had this morning.

If only she would trust him. At first he had tried to get her to talk about herself. He wanted to know everything about her, but she would volunteer nothing beyond essentials. "I lived with my mother and sister in a small town in Texas, near Amarillo." She refused to speak about Floyd.

"What happened to your real father?"

"He walked out on us when I was five. We never heard from him again."

With a dreadful fascination he skirted around her six months in New York. "J.B., did you really . . . I mean, don't talk about it if you'd rather not . . ." He wanted passionately to know, but dreaded to hear what she would say. However, this too she adamantly refused to discuss. "It's gone. It's not part of my life." Which was both a frustration and a relief, for he wanted to think of her life as starting the night of Arnie's party, the night they met.

Anyway, in his heart he just couldn't believe it. J.B. could never have been a hooker.

She undressed behind a locked bathroom door.

She slept chastely in her underwear at night.

She hated to be touched. Yesterday, the sunset bright in their faces, he had watched her struggle to stay awake, her head sinking onto her chest and jerking back up again until the heat and the dusty twilight had finally got the better of her and her tense hands and body relaxed, her cropped brown head sagged onto his shoulder, and she slept, a soft weight against him while he had dreamed his own dreams and smiled, tightening his arm around her, lightly caressing the warm flesh of her upper arm. A mistake. "Don't!" She woke at once, shot him an appalled glance—"Don't do that!"—and edged right up against the door, where, turning her head away, she stared determinedly into an endless, darkening field of beets.

She could change a flat tire faster than he could. When they'd had a blowout she had the car jacked up and the lug nuts half off before he'd managed to drag the spare out of its compartment. It somehow didn't seem a skill a hooker would either learn or need. He'd demanded, "How d'you know how to do that?" She'd replied laconically, "You live in a place like Corsica, you better know."

Finally, would a hooker, necessarily mercenary by instinct, keep a strict tab of debts and personal expenses and vow to pay them back?

"You don't have to do that," he told her time and again. "It doesn't matter."

"It matters to me." And Saint felt certain he would be scrupulously repaid when promised.

Well, he thought hopefully, he wouldn't ask her anything personal again and he wouldn't touch her again, and by the time they got to San Francisco, things would have changed.

But with a sinking in his stomach he knew that in San Francisco he would finally have to tell her what Mr. Friedman had said.

And then what?

J.B. lay very still under the covers, fighting down her regular morning surge of panic.

Where am I?

Waking in yet another strange bed in a different motel at an unremembered spot on the freeway, staring at yet another ceiling of cottage-cheese plaster.

Who am I? For the moment, unsure. She was just a body occupying space; she didn't even recognize herself anymore in the mirror. She would remind herself that she was Jo-Beth Feeney, but what did that mean? Officially she couldn't prove it. Didn't dare. So for now, she was nobody. She had no ID, no driver's license, no money. No personal possessions at all, not even clothes, although Aunt Gloria had insisted on lending a small wardrobe of skirts, slacks, and blouses, all of exceptional quality and the height of style in about 1963, after which Aunt Gloria had bought no more clothes "because I had enough and my closet was full."

J.B. decided she knew how Alice in Wonderland felt, shrinking and shrinking away to nothing. From Josephine-Elizabeth to Jo-Beth to J.B. on the run. I've lost my past, she thought with a queasy feeling of vertigo, and I don't have a future.

Finally, eyes resting anxiously on the stranger in the bed beside her: *Who's that?*

Then she would remember it was Sloane St. John Treadwell Jr., Saint to his friends. She was driving with him to California. He was helping her escape.

At first she had felt nothing but gratitude, both to him and to Vera. But Vera was gone now, and without her for balance, their relationship was far too intense for comfort.

What does he think he'll get out of it? J.B. had learned the hard way that people did not do gratuitous good deeds without expecting something in return.

"There ain't no free lunch, baby." And of course Angelo was right.

Saint hadn't hit on her so far, but she knew it wouldn't be long. Don't look at me like that! she wanted to scream so often. I hate it when you look at me like that, like you're hungry.

But she would have to stay with him until they got to San Francisco, because she had no choice.

Now, from the other bed, Saint asked, "Hey, J.B., you awake yet?"

She gave a grunt of affirmation.

"I'll use the bathroom first, then, okay?"

She heard his bedsprings creak and then the soft sound of his bare feet hitting the floor. The bathroom door opened and closed. She listened to the running of the shower, muffled snatches of song, a flushing toilet, then silence. Saint would be dressing in the bathroom because he knew she preferred it. He was kind and considerate, she had to admit. So far.

They left the motel before seven in the morning and stopped for gas, then for breakfast at a diner beside the gas station, which, with different colored bar stools and curtains, could easily have been Phil's Sandwich Shop back in Corsica.

A waitress who might have been Charlene's sister said, "Hi, folks, coffee? We got fresh Danish, just come in. Still warm."

The customers, too, were the same familiar mix: a salesman checked appointments in a spiral binder; two truck drivers dug hungrily into the breakfast combination plate; a chubby teenage girl sucked iced Coke through a straw and leafed through a tabloid newspaper while her equally stout mother munched on a jelly doughnut. J.B. watched the rich dark flow of coffee into her cup and suddenly felt swamped by a wave of homesickness.

She said abruptly, "I'm going to call home."

The waitress said, "Public phone's by the rest rooms, hon."

Saint raised his head. "No. Don't."

"It's okay. I'll call Charlene. Listen, Saint, Momma's all alone now. I miss her. I just want to know if she's okay, is all."

"Better wait awhile longer."

He was so firm that it frightened her. She even wondered whether he knew something she didn't. She asked, "Saint, if you'd heard anything, you know, about me, you'd tell me, wouldn't you?"

He looked at her. "Of course. Sure I would." Something wasn't quite right about his eyes. She started to wonder what was wrong with his eyes, but then noticed the teenage girl was staring at Saint, down at the front page of her newspaper, and back to Saint again.

"Oh, Jeez." She touched Saint's wrist. "Look."

The headline screamed, "SPRING THROWS TEENAGE SON FROM HOME AFTER DRUGS-AND-MURDER PARTY."

Immediately below, Spring, puffy-eyed and mercilessly wrinkled, glowered at Saint, exhausted and unshaven, climbing from the Jaguar.

J.B. muttered urgently, "How did they get that picture? She wasn't there."

"They faked it." He warned, "Hush."

But the girl had picked up both their sudden interest in her paper and the urgency of their short exchange.

She nudged her mother and whispered loudly, "Hey, Ma. That boy, he looks like the boy in the picture."

Mother and daughter stared down the counter at Saint and J.B. The girl said confidently, "You're him. Aren't you?"

J.B. gazed into her coffee cup. She felt sick.

"Hey, that right? Let's see that." Saint reached for the paper, stared, and scowled. "Nah, nothing like me."

The girl giggled self-consciously. "It *is* you. I c'n tell. Your beard grows the same way."

The waitress, the truckers, and the salesman all turned to stare.

J.B. mentally cursed Saint's fast-growing beard shadow, wishing he'd taken time to shave this morning.

She heard him give a derisive snort—"Oh, sure!"—and saw him jerk his head toward the window at the dusty Ford. "And there's my foreign sports car, right outside." He handed the paper back with a shrug and a scowl of envy. "That kid drives some fancy European car. What wouldn't I give to have wheels like that?"

"Yeah," the mother agreed with a sigh. "Those show-biz kids are spoiled rotten." But her gaze was speculative, eyeing Saint with his beard shadow and J.B. in her lightweight heather suit by Pauline Trigère, which suddenly, J.B. feared, didn't look so old-fashioned and dowdy after all; twenty-five years later, those styles were coming back.

She stood up. She told Saint abruptly, "I'll meet you out front."

As they pulled out of the parking lot she knew everyone was watching through the smeared, steamy windows.

She said, "I don't want to go in those places anymore."

"Then we won't," Saint said.

The flat country was behind them; for the whole afternoon they climbed, winding gently up into the Ozark National Forest, in which Saint decided they would disappear for a couple of days without a trace so J.B.'s shaken nerves could settle down. They rattled across plank bridges over swirling brown streams, meandered through birch groves and stands of pine trees, arriving at the campsite in late afternoon in the premature darkness of an approaching storm.

They set up their tent as far away as possible from the other campers in a site half-hidden by brush, on a ledge overlooking a turbulent little river.

They sat side by side on a rock, their legs dangling over the water, sharing a bag of trail mix.

"Pretty, isn't it?" Saint said.

J.B. nodded. "Real nice."

Thunder growled, long and low. The birch leaves quivered over their heads, the pale trunks standing out ghostly white in the thickening dark.

It was hot and humid; J.B. wore shorts and a pink tank top Saint had bought for her at K-Mart. She had refused to go in, but waited for him in the parking lot, head bent, rereading yesterday's newspaper. The tank top was several sizes too large, the arm holes sagged, and he could see the underneath curve of her breast; the skin was almost bluish white, young and tender, and he wanted to touch her so badly he thought he'd die. He wanted her more and more every day, but he refused to touch her unless she wanted him back. Although she would want him, he promised himself, in her own time. She *must*.

He sat with elbows on his knees, hands dangling between them so his fingertips just brushed his groin and the bar of disconcertingly hard flesh that had materialized the moment he had seen her breast. It was an erection that felt so huge he didn't dare stand or even move in case she noticed. He tried to will it away and felt his body ache and the sweat break out down his spine. He glanced anxiously at J.B. at his side, so close, but she was staring out over the water. She hadn't seen.

A raindrop plopped softly into the humus of dead leaves beside him. Then another. Then, with a soft roar, a sheet of rain rolled up the valley.

"C'mon," Saint said, grabbing J.B. by the arm, "into the tent," carefully positioning his body so she couldn't see the telltale bulge in the front of his jeans.

They lay hip to hip on their stomachs, looking out through the flap into the rain. Wreaths of steam rose from the warm ground. Saint's body felt tense and eggshell tender. He lowered his hot face onto his arms and began to move himself back and forth on top of his massive hardness, slowly and deliberately, angry with himself for doing it, knowing he must stop at once or J.B. would notice and be revolted. He closed his eyes and chewed on the inside of his wrist.

J.B. touched him on the shoulder. "You don't have to do that," she said in a gruff voice. "I'll do it for you, if you want."

In J.B.'s experience, sex was the worst thing to happen to a woman. Look at Momma; look at Melody Rose. Both subjugated to men. Sex turned them into slaves. Didn't they have any pride? She vowed it would never happen to her.

If Saint had come on to her during the past week, if he had tried anything at all, she would have slugged him in the eye and taken off on her own—yes, she told herself, she definitely would have. But he hadn't.

Now she found this lonely, furtive striving rather sad. Did he want it that much, then?

She guessed he did. She didn't understand it. She just couldn't understand why people got so fired up about sex they paid huge sums of money for it. She thought of poor, pathetic Coach, and of Arnie Blaize, who had been prepared to pay a thousand dollars—and that was even more pathetic, because Arnie was young and good-looking.

Oh, shit, J.B. thought, really, what's the big deal?

Then she felt guilty. She thought: Look at all he's done for me. I sure owe him. And after all, I'm not Momma or Melody. I'm me, and I'll never be some man's slave.

She rolled over onto her side as Saint raised his head. The muscles of his cheeks and mouth were tight, his cheeks pale, his eyes very dark and almost feverish.

He whispered, "Are you serious? D'you mean it?"

"I said so, didn't I?" Her fingers tugged at the belt buckle of his jeans and awkwardly worked his zipper down.

She reached inside his shorts and closed her fingers on his erection, thick and warm and gently pulsing under her hand. She touched the tip, so satin smooth, and felt him shudder right through his body. "J.B. No . . . wait."

With agitated movements he writhed out of his jeans, then held her against his chest, crushed in his arms. "Are you sure? Are you really sure? Promise me."

She nodded. "Just don't talk."

He thrust his hands under her tank top, his fingers closing on her breasts at last. "J.B. Oh, God, J.B., I love you."

Yeah, thought J.B. Sure. That's what they all say. I bet Angelo said that to Melody Rose. Floyd might even have said it to Momma, and she believed him. Me, I'll never believe it.

She sat quite still, her body rigid, trying not to feel his touch. Nobody had ever touched her breasts; no one except Floyd; suddenly she wanted to scream and wrench away, but she willed herself to be still. This was not Floyd. This was Saint, she liked him, she was grateful to him, and she would let him do it. She had said so and she didn't rat out on promises.

She felt his fingers touch her nipples very gently, then not so gently; he squeezed them hard; his mouth found hers, he whispered, "I've wanted to kiss you for days, I've wanted you so much . . ."

"I said not to talk."

Now his hands were tugging her shorts down over her hips, his hand was between her legs, searching, and just as she had guessed he would, he gave a sudden hiss of astonishment: "J.B. Oh, my God . . ."

"Yes," J.B. said defiantly, "I'm still a virgin. So what?"

He said incredulously, "I don't understand."

"I'll tell you sometime." Then she was lying under him, he was crouched over her, his back against the roof of the tent; it was very dark as the full force of the storm moved over them; the rain drummed against the tight fabric over their heads; the river was inflated and roaring. They were locked together in their own tight little dark world.

It hurt. It was awful, just as she had known it would be. J.B. closed her eyes. It went on and on, she heard Saint whisper, "I'm *sorry*, J.B.," then suddenly the hurt was gone and she could feel him all the way up inside her body, moving fiercely in time with his gasping breath.

His movements grew faster and more violent, until he plunged with a final wild cry. Then he lay very still, holding her against him, his cheek pressed against hers. He kissed her eyebrow, the corner of her eye, her temple. He whispered, "Thank you, J.B. I'll love you always, forever and ever."

A week later, J.B. sat on the beach at Sand Harbor Cove, Nevada. Behind her, across a meadow of parched grass, towered parapets of sheer rock face seamed with crumbling ledges of shale, where scrawny pines clung for purchase. In front of her sparkled the frigid sapphire waters of Lake Tahoe, and on the far-distant south shore, the high white peaks of Heavenly Valley trembled like a mirage.

She was watching Saint run toward the water with great leaping strides over the burning sand. The water was very shallow in this little bay, a clear Caribbean green over the sandy bottom. It looked warm and inviting, but it wasn't. It was freezing. J.B. watched Saint splash his way through the shallows, then swim with powerful strokes past the raft, beyond the cork floats marking the boundary of the swimming area, and far out into the lake, where the water was very deep and a chill navy blue with windblown white crests.

She envied him. She had said, "I can't hardly swim at all. There wasn't much water around where I grew up."

"Then you can learn. I'll teach you." He was going to teach her to sail too. And water-ski. When they got to San Francisco.

J.B. felt safer in the West. Crossing the Rockies, breasting the Continental Divide, and seeing the jagged peaks marching away from her to north and south, she was completely awed and convinced that, against such grandeur, nobody could spare a thought for her, a petty fugitive.

They spent one night at Caesar's Palace in Las Vegas. They ate a huge steak dinner and had their laundry done.

Here, her sense of insignificance was almost total. Nobody had any idea what was taking place in the outside world, or cared. Reality was the cards, the rolling dice, spinning wheels, and flashing numbers. She felt invisible.

Waiting for the elevator, J.B. spied a long rank of phones, and here she did feel safe enough to risk a call home. Nobody would trace her.

However, "There's too much of a racket down here," Saint said. "Do it from the room."

Once they were in the room, he had undressed her and taken her to bed, so there'd been no time, and first thing in the morning, they'd moved on. . . .

J.B. sighed. She thought: I shouldn't have let him do it that first time . . . I knew I shouldn't have. For now Saint took more and more advantage. Now he made love to her every morning before they got on the road, and many times each night. He couldn't take his eyes off her, couldn't stop touching her, couldn't do enough for her. He loved her. So he said.

He was determined to make her feel the same way. He was desperate for her to come at the same moment as him. He would ask, "Are you ready, J.B.?" "Can you do it now?" And then, with a quickening of breath and a gasp, "I'm going to have to . . . I'm sorry . . . I can't hold on . . . oh, shit! I'm sorry!"

She tried, for if orgasm was that great, she didn't want to miss out, but she didn't know how she was supposed to feel.

She wondered: What *does* happen? What's a woman's body really *doing*? And, when nothing continued to happen, she suspected the whole thing was a fake, that there was nothing more to it than a rubbing together of flesh and that women lied.

Saint grew so disappointed when all his efforts failed that she started to feel guilty again and eventually began to lie too and feign cries and moans of passion. She must have been convincing, for Saint then became so joyous and proud she felt furious.

What am I doing? I'm giving in to him more and more.

However, she did like the coziness of waking in the morning held reassuringly and safely against a warm, strong body.

It wasn't all bad.

After Las Vegas they drove north on I-395 through Carson City to Reno, then crossed the Sierras over the high flanks of Mount Rose.

Tomorrow they would pick up Interstate 80 at Truckee.

Within four hours they would reach San Francisco, and then the journey would be over. Suddenly she realized she didn't want it to end, and not just because she was fearful of the problems she would face on arrival. J.B. wondered: Am I happy? *Could* I be happy? She didn't know what being happy was; she decided, to her complete surprise, that it must feel something like this.

They drove across the Oakland–San Francisco Bay Bridge at sunset the next day. A finger of dense white fog lay up the middle of the bay; the tops of the towers of the Golden Gate Bridge rose above a dense fog bank that trickled like frosting over the hills of Marin County to the northwest.

It was beautiful. She had never seen anything like it. Then J.B. stared at the soaring geometry of San Francisco and thought: Well, here we are, as far west as we can go. The dream's over.

But it wasn't, it seemed. Not yet.

Now they were welcomed and taken care of by Saint's friends.

Jake Plank, ex-roommate, was a likable boy, tubby and cynical and humorous. Mr. Plank was a corporation lawyer, Mrs. Plank was indefatigably social. They lived in Pacific Heights in a tall red-brick mansion filled with antiques and original art.

"They're awfully rich, aren't they?" J.B. whispered. She had never set foot in a house like this, apart from Blaine's Landing, which didn't count, because Arnie, a movie star, was expected to live like that. But the Planks were real people, and this was a real home. Awed, she said little during her visit, but watched, listened, and smiled when spoken to. Mr. and Mrs. Plank thought her a darling girl. She spent a great deal of time bathing luxuriously with bubbles and scented oil in the jade-green-porcelain guest bathtub with the gold fixtures and Jacuzzi. She had never seen such a tub except in magazines.

She told herself she must quit this dreaming; she must get back to reality, tell Saint: Thanks, but I'm going now, it's over.

But it was hard. Both the Planks were genuinely and warmly hospitable and wouldn't hear of anyone leaving. With other guests expected during the next few days, they offered Saint and J.B. unrestricted use of what they called the offshore guest room, which turned out to be a sixty-five-foot yacht berthed in Sausalito, across the Golden Gate Bridge.

Mr. Plank occasionally took favored clients out for an afternoon of gentle cruising, followed by cocktails at the yacht club, but preferred the stable terrain of the Olympic Club golf course.

"It burns me up, not using the boat more. You kids'd do me a favor. Stay on board, enjoy, and make up a list of all the little things need doing."

When J.B. saw the boat, it was harder still to imagine leaving, for the boat was so beautiful, a fifty-year-old floating palace of gleaming brass and varnish, teak and white paint.

Just a couple days more, she would promise herself, then I'm going. She reasoned: I deserve a couple more days, don't I?

She would wake before dawn to the sound of fishermen putting out to sea, make a cup of coffee, and take it on deck. It would be cool, damp, and very calm. When the sun rose above the East Bay hills, the windows of the high-rises in San Francisco glittered as though they were on fire. She would watch, fascinated, as the sun climbed higher in the sky and the tall buildings cast huge blue shadows upon each other.

Living on the boat was like dying and going to heaven. And now, as well as the boat, there was the car.

The rental Ford was long gone; until the Jaguar was delivered from New York, Saint rented a dashing Datsun 240Z. J.B. dared not use her driver's license, but she drove it anyway. She adored that car.

"If you like it that much," Saint said casually, "then it's yours." And confessed he hadn't rented it after all; he'd bought it. For her.

She was aghast. "But you *can't* do that."

"I just did."

"And I can't drive it legally, anyway."

"It's in my name. Listen," Saint said airily (too airily?), "don't worry, everything's going to work out. I can feel it."

For J.B., in retrospect, the three weeks in San Francisco before Saint returned to New York to give evidence at Arnie's trial merged into one endless sunlit day of picnics on the boat, on beaches or grassy mountainsides above Sausalito, gazing down on an endless panorama of lakes, inlets, and promontories; of nighttimes drinking beer in the falling dusk, eating seafood at small waterfront restaurants, and, at Jake's invitation— like his mother, he seemed to be a born party animal—wandering with Saint through huge mansions among young people in evening clothes, drinking champagne, and dancing to society bands.

The night before Saint left for New York and Arnie's trial, Jake's parents gave a black-tie party for their son, about to head south for his freshman year at UCLA.

J.B. gazed through the twelve-foot plate-glass windows into a panoramic view of San Francisco Bay. It was sunset again, the world was gold and fiery tangerine, dark blue and purple. The windows were so wide, they stood so high, she felt she floated in space.

She now possessed a wardrobe of cheap sportswear, antique designer clothes, and six evening gowns from I. Magnin, Saks, and Jessica McClintock.

Tonight she wore the ivory silk, the most expensive dress she had ever owned or dreamed of owning; her other outfits had been bought on sale; not this one. It had cost $950. "That's crazy," she had gasped, shocked, "to spend so much money just for a dress."

"That's nothing," Saint had said mildly, "compared with what Mother spends."

For a moment J.B. thought: He's bought you a car, now he's buying you all these clothes. Clothes, intimate and personal, seemed even more dangerous. She demanded of herself: When's it going to end? When are you going to stop this craziness? But she hadn't been able to resist the dress. It was soft, with sinuous lines, virginal but sensuous at the same time, and people stared at her even with her cropped brown hair. Saint had looked incredibly proud.

She'd said, "Don't be dumb. They're only looking at the dress."

"No they're not. They're looking at you. You look sensational." And, impatiently: "What the hell does it matter? You're with me."

He had bought her a gardenia corsage; the perfume grew more heady as the night wore on. She would always associate the smell of gardenias with that night, and would avoid them for years. As she danced and drank champagne and the creamy petals of the flower gave off eversweeter waves of scent, J.B. felt herself grow light and ethereal, until she didn't even feel the floor under her feet, only the strength of Saint's arms and his hand in hers and his cheek pressed against hers while the candles burned low and the band played the old romantic standards and across the bay an impossibly huge golden moon rose above the Marin hills.

She didn't want him to leave her tomorrow.

Later, entwined in the soft bed in the master cabin of Mr. Plank's boat, she felt the first faint stirrings of real desire. She hadn't sought it; it found her.

In the almost dark cabin, lighted only by the moon, now high and white and cold, J.B. watched the reflection of their two bodies in the tall mirror on the opposite wall as they moved as one, herself kneeling, braced on her arms, her breasts half-moonlit; Saint's dark head lowered against her shoulder, his hands covering hers, his back and straining arms a flowing curve dappled with cool light. Perhaps sex could be beautiful. She thought: I'm giving in. I do love him, yes I do. But now it didn't seem so threatening after all.

She found the days went impossibly slowly without Saint, that she missed him badly. Mrs. Plank invited her back to the house: "Honey, I don't like to think of you over there all alone."

But J.B. needed to be by herself. She had a lot of thinking to do.

She spent her days walking; she drove the Datsun to Stinson Beach and hiked for miles across the sand, or else up the slopes of Mount Tamalpais, wandering through meadows of golden grasses and groves of evergreen oak.

Saint called her every evening on the boat phone.

Everything was going just fine.

Through smart plea bargaining, Arnie's lawyer had had the charge reduced from homicide right down to gross negligence and unlawful discharge of a firearm in a public place; Arnie wouldn't even go to jail, provided he successfully completed two years in a rehab clinic.

Aunt Gloria sent her love.

Spring, initially furious at Saint for what she perceived as unwholesome publicity, had mellowed, for in the end it *was* publicity, right?

The only bad news was that Vera had been fired. Saint had found a letter from her awaiting him at Aunt Gloria's, mailed from England.

Saint said, "I feel really bad; it was my fault. And just the worst luck Mother showed up like that."

J.B. had a momentary vision of the Starfire Trio smashing their glasses in the fireplace, of the empty champagne bottle—it must have looked as if they'd held an orgy—and the drawings. Oh, God, those drawings! She gave an irrepressible hoot of laughter. "Oh, poor Vera!"

"I'll make it up to her," Saint said. "Soon as I get home."

Home. He was coming home. J.B. asked, "When?"

"Tomorrow."

And at once she forgot Vera because Saint was coming home and there was so much to do to prepare for him.

She spent the rest of the evening cleaning up the boat and putting clean sheets on their bed.

Later, her chores completed, sitting on deck alone in the soft purple dusk, she felt a sudden overwhelming need to talk to her mother. To say: Momma, I think I understand after all. I think I understand you, Melody, and all women. I didn't believe in it, I thought all men were like Floyd or Angelo, that they used you or lied to you—but it's not true. Not always.

Momma, I think I'm in love.

I'll just talk for a minute, she thought. Even if the phone's bugged, they won't have time to trace the call. But surely she'd be safe by now. It was mid-September. It had been seven whole months. . . .

She dialed with trembling fingers, knowing Saint would disapprove, that he feared so much for her safety, but if the very worst happened, if the call was traced and she was arrested, well, for the first time, she allowed herself to trust Saint, Mr. Friedman, and Arnie's lawyer to take care of her. They wouldn't let her go to jail.

She listened to the phone ring thousands of miles away in Corsica and feverishly hoped Momma would be there and not out with the Gospel Bearers.

The phone was picked up.

A man's voice said, "Yeah?"

J.B., about to cry "*Momma!*", choked on her own breath.

Then she felt completely winded, as though someone had hit her hard in the stomach. She couldn't make a sound.

The voice demanded impatiently, "Yeah? Whozit, for Chrissakes?" Then snarled, "Asshole," and hung up with a crash.

Floyd Feeney.

And Floyd was dead. J.B. broke out in a cold sweat. It took her three attempts to replace the receiver on the cradle.

He'd been dead for seven whole months. Hadn't he?

J.B. sank into one of the armchairs and forced herself to think logically.

She didn't believe in ghosts. If Floyd had answered the phone, then he wasn't dead after all. She had hurt him but not killed him.

If she hadn't killed him, then she wasn't a murderer. She never had been.

But that made no sense, because the cops were out to get her. She was a suspect for a Murder One charge, her "wanted" picture was posted on precinct and post-office walls. Angelo had told her that, and . . .

He lied, thought J.B. grimly. He knew all the time I'd not killed Floyd, he lied to keep me where he wanted me . . . and I believed him. Jesus God, I believed him.

Oh, the fucking bastard.

Had Melody known? She couldn't stand it if Melody had known too; but in fairness, she was inclined to think not; Angelo would have lied to her too, and Mel would believe anything he told her.

Then, upon the heels of the anger came a marvelous welling spread of happiness.

J.B. thought: I can be me again. I'm safe. I'm free.

She didn't sleep that night, for excitement.

Next morning she drove into San Francisco to one of the most expensive beauty salons in town to have her hair returned to its true color. Now at last Saint would see her as she really was.

It was as she sat there happily staring at her newly familiar face smiling over a rose-pink gown while the manicurist buffed and polished her nails that the first cold touch of suspicion flickered down her spine. She tried to thrust it away, but it returned and refused to leave.

If Angelo knew I hadn't killed Floyd, J.B. belatedly realized, then other people would have known too.

Saint could have known. And now she remembered the times Saint had prevented her making phone calls home.

How unalarmed he had been that she should be noticed.

How casual his promise about the car and the driver's license: *"Everything's going to work out. I can feel it."*

Sure he could feel it, thought J.B. with a sinking heart, because he knew.

Mr. Friedman was in court; J.B. finally reached him two hours before Saint's plane touched down.

He sounded busy and distracted, but was friendly enough. "I don't know why you should want the information again, but you're welcome, for what it's worth . . ." She imagined him searching among papers on his wide, littered desk. "Okay, here I have it . . ." He read over the phone, "The only homicide during the period was a twenty-two-year-old Mexican farm worker who died of stab wounds."

". . . and Floyd?"

"A white male, fifty-two, name of Floyd Feeney, was admitted to County Hospital with head injuries reputedly sustained in a fall while intoxicated. He suffered a mild concussion and was discharged the following day." Mr. Friedman asked mildly, "Didn't Saint tell you all this, J.B.?"

She drove back to Sausalito across the Golden Gate Bridge.

Across the bridge, the highway passed through a tunnel. The entrance to the tunnel was painted in bright rainbow colors. J.B. looked at the rainbow, the golden sunshine, and the blue sky and saw a monotone of gray.

For six whole weeks Saint had lied to her. He had let her go on thinking she'd killed Floyd, that she was a murderer, that she'd go to jail; he'd let her be afraid, and said nothing. . . .

Doubtless he'd had his reasons, but whatever they were, they couldn't justify six weeks of needless terror. Nothing could do that.

Now she felt appalled that she had been so close finally to giving in, to saying, "Yes, Saint, I love you too, I want to be with you always . . .", to being weak just like other women, to losing herself—for nothing. The part of her that had wanted to love so badly and now felt so betrayed hardened to stone.

Now she hated Saint. She never wanted to see him again.

She dared not see him again, he was too cunning, too plausible, too attractive, he'd trick her again, touch her again, and she wouldn't be able to resist him.

She set her mouth into a grim line.

Back on the boat, she'd pack the very few things she considered hers. She would have to use some of the money he'd given her, but she'd pay it back soon enough.

After all, she was free now. Free to work. To make money of her own. There was nothing to hold her back. Nothing to stop her from leaving him.

Chapter
8

Vera was gaining weight steadily now: what else was there to do but eat?

Increasingly she looked forward to meals, her only source of pleasure, and Mum, smugly triumphant, provided better and ever more lavish fare.

The weeks rolled by and Saint never answered her letter. She had put her phone number on it, just in case, but he never called either. After a while she knew she would never see him or hear from him again—he had forgotten her. He had gone off to Connecticut with J.B. and would certainly be sleeping with her by now. How could he possibly remember a fat, dull creature like herself when he was sleeping with J.B.? Vera thought she would die of jealousy.

And anger and frustration, because she couldn't even draw her strip anymore, not now that Starfire had J.B.'s face.

But one morning nine months later, just as she had given up hope, "There's something for you in the post," Mum announced with a suspicious sidelong look. "Airmail. From America."

Vera's heart thudded inside her chest. He hadn't forgotten after all.

She didn't recognize the writing and it was postmarked California, but it had to be from Saint. It must be.

She thrust it in the pocket of her navy pinafore dress to read later when she was alone. Mum made pointed remarks about slyness and secrecy, but Vera ignored her.

After breakfast she rushed away to her room and closed the door.

PAPER STAR

Potrero Hill
San Francisco

March 10, 1981

Dear Vera:

Belated thanks for your letter. Sorry I didn't get back to you sooner; I realize it's been over six months, but my life went into a tailspin for a while.

So, how are you? I felt just totally guilty that Mother showed up too soon and you got stuck with all the mess. What lousy luck. Knowing Mother, she probably charged you for the glasses and champagne. Please let me know so I can pay you back the money at least, though I can't make it up to you for being fired. At least not right now; I can't see myself ever being in a position to employ anybody.

As you see, I'm living here now. J.B. and I drove across the country; she wanted to make a new start in a new place and is doing it pretty well. She's working as a model and is gruesomely successful. I don't see her anymore, except in the papers and magazines. All her problems are over, as apparently she didn't kill her stepfather after all, just knocked him out, so all that worry was for nothing. Ironic, huh?

I'm working on a novel, kind of based on our trip, geographically at least. It's about two people driving across the country and everything goes wrong and gets worse, but they can never get off the freeway. Sort of an Interstate Flying Dutchman. They've actually died in an accident and are in hell. It's called *Right Exit Closed*.

My problem: I have to make them really lousy human beings so they ought definitely to be in hell, but sympathetic enough so the readers care what happens to them. It's tough. I know you'll understand, though, being an artist.

I've rented a studio apartment in a house up here, with a great view, and write evenings and weekends.

Weekdays I'm going to San Francisco State. I'm being a good boy and going to college just like my father wanted. I thought: Why not? Maybe it's not so bad and it'll make him happy at last; maybe he'll decide I'm okay after all. And actually it's great; I'm studying film and having a ball. I think I might be really good at this; maybe I'll be a screenwriter or a director someday.

Arnie's living at a rehab center up the coast called Round Mountain. He seems to be doing okay but can't have visitors yet.

Any chance you might come to San Francisco? It would be fantastic to see you and chew over old times. . . . Remember the Starfire Trio?"

"I don't see J.B. anymore . . ."
What did that mean?
He'd loved her. Or hadn't he?
What had happened between them that had prompted him to write a novel about a freeway to hell? Why didn't he see her anymore?
But how wonderful that J.B. hadn't killed her stepfather after all and could feel free. How great that she was doing so well.
Vera read Saint's laconic letter through and through, but to her frustration, was little closer to understanding what had happened during the past six months, and clearly he assumed a lot of knowledge she didn't have.
But then: *"Any chance you might come to San Francisco? It would be fantastic to see you. . . ."*
Vera flushed with pleasure and excitement. Did he really mean that, or was it merely guilt and politeness? Whatever would he do if she suddenly showed up?
Oh, if only she could go! Write back and say: "Yes, Saint, as a matter of fact I *was* planning to try to sell *Starfire* as a comic strip in America. San Francisco seems like a good place to start, and of course I'd love to see you again."
She imagined Saint meeting her at the airport, how the moment he saw her his face would light up. "Vera!" he'd cry. "How marvelous! You're looking *great*—"
But there the dream abruptly ended, because she didn't look great at all. She looked terrible. She had eaten herself into a size eighteen. She was a fat pig.
Clutching Saint's letter in her hand, Vera locked her bedroom door and took off all her clothes.
She stared at herself and sighed with a sensation of doom. Saint would take one look and shudder. Or laugh. It was no use dreaming. It was much too late.

"Bullshit," Dr. Wheeler said rudely.
Vera stared. She had never heard him swear before. She rather liked it; it made her feel a contemporary, like a grown-up.

"You can do it if you want," he went on, "especially now you're motivated. I'll work out a diet and exercise program for you. And the very first thing you do when you go home right now is throw out all those goodies you've got hidden away in your undies drawer."

Vera's eyes widened. "What makes you think I——?"

"You can't keep secrets from me."

No; she supposed she couldn't. He had known her too long, and much too well.

Back in her room, Vera took off her clothes yet again and shrinkingly made herself study her own body as if she were Saint. Immediately she thought about him driving off with J.B. to Connecticut and then all the way across the country, beautiful J.B., tall, auburn-haired, with the stride of a lioness. It didn't help that he didn't see her anymore. Vera was sinkingly sure that he would if he could. She closed her eyes in pain.

She felt lonely and miserable. Dr. Wheeler couldn't possibly understand how she was suffering, nor even guess how *hungry* she always felt. She opened her underwear drawer and reached under the garments for the chocolate bars she craved, which would make her feel so much better.

She took one out, peeled off the bright foil wrapping, and bit off a huge chunk. Then she watched herself in the mirror, cheeks stuffed, and asked herself defiantly: Why should I bother? What's the point? What difference does it make what I look like? Saint doesn't love me.

But if he really didn't see J.B. anymore, perhaps there was a chance. *And there'd be a much better chance if I was thin.*

She ate the final piece very thoughtfully, then opened the drawer again and took out her whole hoard. Three Crunchie bars, a box of sugar-frosted cookies, six Mars bars, and a hefty slab of Cadbury's fruit-and-nut chocolate.

She packed it all in a brown paper bag and went downstairs.

She called, "I'm going for a little walk, Mum."

Mum replied, "Don't be late for tea. I made a treacle tart."

Vera sighed. She adored treacle tart.

She walked slowly down the street, looking for children. The first ones she saw were Indian or Pakistani, about ten years old, school caps set with mathematical precision on their smooth black heads.

Vera asked, "Would you boys like some sweets?"

They turned to stare at her with enormous eyes like startled fawns, then wheeled away from her and ran.

There, Vera told herself, it's a sign. You can't even *give* the stuff away.

Then she thought sensibly: They've probably been warned a thousand times about taking sweets from strangers. Find someone who knows you . . .

And immediately, walking toward her, along came Laurence Reed, who lived down the block. Laurence, at twelve, had his own computer, took piano lessons, cried at the smallest bump or scrape, and wore glasses thick as the bottom of Coke bottles. Nobody liked Laurence. Vera didn't like him either, but she had a mild kindred feeling for a fellow misfit.

Laurence demanded suspiciously, "What's wrong with it?"

"Nothing."

"Why d'you want to give it away, then?"

"I'm going on a diet. I don't want it anymore."

"Oh." He looked her up and down then said, "That's a good thing. You're too fat. Mummy says being fat gives you blood pressure."

"Well, thank you, Laurence." She watched his prim back view receding down the street, music case in one hand, her bag of candy in the other, and muttered, "I hope you choke on it, you little twerp."

Then, she was committed.

A dreadful few months followed, laced with endless battles with Mum, who felt betrayed and insulted.

The weight came off so slowly, ounce by painful ounce. She would think of Saint. *I'm doing it for Saint. Oh, please, God, let it be worth it.*

The first three months were the worst. Mum and Dad would watch her set off for her run in her gym shoes, tights, and outsize shorts, and sigh mournfully, as though she were doing something dangerous and threatening. She would return in terrible shape and collapse dizzily on a chair, when Mum would pat her face with a cool, damp towel and instantly offer cookies and strong, sweet tea.

"No," Vera would groan. "Leave me alone. Please, Mum. Leave me alone."

For the second time in her life, "Get a job," advised Dr. Wheeler. "Get out of the house."

"A job? What kind of a job?"

"Anything. Can't you do something with art?"

"I can't draw anymore."

"Then sell stuff for someone who can."

She wondered why she hadn't thought of it before. She found a job as assistant and receptionist at a local art gallery that specialized in coy watercolors of country cottages festooned with hollyhocks, kittens playing with yarn, and Jesus Christ looking soulful among lambs. During the frequent absences of the owner, an attenuated elderly man called Christopher, who had, in his own words, a regular *curse* of a chest, she made an occasional sale.

She ran to work, took a sprint during lunch hour, ran home again. She religiously took her vitamins and, to Mum's dismay, lived on a diet of fruit and vegetables and lean meat.

After six months, much more fit, capable of running a mile without effort, Vera found her energy growing in direct proportion to her shrinking waistline.

When she was down to a size twelve, Dr. Wheeler gave her a royal-blue jogging outfit with a white stripe down the side. When Vera put it on she felt slim and racy and quite different.

After nine months, "I wouldn't ever recognize you," Mum said sadly. "You're so different, Vera. I don't understand you anymore. I don't know why you want to be like this." She gave a small, broken sob. "Running, running—I expect you want to run away from us. That's it, isn't it? You don't want to live with Dad and me anymore. We're too old and dull for you."

But Vera was no longer paralyzed with guilt. She said briskly, "Of course I love you and Dad, Mum, but I have to live my life my own way."

By the spring of 1982 Vera had held her weight at one-twenty for six months. She had discarded most of her old clothes, altered those that could be altered, and bought a few new outfits.

Saint had written spasmodically during the year. The book was going fine. School was fun. Arnie was doing well, and Saint had at last been able to visit. J.B. was still around, working hard.

Vera studied her mirrored reflection with pride. She didn't look bad at all.

She looked so good, in fact, she didn't feel threatened by J.B. anymore. It was no longer a problem that Starfire had J.B.'s face.

At last Vera was able to draw again with a free spirit.

After several months of hard work she chose six of the best strips, photocopied them, and airmailed them to Saint.

". . . I thought you'd like to catch up with Starfire's latest adventures. If you're serious about owing me one, and if you have time, maybe you could show these to a paper in San Francisco."

It was a dream, of course. Nothing would come of it. How could it?

But, "It's good to have a dream," Dr. Wheeler said. "If you want to go to California and be a professional cartoonist and are prepared to work for it, then it'll happen." Then he did an unsettling thing. He put two fingers under her chin and raised her face so their eyes met. "At last the attractive girl inside has come out, hasn't she?" And he kissed her very lightly on the forehead.

He had never done that before. She wasn't sure if she liked it or not; if she hadn't known better, and if he hadn't been so old, she might have thought he was . . . flirting. It wasn't quite the right word—there was nothing flirtatious about Dr. Wheeler's somber face and the curious light in his eyes as he looked at her—but she couldn't think of a better one. She hoped he wouldn't do it again. His kiss made her feel strangely uncomfortable, as if a critical balance had shifted between them. She didn't want a shift; she wanted him to stay being Dr. Wheeler.

Her dilemma must have shown. He shook his head. "Why did I do that?" he asked musingly, clearly not expecting an answer from her and abruptly supplying his own: "Because I'm a fool, that's why." Then he laughed gently and was, to her great relief, Dr. Wheeler again.

Vera took a gamble, renegotiated her arrangement with Christopher, and began to work for commission only.

Christopher was delighted. His chest was acting up and the doctor had prescribed time off in a dry climate.

He flew away for a package holiday in Agadir, Morocco, and Vera immediately set to work rearranging the window display, relighting, generally brightening, and accepting paintings on consignment that were not necessarily of sunsets, cottage gardens, or kittens.

She sold nothing the first week except some greeting cards and hand-painted place mats; however, the second week she sold two watercolors and a small oil painting of a sailing ship.

Christopher returned. His cough was better but he had contracted an intestinal ailment that he called the Agadir Trots. Vera was left to her own devices again, and by the third week word seemed to be getting around that the gallery was catering to a clientele other than elderly spinsters and retired clergymen.

Business picked up slowly but steadily, and Vera's spirits with it; in May she had another letter from Saint, and on reading it, her excitement knew no bounds.

". . . maybe nothing will come of it, so don't get too excited, but one of the instructors at State has a friend who knows the editor at Express Features. That's a syndicate owned by the San Francisco *Express*, a local daily. I sent him your *Starfire* package and he seemed pretty impressed. He called me and asked for a presentation. Six weeks of daily comics and six color Sundays. He said you should draw them normal size and reduce them. I guess you know what he wants better than I do. Send them to him direct. To Phil Solway, Syndicate Manager, Express Features . . ." and an address on Market Street.

"I'm leaving soon for Tahoe. Arnie's being released on probation, provided he has blood tests every week and tests clean. His father's rented a place on the lake for the summer as kind of a halfway house, and Arnie wants me with him. I'll go at the end of the semester. It'll be a great place to write." He ended, "P.S. Did you realize how much Starfire looks like J.B.? Did you mean to do it? I've sent a copy of it to her too. Hope you don't mind."

Yes, of course she minded; then, no, Vera thought she didn't mind after all. How petty it would be to mind. After all, J.B. was the apex of the Starfire Trio; of course she should see them.

In the meantime, Starfire grew more real and more assertive every day.

"It's all ever so good," Christopher offered, eyeing the strips with a dubious eye. "I mean, the drawing and all, but isn't she just the tiniest bit *naughty*?"

"Naughty?"

"Well . . . she shows a lot of . . . uh . . . skin. And all those belts and buckles make one think of . . . uh . . . I mean, people like cartoons about dogs and cats and kiddies . . ."

"Probably," Vera agreed, "but I can't do much about it. This is the way she wants to be."

Vera wrote to Saint in Tahoe City. "I'll send the stuff to Mr. Solway as soon as I can. Incidentally," hoping she hit the right note of nonchalance, "I should be in San Francisco myself in August. It would be lovely to see you." And thought: Oh, my God, it's happening. It's really happening. Until an evening in late May, when all her hopes and dreams of going to California came to an abrupt halt.

Dad slipped on some soap in the bath, fell, and broke his neck. He died at once, an intense irony for a man who had devoted his life to disease and had looked forward to a heroic departure following a lengthy illness.

"You can't go now," Mum wailed tearfully. "You can't go away and leave me, Vera. You're all I have left in the world." So that was it. Of course she would stay. In some dark loop in her mind it would make up for the fact that when she heard of his death, her first thought had been dismay for herself and her plans.

"It's not that I didn't love him," she told Dr. Wheeler, anxiously searching her soul, "but I just couldn't see *him* in the end; it was as if he was lost behind all his bottles and pillboxes."

"Don't blame yourself. And don't try to punish yourself either."

"But I can't possibly leave Mum now, it wouldn't be fair."

She wrote to Saint: ". . . I hope I'll be able to come one day, but certainly not yet. I can't leave her. I don't know how she'd manage, all alone."

"Perfectly well, I expect." Dr. Wheeler sighed, then asked, "But couldn't she live with a relative? Doesn't she have any other relatives at *all*?"

In fact, Mum did; her sister, Cynthia, came down from Yorkshire for the funeral. Cynthia was married to a manufacturer of agricultural machinery. She was tall and brisk, didn't believe in poor health, had heartily disapproved of Dad, and made no secret of it. Over the years, communication between the sisters had dwindled to an exchange of cards at Christmastime and birthdays. "Of course we could have Louise if she wants to come. I don't know what else she'll do. He won't have left her a penny, you know. Not a penny."

Louise. Vera blinked. She had almost forgotten Mum had a name. And in fact, to everyone's surprise, Mum also turned out to have considerably more than a penny.

Dad had bought the little house for cash back in the sixties; it was worth a great deal more now. Expenditure over the years had been very slight; Dad, indulging his hobby, had taken full and complete advantage of the National Health Service, spending nothing while his small investments had grown steadily.

Cynthia's grudging invitation metamorphosed into strong encouragement. She persuaded, "Come on, Lou. We have ever so much room."

Mum looked mulish, her lower lip thrust out like an obstinate child's. "No, Cynthia. Of course I couldn't. What about poor Vera, left all alone? She needs me. She needs her home. And her mum."

Dr. Wheeler admonished Vera, "Don't let her do this. Don't let her lean on you. If you do, she'll never stop."

"But she's old. She really does need me now."

His mouth quirked at the corners. "Vera, she's forty-eight years old. She might have a whole new life ahead of her, without you. You'd be doing her a favor."

Doubtfully: "You really think so?"

"I really do."

Cynthia told Mum, "Vera's a grown-up woman. It's time she stopped leaning on you, got a decent job, and took care of herself for a change."

"How can you be so unfeeling?"

Cynthia advised, "She wants to go to America. Let her go."

Mum repeated bitterly, "America."

Chapter

9

Saint watched the wind coming, an arrowhead of darker water rushing toward them across the surface of the lake. He adjusted the mainsheet and reminded his crew member, "Ready to ease off on the jib, Arn."

"Aye, aye, Skip."

Saint was teaching Arnie Blaize to sail. He was also coaching him in tennis and teaching him to water-ski. He felt like a camp counselor.

Arnie had been terrified to leave Round Mountain, and refused to go at all unless Saint was there to help him through his first months in the outside world. "If you'd spend the summer with him, Sloane," Arnie's father said, "we'd be forever in your debt. He loves you, you know, and respects you like an older brother."

The property was quiet and secluded, the driveway winding through a quarter-mile of thick woods down to the big house on the lake. Arnie's parents arrived for weekends; during the week Saint and Arnie were cared for by a married couple called Eve and Vernon. Vernon was general handyman and took care of the cars and boats; Eve was a terrific cook.

There was everything, in fact, to make for a wonderful summer, except for the one thing Saint really wanted—but J.B. was lost to him anyway, and he had only himself to blame. He would still sometimes wake sweating from a nightmare in which he sat once again in the Italian restaurant on Sutter Street, to which he had finally tracked her.

She wore black pants, a white pleated shirt, and a little black bow tie. She looked magnificent and furiously angry. "I don't want to talk with you. Please go."

"J.B., please listen. I love you. I didn't tell you because I knew if I did, you'd leave me. You wouldn't need me anymore. I couldn't stand thinking about being without you. I—"

"I'm not listening. I have other tables to—"

"—thought that in a few weeks I could make you love me too, and then it wouldn't matter. You'd stay anyway." He'd added miserably, staring at the cup of espresso coffee he didn't want, "I'm sorry. I guess I made a mistake."

She had left behind on the boat every single thing he had bought for her, including the white silk dress from I. Magnin. "At least keep that," he had begged. "What am I supposed to do with a dress?"

"I don't care." Her eyes were stony. "Give it to some other girl, who likes being lied to."

"And the car, J.B. The car was for you. You loved that car. . . . What am I going to do with two cars?"

She shrugged. "Not my problem." Then cried, "For six whole *weeks* you let me think I'd killed Floyd. You let me think I was a murderer. You let me be afraid of my own shadow. You can't know what it was like—"

"Because I love you."

"No you don't. You want to own me. You're no better than Angelo. Worse, actually. At least he was honest. He just wanted money, he didn't lay any phony love stuff on me. Now, drink your coffee and get out. And don't come here again. I don't want to see you again. Ever."

He was sure she wouldn't make it; she was alone and young and penniless in a strange town. He waited for her to need him, but she didn't.

J.B. wasn't afraid of hard work, and with murder no longer hanging over her head like the sword of Damocles, nothing could hold her back.

He had kept track of her as best he could.

She was accepted by a model agency; the best in town.

He could imagine it so well, J.B. marching in there with her leonine stride, nailing them with her pale go-to-hell eyes. "You better take me on, because if you don't, someone else sure will." And they had; of course they had.

She had started to get modeling jobs; she gave up waitressing and moved out of the YWCA into a one-bedroom apartment on Telegraph Hill.

He tried to talk to her, over and over again.

If only she would give him another chance, let him try to explain.

He waited for hours outside the agency in case she came in; once a man came down to tell him, "J.B. doesn't want you bothering her. If you hang around here anymore, we'll have to call the cops."

He followed her home and caught her outside her front door. "Give me a chance. Let me just *talk* with you."

She told him, "Saint, I meant what I said. Leave me alone. It's over."

But then, when Saint had finally determined to put J.B. out of his mind, Vera sent the *Starfire* strips.

Saint studied them with disbelief.

It was extraordinary: Starfire *was* J.B.

He typed the address label so she wouldn't recognize his writing, and mailed J.B. a duplicate set. Inside he wrote, "I thought you ought to see this. Vera wants to know what you think." Cunning, involving Vera.

And it worked. J.B. called him at once.

Hardly daring to trust himself, Saint asked, "Do you like them?"

She sounded hesitant and ill at ease at first, but also eager, intrigued, even excited. "Of course. Vera's so clever, isn't she? But it's weird, seeing these. *She doesn't even know I'm blond. . . .*"

She asked for Vera's phone number in England, and her address. And so because of Vera the door was open again, even if by only a crack— although J.B. still, so far, refused to see him.

Saint resolutely gave himself up to work, and in fact, a summer in the mountains suited him very well.

Right Exit Closed was finished. He mailed it to an agent in New York and in the fallow period of waiting while it went the rounds of publishers and the rejection letters rolled in, he decided to adapt it as a screenplay.

The old house was indeed a wonderful place to write.

Saint developed the habit of getting up very early, no later then six, sprinting up the driveway to the gate and back to set his body in motion, then taking a large mug of black coffee to his room and working for three or four hours until Arnie got up.

After that it was difficult to concentrate; Arnie, fragile and anxious to please, needed as much attention as a puppy.

During his stint at Round Mountain he had developed a strong dependency on his counselor, a young man named Lyle, who, like all the Round Mountain staff, was an ex-addict himself. "They know where you're coming from," Arnie explained earnestly to Saint, his phraseology straight from the seventies and already curiously old-fashioned. "They've been there." And of the controversial Round Mountain therapy, which appeared to boast a much higher degree of success than any other method: "It's amazing, man. They reach right down there inside of you, tear you down to nothing, and then build you up again. It puts you truly in touch with yourself. With your feelings. You know."

Arnie expounded at length on the miracles of attack therapy, and Saint listened with skepticism and finally a mild revulsion. "So they all sat around for weeks telling you what a shit you were and how they hated you for being rich and good-looking and famous. Well, fuck 'em. I wouldn't sit still for that."

"Oh, no, Saint. You don't understand. It was done for love. And I'd end up in tears," Arnie went on, eyes glowing. "Every session, I'd cry. It was such a release. It was like a religious experience. I'll never be the same again."

Since his departure, Arnie had had to see his probation officer every other week and have a blood test. "If I test dirty, I have to go right back to Round Mountain." During the first few weeks he had said that with longing.

Now, however, the immediacy of Round Mountain was diminishing, and even though his dependency was transferring perceptibly to Saint, he was definitely making progress.

Arnie had never been athletically inclined; he had been either too fat, too busy, or too stoned. During his sojourn at Round Mountain, however, with its obligatory community services, most of which involved strenuous manual labor, he had developed muscles he'd had no idea he possessed. With his new exercise regimen of tennis every morning, sailing or water-skiing in the afternoons, he had grown tanned and fit.

Arnie's parents were delighted with their son's progress, and so was his agent, who had flown up recently from Los Angeles, bringing proposals, contracts, and the script for Arnie's new project. "You're looking terrific, kid. You look ten *times* better than you did before. And who knows"— in unwitting and unfortunate pun—"being out of circulation for two years may have been a blessing in disguise. It'll mean a smoother transition into adult roles."

The wind shifted slightly to dead astern, then further. "Watch out," Saint ordered swiftly. "Get your head down, Arn, we're jibbing."

The boom swung across the cockpit with a clatter of blocks and a resounding thud. Saint paid out more line. Arnie obediently released his jib. The little boat flew across the surface of the water on white wings and a hiss of spray and, *Goddamn!* came Saint's involuntary silent cry, if only J.B. was in this boat with me now instead of Arnie. . . .

"Saint? Are you busy? Want to hit a few?"

He looked up from the typewriter. Arnie, appearing like an ad for sportswear in a V-necked white ribbed sweater, glittering white shorts with knife-edge creases, and tennis racket swinging loosely in his hand, struck an exaggerated pose and cried, "Anyone for tennis?" Then, diffident: "Oh. Excuse me, Saint. I guess you're not ready yet? Only it's after eleven, so I thought . . ."

"I'll be finished pretty soon now, Arn."

"D'you think about fifteen minutes? Twenty?"

"Something like that. Not much longer."

"That's okay. Whenever. I'll go watch TV."

Arnie turned away and softly closed the door.

Saint sat and stared at the door and sighed. There was no point trying to work anymore. Although Arnie was very good about not disturbing him a second time, thinking about Arnie tiptoeing away to watch a game show on TV was almost unbearable.

Saint wrestled his mind back to Joe and Angela, his characters on their doomed ride on Interstate 80, and spent another five minutes with them before Arnie tapped once again on the door.

This time he came right into the room, holding a bright blue envelope. "Mailman came. It says it's from V. Brown."

J.B. entered the Caffè Trieste on the stroke of one P.M., as planned.

She wore faded jeans and a baggy gray sweatshirt. Her blond hair, much longer now, was tied severely back with an elastic band.

Saint was sitting at a table by the window. She had felt his dark eyes watching her as she rounded the corner onto Vallejo Street.

She ordered a cappuccino, then sat down at the table facing him and gave him a small, tight smile. Saint smiled guardedly back. His face was leaner than she remembered, and very tanned. He looked older, more authoritative, dreadfully eager. She felt a pang of sorrow for him and for herself and determindedly suppressed it.

Saint reached across the table, briefly held her wrist, squeezed, then let her go. "It's good to see you."

J.B. took her hand away and put it in her lap. "Well," she said awkwardly, "so Vera will be here in three hours." She laid the *Starfire* strips carefully between them on the tabletop.

Saint glanced involuntarily from the drawings of Starfire to her own flesh-and-blood face and back again.

He asked, "Would you like a sandwich or soup or something?"

She shook her head. "Just coffee. I ate breakfast late." There was a tense pause. Saint didn't seem ready to say anything, so she asked, "How's Arnie doing?"

"Pretty well. He'll be going back to work in the fall. He has a new project."

"That's good." J.B. found herself twisting her coffee spoon in her fingers, and made herself put it down and leave it alone. "And how about you?"

Saint shrugged. "I finished the book. It's looking for a home. I'm doing the screenplay now, just for the hell of it. It's a lot of fun."

"Great. I'm glad." J.B. carefully didn't look at him. Seeing him again was a mistake. She realized how much she had missed him. How much she still missed him. There had been a period of bitter loneliness after she left him, when she cried every night; after he had walked out of the restaurant that time, she had had to go in back and cry her eyes out. Service had been temporarily suspended out front while the kitchen staff consoled her. "That boy comes in here again and bothers you," Luigi, the salad chef, declared, brandishing a fierce paring knife, "you just leave him to me."

She had even thought of going home again. Not to live in Corsica, but reasonably close, perhaps in Amarillo. At least she could see Momma now and then.

But that would have been pointless, as it turned out, because Momma wouldn't speak to her. "You're dirt," she had spat over the phone. "Don't you call me again. I know all about you, and I know what you tried to do to Floyd. . . . Everyone knows."

Momma had hung up on her. J.B. couldn't believe it. What had Momma meant? What had happened? When she tried to call back, she just got a busy signal.

She called Charlene. Charlene was cold to her just at first. Then: "Oh, honey, I knew it was all lies."

"What's all lies?"

Charlene sounded embarrassed. "What they're saying. That you came on to Floyd . . . you know . . . and he threw you out of the house."

Saint was saying, "I guess you're really doing well."

J.B. nodded mechanically. "I've been lucky, getting so much work. I just got a new commercial yesterday, a soft drink called Breeze. National network."

"Congratulations."

"I had to audition in L.A., but they'll be shooting in San Francisco. Kind of silly." She could hear herself gabbling now. "I'm going to Los Angeles all the time. Actually, I'm planning to go live there in the fall. . . ."

". . . and your momma, honey, you know how she thinks the world of that man. She's gonna believe just whatever lies he tells her."

"Momma wouldn't. She *couldn't*. That doesn't make sense."

"Your momma isn't making much sense lately, honey, and that's a fact. She hears voices, you know, and talks right back to them. Says they're the saucer people."

"The who?"

The flying-saucer people. Out by Mars, or like that. They're going to land on earth real soon, and take folks back to Jesus."

Saint asked, "Why go to L.A. if you're getting all this work here?"

"There's a lot more there."

"Oh. I guess you're ambitious."

That was an understatement. J.B. had determined she was going to do incredibly well, be as independent as she could be, and make a nice home for Momma somewhere where she could collect herself and learn to smile again, somewhere far away from Floyd. She replied shortly, "Yes."

After an uneasy pause Saint said, "Thanks for letting Vera share your place."

This was easier ground. "I'm looking forward to it. We've been talking, you know, on the phone. I said if she wants, she can take it over when I leave."

"I'm sure she'll be very grateful."

J.B. looked down at the drawings of Starfire. "No problem." She leafed through them, one by one. As usual, she felt thoroughly strange at the uncanny likeness of herself to Starfire, a likeness which was not merely physical; Vera seemed to have caught nuances of expression and emotion as well, even in the simplified lines of a cartoon—or perhaps, J.B. thought, more so just because a cartoon *is* simple and all the irrelevant details are left out. . . .

Several hours later, at the airport, J.B. leaned her elbows on the rail, watching the double doors leading to the customs area. People were coming through, so far none of them Vera.

She felt a strange thrill of anticipation. She wouldn't have guessed she'd be so excited.

"Hey," Saint cried suddenly, "there she is. There's Vera," as a slim brown-haired girl emerged, pushing a cart piled high with luggage, topped with a battered artist's portfolio.

J.B. searched for the pudgy teenager from Central Park West. "Where?"

But Saint was already thrusting his way through the crowd. "Vera! Over here!"

The girl turned and saw him. She seemed to glow as though lighted from inside.

That was Vera? Plump Vera? It can't be, thought J.B., astonished. Why, she's lovely.

"Hey!" Saint hugged Vera. "Welcome to California. It's great to see you. God, you're just the same."

Vera looked suddenly stricken and bitterly disappointed.

J.B. told Saint silently: You moron, can't you see she's beautiful now? Can't you see she lost about fifty pounds? She hugged Vera in turn. "You're looking just great. Gorgeous! Doesn't she look terrific, Saint?"

Saint was pushing the cart rapidly through the terminal toward the garage. "Sure. Terrific."

"And she's lost a lot of *weight*."

"Well," Saint said briefly, far too late, "so you did. Good for you."

J.B. gave an inward sigh of frustration. She thought: She probably did it all for you. And realized: You fool, Sloane St. John Treadwell, she *loves* you.

J.B.'s apartment was on the second floor, in a colorful alley containing an art gallery, an Indian restaurant, and a cheerily noisy bar with a jukebox and dance floor frequented by clean-cut stockbroker bikers as well as their not-so-clean-cut brethren. However, the bedroom was in the back and overlooked a small untended yard where trumpet vines and nasturtiums tangled together in cheerful confusion over a sagging grapestake fence and a discarded iron bedstead.

Saint stood quite still, holding Vera's bags, hungrily looking around at the tidy room, at the pine bureau upon which hairbrushes and cosmetics were arranged, the narrow white bed with its inexpensive floral spread from Sears, the sofa bed made up for Vera and camouflaged with colored pillows. He was overwhelmed, seeing where J.B. slept. He was searching for something personal for his hungry soul to cling to, although there wasn't much, not even a family photograph.

"How could there be?" J.B. might have asked. "That's three times now I've had to run off and leave everything behind."

She had had almost two years now to accumulate possessions, but had lost the habit. She bought very little for herself, for most of her money went directly into her savings account.

She felt uncomfortable, seeing Saint staring at her room. She moved him out of there as soon as she could. "Vera has to unpack and shower and stuff."

They went out to dinner at an Italian restaurant down the street. J.B. chose it specially, not just for the food, which was excellent, or the price, which was reasonable, but for the noise, the distractions, and the activity. Waiters wearing rumpled aprons slammed great steaming platters of pasta and unlabeled bottles of dark red wine on long, scrubbed trestle tables; salami and Chianti bottles swayed from the ceiling in the garlic-laden updrafts of hot air; Puccini and Verdi arias blared; and everybody shouted.

There was no danger of intimacy amid the noise and confusion, and right after dinner she would take Vera home to bed.

Already Vera looked pale, tired, disoriented, and rather forlorn as she raised her glass. "Cheers! Let's drink to the first reunion of the Starfire Trio!"

J.B. hoped Vera didn't notice that she and Saint touched Vera's glass with theirs, but not their own.

Vera was doing her best, but clearly the reality was falling short of expectation and the restaurant was too much for her on her first night. J.B. watched her give an appearance of appetite, pick through her linguine, nibble the clams and push aside the pasta, nervously drink a little too much of the dark red wine, and watch Saint, who didn't notice. Please, Saint, J.B. begged silently, please look at her and stop looking at me.

"You'll have to come up to Tahoe, Vera," Saint was saying. "It's beautiful. J.B. can bring you up. You will," he said, watching her, eyes kindling, "won't you?"

J.B. smiled thinly. "I have a pretty full schedule. But that's no reason why Vera can't come . . . it's an easy bus ride."

Saint's eyes were demanding. J.B. ignored the message. It makes no difference, she wanted to cry; just because we're all together again, and in spite of Starfire, nothing's changed between you and me.

Vera looked from one to the other. She started to say something, which was drowned in a wave of applause and shouts as three waiters burst out of the kitchen carrying a panettone with a candle stuck into it, singing "Happy Birthday to You!" in operatic chorus.

J.B. sighed. Shit, she thought, why can't people love right? There was a phrase she had heard, it came from a play, she guessed, though she didn't know what it was. Star-crossed lovers. It seemed to fit.

Vera loved Saint. Saint loved her, J.B. And she? Whom did she love? She told herself steadfastly: I love Momma and I guess I still love Melody Rose, they're my kin no matter what, they can't take care of themselves, and I'm going to do my best for them.

She thought that was the only real kind of love, after all.

Chapter

IO

It was an afternoon of quiet, solid heat; San Francisco Bay stretched smooth as a polished mirror; boats rode the water with drooping sails; a freighter glided silently up the channel toward Oakland, pushing a bow wave like twin silk ribbons.

Vera sat cross-legged on the grass at the Marina Green beside the yacht harbor, watching the shooting of J.B.'s commercial. The product was a carbonated soft drink called Breeze, whose image was supposed to be young, sassy, and sporty.

The set was blocked off by road barriers: an outdoor café, erected just that morning but looking quite authentic and permanent, with little white tables and chairs under striped beach umbrellas, pots of brightly colored geraniums, and a Coca-Cola vending machine.

J.B., golden and gorgeous in a brief tennis skirt and white tank top edged in pink, sat at one of the tables with a handsome young man. She was absently bouncing a Prince Pro tennis racket off the toes of her flawlessly clean sneakers. The young man lay slumped in his seat, apparently sound asleep. They were waiting between takes, as usual, thought Vera, surprised how slow and dull it all was, glad she had brought her sketchbook so she had something to do.

She had drawn a cameraman with butterflies tattooed on his brawny shoulders; a cop leaning on the trunk of his patrol car, somnolently manning the barricades; a young woman trying to control three dogs on intertwined leashes as they milled around her legs; J.B. at the table, chin resting pensively on her hand, gazing at nothing, thinking.

What was she thinking about? Vera had lived with J.B. for almost two weeks now. She liked her very much. J.B. was kind and considerate, but she was a very private person. Vera would have given almost anything to know what J.B. thought, especially how she felt about Saint.

He had called again this morning. "So what about it, Vera? When are you and J.B. coming up here? There's not much time left."

"I'll talk to J.B. again."

"Try to make it this weekend."

"I'll do my best."

On the set J.B. raised her head as the director strode purposefully forward and struck an attitude of command. He held an old-fashioned megaphone, through which he boomed a stream of instruction.

"Okay, ready to roll. Places, now. That means you, Roy. Wake up. And, Roy, you and J.B. are too widely separated. Get your chairs closer together. . . . Okay, people. Fifty frames. Slate it . . ."

A boy held a black-and-white-striped board in front of the camera.

". . . and rolling. . . . Action!"

J.B. and Roy stood up and wandered toward the vending machine. They exchanged glances of resigned gloom.

"Cut! Great!"

Now another long wait. Vera watched the Coca-Cola machine being taken away and another machine bearing a conspicuous Breeze logo trundled center stage on a dolly. A girl in jeans sprayed it with an oily substance and began to polish it to a high gloss. There was a lot of activity with a new lighting setup. One of the lights was huge and rolled back and forth on a track like a small train.

Vera sighed and lay back in the grass. She felt languid and tired. She tried to tell herself it was jet lag, but that was unlikely after so long. No, she knew what the problem was: she was suffering a severe reaction to dashed expectations.

How she had dreamed of her arrival in San Francisco and her first night with Saint.

But in her dream she had been alone with him in some dim, romantic little hideaway, not sharing a long family-style table with J.B. and a dozen raucously celebrating Italians. "Happy birthday to you . . . happy birthday to you," the waiters had sung, "happy birthday, dear Giulio . . ." Everyone had laughed and screamed and applauded Giulio, a toothless, wrinkled gnome who looked at least ninety, while he blew out the candle on his little cake.

Vera had made herself laugh and smile and applaud too, and she had toasted the reunion of the Starfire Trio, although it had fallen horridly flat. She had felt exhausted from the long journey and her nerves were stretched to the breaking point. So Saint and J.B. were supposed to have broken up. Well, it wasn't true; J.B. might have left Saint, but so far as he was concerned, nothing had changed. He still loved her.

Vera hadn't been able to sleep much that night, her dreams a turbulent parade of faces and images against an endless loop of old Giulio's birthday song, now discordant and mockingly brazen.

The next morning Saint arrived early to take Vera on the promised tour of the city, but he had clearly been hoping J.B. would come too, and was disappointed to find she had already gone out. He tried not to show how disappointed he was, and did his best to give Vera a good time.

He would have succeeded if she hadn't loved him and wanted so much more than just a friendly tour. As it was, it all merged into a featureless jumble of breakneck hills, monuments, boats, and bridges, ending across the Golden Gate Bridge for lunch in Sausalito so she could see the city skyline. "It's really beautiful," Vera admired dutifully.

Saint had ordered the house specialty, bayburgers on sourdough bread, which arrived on gigantic oval platters heaped with garnishes. Vera had a sudden urge to stuff herself, to eat every single thing on that enormous plate, but managed to control herself and eat only the meat and a slice of tomato.

During lunch they talked about *Starfire*.

Saint had called Mr. Solway again the day before Vera arrived. He wanted to hear from her as soon as possible. "Looks good," Saint said. "He seems really interested."

"That's great." Vera was thinking: If I was Starfire, this day would be so different. I'd be fascinating, captivating, I'd make things go just how I wanted. She'd been able to do that once; as Starfire she'd brazened through her interview at the Dorchester and got the job with Spring Kentfield. She had been brave enough to stand up to her parents and go to New York. But now she was completely tongue-tied. Starfire had lost her power. She added, "You've been wonderful. Thank you so much."

"Hey, listen. I got you fired and deported." Saint grinned absently. "It's the least I can do."

On the way back he said, "Don't forget about Tahoe, Vera. It'll be the end of the summer soon. Arnie's going back to work and I have to go to New York."

Her blood ran cold. "New York? You mean . . . to live?"

He shook his head. "Just business."

Vera felt limp with relief. What an irony, to come all this way to find Saint leaving almost at once. She asked, "Something to do with your book? Have you heard——?"

"Nothing. No, I could wish. It's only family business. It's my birthday. I'll be twenty-one, and I come into a trust fund."

"Oh," said Vera. "That's nice. Are you having a party?"

"No, but . . ." buoyantly, "I'm having dinner with my father. Just the two of us. He says he wants to talk to me. He called me himself. It's the first time ever; usually it's Aunt Gloria who calls, or that bitch Miss Gerrity."

"I'm so glad. That's wonderful."

"It'll be the first time we've had dinner alone together. It's my going to college turned him around, I guess. If only I could have told him I'd sold the book, that'd really be something."

Vera said, "There's still time."

When they returned to the apartment, J.B. hadn't yet returned.

Saint shrugged resignedly. He kissed Vera's cheek. "See you soon. It's great you came back."

"Thanks for lunch. I had a wonderful time."

"So did I. And, Vera . . . don't forget to talk with J.B. about Tahoe."

J.B. stood patiently while a girl in a smock dusted more blush on her cheeks, her mind far away and fully engaged.

She had been trying to calculate for most of the afternoon how much money she would make from this series of commercials. Quite a lot. And God, she needed it.

A recent call to Charlene had revealed more disturbing news. Floyd had walked out on Momma.

"He took up with this woman," Charlene explained. "And no, honey, let me tell you, she's not exactly Marilyn Monroe. She's pushing fifty if she's a day, and real heavyset, but he's crazy about her. He's even cut back on the liquor."

Good riddance, was J.B.'s first relieved thought. Floyd's out of our lives forever, with a bit of luck. She asked, "How's Momma taking it?"

"Not good, honey. I guess she really loved that man. But he's saying she drove him to it, making him crazy with her saucer people."

"Oh, no. Oh, poor Momma."

"And between you and me, honey, I think she's hurting for cash."

J.B. sent a money order to Momma at once for two thousand dollars; a postcard came back: "Don't send no more of your derty money i pray for you," although the money order was not returned, presumably cashed.

So soon afterward it couldn't have been a coincidence, Melody Rose called from New York.

"Hi there, sugar, how're you doing?"

J.B. hadn't spoken to Mel in a long time, and then she had hung up on her in a rage. Mel *had* known. J.B. said coldly, "Okay, thanks."

"Yeah, I'll bet. I see you on TV all the time. Must be doing *real* well." A sigh. "I'm not doing so good myself, though, and that's a fact."

"Sorry to hear that, Mel. Isn't Angelo taking care of you?"

"Jeez, Jo-Beth, he's history."

"That's something."

A pause, then a sound halfway between a choke and sob. "Yeah. The son of a bitch threw me out, Jo-Beth. I'm working in a club, kinda, off of Times Square."

J.B. could imagine the club.

"What'm I gonna do? He took everything. Even my clothes. I don't even have any fucking *clothes*. And I'm flat broke. Oh, sugar, I miss you. I miss you real bad." Her voice rose in a wail. "I was thinking, after all, you're my sister. I helped you out when you needed me. Took you in, and all. Jo-Beth, you're doin' so good now. I need some money, you gotta send me some money. . . . like about ten grand would help about now—see, there's this guy gave me this loan, and he's gettin' real heavy and I'm scared shitless, Jo-Beth. . . ."

J.B. sighed. She should have told Melody Rose, "I owe you a big fat zero, Sis. Forget it." But she hadn't the heart. Melody was the only sister she was ever going to have. And she was a victim too, just as much as

Momma. They were both victims of rotten men. So she'd said, "Okay, Mel, I'll do what I can."

Oh, yes, J.B. thought, I need money, all right.

It's time to move on and up.

"You'd be crazy not to go to New York or L.A.," her agent said. "That's where the real action is."

New York? Forget it, she wasn't going back there again, no way. But Los Angeles—she was flying down there once a week at least. She would save on air fares and rental cars, if nothing else. . . . Yes, it would be Los Angeles, and soon.

The director was shouting and waving his arms. "Okay, folks. Let's go."

The lights flashed on. The cameras rolled. "Action!"

And there it was—the magic machine fallen gleaming from the sky, Breeze, the answer to everyone's deepest desires.

J.B. and Roy exchanged delighted glances and flung up their hands with excitement.

Roy pulled the lever on the machine. Nothing happened.

"Shit!" Roy moaned. "The fucking thing's stuck."

"Cut!"

And as the cameras died, and a cascade of beautiful glittering Breeze cans thundered out onto the ground, "Well," he sighed philosophically, "wouldn't you just *know* it!"

Afterward Jo-Beth and Vera sat on the grass drinking Breeze while the café was dismantled and loaded into a truck.

Vera swirled the remains of her drink around in the can. "Do you like this stuff? I think it tastes awful."

J.B. shrugged. "I just sell it. I don't have to drink it." She asked, "Did you have fun? Was it interesting?"

"When something actually happened."

J.B. laughed. "Every couple of hours. Still, you did some drawing."

Vera showed her the book. J.B. flipped the pages, exclaiming with admiration. "God, you're so good. When are you seeing the syndicate people? *Syndicate*." With a wry grin, "Sounds like the Mafia."

"Tuesday next week."

"Jeez. Are you nervous?"

"A bit."

"What do they want? What are you going to say? They've already seen the strips . . ."

"I have to tell them stories. They want to make sure I have stories worked out for the next six months."

"Do you?"

"As far as I can until I actually do it. Then I really have to go with what Starfire wants to do."

J.B. stared at Vera in surprise. "How's that?"

Vera explained patiently, "If she feels things should go differently, then I have to do it her way."

"But, Vera . . ." J.B. knit her brows. "She's just someone in a story. She isn't real. Is she?"

"She's real enough."

Feeling curiously excited, J.B. said, "Tell me about her, then."

Vera answered slowly, "She's beautiful, and she has special powers . . ."

J.B. nodded. She already knew that.

"But she's also very . . ." Vera paused, as though searching for the right word. ". . . insecure, I suppose. I mean, with her body. She's not used to having one. In her own world she's just a creature of light and energy. She can go anywhere in the universe, do anything. Now she feels trapped."

"Doesn't she like being human?"

"Sometimes. Maybe most of the time."

"Do humans know she's an alien?"

Vera shook her head. "Not unless she wants them to. They find her fascinating, though they all feel something strange about her. Something they can't identify."

J.B. asked curiously, "Can Starfire fall in love?"

"With an Earthman? I'm not sure. She hasn't let me know yet. Emotion confuses her, you see. She doesn't know how to handle it. She doesn't understand how humans think and feel. How can she? She looks human, but she's not. She's an alien . . ."

"Yes." J.B. nodded. "Oh, yes."

"And of course, she's lonely. Her home is so far away, light-years away, and she can't go home till she's finished her mission."

"What happens if she fails?"

"She can't. If she fails, her world is destroyed."

J.B. found she had been holding her breath. She reminded herself again that Starfire was just a character in a story.

Still, she said compulsively, "I know just how she feels, poor thing. I feel sorry for her."

Vera replied with unaccustomed sharpness, "Then don't. She'd hate that."

"You seem to know her very well."

"And so I ought. At least . . ." uncertainty creeping into her voice, "I thought I knew her."

She poured the rest of her Breeze away. They both watched the brownish liquid fizz as it sank into the grass.

J.B. observed, "Good thing the client isn't here."

"Yes." After a moment Vera said, "Saint called again this morning. About going to Tahoe."

J.B. stared at the ground where the Breeze had sunk into the dry grass without a trace. "What did you say?"

"That I'd ask you."

"Well," J.B. sighed, "nothing's changed. I'm not going. But that's no reason why you can't go. Why not? It'd be terrific. Seriously."

"It wouldn't feel right, going alone." Vera drew a deep breath and said, "It's you he wants to see, not me."

Very slowly and deliberately J.B. crunched the empty can of Breeze in her hand. "I wish he didn't." She whispered, "It hurt, you know, when I found out he'd lied to me. I thought he was different than other guys. I really did. But he's just the same, after all. They're all the same. They want to own you." She added, "Then, when they get you, they use you and dump you."

"Not Saint."

J.B. looked away. "Of course Saint. He's a man, isn't he?"

Arnie knocked on Saint's door at eleven o'clock as usual, but, seeing Saint busy working, silently mouthed "Anyone for tennis?" and departed at once with a token wave of his hand.

Saint worked on for another half-hour; then, sighing, he put on his sneakers, collected his racket, and went to find Arnie in the game room.

But Arnie was not there. Vernon and a repairman hunched over the television set, whose screen was a blaring rectangle of dots. "On the fritz," Vernon told Saint. "Arnie went on ahead. Said he was gonna work on his serve till you were ready."

"Okay. Great." Saint wandered out the front door, both encouraged that Arnie had gone on without him and glad the television had died; he hoped it would be on the fritz for a while.

Arnie liked to watch every evening, and all too often, without warning, J.B.'s face would suddenly flash onto the screen advertising milk for healthy bodies, lotion for baby-soft skin, or Swedish salon treatments for silkier, more lustrous hair.

And she wasn't coming up to Tahoe. "I'm sorry, Saint," Vera had said on the phone. "I tried."

He paused outside the house, staring toward the lake, which glittered blue and silver between the trees. The aspens were starting to turn. There was a new fall crispness to the air. It was beautiful here.

Wouldn't J.B. forgive him? Ever?

Saint closed his eyes, blanked his mind, then silently and intensely willed J.B. to his side with such force he knew he would open his eyes again and find her standing on the path facing him, looking astonished and perhaps a little scared. He willed it so hard he felt actually giddy.

He opened his eyes, filled with irrational expectation . . .

But of course the path was empty.

Saint moodily banged his racket against the side of his leg. He told himself not to be a fool.

He resolutely squared his shoulders and marched down the path toward the court to play tennis with Arnie.

Now he could certainly hear him working on his serve; crack, crack, crack—he was working like the very devil. He sounded like two people.

And as Saint emerged through the trees, why, there *were* two people on the court.

Arnie and a girl.

And—oh, God—the girl was J.B.

His heart turned over with a floundering thud which left him breathless. It had worked! By some miracle she had actually appeared. And then the girl turned to face him and he thought he would be sick with disappointment because it wasn't J.B. at all, just another tall girl with blond hair.

She smiled and waved at him, then turned back to the game.

Arnie served and she whacked it back an inch above the net.

Arnie returned it too high. She volleyed and put the ball away. It struck and bounced way out of reach. Arnie leapt and missed and stood with hands on hips, panting.

The girl laughed. *"Game!"* Then came loping to the sidelines with outstretched hand. "Hi! I'm Fletcher McGraw."

From the back she could so easily have been J.B. The same build, height, hair, and a similar easy stride. But from the front, no, not in a million years. This girl had a conventionally pretty, pouting face, round blue eyes, and a meaty upper lip exaggerated by a slight overbite.

She angled him a look of comprehensive appraisal, from the crown of his tousled black head to his faded purple tank top to the frayed toes of his sneakers.

Arnie said, "She's our new neighbor. Her father rented the place next door."

"Yeah." Fletcher smiled. "We live in the Valley and it's real *hot* there now—I heard Arnie playing, all by himself, and just wandered over . . . he didn't seem to mind."

"I do now," Arnie complained to Saint. "She's too good for me. You play with her."

"No," Saint said, but Fletcher was back on the court, waiting, her posture one of expectancy and challenge.

He felt irrationally upset that Fletcher was not, after all, J.B., and in his intense disappointment he played ferociously and without chivalry, slamming his power serve at her full force, making no concessions, playing to win.

He quickly realized that the joke was on him, for although he did win, it was quite a fight.

By the end of the set, which he took 6-4, he was panting with effort and his purple shirt was soaked with sweat. Fletcher herself was flared with the excitement of battle, her eyes gleaming, lips curved in a satisfied smile. Saint couldn't help noticing how her nipples showed hard as pebbles under her top, and realized she wasn't wearing a bra. She shook his hand over the net. Her fingers were hot and very strong.

Arnie said, "She's lucky to be alive. You were out to kill her."

Saint said, "She can take care of herself." He gave Fletcher an uneasy smile, for he hadn't behaved well at all. No gentleman he. And it really *wasn't* her fault she wasn't Jo-Beth.

Fletcher smiled back, rather an odd smile, as though she and he were secret conspirators. "But that's the way I like it. No holds barred. Fight to the death."

Later, after Fletcher had collected her bathing suit and Eve had prepared a picnic lunch, they took the ski boat out on the lake.

Saint had asked Arnie, "Wouldn't you rather I didn't come?"

Arnie stared at him in shocked surprise. "Why?"

"She's pretty. I thought you'd like to be on your own."

"Is she? Comes on too strong. Anyway," Arnie said flatly, "she prefers you."

They took turns skiing—Fletcher was as good as Saint expected—then stopped the boat in Carnelian Bay. She said, "It's not as pretty here as it is at Sand Harbor Cove. It's not far. We could ski on over."

"No," Saint vetoed with such finality and such a hard look that Fletcher's flax-blue eyes opened wide.

Arnie glanced at him anxiously.

Saint ordered himself: Idiot, lighten up. She didn't say it on purpose. How was she to know?

He told himself to be easier on Fletcher. She was a nice girl, a hell of a tennis player, and actually didn't look at all like J.B. Her body was different too; more muscular, more rounded. She had changed into a white bikini, just tiny triangles tied together with strings, which barely covered anything. There was a small red-brown mark on her left breast about two inches above the nipple. For an instant Saint wondered about the mark: was it a scar or a burn?

She certainly had none of J.B.'s natural reserve, either. Fletcher sat up on the rail, swaying easily with the motion of the boat as she ate her sandwich, long legs unself-consciously splayed so that Saint could clearly see the light brown pubic hairs curling around the crotch of her bikini. Arnie noticed too; always shy with girls, he flushed and turned his head.

Saint looked up and found Fletcher watching him. She gave him a long, lazy smile and nibbled at her lower lip.

*   *   *

Saint couldn't sleep that night.

He lay on his back in the soft darkness, knowing the moon was casting a wide light trail down the surface of the lake. He could both feel and hear the beat of his heart and the pulse of the blood through his body as he thought about J.B.

It had been so long, so very long, and he had been living like a monk. His blood thundered. He needed—wanted—so badly to make love to J.B., but if he couldn't, he didn't want anyone else.

Then suddenly, hot and turbulent, his need turned to anger. What right did she have to make him feel so miserable?

It would serve her right if . . .

Yes.

He watched J.B.'s image slowly fade, to be replaced by the face of Fletcher McGraw.

Now, in the dark and safely alone, he examined her pouting, knowing mouth, the little white teeth and pink tongue, nipples showing dark under her sweated tennis top, those curling hairs between her legs and the curious scar, which now, in his mind, had assumed a raffish quality, even a hint of perversity.

Once again he saw her feline smile while she watched him look. Oh, yes, he had been meant to look. He was definitely meant to do something about it too.

Well, he was only a human. Not a saint. That wasn't even his real name.

Angrily he told J.B., "It's your own fault. You have only yourself to blame."

Chapter

II

"I divorced your mother as soon as it was decently possible after you were born," Sloane Treadwell Sr. told Saint.

Saint didn't know what to reply to that, or if indeed any reply was called for. Instead, staring down at his plate, he carefully counted the strips of wild duck meticulously arranged in a flower pattern around a cone of wild rice. There were seven pieces of duck, interspersed by two segments of orange, three asparagus spears, and a garnish of watercress. His father had steak tartare. It had arrived, a crimson mound, with a globe of bright orange egg yolk glaring dead center, which Saint involuntarily perceived as a ghastly parody of a female breast.

He watched his father plunge his fork into the top of the egg yolk and mash the orange goo methodically into his meat, winced, and looked away; then shrugged his shoulders inside his new Versace jacket, speared a fragile sliver of duck, and wondered how soon he could decently excuse himself and leave.

Just at first Saint had allowed himself to be both touched and enormously pleased by this dinner invitation upon his coming of age; such a traditional, rite-of-passage, father-son affair in which typically the father would accept the son, not as an equal exactly, but certainly as a legitimate, rational adult. Perhaps he would at last decide Saint was worthy of his time and attention; perhaps they could finally begin to know each other; his father might even be secretly proud that Saint had never taken advantage of his privileged position and now appeared to be succeeding in his own chosen field, for Saint *had* sold his novel. His agent had called the day before he left for New York.

"Congratulations, Sloane. We've had quite a nice offer come in. Not at all bad, for a first book."

Arnie was thrilled. "I want the movie rights! I want to play Joe."

Aunt Gloria was pleased as Punch. "I knew you could do it, Sloane." He had asked her not to tell his father; he wanted to spring it as a surprise at dinner.

Saint had forgotten his anger with J.B., and called her next. She wasn't there, of course, but at least Vera was happy for him. "That's just wonderful, Saint. You must feel on top of the world. And guess what," she'd added shyly, "I've had some good news too about *Starfire*."

"As soon as I get back," Saint promised, "we'll have a celebration. The three of us. The Starfire Trio is alive and well."

His first morning in New York, he went to visit his new editor, who turned out to be a dashingly dressed, enthusiastic blond in her forties. "We're very excited about *Right Exit Closed*. Spare me the haunted houses, things that walk, psychic kids, and all that shit; this is *real*, hitting right below the belt at everyone's nightmares. *Today* horror; on the freeway, yet. We'll market it as horror for the eighties. And you're so young! How old are you?"

"Almost twenty-one."

She grinned ruefully. "I *think* I remember what it was like, being almost twenty-one."

If only J.B. had been with him, it would have been perfect. As it was, it was pretty damn good.

Two days later, twenty-one in actuality, Saint assumed personal control of approximately five million dollars upon the maturation of his grandfather Treadwell's trust fund. There had been a small ceremony in Mr. Friedman's office and Saint had signed his name on several dozen documents. Afterward Aunt Gloria, glowing and proud of him, took him to lunch at the Colony. She wore a slightly battered straw hat over carelessly pinned-up hair, and the pink Chanel suit she had worn to summer lunches in town for the past twenty-five years; it had fresh mud on the hem; Saint guessed she hadn't been able to resist one last foray into the garden before leaving for the train.

His father had not joined them. He'd said, "I'll see you at dinner, Sloane. Wear something suitable."

Saint did not own a suit and had no intention of buying one; however, he had dressed carefully for this evening in his brand-new jacket—pearl gray with a thin pink stripe—a navy-blue Ralph Lauren shirt, and white slacks. He had even had his hair cut. His father was not impressed: "You look like an Italian gangster, Sloane. Or a drug dealer. And where's your tie?" Upon discovering there was no tie, nor would there be a tie, he instructed Miss Gerrity to change their dinner reservation.

So instead of his father's preferred locale, a place of comfortable leather seats, hearty steaks, and solid oak booths filled with middle-aged gray-suited power moguls like himself, here they sat in a trendy little place with pink linen, glass bricks, fancy little dabs of color-coordinated food upon oversize plates, the silent reproach being more articulate than words.

Saint gazed at his father, square and gray and powerful, as incongruous in this setting as a granite monument in a greenhouse filled with tropical flowers, determined not to allow this euphoric time to be spoiled. He asked, "If Mother was that bad, why did you marry her in the first place?"

His father said stolidly, "Because she was pregnant."

Saint give a mental whistle of surprise. He had never seen his father betray emotion at any time. Never excitement, never warmth, never fear. He was a corporate machine receiving all the satisfaction and pleasure he needed from balance sheets and ratings. But once, after all, he must have been young and careless and human enough to fall romantically in love with a beautiful actress, even if only for one night. Saint laid down his fork and studied his father with more warmth and even sympathy. He asked carefully, "With me?"

His father nodded.

"Well," Saint said. "I guess you did the right thing, then, marrying her."

"I had no choice." His father snapped a breadstick in half and crunched one end between strong teeth. "She refused to have an abortion."

Saint opened his mouth to say something, then realized he had no idea what to say. He played for time, dabbled a stick of asparagus in the floret of hollandaise sauce, and stared at it with concentration.

Logically, of course, he could understand. He tried to put himself in his father's position. It was 1961. Attitudes were different then. He must have been truly appalled, knowing Spring was pregnant. Of course he would have wanted her to abort the baby. . . . But on a different, very primal level he thought: How dare he! That baby was *me*! My father wanted my mother to get rid of *me*. And then the ominous little question crept into his mind: *Why is he telling me this?* It's a cruel thing to say. And what's the point, anyway? At least Spring had said no. Thanks, Mom, Saint thought wanly, perhaps you're not such a selfish old bitch after all.

His father went on, "It was against her interests, clearly, to have the operation. You were an essential bargaining chip."

"I don't understand."

"Oh, Sloane. Think. She held all the cards. If I did not marry her and settle a considerable sum of money upon her, she made it very clear I would regret it bitterly."

"What would she have done?"

"She would have run screaming to the tabloid papers, of course. Treadwell Communications was just starting to get off the ground, and a scandal was the last thing I needed. I had made a few enemies."

No kidding, thought Saint.

"I couldn't afford the risk. I married her, as she demanded, and paid her off. We separated as soon as you were born, and I began proceedings six months later. She was very rapacious."

Saint had drunk a glass of wine with dinner and it now sat flat and sour on his stomach. He asked, "Why are you telling me all this?"

"Because it's time you learned the truth, Sloane; you're of age. There are things you must understand."

"Well," Saint said mechanically, "thanks. I guess. I understand everything. I was a bargaining chip, you felt tricked, you never liked me. Quite reasonable. I don't blame you." He folded his napkin, placed it beside his plate, and pushed back his chair; all he wanted now was to get out of there. He rose and said politely, "Thanks for dinner. I think maybe I better go."

"No, Sloane. Sit down." His father spoke as if to a junior and insubordinant employee. "I'm not through."

"You mean there's more?"

"Certainly there's more."

Unwillingly Saint sat down again.

His father steepled his fingers and stared fixedly over the top. It was one of the few times he had looked Saint directly in the eye. He said, "When your mother told me her news, I understood her to be two months pregnant."

Saint looked back at him, puzzled. His father's eyes were a flat gray, the color of zinc. "So?"

"She was lying. She was four months pregnant, or even more. You understand, she had good muscle tone. She was a trained dancer. Her pregnancy was not really obvious until at least six months. Even seven.

"It wasn't until you were born, allegedly two months premature but clearly a full-term baby weighing close to nine pounds, that I realized she had pulled one of the oldest tricks in the book. And I'd fallen for it."

Saint blinked. After a moment of silence he began, "So, what you're saying is—"

His father said harshly, "She passed off some other man's brat as mine."

"So you're . . . you're not my father?"

"I thought I had spelled it out for you, Sloane."

The noise and clatter of the other diners fell away. Saint could see their lips moving, watched silverware being wielded, waiters clashing piles of plates and glassware, and heard nothing but a distant humming in his ears. Finally, he asked, "Couldn't you have . . . disowned me or something? You didn't have to pretend I was your son."

His father's lips turned down in a chill smile. "At that particular moment I was not equal to the scandal, or the ridicule. Or, frankly, the inescapable vituperation from your mother. I bowed to the inevitable. I made you my heir, gave you my name, which, I am amused to see, you have always had distaste for, but I saw you as little as possible. Frankly, I couldn't stand it."

He sighed and rested his chin contemplatively on his fingers. "Not an attractive story, but I felt I owed it to you. So you should know why I have been less then attentive all these years."

A waiter hovered. "Would you gentlemen care to see the dessert trolley?"

"Sloane?" asked his father—or, no, *not* his father. "The cheesecake doesn't look too bad."

"Dessert?" Saint stared. "You're offering me *dessert* now?"

The waiter said, "We have a lovely strawberry mousse tonight. And the pecan pie is simply yummy."

"No, thanks." Saint shook his head. He felt a bit queasy.

He heard his father—*him*—say, "I'll have coffee. Decaffeinated. Sloane?"

Saint shook his head.

The waiter bowed and withdrew.

After a moment Saint asked, "Well, then, so who was he? *Is* he? My real father?"

The man across the table shrugged. With a slight grimace of distaste: "I haven't the slightest idea. You'll have to ask your mother. Perhaps she'll remember."

Oh, boy, Saint noted, you've shoved the knife in, now twist it. Good for you. He looked across the table with pity. How could anybody be so calculatingly and pettily cruel? It wasn't even cruelty; it was meanness. And from now on, he thought, cold in his turn, I owe you nothing. I did my very best. I loved you. But that's all over now.

"I'm sorry to have perhaps been a little hard on you, Sloane, but I thought I owed it to you, the truth. To clear the air."

Saint folded his pink napkin into a tight little wad and placed it tidily upon his bread plate.

"No you didn't," he said quietly. "You wanted some revenge, is all."

"Revenge? Certainly not. Don't be melodramatic. That's your mother speaking."

"Oh, you poor, sorry man." Saint stood up very slowly and braced himself on the back of his chair, locking his knees so his legs wouldn't shake. The supreme irony, he thought, would be a battery of singing waiters bringing in a birthday cake. "Why didn't you say all this a couple of days ago? I assume you'll want to transfer the Treadwell Trust. I don't know what's involved here, but if I'm not your son, then obviously I have no claim to that money."

Saint remembered that wintry afternoon almost three years ago, ripping up a thousand dollars and dropping it on the rug in front of Miss Gerrity's shoes, and how satisfied he had felt. Well, figuratively ripping up five million dollars should make him feel five thousand times better.

"You're still my legitimate heir, Sloane. Of course it's yours."

"I'm making my own living now. I don't need it."

"Oh, yes . . ." The voice assumed a slightly petulant edge. "Ten thousand dollars advance. I wouldn't call that a living."

"It's a beginning."

Saint turned and walked away.

"Sloane, come back here. Don't be a fool." For the first time Treadwell Sr. sounded less confident, unsure, even afraid.

"Sloane! Remember who you are!"

Saint leveled one last gaze at the man whom he had loved and tried and failed to please all these years and said blandly, "If I knew that, I'd give it a try."

He walked.

It was an updated version of that enraged journey three years ago.

He found himself supplying script direction.

Exterior, street, night. The air is hot and humid. Pedestrians throng the sidewalks, lovers, joggers, dog-walkers, window-shoppers. A young man wearing a fashionable Italian sport jacket marches angrily up Fifth Avenue.

Track with the young man past various well-known landmarks until he abruptly swerves into Central Park at Nintieth Street. He crosses the dark, deserted park from east to west in a direct line, striding with total unconcern for danger, as if certain he is protected and rendered untouchable by the aura of fury which surrounds him . . .

Saint walked as far west as Amsterdam Avenue and then cut downtown again. He walked until he was exhausted, returning to his mother's apartment about two in the morning.

Back in his room he found himself still too strung-up to sleep. He decided he couldn't wait until morning to get away, and there was nobody home anyway. He packed his bags and took a cab to Kennedy Airport. From there he boarded the first available flight to San Francisco.

He arrived midmorning, picked up the Jaguar from the long-term parking lot, and drove through the windy sunshine of the bayshore freeway into the swirling fog of the city, his body and brain aching with hurt.

It was a desolate thing to find out he was not a Treadwell, that his father had never been his father after all, and that Aunt Gloria was no longer—had never been—his aunt. It was a bitter thing to have had it told with such cold triumph, and even more bitter to realize that his love had been wasted all these years. He felt like a fool—which brought in its wake a wave of intense anger.

By the time he reached the city his tangle of emotions had warped together into a single strand of aching need.

He drove to Telegraph Hill as if his car was fixed in a homing beam. He knew there was only one person in the world who could help him now.

He parked in the alley and stood outside her house.

He pressed his finger on the door buzzer and leaned on it.

J.B. opened the door.

Later he would wonder what would have happened if it had been Vera who answered the door—Vera, who was nearly always home but who today had gone to the laundromat—but J.B. opened the door, and so abruptly that he almost fell over the threshold on top of her. "Good grief, Saint," she said crossly, "I'm not deaf."

"J.B., I have to talk with you." He gripped her so hard by the upper arms that she gasped and thrust him away. "*Stop* that! What's wrong with you?" Rubbing at her flesh, where red marks already showed. "That hurt. Jesus, Saint."

He paid no attention. "I need you, J.B. Let me in."

"You're already in."

"Yeah." He swung precipitately through the living-room door and stumbled over an open suitcase. "What's this for?"

"I'm starting to pack."

"Pack? Where're you going?"

"Los Angeles. At the end of the week. I'm moving." At Saint's look of stunned surprise, "I *told* you."

Everything went to pieces then. He lost it. In his precarious state Saint saw J.B.'s departure as yet another massive breach of faith. "You can't go. I won't let you go."

He shouldn't have said it. He knew that at once, when J.B.'s eyes flared with anger, but he couldn't help himself. "I won't let you."

She cried, "You don't own me. I'll do what I want."

"But I need you here. J.B., you don't know what happened . . . God, J.B., I love you so much I have to have you . . . ." And he caught her and crushed her up against him, feeling her muscles tense in his arms, her body recoil, her face turn away from his kiss. He was unaware of the sudden pain as she grasped him by the hair and dragged his face away. "J.B., please, for God's sake . . . J.B., I know you love me too. You want me as badly as I want you. I know you do. You've got to come back to me. You *have* to—"

She flung herself away from him in fury. "I don't have to do anything. And I don't love *you*. I never have. Don't touch me again."

He moved purposefully toward her. She backed away.

He said, "If you go to L.A., then I'm coming too. I'll follow you."

"No way. Saint, for the last time, leave me alone. I don't want you."

"Yes you do." He laughed shortly. "Come on, J.B. That last night on the boat. That last time, that was real. I could tell. You can't pretend it wasn't."

She laughed too, a cold, mirthless sound. "That was acting. Don't you get it? I was pretending, like all the other times. I was using you because I needed you. But I don't need you anymore. I'm doing just *fine*. Now, for God's sake, go away and never come back. Leave me alone. I can't stand this anymore."

He drove through parched heat up Interstate 80 toward Truckee and Lake Tahoe, the scorching wind blasting in his face. He roared past the more decorous drivers, cutting in and out with brutal unconcern, foot hard to the floor, at seventy, eighty, and up to one hundred miles per hour, watching the rearview mirror with slitted eyes, waiting for that inevitable wink of red light far behind—although knowing that he was still invulnerable, still protected by his red aura, now intensified a thousandfold by this latest and most devastating rejection, knowing that there would be no police pursuit, that nobody would or could stop him.

Saint didn't slow down until the turnoff onto Route 89 for Lake Tahoe, when he followed the twisting banks of the Truckee River with no awareness of the cool green shadows and tempting stretches of sparkling water.

He unlocked the big gates to Arnie's house, drove through, lurching unevenly down the lumpy driveway, and now he could catch glimpses of the lake between the trees and smell the sharp pine scent of the trees.

Thank God there was nobody here.

Arnie was in Los Angeles.

Eve and Vernon had the week off.

Sanctuary. Why hadn't he had the sense to come here first?

Saint braked sharply in a spurt of dust. He flung his bag onto the porch, ran down to the lake, and crunched across the small shingle beach to the deserted dock.

He needed to swim as far and as hard as he could, to cleanse himself of useless emotions, to swim to exhaustion.

Saint stripped his clothes off and dived naked into the frigid water. It was a shock on his hot body and he gasped for breath as he surfaced. Then, striking out toward the center of the lake, not sparing himself, he forgot the cold as his skin grew numb. He swam until his arms ached, then stopped, rolled on his back, and floated, staring up into the hard bright blue sky. The water was glassy smooth. It was so quiet the thin air seemed to vibrate.

He floated for five minutes, until the cold took him once more. He stared at his arms, pale and goosefleshed; through the water his feet gleamed greenish white.

Saint swam violently back toward the dock, pushing himself with all his strength.

He hauled himself out on trembling arms, the dry heat of the sun prickling on his back. He shook his head, the water flying in an arc of cold droplets and . . .

"You sure did swim a long way," said Fletcher McGraw.

Saint gathered his feet under him and moved into a half-crouch. He pushed the wet, tangled hair from his eyes, and there she was, cross-legged on a striped beach blanket, observing him smilingly through heart-shaped sunglasses.

He demanded angrily, "What the hell are you doing here?"

She shrugged. "I heard your car. I wanted company. I was bored."

He crouched on one knee. He begged her, "Leave me alone, Fletcher. I'm not good company today."

"It's been awful dull, just Dad and me. And now he's gone down to Sacramento on business." She gazed up at him with ingenuous blue eyes, reached out her hand, and touched him on his wet forearm. "I don't know how you can swim in that water."

"Fletcher, listen to me——"

"You're a pretty good swimmer, aren't you?" She gazed at his naked chest, still heaving with exertion, at his nipples, hard and erect with cold, then downward to his flat stomach and bunched, muscular legs. She said meaningfully, "I'm sure you do everything well. . . ."

Saint warned, "Fletcher, go home."

"Why?" She licked her lips with a pointed pink tongue, and without apparent movement, one little triangle of her bikini top slid sideways, exposing a beige half-moon of nipple.

"Because I'm just not in the mood." Saint glared at her. "I mean it. Get out of here."

Fletcher licked at her lips again, and now her entire breast was free. It was hard and round and brown and white. She said, "My, you're real angry. What's the matter, Saint?" She squeezed her nipple gently with her fingers, then rubbed it slowly with the palm of her hand.

"Don't do that, Fletcher. Not now."

"You remind me of some kind of wild animal with bared fangs. . . ."

"Jesus Christ, *will* you stop it. I don't want you."

"Come on, Saint. Nothing's that bad." She unhooked her bikini top and cupped her breasts for him.

Saint looked at them, then raised his eyes to her face. She stared back at him, smiling that odd smile of hers.

He moved toward her, very slowly, and pushed her backward, flat on the hot, splintery boards of the dock. He braced himself on his arms, his palms laid flat on each side of her head. He tore her expensive dark glasses off and tossed them over the side into the water. Fletcher's blue eyes were glazed with an expression he had never seen before, and once again she ran her tongue over her full lower lip. "You're really exciting when you're mad."

He had long ago lost his capacity for thought, for reason. Now he was a creature of pure raw anger, although a tiny warning was sounding somewhere deep in his clotted brain. Stop it. Stop it. Stop it.

"And you do, too, want me. You wanted me that last day on the boat. You can't pretend you didn't. I could tell, you know. It was for real. . . ."

Almost word for word what he'd said to J.B.

It was the final straw. He held Fletcher's head down, crushing iron fingers across her throat, pinning her painfully to the hard dock. Fletcher had stopped being Fletcher. Now she was J.B. and he wanted to hurt her. He wanted revenge for all the hurt she had dealt him.

Fletcher writhed under him, kicking, screaming, cursing, beating her fists on his back, on his face. "You fucker!" Fletcher screamed. "Oh, you shit fucker!"

To stop her screaming he bit her lips savagely enough to draw blood, after which she fought him steadily with muffled throaty cries until he had finished. It was horribly, thoroughly satisfying.

He lay across her body, panting and only half-conscious. Through half-open eyes, the landscape swirled dizzily around him in shades of red and black, which slowly lightened and took on ordinary colors as the thudding of his blood calmed, rational thought returned, and . . . "Oh, Jesus Christ," Saint said painfully through bruised lips.

Fletcher lay quietly under him, her body marked with livid red patches that by tomorrow would turn purple and black.

"Oh, God," Saint whispered, "Oh, God, Fletch, I'm sorry." He leaned over the edge of the dock and retched, although he hadn't eaten since last night and all that came up was acid stomach fluid. "Oh, God. I don't know why . . . I couldn't control . . . Oh, Christ . . ."

Fletcher lay curled on her side, facing him. She looked dreamy and peaceful. She smiled at him, actually smiled. Astonishingly: "Oh, that's okay," he heard her say contentedly, "it was great. It was the most exciting thing ever happened to me. I loved it. You're like a fucking stallion when you're mad."

Saint leaned his head into her soft, bruised stomach and began helplessly to cry. He thought he felt her stroke his hair.

Chapter

12

Vera breakfasted quickly on black coffee and a slice of honeydew melon and went to work.

Nowadays she did little else but work.

Her meager savings were running very low. J.B. had offered to continue paying the full rent for a while, even though she would be living in Los Angeles; "I'd like to know I have a place to come back to if I'm in town, and anyway, I feel like I have a stake in *Starfire!*"

But although it was very generous of her, Vera hadn't liked that idea much; *Starfire* seemed to be less and less her own property. Nor did she wish to feel too indebted to J.B. In the end they decided to split the rent fifty-fifty.

Starfire was going to be a great success. "We have faith in *Starfire*," Phil Solway had said, "and we have faith in you." But faith alone wouldn't pay the rent; she wouldn't earn a nickel until *Starfire* was launched and running in newspapers across the country, and that wouldn't happen for months.

It had never occurred to Vera how long it would be before she got paid.

The Express Features salesmen wouldn't even show the *Starfire* proposal around to the syndicate's member newspapers until the beginning of the year. Provided all went well and enough subscribers bought *Starfire*, the release date wouldn't be until March of next year at the earliest.

In the meantime she would have to find a job—something in the evenings so she could draw during the day, which raised the next problem:

Vera didn't have a work permit. She must find an employer prepared to pay cash and not ask too many questions. That was another reason J.B. was being so generous with the rent; she knew just what it was like to need work and have no papers.

Thank God for Dr. Wheeler, who was arranging funds for Vera here through his California bank. She had hated to take his money, but he was adamant. "You can pay me back when they bring out the Starfire T-shirts."

"It's real nice of him," J.B. observed suspiciously. "Too nice."

"He's just a nice man."

"I'll bet he's got something on his mind. He'd never do that otherwise."

Vera, who was afraid of that very thing but hadn't wanted to think about it, said sharply, "I'll pay him back and that'll be that."

J.B. nodded. "That's okay then." Then asked casually, too casually, "You heard from Saint lately?"

"No. Why?"

J.B. had drawn breath as if to reply, but apparently changed her mind and left a few minutes later for a hair appointment.

Vera sighed, made herself not think about Saint or her money problems, resolutely pushed her cup of coffee to one side, and began to block out the opening of her new story.

She drew Starfire, light hair rimed with frost, glaring angrily at the oily sludge lapping around the base of once-pristine icebound cliffs and at the tarry corpses of birds, seals, and fish tumbling stickily in the soiled water. "How dare they do this," raged the bubble over Starfire's head. (Vera ringed the bubble with Jack Frost icicles, identifying the intense Arctic cold through which Starfire could walk unscathed and relatively unclothed.) "Somebody's going to pay for it."

The deep rumbling of a high-powered engine echoed up from the street below, but Vera was accustomed by now to the bikers and their comings and goings and paid no attention. She was absorbed.

Here was a wonderful opportunity for special effects—towering mountains sheathed in icy cloud, glaciers tumbling down into an obscene ocean of tar, the ominous bows of a black ship bearing down upon Starfire riding her ice floe. . . .

CUT TO: *The President of Calco. Suave and handsome, fiftyish, a big cigar, smooth as his own oil. He addresses an executive meeting.*

President: If we play our cards right, we'll come out smelling like a rose. It's the government will take the rap.

CUT TO: *Starfire*, CLOSE-UP.

Starfire (commands the tanker): Don't come any closer or you'll regret it!

The bike's roar eased to a steady rumble. Vera glanced out the window. Then she saw it was not a motorcycle at all, but a sports car, its white flanks travel-stained and dusty, the windshield smeared with dead bugs. It was parked half on the sidewalk in defiance of a no-parking-anytime sign. Saint sat quite still in the driver's seat, staring up at her window through reflecting sunglasses. Something was strange about the angle of his head, the tired set of his shoulders, the line of his mouth, but Vera's mind filed that knowledge away for examination later on. For now, it was enough that he was here. Even though, she reminded herself, he hadn't come to see her but J.B.

Eventually he switched off the engine and picked up a bottle-shaped brown-paper package from the passenger seat.

"Hi, Vera," Saint said on the doorstep when Vera opened it to his ring and pretended she hadn't been watching him. "Just happened to be passing." He drew a breath. "Is J.B. here?"

Her breath came a little short with her disappointment while she told herself not to be so stupid. "Sorry. No."

He closed the door behind him. "Good. I wanted to see you."

Her heart lifted.

Saint went on, "We have celebrating to do, remember? *Right Exit Closed* and *Starfire*. Sold the very same week. Stars must be right or something. Right?" He took off his dark glasses, which left clean pale patches in the dust on his face. The skin around his eyes looked tender and bruised. "She coming back soon? J.B.?"

Vera's heart sank again. Too good to be true. "No," she said evenly. "She has a shoot at Fort Cronkite. She'll be late."

But again, curiously, he seemed relieved. "That's good." He seemed very tired. He walked into the living room with exaggerated care, which was when Vera wondered for the first time whether he was also drunk, but no, that was surely not likely, it wasn't even eleven o'clock in the morning.

"Congratulations," Saint said. "Happy birthday."

"It's not my birthday."

"I know. But it's mine. Was mine. Close enough." He pulled a bottle of Domaine Chandon Brut from the bag, flourished it, and untwisted the wire around its neck. Warm from the journey and well-shaken, the cork shot out with violence and cracked against the ceiling. Saint stood quite still, solemnly watching the foam flow over his fingers while Vera rushed for glasses.

"And I'm twenty-one," Saint reminded her. "Don't forget I'm twenty-one years old. I can go into a bar and order a drink. And they have to give me one." He added portentously, "I can pay for it too. I've got lots of money."

"That's nice." Then Vera asked, "How was your birthday dinner? With your father?"

Saint raised his head and stared at her. She looked back into emptiness. "I had duck," he said after a moment. "Wild duck. Seven pieces. My . . . " He frowned as though in deep concentration. "*He* had . . . He ate a woman's breast."

Vera gave a small reflexive shiver. She decided she must either have misheard him or he had misheard her and replied to the wrong question. However, the birthday dinner seemed an uncomfortable topic, and she decided to stick to safer things. "Well, tell me all about it. The book, I mean."

Saint obliged. Talking about the book, he became more focused. He drank his champagne, grew enthusiastic, gestured and paced with almost his normal verve. He liked his editor, he trusted her, she had good ideas, he had to do some rewriting, but no big deal, he agreed with the changes she proposed. He thought they would strengthen the book. "And they're bringing it out next fall. She said October's a good month."

"That's not for a year." Vera mused yet again how long everything took. "What're you going to do now?"

"Do? I'm doing it!" Saint set his glass down with a crack. "The screenplay. I'm halfway through and it's going just great. I like it better than writing books. It's fun to create something you can *see*." He looked up, his eyes bright, his smile real now. Vera relaxed. "And now," Saint prompted, "it's your turn."

Vera obliged, telling about her meeting at Express Features. "It went really well, except I have to watch my language."

"Well, sure you do. You're writing for Mom and Dad and the kids and Great-Aunt Edna. You can't use foul language."

Vera gave a slightly wild giggle. "No, Saint. They mean the *words* I use. Starfire sounds too British. And I get my slang wrong."

"This your contract?" Without waiting for her consent, Saint picked it up and began to read. " '. . . *agreement between the author and the Express Publishing Company, a corporation . . .* ' Have you read all this, Vera?"

"Of course."

"I got you into this. I want it to go right. *'Express Features agrees herewith to pay the author fifty percent (50%) of the gross revenue . . . actually received by Express Features from purchasing publications after deduction of production expenses.' "*

He frowned. "They get fifty percent of everything. You understand that?"

She nodded. "They said that's normal because they take the risk. Isn't it?"

"I guess. But it seems like a lot to give away. Will you make much money?"

"Not for a bit. Just a few hundred dollars a month, after they've sold to about fifty papers. They said the real money's in the books, dolls, and stuff."

"Provided *Starfire*'s enough of a hit." Saint read the contract through carefully, then tossed it back onto the table. "I guess it's fine and legal, all right. If you sign it."

"Of course I'll sign it."

"Mm." Saint was now leafing through the new *Starfire* drawings: Starfire in the Arctic forcing a supertanker away from the coast by power of will. He looked at them closely, then went through them again, his brow puckered into a frown.

Vera drank a little more champagne. It didn't taste as good as it ought to, warm. Perhaps she should make some coffee. It would be better for Saint anyway, if he was driving, especially if he'd already been drinking. She rose. Outside, a meter maid stood behind the Jaguar writing on a pad. "Saint! Quick. You're getting a ticket."

Saint didn't look up. He was carefully scrutinizing Starfire's face as she gazed at a pathetic heap of oil-blackened dead animals. He said absently, "Long as they don't tow me."

"But—"

"Not now. Listen, Vera—"

"—you could still—"

"It doesn't *matter*. Now, come here."

Obediently she leaned over his shoulder. He touched Starfire's face with the tip of his finger. "You get precisely the right expression with just a couple of lines. I know exactly what she's thinking. What she's feeling. That's what I try to do with words."

Vera flushed with gratitude. "Thank you."

"And the eyes. The eyes are . . . profound." Then Saint said, "But I agree about the writing. It isn't nearly as good as the art. You shouldn't do both. You need a writer."

"Yes," Vera agreed, "but I can't afford to pay one."

"Doesn't matter. You don't need to."

"But how—?"

"I'll do it."

"You *will*?" Vera's smile threatened to split her face. "You're serious? That would be wonderful—"

"On one condition."

"Of course."

"Okay, then. You call Express Features and say thanks but no thanks. You got a better offer."

"A better . . . " Vera stared at Saint in total perplexity. "What offer? I don't understand."

"Starfire's much too good for the funny papers. She shouldn't be owned by a syndicate either, she needs freedom to be herself. What I'm proposing to you," Saint said with deliberation, "is that we go into business, you and I. We're going to be comic-book publishers. We'll bring out a book that's going to knock 'em dead. A 1990's comic book, with real characters, not just cardboard-cutout heroes and villains. We'll give them beauty and horror and sex and imagery that'll knock their eyes out. We'll set the stories against the issues of the nineties, like you've begun it, in the Arctic, in rain forests, radioactive-waste-disposal dumps . . . Starfire has to save the planet or die along with the rest of us. Oh, Starfire's going to be great, Vera, she's going to be our generation's hero, she'll step up into the classics." He smiled, but his smile was old and sardonic and somehow chilling. "I just got a lot of money, Vera. Five million dollars. I was wondering what to do with it."

He picked up the contract again and tore it in half. He tossed the torn pages on the floor and said, "This'll have to do instead of the thousand bucks, this time."

Vera had no idea what he meant. She shook her head in confusion. Definitely he must be drunk, although he didn't sound drunk anymore. And drunk or not, she trusted him absolutely.

"So we'll have to have another toast," Saint said. "To partnership."

Partnership. Vera dared to allow herself to think: We're partners; I'll see him all the time. We'll work together. She reminded herself he hadn't wanted to see J.B. this time, just her. Oh, it was going to be wonderful. She ignored the tiny warning voice inside her head which warned her that something was wrong, wrong, wrong.

Saint filled their glasses again. "Partnership," he repeated, and clinked his glass against hers. "What a day. Happy Birthday, Success, Partnership. And one more thing . . . Gee, I almost forgot." The corners of his mouth tightened.

"Congratulate me, Vera. I'm getting married."

Vera sat there in shock, staring at the closed door, listening to the sound of the Jaguar's engine fade away down the hill. Married.

Then, acting from sheer instinct, she rushed blindly for the refrigerator as though to a long-neglected but much-loved friend, the only friend she could count on in times of trouble. However, J.B. was still around, and all Vera found was diet Seven-Up and yogurt.

When J.B. returned late in the afternoon, carrying a pile of packing boxes, "Guess what," Vera told her, "Saint's getting married."

J.B. didn't react just at first. Vera watched her take down a rack of hairpieces from a high shelf and toss them onto the bed. Finally, in a tight-sounding voice: "I don't believe you."

"It's true."

J.B. waited, obviously expecting to be told it was all a joke, but when Vera said nothing, just stood there with arms folded, watching her, she asked in a strangely muted voice, "You aren't putting me on? This is for real?" And finally, when Vera still said nothing: "How do you know? Who told you?"

"He told me himself. Her name's Fletcher McGraw."

"But who is she? I never heard of any Fletcher McGraw."

"Someone he met at Lake Tahoe. Arnie says her father rented the house next to them on the lake. He breeds racehorses. She's blond and has a great backhand."

J.B. repeated slowly, "A great backhand."

Vera wondered, "Do you know something about this? You seem surprised—but not surprised, if you see what I mean."

J.B. shook her head. "How could I?"

"Arnie's very worried. He doesn't think Saint should marry her."

Arnie had, in fact, said, "There's something wrong with Fletcher, Vera. She seems like an okay person, and she's pretty enough, but there's something underneath that's weird."

J.B. said, "It's real quick. Much too quick."

"Arnie said he'd only met her a couple of times," Vera agreed, "and didn't even really seem to like her that much."

J.B. wandered toward the window, her face pale, absently grasping a pair of corn-colored hairpieces, which flowed between her hands like the tails of palomino ponies. Vera glanced at her covertly. She *did* know something. Something must have happened between J.B. and Saint that she, Vera, didn't know about.

J.B. finally said, "Maybe she's pregnant."

"No. It's not that."

"How d'you know?"

"She couldn't be pregnant," Arnie had explained, "or if she is, she couldn't possibly know yet. Anyway," sounding curiously old-maidish and more than a little embarrassed, "I didn't even know they'd . . . uh . . . gotten together."

Vera stared at J.B.'s rigid back. What *happened?* she wanted to cry. And *when?* But she knew J.B. wouldn't tell her. J.B. never talked about things that mattered.

At first, the shock of Saint's news seemed unbearable; however, the days passed as usual and the wedding was not to be for months, not until halfway through next year.

"Late spring," Saint said on his next visit. "That's the earliest the designer can do it."

"Designer?" Vera asked, baffled. It had never occurred to her that a wedding needed more than a bride and groom, with a presiding minister or justice of the peace. "But what for?"

"For the look," Saint explained patiently, "The theme, color coordination, that kind of thing."

"It sounds like making a film."

Saint nodded. "Exactly. She wants it to be Southern, a blockbuster like *Gone with the Wind*. Crinolines, gallant Southern gennelmen, barbecue pits, azaleas, the whole shebang. And it has to be in May or June, so the foals will be around, looking cute. But that's a long way off," he said impatiently. "Let's not talk about it. Come on, Vera, we have work to do."

With the numbing word "wedding" thus reduced to a vague event far off in the future, Vera was able to convince herself it would never really happen, and almost managed to forget about it.

As the weeks passed, Fletcher was increasingly occupied with fittings, publicists, magazine editors, invitation lists, and gift selections, and Saint, apparently uninvolved and uninterested in his own wedding, had a great deal of time to devote to *Starfire*.

He only saw Fletcher on weekends.

He didn't even want to talk about her, which was fine, because neither did Vera. During the week she had Saint all to herself, for J.B. was gone too.

Vera cautiously allowed herself greater and yet greater rations of happiness. And Saint seemed happy too. He enjoyed being with her, and certainly he thoroughly enjoyed being a publisher.

He created a company called Starfire Incorporated, capitalized it with three million dollars, and put Vera on a salary of four thousand a month, which appalled her—"I can't take that much . . . and it's your *own* money"—and accepted only when she realized she would be able to pay Donald Wheeler back at once, and when Saint himself insisted, "You don't understand, Vera. One has to pay for *real* talent. It doesn't come cheap. Or shouldn't."

"But it doesn't feel right to be paid for something I enjoy and would do anyway."

"Stop being so righteous. Just draw."

He located a graphics company, not only new and eager for work but also with a fine new offset press. Vera had adapted her cartoon strips to comic-book format, and with production efficiently in hand, Saint spent hours on the phone arguing over paper grades, print runs, and deadlines. He met with distributors. Began to set up an advertising campaign and launch. "So much to learn, so fast," he said with satisfaction, cramming each moment as full as possible.

Then, of course, there was the writing. He bought a computer with a sophisticated color graphic software program, which terrified Vera. "I'll never be able to run that thing. And what the hell do they mean by a microsoft mouse?"

"You'll learn. It's easy."

For Saint, perhaps. Driven, he was soaking up new information much faster than a computer. He would sit there staring at the images on the screen, at his captions, dialogue balloons, thought balloons, and stage effects. He would cut and switch and juxtapose, now and then crying, "Got it! That's *great*." Or, "Won't work. Hold on . . . " Or, "Look, Vera, how about this—a two-shot, Starfire and the senator, colored in muted blues and grays to show we're in her head, in a flashback, *then* cut to Starfire alone in the oil with the dead animals: 'Someone's going to pay for this . . . people like this shouldn't be allowed to live. . . .' Think of it as a film," Saint said. "It's really just another screenplay, after all."

The days rolled by very fast. Vera and Saint worked and learned, sparred together in verbal warfare, and sparked ideas off each other. Vera's drawing grew steadily cleaner and bolder, Saint's dialogue increasingly honed.

Then Christmas rolled around and Saint disappeared to the Central Valley to spend the holidays with the McGraws. It came as an unpleasant shock to Vera, although she knew she should have expected it. However, by now Vera didn't think of Fletcher and her father as a future bride and father-in-law, just as the McGraws, whom Saint visited on weekends.

As his departure drew closer, he grew increasingly moody. Clearly, Vera thought with a certain guilty satisfaction, he didn't want to go. Fortified by several gin and tonics, she finally nerved herself up enough to demand, "Why, Saint? Why are you marrying her? You don't love her, do you?"

"I like her."

"That's not enough."

"All right, then. I owe her."

"That's still not enough to marry somebody. And what do you mean, owe her? What for?"

"Because when I was . . . upset once and did something really pretty bad, she was real good about it. She didn't have to be."

"Bad like what?"

His face closed. "Sorry, Vera. That's my business."

"But, Saint——"

"I said it's my business." And that was that.

However, as the holidays grew closer, he in turn worried about Vera, which touched her. At least he cared. "I don't like leaving you alone, but I can't take you to the McGraws'. Even if you wanted to come."

"Which I don't. But thanks."

"But what are you going to do, by yourself? I've taken up all your time. You don't know any other people."

Vera had thought of going back to England for Christmas, but had dismissed the idea quickly. She didn't dare leave the country; her visa was not yet through, and without it she didn't know whether she would be allowed to return. She had tried to explain that to Mum.

Mum resolutely didn't understand. She wrote a long, rambling letter designed to fill Vera with guilt. "I feel as if I've been farmed out, just like an old dog that nobody wants. What's the use of having children if they leave you the minute you need them? Of course, I know you never really loved me, but . . . "

Vera had a catalog company send Mum a huge and very expensive hamper filled with Christmas goodies.

"A very nice idea, I'm sure," Mum wrote, "but not what I wanted. I just wanted my girl back."

It should have been a depressing, lonely time, but it wasn't, because Donald Wheeler came home for the holidays and invited her to visit with his family in the Napa Valley.

Saint observed narrowly, "Dr. Donald Wheeler seems like a pretty close friend."

Vera hurriedly explained, "Oh, yes. He's taken care of me most of my life. He's been wonderful. Helped me with my weight, lent me money . . ."

"Is he a boyfriend now?"

"Of course not."

"Does he want to be?"

"Good lord, Saint, what an idea. He's old. He's nearly forty."

However, to her surprise, she found herself astonishingly pleased to see Donald Wheeler, and loved her week at his mother's Napa Valley ranch—right up until New Year's Eve.

Donald's mother was Anna Bardelucci Wheeler, of the famous Napa Valley wine-growing clan. She had met and married Donald's father, an English doctor, during his period of recuperation in California following a long stint in prison camp in the Philippines during World War II. Donald was born in London, whence his father returned to resume his long-interrupted medical practice, although Anna never properly adapted to the climate, the food, or the people. When her husband, always frail, died of bronchial pneumonia following a grinding work schedule through-out a long, freezing winter, Anna immediately brought her young son back to California and eventually took over the management of the family wine business, which she still ran with flair and energy. She was now a youthful woman of sixty-five, her red hair barely showing any gray, spending most of her time careening around the property in a mud-splattered jeep.

Vera found her slightly intimidating, but from the moment Anna discovered Vera knew next to nothing about the growing of grapes, she promptly lost interest in her houseguest beyond a vague politeness. Donald found the situation comical. He urged, "Don't worry about it, Mother's a fanatic. She's given up on me as well."

In fact, it was so good to see him again that Vera even began to call him Donald rather than Dr. Wheeler, and it was so good having someone to talk to. Donald was delighted with the progress of *Starfire* and com-plimented Vera both on her success and on her continued slimness. She told him all about the new production company, about J.B.'s increasing success in Los Angeles, and about Arnie, apparently fully rehabilitated, on location in Sun Valley, Idaho, where he was making a ski movie.

However, on New Year's Eve, the last night, Donald almost wrecked everything when he observed, "So you're still in love with Saint."

It came from out of the blue. Her face must have given her away.

He said gently, "He's the only person you haven't talked about, you know."

"He's getting married."

"Yes. I kind of picked that up along the way."

He kissed her at midnight under the mistletoe among a large crowd of celebrating people. It was a determined kiss that left Vera thoroughly shaken. "Please, Donald. Don't do that."

"You know how I feel about you, I guess. How I always have." Lightly: "What does that make me? A pedophile or something? Chasing after little girls?"

She flushed, shook her head, and looked down at her feet. She liked him so very much. Oh, why did things have to change? She didn't want him to feel this way. She said slowly, "I wish you wouldn't . . . because I can't—"

"It's okay. I'm not going to press you. Not yet. But bear me in mind, please. And that I'll be coming home in the not-too-distant future." He added wryly, "I've about had it with the National Health Service anyway."

The next day he was gone. She returned to San Francisco.

Saint came back.

Vera happily picked up her old routine with Saint and the plotting of Starfire's adventures, and the months rolled happily and busily by—until early May, when the ornate invitation arrived in the mail, its beautiful calligraphy on antique ivory parchment spelling out its message of doom: "You are invited to celebrate the marriage of Fletcher Roscoe McGraw and Sloane St. John Treadwell Jr. . . ."

No, Vera told herself, shaking her head. No.

By now she had persuaded herself Fletcher was not even real, just a faint blond shadow with a great backhand.

"What's the problem?" Saint said. "It won't make any difference to us."

"Yes it will," Vera said. "It will make all the difference in the world." All this would end. Surely Saint couldn't spend much time with her after he was married.

There was only one answer. After Saint had left for his weekend with Fletcher, in the deepest and darkest despair she had ever known, Vera rushed to Lucca's Bakery around the corner, where she bought a fat pastry stuffed with cream cheese.

It helped a little, but not nearly enough.

Afterward she went to the local market and stocked up on doughnuts, ice cream, candy bars, chocolate cake, and various frozen pies, although she knew it was useless: there weren't enough goodies in the whole world to fill the aching void inside her.

Saint at last woke up on the day of his wedding, when he realized that reality was Fletcher McGraw, her father, and an ambiguous position as prince consort in a powerful Valley family.

That was when he at last admitted to himself he was marrying Fletcher McGraw for all the wrong reasons and that he was bound to hurt a great many people but that by now it was much too late to get out of it.

Just as he had predicted to Vera, the wedding was an astonishing production with a cast of thousands. It was a majestic feat of organization, its momentum so unrelenting that the very thought of stopping it all, of crying out, when challenged to "speak now or forever hold your peace," that this was a farce, it was unfair, it should never be happening, was so unthinkable that it brought him out in a clammy sweat.

It seemed half the country was there to see him married to Fletcher McGraw. The parking area was packed with expensive vehicles, the aggregate cost of which would probably equal the gross national product of a small country, and beyond it the McGraw airstrip hosted an assortment of aircraft, including two Lears, a Gulfstar, and the four-engine Cessna piloted from Scottsdale, Arizona, by the mother of the bride.

The McGraw homestead was a pillared mansion certainly reminiscent of Tara, backed by green pastures dotted with mares, each grazing contentedly with a foal at her side.

With such excellent material to work with, the famous Beverly Hills wedding designer had had a field day.

The gently sloping lawn in front of the house was transformed into a romantic formal garden with trellises, gazebos, and banks of flowers, the tables swathed in lavender, white, and dark blue (Harlan McGraw's racing colors), with more tables and chairs set up around the dance floor and overhead a tracery of garlands, ribbons, and love knots—also lavender, white, and dark blue. Thousands of butterflies should have fluttered into the sky when Harlan McGraw made his formal toast to the happy couple, but by then things were running late, the sun had already set, and the drowsy butterflies refused to leave their containers. They had cost well over ten thousand dollars, but most people had forgotten about them anyway in a welter of food, expensive liquor, and bonhomie.

Aunt Gloria, wearing a very good but outdated beige linen suit that she had worn to every summer wedding since the fifties, greeted Saint with bewilderment. "I don't know anybody here, Sloane. Who are all these people?"

Fletcher's mother, a leathery specter of a woman with a tennis tan, whose pink silk dress hung straight down from her bony shoulders as if still on its hanger, greeted him with a bone-crushing handshake and, standing so close he could smell the gin and cigarette smoke on her breath, demanded with a rasping chuckle like the rattle of bones, "Know what you're in for? My gal chews 'em up and spits 'em out before breakfast."

Harlan McGraw, burly-shouldered, champagne glass appearing thimble size in his huge hands, admonished, "She's high-spirited—all blood and temperament. Keep a light hand on the rein and everything's gonna be all fine and dandy."

"Yes, sir. You bet."

"And you be good to my little girl, you hear? She means everything in the world to me."

Vera looked tired and listless in an unbecoming, fussy dress like a royal-blue lampshade. Saint introduced her to Fletcher, who looked her up and down and smiled lazily. "So *you're* the woman I share my husband with!" As though Vera were too plain and negligible to count. Saint felt a stab of fury.

Arnie, his best man, looked very handsome in a dove-gray cutaway jacket, lavender cummerbund, and dress shirt with dark blue ruffles. He was purportedly terrific in *Snowbirds*, which would be a big Christmas release. The invited press from *Town and Country*, *People*, and *W* followed as closely as though yoked in harness. He had a dashing white smile for everyone, but his emerald eyes were watchful and strained. He told Saint, "I hope you know what you're doing."

"So do I."

"Why isn't J.B. here?"

"I didn't invite her." And at Arnie's look of inquiry: "I didn't want her to come. Now, leave it alone."

Arnie's eyes turned hard. "What did she do to you? She did something, didn't she? That's what started all this. Vera said there was something."

Saint ordered sharply, "I said to drop it."

"Okay. Sorry." Arnie's shoulders slumped slightly under his elegant jacket. "But remember, I'm always around." With an echo of Round Mountain: "I'll always be there for you."

Fletcher herself, of course, looked breathtaking, delicate as a magnolia petal in yards of taffeta and lace crinoline, her gossamer-light veil rearranged in puffs behind her head. But although they had played tennis together, swum, ridden horses, and danced, and although he had slept naked with her countless times and found himself darkly aroused by some of the things they did together, he didn't know her, really, at all. Nor, he had a sudden queer frightening feeling, did he want to.

However, amid all the people, the tangled conversations, and the gaudy confusion, it was the confrontation with his mother that would stand out in his mind for years to come.

Saint hadn't seen his mother in a long time. Although he had tried to track her down, to wrest the truth from her—"All right, Mother, who is he? Who's my father?"—she had proved elusive and finally, involved with Vera and their new venture, he hadn't thought it was so important anyway—until now. It was important now because if it hadn't been for that dinner with his . . . with Sloane Treadwell Sr., none of them would be here today and on Monday morning he would return to Vera and *Starfire* instead of . . . But he pushed the thought of his honeymoon far to the back of his mind.

Spring Kentfield was dressed fully in character for today, gold ringlets tumbling under a sapphire-blue bonnet, swishing crinolines swaying over a froth of petticoats, and a tiny parasol shielding her face from the sinking sun. She had had liposuction and a second face lift, and in the dusk, from a distance, didn't look a day over thirty.

Ironically, she raised the issue herself. "What a shame your father couldn't be here today."

"How odd you should say that, Mother."

"Really, dear?"

"I mean, I didn't ask my father to my wedding. Because I didn't know whom to send the invitation to."

Her plucked eyebrows raised. "Sloane. Dear. What in the world are you saying?"

"Sorry to shock you, Mother, but Father—*your ex*—told me himself at my birthday dinner. He made quite a thing of it, how he wasn't my father after all. He told me to ask you about it. And I'd really like to know who he is, if you don't mind."

For an instant she was quite silent. Then: "Sloane, *Really*! That sarcastic tone is *not* called for." She tossed her golden ringlets and swirled her crinoline so that it made a vexed rushing sound over the layers of lace. "And what an incredibly vulgar suggestion."

"Don't pretend you don't know."

She turned wide blue eyes upon him and twirled her parasol. "Oh, Sloane. *Surely* you didn't believe him?"

"Why shouldn't I?"

"Because you know how he hates me. Darling, he's a horrible man and he just wanted to hit back at me through you. To make me miserable. Now, really"—laying a hand on his arm and raising a delicate hand in a lavender kid glove to tidy the black hair that had tumbled untidily forward onto his forehead, such a tender, motherly gesture that he was sure she must have noticed a photographer close by—"don't frown." She tried to unpleat the taut skin between his brows, and cried merrily, "It's your wedding day! And I do believe it's time to go cut the cake!"

She had almost pulled it off. Spring Kentfield was quite a competent actress. But that fraction-of-a-second pause had given her away.

Not that it changed a thing. He had just made the mistake of his life, and it wasn't much comfort to reflect that the only person truly to blame was himself.

Chapter

13

In April 1984, almost a year after his wedding, lying alone in bed in an Acapulco hotel whose name he couldn't remember, Saint knew his marriage was finally over.

It had been a terrible year, which, in retrospect, he decided could be summed up in four representative scenes, the memories of which coiled together in his mind like poisonous fumes.

July, playing tennis together at the ranch . . .

The red-clay court was fiery in the late-morning heat. A reddish glow burned behind Saint's eyes; he wiped the sweat from his forehead and narrowed his eyes against the glare.

Fletcher was serving. She arched her back and raised her racket behind her head. Her breasts tautened and lifted. She wore a terry-cloth headband, wristbands, tennis shoes, and little socks with powder-blue bunny tails at the back to hold them in place. Apart from that, she was absolutely naked.

She served, hard and straight. Saint cracked the ball back and ran to the net. He was playing wildly, disturbed by her bouncing breasts. Fletcher returned the ball high and Saint swiped it out of court, right over the high fence and into the oleander bushes. Fletcher laughed. A male voice beyond the hedge cried, "You'll have to stop your game now, Mrs. Treadwell. They're bringing up the stallion."

Fletcher stood on one toe, poised and alert, head to one side, then flung her racket on the bench and ran for the gate. She beckoned Saint. "Quick."

Saint shrugged, then followed her off the court and into the dense growth of oleanders, through which ran a faintly marked trail. Fletcher stopped just short of a split-rail fence the other side of the hedge and cautiously parted the foliage. Saint peered over her shoulder. Framed with slender leaves and bright pink flowers was a small corral. Inside, a tall roan mare shifted edgily from foot to foot, a very young foal thrusting its nose under her belly. A burly man—the vet, Fletcher whispered— stood beside the mare, his hand on her neck, soothing.

Peering over Fletcher's shoulder, not sure what to expect, Saint saw the vet's shoulders stiffen; there was tension in the way he turned his head. Something massive, even dangerous, was approaching. Saint heard a muffled beat of hooves on dirt, which made the ground tremble; men's voices, pitched low; thumps; the creak of leather; muttered Spanish oaths.

And then the stallion exploded into the corral, Trumpet Call, seventeen hands at the shoulder, a ton of meat and muscle, barely controlled by the two Mexican wranglers, who hung on, one on each side of his great, tossing head.

"He's a bastard," Fletcher murmured admiringly, "a real honestagod fucking bastard. Almost bit a guy's arm off once. I wouldn't go within ten feet of him."

For a second Saint forgot Fletcher, forgot everything. Trumpet Call was such a beautiful animal, he was lost in helpless admiration. The stallion's black hide glistened with health and attention. At the height of his sexual display, the crest of his mane had risen and his neck curved in an exaggerated arch that reminded Saint of horses in old Flemish tapestries. Trumpet Call was already enormously aroused by the scent of the mare, his rigid penis reaching almost to his fetlocks.

"Ain't that something?" Fletcher moved behind Saint and rubbed her sweaty breasts against his bare back. She found the zipper of his shorts, reached inside, and began to massage him to erection. "Did you ever see such a big cock? I wish I was that mare, getting a cock like that—"

"Don't." Saint tried to pull her hands away. The scene unfolding in front of him both fascinated and appalled him. What Fletcher was doing seemed a humiliating parody compared with the catastrophic coupling about to take place in the ring. "Don't do that. Not here."

"Why not?" Fletcher hissed. "Don't be such a prude. The horses can't smell us; we're downwind. No one can see us. Nobody'll know."

But Saint had been married two months now, and with a shrinking feeling he thought: Sure they know.

Certainly the vet, most likely the Mexicans too. He was already imagining the sly looks and hidden smiles; he was undoubtedly the butt of many jokes among the wranglers and stableboys. Fletcher's latest stud. He was glad he didn't understand more than a few words of Spanish.

By now Saint had found out what everyone in the county, perhaps in the state, had known for years: Fletcher McGraw was sexually ravenous; she kept lists of all the men she had used and discarded, complete with statistics. She had complained about the vet's performance during the first week of their honeymoon. Apparently, now they were married, there was no need to pretend any longer. "I tried him once and dumped him. What a wimp. Said he loved me, wanted me to go off with him. Can you imagine? I treated him like shit and he kept coming back for more. I guess some people, they really enjoy it, you know? Getting kicked around?"

"Not me," Saint said tensely. "You better not try any of that shit with me."

"No," she promised, eyes suddenly wide, "not with you." She had moved against him, her body pressing into his, and ran her fingernails down his spine. "Fuck me now, Saint, right now, show me how I'd better not try any shit with you, do it against the wall, right here, now, Saint . . ."

"Here? Are you crazy? Someone will come."

"Who cares?"

And he had, too; in the walkway right outside the hotel lobby at ten o'clock at night. Miraculously, nobody had come, although possibly he wouldn't have cared, for he found her frenzied impulses darkly and humiliatingly arousing.

The stallion was approaching the mare, lifting his hooves with delicate precision, as though performing dressage. The mare sidestepped and cavorted, the foal cowering at her side.

One of the Mexicans led the foal away. Another man grasped the mare by her halter and held her still, stroking her nose. She snapped at him and laid her ears flat.

Trumpet Call, mane flying, nostrils flared and scarlet, rubbed his nose across her silky neck and nuzzled her withers. Threatening sounds rumbled up from deep inside the mare's chest. The stallion attempted to position himself for mounting, and immediately she seemed all teeth and flying hooves. The men holding her shouted and swore; one was flung to the ground on his back and narrowly missed being kicked in the head.

Behind Saint, Fletcher gasped and sank her teeth into his neck. Then she squirmed around him, bent over, and gripped her knees. "Go on. Pretend I'm the mare. Do it. While he's doing it to her. Come on, for Chrissakes . . ."

Saint stared at the tanned buttocks offered in front of his face. His head swam.

Helplessly, with a stifled groan at his involuntary response, he grabbed her around the hips and rammed deep inside her into a turmoil of frantic heat. He closed his eyes. Fletcher ground her behind tensely against him, clenched her strong vaginal muscles around him as he drove into her with enough force surely to drive through her body as far as her throat, while his hands closed on her hard round breasts, his nails tearing into her flesh, and he knew that afterward she would examine the purple tracery of broken blood vessels and bruises and smile with contentment.

The coupling of Trumpet Call and the mare reached its violent climax. The mare was blowing bloody froth through her lips. The foal bleated sadly in its corner, where it was tethered to the fence. The stallion roared and grunted, and, "Yes," Fletcher was groaning, "yes, yes, yes." Saint clenched his hand over her mouth to stop her noise. She bit down hard on his fingers.

September, in their bedroom . . .

"If you ever leave me," Fletcher said with a trilling little laugh, "I'll kill you. You know that?"

She lay back on the bed, naked but for a wispy black lace bra, which she immediately unhooked and tossed aside onto the floor. "And then," she announced, running her hands across her nipples, "I'll kill myself. I have my darling little friend." She swung her long legs off the bed and strode for her closet. "Want to meet my friend? Look. Here's where she lives. Cute little devil. Don't you think she's cute?"

"No," Saint said flatly, staring at the decorative pearl-handled Mauser nestling among silky panties, vibrators, half-slips, and filmy brassieres. "No, I don't. Where the hell did you get it?"

"Daddy gave it to me." Fletcher pouted. "Daddy wants me to be able to protect myself. Daddy loves me."

Saint accosted Harlan McGraw the next day.

It was the first time Saint had been able to catch his father-in-law alone in a month. If he'd been asked, he would have sworn the older man avoided him.

"Mr. McGraw, I've been wanting to talk to you."

"Sure, son. Anytime."

"It's about Fletcher."

Immediately Harlan McGraw's stride lengthened. "Better move it along . . . gotta meeting with an owner . . ."

"I don't like her having a gun."

"Now, listen, son. I gave it her myself."

"I know."

"With me gone so much, and you away too doing whatever you do in San Francisco, a girl needs some protection."

Saint hurried to catch up. He blurted, "She doesn't see it as protection. It's fun. She sees it as a toy, Mr. McGraw."

"Harlan, boy. Call me Harlan. Keep telling you that."

"Harlan. I'm serious. I have to talk with you. Can you slow up a bit? Listen to me. Fletcher needs help. She's *sick*."

"She looks fine to me. What's wrong with her?" The heavy face took on a rosy flush. For a man who spent his time overseeing the breeding of horses, he was extraordinarily prudish, Saint found, when it came to people. Especially his daughter. "Is she . . . did you . . . ?" In a rush: "She in the family way?"

Saint almost screamed with exasperation. "She's not pregnant. She doesn't need that kind of doctor. She needs a psychiatrist."

Harlan McGraw stopped dead in his tracks. His face darkened to an outraged magenta. "What're you saying to me? That my daughter's not right in the head? She's as sharp as a tack and sane as you or I."

"It's not like that, Mr. . . . . Harlan. It's a sexual thing. She—"

"Sexual?" Harlan McGraw shook his heavy head. "Well, sure, boy. She's been a wild gal, played around some, but that's over now. She's married. She'll settle down." He regarded Saint carefully. "You're not one of . . . uh . . . you do *like* women, don't you?"

Saint nodded.

"Well, that's all right, then." Harlan McGraw vented a sigh and reached for his shirt pocket. "Have a cigar."

"No, thanks."

McGraw looked suspicious for a moment, as though the masculinity of anyone who refused a fine cigar was automatically suspect. "Your wife's a beautiful woman, I guess you noticed? Be strange if she hadn't sowed some wild oats. The fellows been hanging around since she was eleven, twelve years old."

Saint nodded. "I bet."

"But that's over now. She's your wife, so you be good to my gal." McGraw added, "I've said it before and I'll say it again. Be good to her— if you know what's good for you."

December, at Bally's, Reno, at a convention of thoroughbred owners . . .

It was a surreal experience, staying in that great hotel which boasted the largest casino in the world. It was a world of its own, where day and night merged seamlessly together, where time was irrelevant, where the lobby doors onto the outside world were tinted a deep purple to create an illusion of perpetual twilight.

The gala dinner was on the third evening. Fletcher looked glowing, wholesome, and sumptuous as a peach in high summer, wearing a five-thousand-dollar dress of pink and gold beadwork. Harlan McGraw had been so proud of his pretty daughter in her beautiful dress; he had smiled and patted her, called her baby and honey.

Before the dinner Fletcher had wanted to play with her new toy, real police handcuffs. She demanded Saint handcuff her to the bed and beat her. He refused. She shrieked at him in fury and ran from the room, crashing the door closed behind her.

She was cool to him during dinner, smiling only for her father, and afterward declined to dance or watch the show. "I'm going to the tables with Pop," Fletcher told him dismissively, "and win a bunch of money."

Half an hour later he saw her at her father's side at the roulette table, a pile of one-hundred-dollar chips in front of her.

McGraw urged, "Come on, son. Park yourself and pitch in."

Saint shook his head. "Not tonight."

His father-in-law angled him the same dubious expression as when Saint had refused the cigar.

Saint explained, "I guess I'm just not a gambler."

Five hours later Saint leaned his forehead against the coldness of the window, watching, far below, the everlasting belt of traffic looping away south into the desert on I-395. To the west, Highway 80 arrowed off into the Sierra Nevada, a vast black rampart above which hung a cold, glittering moon.

He had not been able to sleep. At two A.M., mildly alarmed, he had returned to the casino looking for Fletcher, but she wasn't there. In the predawn darkness of a freezing Wednesday morning, "Where is she?" Saint demanded of the moon, the mountains, and the icy wind. "What's she doing? Who with?"

There was a soft slithering sound against the door.

His hair lifted on the nape of his neck. It was so stealthy, so weird. He turned away from the window.

Now a scraping at the lock.

He ran across the room, bare feet sinking deep into the carpet, and flung open the door.

Fletcher stood there, gilt-framed studio portraits of Judy Garland and Lana Turner smiling from the wall behind her. Her face was swollen and bruised. There was blood on her teeth. Her pink-and-gold dress was torn.

"Oh, Christ." Saint picked her up and carried her to the enormous round bed and carefully eased the dress off. There were blue-black marks all over her breasts and a bleeding gash at the base of her neck. "It's okay, Fletch. You just rest right there. I'll get the doctor. And the cops." What was the emergency number to call in the state of Nevada? He must . . . He cried, "Who the *hell* did this to you?"

Fletcher mumbled through swollen lips, "Not cops. Don't call cops."

"My wife's hurt," Saint barked into the phone. "She's been badly beaten. She needs help right away." He gazed at her, appalled. "Oh, God, Fletch."

She looked up at him. Her eyes could only open to slits, but they were drugged and dreamy and contented. "Dunno who he was," she managed with an unmistakable note of satisfaction. "Met him at the tables. Think he was Mafia. Don't want cops."

Saint stared at her helplessly. He asked, "Fletch, why do you do it? Just tell me that. Why?"

"Because you won't."

"What do you think I am?"

"You'd do it if you loved me. You don't love me, do you? Never have." She began to cry.

And now, in Acapulco, in April, it was the end.

Saint had sought refuge the rest of the winter and early spring working on the *Starfire* strips with Vera. Fletcher had grown increasingly suspicious of Vera. "Do you have some kind of sick thing going for fat people?"

By now Saint knew he must escape, and soon. His days in San Francisco were oases of contentment, and he dreaded his return to Fletcher a little bit more each time.

It was harder and harder to recall the good times they had had—they must have had good times, hadn't they?—to remember she had been kind and gentle to him once; but now he realized that that had only been a reward for passing her test, for giving in and raping her.

In early April he told her, "I can't go on like this."

Fletcher agreed. "Glad you see it that way too. It's time we moved out. Got our own place."

"That's not what I mean."

"I thought maybe Palm Springs," Fletcher said. "It's gorgeous there. And no smog. Great tennis."

"We need to talk. Fletcher, I have to talk with you."

So they had come to Acapulco, to a beautiful hotel with private guest cottages and individual swimming pools, built in the 1930's as a discreet hiding place for the very rich.

The second afternoon it was hot, tranquil, and very quiet, so quiet that Saint could hear the sounds all the way across the patio.

He followed the pathway of white stones between the pool on his left and the line of miniature palm trees to the right.

The front door to their cottage was open. Saint went in, still following the sounds, his sandaled feet silent on the tile floor. He stopped dead in the open archway leading to the bedroom while the scene seared onto his brain like acid. He would never forget it.

Fletcher was lying on her back across their bed, arms flung out to either side, her long athletic legs spread wide. A naked man crouched between them, his face buried in the blond fur of her crotch. Saint could see only the back of his head, his thick, lank black hair, and could hear the sucking gurgles of his mouth and tongue. The man held a knife in his hand, the point resting on the left side of Fletcher's stomach. Fletcher, face contorted, eyes closed, gasped, "Yes, yes, yes, do it, do it now," and Saint watched in frozen fascination as the man delicately drew the knife across her stomach. A thin red line slowly appeared and Fletcher began to scream in climax.

The man raised his head, turned, and saw Saint standing there.

And he wasn't a man at all, he was a boy, not more than sixteen. Saint watched the shock flood the kid's eyes, his mouth sag in horror, and his face turn greenish white. He released a torrent of frantic Spanish through shaking lips, terrified, even though he still held the knife. Saint thought he was telling him that Fletcher had ordered him to do it. That she had even paid him.

Saint believed him. He found he could move at last. He nodded dumbly and stood aside. He licked his dry lips. He jerked his head toward the door.

The boy crept past, the knife dangling harmlessly in his left hand, his eyes rolled back in his head. It could have been almost comical, Saint thought distantly. Once the boy was through unharmed, he took off in a wild, plunging run.

Fletcher rolled languidly onto her side, rubbed her hands over the thread of blood on her stomach, licked at her fingers, and laughed.

Saint said, "You're crazy. Absolutely crazy."

Fletcher said, "Just flying. Wanna hit? There's some stuff in the bathroom. He got it for me."

Saint went into the bathroom. He found a small pile of white powder on Fletcher's hand mirror.

Oh, great. This now, too?

He tipped the cocaine down the toilet. The powder spread out milkily on the surface of the water. He flushed it.

"Hey," Fletcher cried, voice slurred, "what didja wanna do that for?"

He returned to the bedroom and stood by the bed, looking helplessly down at his wife. Finally, "Oh, God," Saint said, "you poor bitch." He sat down and took her hand. "You've got to get help this time. I'm not letting you go on like this. We're going back to California in the morning."

Her eyes narrowed. "What did you say?"

"I said you're going to get help."

"No. Before."

"I said, you poor bitch. And I mean it. Fletch, I am desperately, truly sorry for—"

She swatted him hard across the face. "You fucking bastard. Don't you dare say that. Ever. Nobody feels sorry for me."

"Fletch—"

Her face contorted. "Get out of here."

"No." He shook his head. "I'm not leaving you."

"You better. I don't want you. You stay, and I'm gonna scream. I'm gonna tell them it was you cut me." She flung herself at him, nails aimed for his eyes. Saint dodged, caught her by the wrists, and forced her back down on the bed. She lay under him, struggling so strongly he could barely hold her, her eyes blazing slits of rage. And then suddenly the rage was gone, wiped out, replaced with glittering expectation.

She licked her parted lips and smiled and reached between his legs.

Shaken with revulsion, Saint let her go abruptly and stood up. "Cut that out."

She moved fast. She swung her legs to the floor and grabbed for his arm. "Hey, no, Saint, I didn't mean it. There's no need to go."

He muttered, "I'm sorry, Fletch."

Then he was through the door, striding across the patio, down the walkway toward the main hotel building, through the cool lobby with its thick adobe walls, decorated cathedral beams, leather furniture, and long reception desk where a group of brightly clad tourists were making reservations for tomorrow's deep-sea-fishing trip. Fletcher, still nude, padded behind him. "Saint. Stop. Wait . . ."

Saint ignored her. He emerged into the blinding white street. Several cabs were parked under the shade of frangipani trees. He climbed into the first one and slammed the door.

Fletcher pounded on the window. The driver looked anxiously from her to Saint.

What he saw on Saint's face must have decided him not to argue. He pulled away. Fletcher's bloodstained fingerprints smeared the window glass, and the echo of her voice, raised in an eldritch shriek, trembled in the air. "You'll be sorry, Saint. Nobody walks out on me. I swear it, you're gonna be real sorry."

He hadn't taken her seriously. He should have.

Much too late he realized that when he left Fletcher he should have ordered that cab to take him directly to the airport. He should have taken the first plane out of the country, no matter where it was going. Instead, he just went to another hotel.

He couldn't just abandon her.

He called from his new room to check up, to see whether she was all right, but there'd been no answer from the room. Saint almost went back there, but didn't; however, he left word where Fletcher could reach him if she wanted. He felt sad and guilty and anxious, and when the hours passed and she didn't call, he went out and walked alone for miles, returning to the hotel at midnight.

He went to bed . . .

. . . to be woken at three in the morning by a gun barrel stabbing into the side of his neck.

Completely disoriented, he stared up at the two men who leaned over him, and shouted.

The one with the gun told him in poor English that they were federal police, drug-enforcement detail, and demanded to know where his stash was.

Saint shook his head in bewilderment. "What stash? What're you talking about?" The gun barrel smashed against his cheekbone and he tasted blood inside his mouth. The other man went into the bathroom. Saint licked dry lips. He croaked, "Listen, you guys are making a mistake." He was still too confused to be seriously frightened. It was just a mistake, it would be cleared up. Of course it would be.

Then the man came out of the bathroom carrying two plastic Ziploc bags of white powder. He held them up for Saint to see. There was a knife too, he told his partner, lying on the countertop.

Saint began to feel sick. "That's not mine. I never saw it before. And I don't even *have* a knife."

They ignored him, just dragged him out of bed and ordered him to dress. Then, handcuffed, he was prodded into the elevator at gunpoint, dragged across the lobby under the eyes of a nervous night deskman and several late-night revelers who all turned to stare, and into a waiting car.

They drove through humid night streets to police headquarters. Saint was handcuffed to a hot-water pipe for what seemed hours, until eventually a paper was produced, smudgily typed in Spanish, for him to sign. They told him it was his confession.

Saint shook his head. "No way. This is crazy. I'm not signing that thing. I want a lawyer."

He was urged to sign; it was explained at first with patience how much easier that would be for everyone, especially for him. After all, why would he not wish to sign? The evidence was all there. The cocaine. The knife. And witnesses too, to tell about the poor girl running naked and bleeding through the lobby.

"No," said Saint. He still didn't quite understand. He was Sloane St. John Treadwell Jr. of the United States of America, young and smart and rich and well-connected.

He couldn't seriously be in deep trouble. Could he?

His interrogator shook his head. "Not smart."

There and then, still handcuffed, he was flung on his back across a scarred wooden desk.

Several men gripped his legs, two more held him firmly by the ears and hair, while another forced his mouth open and stuffed some foul-tasting rags inside. Another stood over him contemplatively shaking up a bottle of soda water while holding Saint's nostrils pinched tightly closed. Saint began to struggle and fight for air. The blood roared through his head. His lungs burned. The man's face, the hand, and the soda-water bottle faded into darkness. Then mercifully the hard fingers loosened. Saint took a huge involuntary breath. The bubbling soda water, which he learned afterward was loaded with Tabasco sauce, shot up his nose and exploded through his skull and chest in a huge flare of pain. Through the roaring in his body he heard incredible sounds, which he finally realized were his own muffled shrieks. His body reared up from the table in uncontrollable spasm; it took four men to hold him down.

After a long-enough interval, when he lay there wrecked, sobbing, blinded, burning, they suggested he would probably be ready to sign now.

Saint gasped, "Fuck you."

So they did it again.

And again.

After a third, more prolonged period of agony, barely conscious, he understood it really didn't matter what he said. They would have the confession one way or another. And they could go on much longer than he could. They could go on forever. And they would, too.

After he signed, everyone relaxed and became almost friendly.

As soon as he was able to speak, he again demanded a lawyer, to be told of course he should have one, wasn't that his right?

In the meantime he was thrust into a holding cell, the sixth man in a space designed to hold two.

Saint reassured himself: This can't be happening to me. I don't believe this. They can't do this.

But they had; and, he thought with sudden terror, they could do what they wanted with him and nobody from the outside world could help him because nobody even knew he was there.

However, he had at least been promised a lawyer. Saint began to pin all his hopes on the lawyer, certainly his only chance. The lawyer would listen. He would understand the truth, how this was a terrible mistake. Saint would have justice . . .

The lawyer, Abogado Domingo Beltrán, was soft and pear-shaped, wearing a blue nylon suit and lots of rings. Throughout their interview, his feet, very small in shiny black shoes, stayed meticulously planted side by side on the floor in front of him. His command of English was poor.

He listened to Saint's story and buffed his nails with a monogrammed handkerchief.

Afterward, studying his manicure with close attention, he murmured, "You tell me the cocaine is . . . plant? By your wife?"

"My wife must have arranged it. We'd had a . . . misunderstanding." He leaned forward urgently. "Señor Beltrán, I knew *nothing* about it at all. It's lies. Can't you understand? It's a setup. She wanted revenge."

Señor Beltrán made clicking sounds with his tongue. They could have signified anything—sympathy, dismissal, apathy.

Saint drew a deep breath. "Señor Beltrán, I want to change my plea. I'm not guilty. I'm innocent."

The lawyer spread out his fingers and studied his rings. "But

Mr. . . . uh . . . " He squinted at a paper in front of him. ". . . Treadwell."
He had trouble enunciating the W. "Sorry. Impossible. You already sign
the confession."

"But you know goddamn well why I signed it. They tortured me to
get that confession."

"Torture," Señor Beltrán said mildly, "is a terrible thing."

"My confession's invalid," Saint insisted. "And I'll say so at the trial."

"*Claro.*" The lawyer nodded. "And you show the court the marks on
your body, yes?"

Saint sat very still and stared at him. He said slowly, "Oh, Christ."

The lawyer nodded politely. In suddenly excellent English he said,
"You have my deepest sympathy, Señor Treadwell. . . ."

The sentencing was very quick. It was all over within ten minutes.

The charge was made; he was accused of a *crimen contra la salud.* A
very serious offense. His confession was read out; he was asked whether
he had any comment. He had plenty. He raged at length on this parody
of a court of law, this mockery of justice. Everybody looked bored and
annoyed with him for wasting their time. A fat girl wearing too much
makeup was already doing the paperwork, clacking away on an ancient,
very noisy typewriter.

The completed form was presented to the judge.

"*Quinze años,*" said the judge, signed the form, and passed it to the
court clerk, who stamped it. *Thud.*

Fifteen years.

And life, as Saint had known it, was over.

PART THREE

PART THREE

Chapter

14

It was a Wednesday. On Wednesday and Friday mornings, punctually at 8 A.M., Victor Diamond breakfasted at the Polo Lounge with Jason Brill, his personal assistant. By tradition they always occupied the same banquette and ordered the same breakfast: fresh-squeezed orange juice, a bran muffin, and herbal tea for Diamond, while Brill, nursing an ulcer, drank a glass of buttermilk.

Diamond was immensely tall, silver-haired, with the dark, hawklike features of a Gypsy king. Brill was a pallid, spectacled gnome in a black silk suit. Together, however, they made a formidable team, and here, for an hour and a quarter precisely, twice a week, Diamond held unofficial court, although only a chosen few dared approach him—and then still had to run the gauntlet of Brill's chillingly expressionless stare.

On the stroke of nine-fifteen they would leave for Omega Studios, where Diamond, as one of the most successful producers in the country, ran his own little empire and enjoyed even more power and privilege than David Zimmerman, chief executive officer.

So far this morning two people had visited the table.

The first visitor was Max Frank, packaging agent, sounding out Diamond's interest in a British joint venture with West German financing.

Frank was followed by Sidney Farrell, female lead in *Danger Wind* at Omega, anxious for a particular costar who was having scheduling problems. "We work together so well. I can't stand it that he can't get out of this stupid TV thing. Could you pull strings? I know you could if you wanted!"

Diamond smiled. Pulling strings was something he did well. "Count on it."

Sidney departed on a breathless cloud of thanks.

Brill murmured. "Arnie Blaize's on his way over."

"No," said Diamond. Arnie Blaize had become a pest. He had a science-fiction property he had decided needed Diamond's unique touch. He had been besieging Brill for an appointment for weeks now. "There's room for just so many space epics," Diamond declined firmly, "and then the party's over. Look at *Dune*." But Arnie was infuriatingly persistent. He had even used Spring Kentfield's name as a potential key to open the door. He should have known better. Diamond was never bought, and especially not through the influence of a sitcom actress for whose work he had no respect.

"Good morning, Mr. Diamond."

Diamond nodded without enthusiasm. Jason Brill bored Arnie with a look that would have vaporized granite, but Arnie appeared impervious.

He smiled pleasantly at Brill and slid uninvited into the banquette seat beside Diamond, simultaneously opening a black leather briefcase, taking out a thick manila envelope, and placing it on the tabletop. He held his hand out politely to Diamond. "We haven't formally met. I'm Arnold Blaize. Call me Arnie if you like."

Diamond said, "Yes, I know," and shook the offered hand with reluctance. He did not wish to have anything to do with Arnold Blaize, a lightweight bland teen idol who, in Diamond's opinion, epitomized everything reprehensible about the motion-picture business. He and Spring Kentfield made a good pair. Nor did he wish to be harassed about some banal property which would neither enhance his reputation nor make money. He said quellingly, "You've already spoken with Mr. Brill, I think. He'll have told you——"

"I want you to see it, Mr. Diamond. If you're still not interested, I won't bother you again."

Diamond sighed. "All right." He checked his watch, a heavy stainless-steel Rolex. "You have five minutes."

"Fair enough." Arnie's green eyes held hard and steady as he took a comic book from the envelope and laid it beside Diamond's plate. "Here it is."

Diamond laughed aloud. "Oh, come, Mr. Blaize. Don't waste my time."

"You gave me five minutes. Look at it, and listen to me." Arnie's light voice held a note of determination that surprised and almost intrigued Diamond. But even so. A comic book.

"Starfire already has a following—she's becoming a cult figure. Now, the concept needs to expand, reach a wider audience. It's time for the motion picture. We need the backing of a big studio like Omega with the publicity machinery and the distribution. But most especially, we need a producer with vision."

Diamond had to respect Arnie's audacity. He said dryly, "I'm flattered that I came to mind, but there's nothing I can do, even if I wanted to. I'm fully committed for the next three years. If you want to take this project to the screen, I strongly suggest you think of the Japanese market; they are producing superior animated cartoons now. I can put you in touch with someone who—"

Unheeding, Arnie swept on. "This is number four in the series. Each episode has a great story line, great characters, terrific art. A screenplay is in development." He urged, "I came to you first, Mr. Diamond, because I knew you'd have the imagination and the ability to do *Starfire* justice."

"Justice? To a . . . to some kind of pop-art fantasy?" Diamond's thick brows drew together. "Are you *serious*?"

"More than I've ever been in my life. We have two minutes left."

Diamond's mouth twitched in a half-derisive smile. He glanced at Arnie, then down at the cover, which to his surprise was actually not bad and quite imaginative. The title "*Starfire: The Interrogator*—No. 4 in the Saga," sprang out in bold script above a computer screen set inside a block of ice. The block floated in an extraterrestrial landscape of weird geometry and sinister colors. On the screen, in deftly depicted graphics, was the face of a woman with wide silvery eyes, a broad brow, and abundant shimmering hair. Incorporated into the graphic was the information "Drawn by V. Brown; Written by John Saint."

Diamond stared into the woman's eyes. It was just a cartoon drawing, but something about those eyes caught and held him.

He poured himself another cup of herbal tea and began slowly to leaf through the book.

At once he had to admit that yes, the art was indeed superior and John Saint's dialogue surprisingly literate for such a medium. He asked, "Who owns the rights?"

"Vera Brown owns the rights to the Starfire character on her own. Otherwise, it's a partnership between Saint and Vera.

"And what does Spring Kentfield have to do with this?"

"She's John Saint's mother."

"And his father?"

"Sloane Treadwell. Of Treadwell Communications."

"I see." Diamond thoughtfully turned pages. "Tell me more."

"I've known Saint a long time—we were in school together. He's a great guy . . . very talented." He described Saint enthusiastically, concluding, "He's an established writer now—he has a book out, *Right Exit Closed*. It did really well for a first book. Well-reviewed and everything."

"It takes more than one book to establish a writer."

"He's working on the screenplay now for *Starfire*."

"Is that so? What makes him think he can do it?"

Arnie said ingenuously, "You said yourself he writes good dialogue for comic books."

"Unh," murmured Diamond, "give me a break." But he went on turning pages, scanning panel by panel. The outlines were bold, the color blocking imaginative. Briefly he wondered how it would occur to an artist to view scenes from such unusual perspectives.

Starfire herself was remarkably well-defined for a comic-book character. Diamond studied her where she crouched naked on a sandbar, surrounded by exotic vegetation, body partly shrouded by vapor. Her face conveyed deep emotion. Shock, distress, dislocation, confusion. Diamond knew at once how she felt, that she was lost both in space and in time. He could sense her thoughts, almost hear her voice. She could almost be real.

He asked abruptly, "Does Brown use a model?"

Arnie nodded. "J.B.," he said with confidence, clearly expecting to impress, for J.B., known only by her initials, was famous now. "Well," he asked, when Diamond didn't immediately react, "what do you think?"

Diamond set his cup very deliberately in the saucer and pushed it away from him across the tabletop. An attentive waiter swooped upon it and spirited it away. "Will there be anything more, Mr. Diamond?"

Jason Brill gave Arnie a hard look. "It's getting late. It's nine-sixteen." And immediately *Starfire*'s spell was broken.

Diamond ran an elegant hand through his hair. His eyes grew opaque, his manner newly distant. The interview was over and his mind on other matters. "You're right, Arnie. It's worth a look. But I have to leave now, I have a meeting. Call my office and we'll talk." He picked up the envelope. "I'll look through these."

He had reached the main entrance, where his car waited for him, a navy-blue Jaguar XJ-S polished to a mirror glitter, before he realized Arnie was following him. Diamond turned with controlled impatience. "Arnie, I have no more time. Please call the office."

"I'm not through. I'll ride to Omega with you."

The assurance and effrontery were too much. Brill looked scandalized and Diamond opened his mouth on a blistering retort, but by now Arnie had been noticed. A small cluster of tourists was whispering, nudging one another, and staring. He heard somebody say, ". . . and that's Victor Diamond, the famous producer." Any moment now autograph books would be brandished, a hysterical crowd would materialize from nowhere, and Diamond wanted none of that.

"Oh, God," he sighed. "Get in."

Diamond drove with ruthless precision, weaving in and out of traffic down Sunset Boulevard.

Arnie was saying, "The way we visualize this, we integrate the cartoon images and animation with live action and terrific special effects. It will be something unique. And with your name and reputation behind it, 'A Victor Diamond Film,' everyone will know this isn't just a one-dimensional cartoon adventure. They'll know this is an adult film for real grown-ups, with depth and character and eroticism. . . . Only you have the vision to do it right."

It was an unabashed appeal to his vanity, and Diamond couldn't help but feel a glimmer of satisfaction. Yes, he had a reputation for sophistication and quality. He took fearless risks with his erotic scenes and was frequently compared creditably with the great European filmmakers.

"And with the package we have——"

Now Diamond exclaimed impatiently, "Come on, Arnie. What package? You're trying to unload a bunch of unknowns. I can't go to the bank with John Saint and J.B. Come on, be real."

Arnie said simply, "You can. You can do anything. That's why I came to you first. You have the power."

Diamond nodded in simple acknowledgment. Yes, he did have the power. Omega Studios dared refuse him nothing. He had built his empire very carefully. He had long ago realized that all the talent in the world was useless when a project could be wrecked by one electrician walking off a job or a government permit withheld. He had spent thirty years cultivating the right people, from union leaders to politicians to international bankers. He knew everyone, he knew the right buttons to press, he knew where a great many bodies were buried, both literally and figuratively. He was a giant manipulator, and a master puller of strings.

"I mean," Arnie said, "take J.B., now. She has potential as an actress, and she has a lot of presence. And after all, she *is* Starfire. Saint doesn't exactly have a track record, but he will soon. I bought the rights to *Right Exit Closed*, you know. It'll be a winner. And then you have me. You can take my name to the bank, all right. I'll costar and I'll work for scale. Less, if necessary."

Diamond demanded, "Why?"

"I believe in the project."

"And presumably in John Saint."

"Always."

The car phone bleeped. "No," Diamond said curtly, "I'm in conference. Tell Mr. Zimmerman to get back to me."

He shifted gears and nudged the Jaguar effortlessly into dense traffic on the freeway. Brassy light glared from long lanes of curving metal roofs. The ride would now take ten more minutes, give or take one or two. The heat was mounting; he turned up the air conditioning, and as frigid air blasted through the vents, he began to visualize.

The girl—J.B.—in close-up, then a dissolve to the painted eyes of Starfire. Pull back into an animated sequence, Starfire, arrogantly sensuous, nearly nude, taking aim with a . . . an extraterrestrial crossbow at a monster, all claws and razor fangs, hurtling upon her through billowing magenta clouds. He would approach Ralph Bakshi for the animation, Diamond thought, yes, perfect, for the precise blend of ominous beauty—

The phone rang again and he ignored it.

Yes, it *was* an intriguing idea; approached right, an erotic fantasy with animation and special effects, and with some *weight* to it, saying something more . . . intelligence—the oil-spill concept was good, involving a groundswell of global awareness of environmental danger—yes, perhaps it could be a winner.

The gates of Omega Studios swung open at his approach; he swept through without slowing. On for another quarter-mile. A red-and-white-striped barrier rose for the Jaguar, and Diamond entered his own compound.

He drove up to the main office building and into his personal space, stenciled "VICTOR DIAMOND."

He switched off the engine. "All right, Arnie," he said after a moment of silence. "Why don't you get the principals together and we'll talk."

"You mean that?" Suddenly Arnie's voice lost its steely determination. It was boyish and eager and almost trembled with gratitude.

"Send me over a treatment. Then have your people call Jason Brill and set up a meeting for next week. You, Brown, and John Saint. And J.B., of course." Diamond opened the door onto the murky heat.

"Sure," said Arnie. "I'll fix everything—except there's a problem with Saint . . ."

Diamond ran, as usual, on the beach in late afternoon, but today for longer and much harder. Afterward he swam for half a mile against the crosscurrent just outside the surf line before returning to the house.

Long ago, after his wife had entered the institution forever, blinded from her search for God's face in the white blaze of the desert sun, her brains fried from LSD, Diamond had bought three of the densely packed houses at the Malibu Beach Colony, pulled them all down, and built himself a redwood Mayan pyramid, which he surrounded with sculptured Japanese rock gardens.

It was rumored that the strange house was a memorial for his lost love, but when invited to comment, Diamond only scoffed. It had nothing to do with Vangie. He merely wanted to live at the beach, "and if you buy million-dollar real estate," he pointed out, "you shouldn't have to hear your neighbors on each side flush the toilet."

He never mentioned his wife again, and by now, almost twenty years later, the scandal and tragedy of the once-dazzling Vangie Sellors had been forgotten by all but a few.

Diamond visited occasionally to make sure she continued to be well cared for, but lost in the wasteland inside her head, she had no idea who he was, who she was now, or who she had once been.

In the meantime, his hatred for drugs had become legend.

*　　*　　*

Diamond showered, then retired to the windowless meditation room in the core of the pyramid, where he assumed the lotus position on his black carpet and opened his mind to the void. Afterward, changed into loose cotton slacks and a terry-cloth shirt, he stretched out on a lounger among the meticulous arrangements of rocks and gentle fountains of his outer patio with a glass of iced Perrier at his side.

The sun, momentarily a perfect orange disk poised on the gray knife edge of the calm horizon, began its slide into its own reflection until it was a hemisphere lying in a puddle of molten gold.

This was the time of day Diamond enjoyed the most, this half-hour of peace and contemplation until his servant, Hamura, appeared to serve an excellently cooked light dinner, after which Diamond would retreat to the projection room, also in the core of the building, immediately below the meditation room, to watch a selection from his huge film library. Tonight it was *The Maltese Falcon*, one of his favorites.

The sun shrank to a tiny point of crimson light and then winked out. After that, dusk fell quickly. Hamura appeared pushing a trolley loaded with crystal, china, linen, a covered platter, and a bottle of dry Meursault in a silver ice bucket. He set one place at a glass-and-wrought-iron table and lit the lamp, a stylized steel woman, arms raised above her head, grasping a torch shaped like a flower. The lamp was art deco but blended pleasingly with the whole. Next Hamura held out a chair for Diamond to sit, and arranged a large white napkin across his lap. He served slivers of raw albacore tuna, giant shrimp lightly sautéed in olive oil and garlic, rice rolled in seaweed, poured the wine, smiled, and bowed slightly from the waist.

Diamond said, "And the telephone, Hamura."

The telephone arrived instantly. Hamura bowed again and departed, his slippered feet making no sound on the stone.

Diamond took a first sip of his wine and stared into the gathering darkness, memories crowding into his mind of Vangie Sellors, aka Evie Selz, seventeen-year-old preacher's daughter from Lubbock, Texas, with the naturally flaxen hair and the huge smoky eyes, raw clay from which he had created a star reputed to be the most beautiful woman in the world—a goddess who had run away with a renegade director to a commune in New Mexico to make the definitive movie, the greatest film of all time. Only the moviemaking had resulted in ten thousand feet of drugged-out garbage, the director had walked off a cliff and killed himself, while Vangie herself had taken a trip from which she would never return.

"There's a problem with Saint," Arnie had said. "He's in Santa Paula," explaining that Santa Paula was a federal prison in the state of Guerrero in Mexico.

Diamond gave a grim smile. He could see himself now, slamming his car door shut and facing Arnie across the Jaguar's scorching roof demanding, "Why?"

And it was drugs, naturally. John Saint had been sentenced to fifteen years for dealing, smuggling, and corrupting a minor, and naturally Arnie explained that it was a setup, that he was innocent.

"And I'm the one you choose to get him out. You should know better, Arnie." Diamond said coldly, "You'll have to spring your Mr. Saint by yourself."

Arnie cried, "I've tried. I've been trying for over two years. But who's going to listen to me, with *my* record? Listen to me, I swear he didn't know the stuff was there, he——"

Diamond smiled grimly. "Please, Arnie, don't waste my time anymore. And don't call me again. Ever."

The uniformed doorman greeted him outside the thick green glass portals of his lobby. "Good morning, Mr. Diamond."

Diamond entered without looking back, and the doors whispered closed behind him. "It was his wi——" But Arnie's despairing cry was cut off in mid-phrase.

Diamond finished his dinner, gazing thoughtfully at the flickering art-deco nymph. He poured himself another glass of wine and reached for the phone.

He pressed number two on the automatic dial.

When it was answered, he didn't identify himself but merely said, "I want information. A run-down on John Saint, approximately twenty-five years old, son of Spring Kentfield. Everything you can get."

Then, carrying the wine bottle and his glass and a manila envelope, he went into the projection room and closed the heavy padded door behind him.

The Maltese Falcon was all set up and ready to roll. Diamond put it back carefully on the shelf.

He threaded a film called *Terry's Image* onto the projector instead.

Terry's Image was a virtually plotless, pretentious, grainy black-and-white piece shot in 1962 involving a photographer, three models, and some ill-defined, never-disclosed threat. It was filmed mostly in the New York subway. The only saving grace was a luminous five minutes of Vangie Sellors. While the credits rolled, he opened the envelope and took out a comic book. He opened it to the page where Starfire crouched on the sandbar.

When Vangie finally appeared, he looked from the screen to the page and back again, and nodded briefly to himself.

Chapter

15

It was suffocatingly hot. The sweat rolled down Saint's back and dripped off his ribs.

He huddled against the slimy wall of the cell. It was hard to breathe; the thick air was rank with dreadful smells. The light glowed a sullen red, a refraction of the dawn light through a high narrow grating that would make a ten-minute crawl across the flaking plaster of the opposite wall.

He had been woken from fitful sleep by a terrible scream followed by a heavy thud and a jeering howl of laughter.

El Burro occupied his usual position slumped beside the toilet, which was just an open drain, its edge encrusted with layers of decaying filth. Beto held him fiercely by the hair and was pounding his head against the wall. El Burro was a deranged vagrant and inclined to scream at unnervingly unexpected moments. Beto was a street-gang leader and had murdered a lot of people. The other three men were thieves. They crouched on the two concrete bunks muttering with resentment at being woken.

Saint buried his face in his arms in a vain attempt to shut out the noise, the waves of despair crashing through his brain for the thousandth, the millionth time. He would be here forever, abandoned and forgotten, his world shrunk to this tiny cell and its terrible inmates, until he died or went crazy, just like El Burro.

The madman howled again; Beto punched him in the mouth and slapped his face. The thieves laughed. The red light finished its crawl and faded out. Above the groans and jeers Saint could now hear a metallic clang and crash and hoarse yells.

The torero was here.

"El Toro" was the derisive name given by the inmates to the disgusting concoction of slimy soup dotted with shreds of half-rotten vegetables and the occasional piece of gristle which, with tortillas, made up their entire ration. It was wheeled along on a greasy cart and doled out by the torero, a bulbous giant with a smashed nose.

The door to their cage swung open. Moving bodies rustled past Saint like rats; he could hear the scuffling of their bare feet on the stone. He ran with them through the darkness. When the torero called, one obeyed or one starved.

Saint ran and ran and ran, and behind him the madman began to howl again.

He ran faster; the howls rose in volume.

Then someone was calling his name. "Santo! Please!" One of the thieves grasped Saint's shoulder and shook him.

Saint struggled, shouted, then opened his eyes.

He realized blearily that it hadn't been El Burro howling, but himself.

"This is too much," said his cellmate reprovingly. "Santo, have mercy on an old man's nerves. This is seven nights now, all in a row."

Javier Gallegos, his cellmate in the state prison to which Saint had been sent after a month in the holding cells, was a plump, cynical restaurant owner who had been running a profitable prostitution business from his upstairs rooms. He was quite philosophical about it; it was a setup pure and simple, "the same as your own unfortunate situation, Santo. They were out to get both of us."

His attitude was a comfort to Saint.

He was just as matter-of-fact about the torture. "Of course. The nose trick. That's the most common method. Doesn't leave marks, you see, simple and most effective."

Saint said in a strangled voice, "Soda water and Tabasco sauce. I never felt so humiliated in my life."

"You would have preferred a cattle prod on your private parts? Relax. It's over now. You have been through hell and survived. Hell is over." The plump restaurateur spread his arms to encompass the courtyard around them, in which the other inmates wandered, bickered, haggled over purchases from vendors, or slept.

"Welcome to purgatory. Now, calm yourself and sit down. I have some nice calvados somewhere. . . ."

From the beginning, Javier Gallegos had been nothing but pragmatic. An aristocratic American to share his quarters in the privileged section of the jail endowed him with a certain status, and the fact that Saint was also rich didn't hurt either, for here, for a price, one could buy almost anything, "all the comforts of home," Gallegos declared placidly. "We can be of use to each other, and the time will pass quite pleasantly."

Saint was glad to turn over a fairly large sum of money each month in return for the excellent meals and other favors. He was certain Gallegos cheated him much less than others would have done.

Now, at a rattling of locks and confused clattering, "*Desayuno*," Gallego announced with contentment as one of his own waiters wheeled a trolley into the cell. "Breakfast time." He lifted lids from dishes and sniffed. "*Huevos rancheros. Muy bien.*"

He was already dressed, dapper in a dark gray silk suit, ready to start his day. The waiter tucked a large pink linen napkin around his employer's neck, poured coffee, and handed him the morning's *El Diario*. Gallegos turned at once to the financial pages.

Saint looked at breakfast, arranged nicely on the trolley with linen and coffeepot and fresh orange juice, and reflected that this was certainly a great improvement over El Toro. In fact, if one ignored the weeping stained walls and the bars on the small window and the locked door, one could almost be staying in a hotel where the service and food were above average.

Saint's first action, arriving in these more palatable surroundings, had been to hire a new lawyer.

The lawyer promised everything and did nothing. He was smoother and richer and, Saint now suspected, more corrupt than Señor Beltrán, but what choice did he have?

In the United States his affairs were in a turgid mess.

Arnie was trying his best, but got nowhere. Mr. Friedman had no power outside the country, especially when the authorities in the state of Guerrero refused to cooperate. "Fletcher and her father will have paid everyone off." Saint pounded his fist against the scabrous plaster of the wall. "They can afford to keep me here till I rot."

"At least two years." Gallegos nodded. "Almost no matter who you are." He explained with a resigned shrug. "Once the machine is set in motion, it must run its course. It's useless to fret. Bureaucracy is a fact of life and one must make the best of it." He lit a cigar and leaned comfortably back in his chair.

Saint snorted disgustedly, "Make the best of it!"

"Why not? What else is there to do? The time will pass. Time always does. Relax, Santo. Don't beat your head against the wall. There's plenty of diversion here if you look for it."

During the endless months that followed, Saint forced himself to fill his time as Gallegos suggested. He bought a cheap guitar and learned to strum on it. He didn't sing because his voice now sounded harsh to his ears and his damaged throat hurt. He picked up Spanish quickly from prostitutes, embezzlers, thieves, drug dealers, and hit men. He learned to fight, acquiring many useful tricks that surprised him. Still, the days were very long, a grinding succession of light and dark, bribery, intrigue and conniving, the only high spots being the meals supplied by Gallegos' restaurant.

At least, now there was mail. Letters came from Vera, Arnie, Aunt Gloria, the production people at Starfire Enterprises. He even had a postcard from his mother. He no longer felt abandoned and forgotten, but the reminder of the outside world continuing without him frustrated him more unbearably than ever.

He heard nothing from J.B., although that wasn't surprising.

As the months rolled by, however, he managed to forget that last dreadful encounter. It was as though, for him and J.B., the years had rolled back, and to Gallegos' increasing boredom, he endlessly described their magical journey across the country and the blissful weeks on the boat. At night in the dark Saint would try to summon up her face in his mind; he ached to dream about her, but her image would never quite materialize, and in dreams she was maddeningly elusive. Well, he told himself, he wasn't really surprised; she didn't belong in a place like this; he shouldn't think about her while in jail.

"That's right. Don't waste your time," Gallegos advised bluntly. "She doesn't love you."

"What do you know?"

"Women are my business. I know."

Six weeks after Saint's arrival, his plump little cellmate erupted into the cell, face wreathed in smiles, crying, "Santo. Hey, Santo! You have a visitor!"

J.B. Saint clenched his hands and his blood thundered.

Perhaps it was J.B. Perhaps she had decided to come back to him after all. Within seconds he had persuaded himself that of course his visitor must be J.B.

But it wasn't.

Gallegos ushered Vera through the door with a flourish, as though she were a visiting duchess. Then, with heavy tact, he left them alone until visiting hours were over.

Vera was flushed both with heat and with pride in having successfully completed her long and difficult journey. She was clutching numerous packages. She was very fat.

Saint hugged her in his arms. The disappointment was crushing, but after the first terrible seconds he was aware of a powerful relief. He didn't want J.B. to see him here, like this. With Vera, he didn't have to feel shame. In fact he was so pleased to see her he almost cried.

Vera did cry. "Oh, Saint, it's so awful. I'm so sorry."

After she had dried her tears, looked around, kissed him again, and sworn explosively about Fletcher's unbelievable treachery, she handed him his gifts one by one and watched with pleased expectancy as he exclaimed over each item.

There were candy and peanut butter and jars of his favorite jelly. Toothpaste, shampoo, soap, an electric razor, a Spanish dictionary, language tapes, and a tape recorder. Most important, some of the books he had asked for—"I couldn't carry all of them, and I didn't dare trust the mail"—and the new *Starfire* layouts.

"I need help, Saint. I wish you'd check through all this and put me straight with the dialogue. It's not sounding right. I'm a couple of issues ahead with the art, so I could bring it all down at once . . ."

So they had a production meeting. Saint's spirits rose.

Starfire was selling well.

"Terrific sales," Vera said. "Well over 300,000 for the last issue."

Saint saw that as a good omen. Surely if *Starfire* was such a success, that boded well for his own future. But now Vera's face clouded. "Oh, God, Saint, we're all doing our best, but your . . ." She found it next to impossible to say the word "wife." "*She* and her father won't talk to us. They could stretch everything out forever." She said with despair, "How that woman must hate you to do this. Such horrible lies. And as for stabbing her . . ." Vera's face twisted. "I'd bloody well stab her myself if I had a chance."

She sniffed, wiped her nose on the sleeve of her caftan, and went on, "She certainly paid to have you put away, and apparently her timing was good. Arnie checked up. There was a drug sweep at that time. The Federales were supposed to fill a quota of arrests to make a showing. Obviously they couldn't nail anyone important, so they picked up all the little people."

"Like me."

She nodded. "Minor-league dealers and social users, and you, a convenient gringo. A scapegoat. And they got paid for it too. Oh, Saint," she wailed, "what a horrible mess."

Saint found himself in the position of consoling Vera. "There, there. Calm down. It's okay."

"No, it's *not* okay. It's lousy. And you won't believe this: I called your father, and what a son of a bitch. He didn't want to know. He was even angry with me for calling. All he'd say was: how like you, to waste your inheritance on a comic book, and you probably deserved it all. Honestly, Saint! Your own father! He won't do anything, and think of the strings *he* could pull. That's what Arnie says we need more than anything, more than money, even—strings. Someone with influence. More than the McGraws have."

Later, Gallegos asked, face wreathed in smiles, "You had an enjoyable visit?"

"Of course."

The Mexican gave a gusty romantic sigh. "In bed, that one would be a mountain lioness on heat."

Saint looked at him in astonishment.

"Yes," Gallegos went on dreamily, "a lioness. And she loves you. Believe me." He nodded sagely. "I know what I'm talking about."

Saint snorted. "Don't be dumb. That was Vera. She's just a very good friend."

Gallegos looked at him pityingly. "You have a lot to learn about women, Santo."

The days, weeks, and months rolled by.

For a while after Vera's visit Saint had dared to hope. When nothing happened, his emotions plunged to despair blacker than any he had known before.

Gallegos grew impatient. "You're being stupid. There's nothing you can do. Why tear yourself apart?"

Saint snarled, "It's okay for you. You'll get out of here soon."

"Certainly. But I'm not talking about me. Now, listen, Santo." They had been locked in for the night. Gallegos poured them both small glasses of expensive cognac. "Wasn't it one of your American writers who said: The best thing about being a writer is being able to turn even your worst experiences into money?"

Saint shook his head in numb resignation. "Maybe. Who cares?"

Gallegos persisted. "Spare me the self-pity. You're a writer and you have great advantages. You can escape with your mind. Every day, every night, you can get out of here. And one day, even *this* you can use. Thank Christ I was in prison, you can say. It's great material."

"Yeah." Saint sneered. "Sure."

The Mexican shrugged plump shoulders under his expensive silk shirt and tossed back his drink. "Santo, you're being tiresome. And stupid. I'll say it again, and I'll say it every day until you see sense: you are a writer . . . so write something."

Grudgingly, to keep Gallegos off his back, Saint went to work.

Thanks to his cellmate's arrangements, the mechanics were simple; he could buy paper and pens; he could even have a typewriter sent in if he wanted.

"There is no pressure," Gallegos pointed out, as though it was a great asset. "You have all the time in the world."

Saint started to say something obscene, but the words trailed off, for an idea did seem to be forming.

Gallegos left him alone.

Saint stared at the blank white paper in the typewriter and waited. After a while he wrote: "*Starfire the Wanderer.*"

After five minutes of thought he wrote: "A Screen Treatment."

The ingredients for a story began to jostle inside his head, and soon he started to jot down notes:

Starfire, interplanetary ambassador, returns to her own galaxy to find the star of her old system has become a supernova; it has exploded and swollen through billions of miles; it is now a red giant; it has swallowed its planets, their satellites; its entire system has been incinerated.

She cannot believe it.

Why did she have no warning? How long has she actually been gone? Through some warp in the fabric of time, she must have been gone for aeons. . . . And with the destruction of her home planet, with its sustaining forces, she has lost her old ability to change her shape. She can no longer move objects with the force of her mind. Now she is either disembodied energy or else forever locked into the inadequate body of Diana Starr. . . .

She is also locked into the vector which draws her back to Earth, now her only hope for a future.

Saint's mind ranged through the universe. With Starfire he soared unharmed through cataclysmic explosions, black holes, and billions of miles of cosmic dust.

In jail, he wrote on into the evening.

Riding the vector, Starfire returns again to Earth, but once again apparently too late.

In her absence there has been a nuclear war.

Much of the land is black and charred and crystalline; steam rises from holes in the ground; mud boils; on the horizon a black mountain range towers into the sky—or is it the burned-out rampart of a ruined city?

Starfire is appalled because Earth is now, perforce, her home forever. She vows to save it if she can; she will not allow it to spin endlessly as a stripped-down husk of barren rock. . . .

"Good," Javier Gallegos said in approval. "It's going well."

"I should finish the treatment in a few days."

His cellmate nodded and smiled. "Take your time. Do it right."

*   *   *

The second year rolled by. 1985 became 1986. In May, Vera returned to Santa Paula for another staff meeting. She took a hotel room for a week and visited the jail whenever possible.

She had quickly grown accustomed to the visiting procedures and by now was quite friendly with some of the inmates.

She offered determinedly, "It's not that bad, really, so long as you have money."

"Try it sometime."

"It's probably more human than an American jail. It's sort of like a village, really," she said, gazing at the courtyard filled with small stalls, at milling families including small children, at a woman in a brightly striped serape cooking tortillas.

"The families leave. And you get locked up at night."

Vera explained that Arnie wanted to come but he was in production and the insurance carrier wouldn't cover the risk. "Personally," Vera surmised, "I don't think he wants to see you here. It would make him too angry."

Endless petitions were circulating for Saint's freedom; there were endless promises, continuous frustrations. His mother had advised Arnie to contact Victor Diamond, whom she had once known, although under what circumstances was unclear. "She's very upset that nothing's happening, and she says this Diamond has unlimited influence."

"Why should he help?" Saint demanded. "What's in it for him?" Vera had no idea.

When Saint said his final good-bye to her, amid a tide of women and children and a few men streaming out of the great gates into freedom, "It doesn't look good, does it," he said bluntly. "I'm going to be here a very long time."

"Don't say that," Vera said fiercely. "We're all trying. Even your *mother's* trying. She's thinking about somebody else for a change."

"I wanted to ask you. Could you . . ." . . . *ask J.B. to write to me?* But he couldn't say it and with a mental sigh thought: What's the use, anyway?

Afterward he was glad he hadn't.

It was much better to forget J.B., to set her aside in a locked drawer in his mind and turn the key.

That night Saint sat down at his typewriter and rolled in a fresh piece of paper. He watched the words appear: *"Starfire. An Original Screenplay by John Saint."*

Black, deep space pricked with tiny distant stars and the thin sound of perpetual dust-laden wind.

We close very slowly on one star center screen, which visibly trembles, then soundlessly explodes in a convulsion of energy to become a spreading cancer of pulsing red light, swelling outward, bigger, huge, spreading steadily, until, in one burst of cacophonous music, the screen is entirely red.

The red fades once again to black, the wind song persists, the stars reappear, then realign to suggest human features. The wind gives way to muted music, quiet jagged notes in a minor key, suggestive of alienation and loss.

A woman's face gradually forms from out of the stars, clearer and drawing ever closer, until the eyes alone fill the screen. They are extraordinary eyes, silver but trembling with incandescent colors like a fire opal. The pupils pulse with starlight.

The main title rolls:

Starfire. . . .

Chapter
16

"Dear Donald," Vera wrote. "I was so sorry to miss you again when I was back in England, but it was all such a rush and I had to go straight up to Yorkshire. Mum hasn't been well, you know . . ."

. . . although there wasn't much actually wrong with her. "She needs someone to take care of," Cynthia had said. "She has no one to worry about. Nothing to do." Mum had been pathetically grateful that Vera had come home, "and so happy, dear, that you're not trying to look like a mannequin anymore. It's simply not our Vera, you know." When it was time to return to California, Mum took to her bed complaining of terrible pains. "I can't believe that you'd go back there again and leave me like this. You've grown hard, Vera. Dreadfully hard. What is there for you to go back to, anyway? It's not as though you've got a young man waiting. . . ."

"I'm so glad you're coming home to California at last, and your replacement looks as though he'll work out well in the practice. I'm away for the next few weeks, so can't, unfortunately, meet you, though I'm sure your family will be so excited to have you back they won't want me intruding anyway."

No way, Vera thought, did she plan to meet him at the airport as he'd asked, she didn't want to see him at all, not looking like this and not right now, when her whole heart and mind were so focused on Saint.

"There's been no change in Saint's situation; it seems to be the ultimate Mexican standoff. However, Arnie and I haven't given up, and a new plan is in the works. I'm staying with him for the moment, as you can see from the Beverly Hills address, to help plot. This is an amazing place, a fantasy penthouse with everything one could ever need, including a projection room, spa, and gym though Arnie really uses only two rooms, the library, where he works on scripts and listens to tapes, and his bedroom . . ."

And what a strange place that was, a decorator's idea of a teenage boys' den. A single bed with storage units below; sensible plaid wallpaper and draperies; and on the walls, school pennants and ten-year-old photographs of sports teams, Saint's face visible among rows of other grinning fourteen-year-olds.

"Arnie doesn't actually live like a movie star at all. He hardly ever goes to parties or even out to dinner . . ."

Thank goodness. Vera felt like a pale slug beside the thin, tanned, beautiful women of Beverly Hills. She dreaded going anywhere with Arnie, who would always be recognized, while she would be stared at with outraged amazement: *"Who does that fat cow think she is, hanging around with Arnie?"*

". . . he prefers to stay at home. His meals are sent up by the Italian restaurant downstairs. . . ."

And it was a very good restaurant, too. She would probably gain even more weight, but what the hell, Vera thought, what did it really matter?

She sighed and shifted restlessly on her chaise. She seemed to have been writing this letter on and off all day.

She reflected that she could much more easily have called Donald on the phone, but then she would have had to answer questions, think fast, make snap excuses, whereas with a letter she could take her time and avoid him for longer. Anyway, it gave her something to do while she waited.

Oh, if only Arnie would come home.

She stood up and paced from one end of the terrace to the other.

What was taking so long? He had planned to see this man, Victor Diamond, at 8 in the morning.

Spring had seemed certain that if anyone could help, he could. "He's made films in Mexico and has important friends in government. He has all the power and connections in the world."

Vera had asked Arnie, "Was she married to him once? Were they lovers?" for Spring had been unclear about her connection with Diamond.

"I think they worked together," Arnie replied vaguely, "a long time ago."

"Well, at least she's doing her best for Saint. She's acting like a real mother."

Arnie said sourly, "Don't be too impressed. She's getting a lot of mileage out of it. Suffering mother. Wearing yellow ribbons till he's released. All that."

"Oh, Arnie. So cynical."

"So true."

But for whatever reason, Spring had pointed the way to Victor Diamond, a man of power, and Arnie had left early that morning with high hopes.

But he hadn't called all day. It was a bad sign.

Vera's stomach rumbled. She was hungry again, but it was only five o'clock and dinner wouldn't be delivered until after seven.

She returned to her chaise. She laid the three pages of her letter on the table beside her and weighted them with a terra-cotta fish. She would return to it later. She wished Arnie had something to eat in his sterile refrigerator.

She could use a large slice of chocolate cake right now, with fudge frosting.

"Well," Arnie said tiredly, "it didn't work. Boy, how it didn't work. I just couldn't stand to call you." He had showered; his light hair was still damp and slicked back behind his ears. He wore white slacks and a white lawn shirt. He looked clean-cut, sharp edged, and brittle as a character in a Noël Coward play.

"Well," Vera pointed out, trying to hide her crushing disappointment, "he probably thinks cartoons are for kids."

Arnie shook his head. "It wasn't that. I almost had him. For just a minute there he could see it and *taste* it. His eyes got that certain look; his juices were running . . . But I screwed up. I should have known he's a fanatic about drugs." He looked about ready to cry. "I thought his wife was institutionalized after a *breakdown*. I assumed she was a schizoid or something."

"But . . . ?"

"She fried her brains with LSD back in the sixties. She's a vegetable. God, Vera, a fucking *vegetable*. The second Diamond heard about Saint in jail for drugs, it was thumbs down all the way. He wouldn't listen. If he had, he wouldn't have believed me. Who blames him? But I'm not giving up." Arnie swung on his heel and leaned his elbows on the parapet, staring across the sultry cityscape. "I know now he's the right man. There must be a way of getting to him. We must think of something, you and I."

Vera felt like crying. "It goes on and on. Whenever we think there might be a chance, the door slams shut on us. I go down there and I see him in that awful place and I try to be cheerful, but it's harder every time. And then I think what it must be like for him. Oh, God, Arnie." Vera began to arrange the thin cotton fabric of her caftan into tight accordion pleats. "I don't know how long I can go on." She thought of Saint wasting the best young years of his life in limbo and whispered, "I can't stand it. I love him."

Arnie patted her absently on the shoulder as though she were a pet dog, stood up, and paced across the terrace. He leaned on his hands and gazed across the murky city toward Santa Monica and the ocean.

"I love him too," Arnie said evenly. "Ever since I first met him. He was my roommate. Nobody else wanted to be my roommate. He was a transfer and got stuck with me. I was a fat little nerd with glasses that everyone picked on. He was handsome, good at sports, bright, and popular, and everybody wanted to be his friend. He was even rich. The minute he walked in the door, I thought: He's going to take one look at me, laugh, and walk right out and demand a different roommate. I was totally afraid of him. But he didn't do it, just treated me like I was handsome and popular too. He was a real friend. He stood up for me, always. Anyone picked on me, he told them to go fuck 'emselves. He'd have fought them too, all of them, and they knew it. They left me alone when I was with Saint. I'd have done anything for him . . ."

The sun had dropped now; the sky was dark behind the mountains; Vera thought she saw the flicker of lightning. A hot breeze skittered across the terrace. It was Santa Ana weather. Arnie turned back to face her and drew a deep breath. "And now it's my turn to help him, and I swear nobody's going to stop me."

Vera went to the bathroom and bathed her aching eyes with cold water. When she returned, calm: "Well, back to square one, I suppose. What now?"

Arnie leaned back in his seat and hooked his toes under the base of the table. The lamplight struck sparks from his eyes. For a moment Vera thought she had never seen anyone look more determined.

"What now?" echoed Arnie. "Well, now, as I see it, we start to get serious with Vic Diamond. We bring on the heavy artillery."

Vera stared at him. "Like what, exactly?"

"Starfire herself."

At first J.B. stormed, "Are you crazy? I'm not doing something like that."

Arnie said coldly, "Yes you will. Diamond won't talk to me. He won't answer my calls. You're Saint's only chance."

"So I'm supposed to take Diamond to bed and turn him on so much he springs Saint."

"I didn't say that. You're supposed to impress him so much he will make the film at all costs. Listen to me, J.B. He's a professional. He was fascinated by *Starfire*. He just has to *see* you. Believe me. Anyway," Arnie said in a dangerous voice, "d'you want Saint free or not?"

"What do you think I am? Of course I do, but . . . listen, Arnie. Don't make it be my fault now, that he married Fletcher and went to jail."

Arnie said ruthlessly, "He went to Fletcher because of *you*. Something you did, something you said. I don't know what it was, and I don't want to know. But only you could have stopped him marrying her. And now only you can get him out."

On Friday night, two weeks later, Arnie was readying J.B. for the party where she would meet Victor Diamond for the first time, applying her makeup himself, his fingers deft and knowing.

He stood back to review his handiwork and shook his head critically. "Foundation's too dark; needs toning down." He busied himself yet again with shading and contours, glancing continuously from a panel of *Starfire: The Interrogator* pinned on the wall, then back to J.B.'s face. "We have to get it *right*."

Arnie had hired a private detective to check on the movements of Victor Diamond. Today's events had revealed:

Breakfast at Polo Lounge.

Production meetings, Omega, in a.m.

Lunch with David Zimmerman and visiting chairman from corporate headquarters in New York.

Meetings in p.m.

Rubin Zeff, M.D. five o'clock (cardiologist).

Romano cocktail/buffet eight o'clock.

Note: Subject seldom attends these functions but plans to make exception here. Subject habitually arrives after food has been served, drinks one glass of wine, two at most, conducts relevant business, and leaves within the hour.

"I won't go," J.B. had said flatly. "Think of something else."

Arnie had in fact thought of and dismissed all kinds of ways of attracting Diamond's attention, including a billboard of Starfire's face on the Ventura Freeway or a full-page ad in *Variety*, "but meeting him at a party is much more natural."

"Natural? With me looking like this? And I'm not even invited; I'm a gate-crasher. Suppose they don't let me in? There'll be a guest list. There'll be guards——"

"Who'll have instructions to let in all beautiful unattached women. Don't worry, J.B. Romano's a satyr."

"A what?"

"Sex maniac."

"Great. Just what I need. Listen, suppose Diamond doesn't show up after all? Or he does and I miss him? Or he's late and Romano makes a hit on me? What do I do then?"

"You play for time," Vera said slowly. "And confuse him. Explain who you are; you're Starfire, from the system of Rigel."

"Oh, *sure*."

"You're Starfire." Arnie moved behind J.B. and tilted her chin up, peering into the mirror, where her smoky gaze stared back at him, framed with the new mane of silver hair, the coloring of which Arnie had supervised personally at Mr. G's. "You're Starfire and you are very—no, *extraordinarily*—beautiful. You also have power and you can handle Steve Romano all right. Vera, tweezers. Her eyebrows are too thick."

J.B. drew a sharp breath. "You're not going to *touch* my eyebrows."

"Hold still," Arnie said ruthlessly, "or I might stick you."

Next, the application of silver eye shadow with dark gray liner carefully drawn out along the lids.

Vera shifted uneasily from foot to foot. It was almost eerie. Arnie was an excellent makeup artist. Too good. J.B. herself was vanishing; Starfire was becoming more real by the minute.

Arnie drew back again to study his progress. "Looking good."

J.B. said, "I want a drink."

"No way," Arnie said. "You'll smudge your lipstick."

Finally, there was the dress. A brief metallic tunic, and silver kid sandals with thongs crisscrossed to the knee. J.B.'s only jewelery was a heavy silver ring shaped like a snake coiled about her left index finger.

Arnie caught her by the shoulders and turned her toward the three-way mirror. "All right, Starfire. Look at yourself."

J.B. stared speechlessly into the mirror, at a warrior princess with luminous skin and huge lambent eyes. She said in a small voice, "It'll be a shock. Diamond's old. He could even have a heart attack and die. He'll never help Saint then."

"He's only fifty. That's not old. And he's a health nut."

Vera pointed out, "He sees a cardiologist."

Arnie shrugged. "So what? The guy leads a high-stress life; he takes precautions and has checkups."

J.B. said, "Even if he doesn't have a stroke, he's going to be mad as hell that someone would pull a thing like this. Same result."

Arnie leaned forward, his hands on J.B.'s shoulders, meeting her eyes in the mirror. His own eyes were intent, almost mesmeric. "Whatever happens," Arnie said in a quiet but oddly vibrant voice, "you can deal with it. You have power. You're Starfire now. Look at yourself again."

Vera took a step backward. She felt breathless and a little frightened. For a second she thought she felt something pass among the three of them, some transference of energy that, in its path, left her bereft. I've lost her now, thought Vera. I've given Starfire away. J.B. really is Starfire now, and I'll never have her back, ever. And if Diamond doesn't get Saint out of jail, I'll have done it for nothing. She said in a strangled voice, "This had better work."

Arnie said, "Starfire will make it work. Of course she will." And to J.B., "You can reach into Diamond's mind and make him do what you want. Your mission is to save Saint, and you can do it. You know you can. You can do anything."

In the lobby, among mere mortals, J.B. really did look like an exotic creature from another planet.

People turned and stared; an awed silence fell.

J.B. muttered, "*Christ.*" Her hands began to shake. She dropped her little silver evening purse. Arnie picked it up and hung it over her shoulder.

He touched her briefly on the arm. "Good luck."

J.B. gave him one last glance of real human terror with her fantasy eyes. Then she tightened her lips, squared her shoulders, and followed the chauffeur outside.

Arnie and Vera watched him hand her into the long silver car and close the door.

They watched the limousine pull out into traffic in stately fashion, heading for Coldwater Canyon, carrying Starfire on her mission.

Vera said, "You didn't have to be so rough on her."

"I'll do what it takes." Arnie grasped Vera by the wrist and towed her into the elevator. "And now I'm going to break my rules. There couldn't be a better time. We're going to get drunk, you and I."

Chapter

17

"I'm Starfire. I have power. I'm Starfire. I have power." J.B. muttered the words like a mantra, perched tensely on the edge of her seat in the dark limousine, her body rocking with the sway of the vehicle as they turned first off the freeway onto a major street, then onto a lesser road, then up into the mountains. She felt as lost, lonely, and cut off as though she really were riding through space.

Eventually they pulled up at a pair of floodlit wrought-iron gates manned by no fewer than four security guards.

Her overpowering impulse was to run. To open the door and just take off before anyone could stop her. But after a brief exchange that she couldn't hear, the big gates swung open and they were waved onward, to whisper to a stop in front of tall vermilion-lacquered doors.

Behind her the car pulled away; it was too late to run. J.B. stepped through the bright doors of Steven Romano's house into an immense atrium two stories high, where tropical vines and flowers trailed from high balconies and music played in unfamiliar electronic cadences that heightened her sense of doom.

I'm Starfire, J.B. told herself fiercely. I'm Starfire and I have power.

She accepted a glass of champagne from a white-jacketed butler, then followed him across the hall, through an arch, and outside into a Japanese stone garden of sculptured lava and white gravel. Down moss-covered steps past a sinuously shaped swimming pool, over a waterfall across a narrow stone bridge, and down steps again, past walls hung thickly with jasmine and clematis. Some other time she would have found it all very beautiful.

Steve Romano held court on the lowest terrace, which was paved with marble and filled with delicate white-painted wrought-iron furniture. He wore narrow-legged black leather pants and matching vest with no shirt. A small ivory skull hung against his bare chest from a wide-linked gold chain. He saw J.B. at once, his brows lifted, and he moved to her side with fluid grace. "Welcome, lovely stranger." Steve coiled a lock of her silvery hair around his finger. "You look as if you should be slaying dragons with a spear."

She deftly reclaimed her hair and attempted a relaxed smile. "Hello. I'm J.B." She glanced quickly around. None of the other guests was Diamond. Well, here she was, in place. She didn't feel like Starfire the warrior at all. She felt more like a sacrificial goat pegged out for the tiger—who would arrive any moment now.

"I know exactly who you are," Romano said pleasantly, "but not who you belong to."

Belong to? A dangerous spark flashed in J.B.'s eyes. "I belong to my*self*."

"You're *alone*? Well! That's the best news I've had all week." Steve dealt her a slow, predatory smile and squeezed her shoulder. "I'm bored as hell. This is a godawful party. I don't know why I do this. It's not my kind of thing at all." He clinked his glass against hers. "Welcome. Make my evening sing."

J.B. thought furiously: I can't deal with this. I *won't*!

But then she thought of Saint and her own guilt and Arnie's anger and Vera's love, sipped her champagne, and regarded him coolly over the top. "I can't help you," Starfire replied, "I'm tone-deaf."

"But quick with your tongue. I like that in a woman." Romano's expression was that of a famished diner eyeing a piece of succulent filet mignon. "And my personal preference in parties is something much more intimate. Why don't we take our drinks to bed? By the time we're finished, perhaps they'll all have gone away." He placed his hand possessively at the nape of her neck under her hair. She took an involuntary step backward. "It's the least you can do," he said pleasantly. "Standard price of admission."

Starfire decided Arnie was certainly right about Romano being a sex maniac. Wham! Just like that. "You certainly don't waste time, do you?"

"No," Steve said pleasantly, "why should I? This is my house and my party."

"That's an honest answer," Starfire replied. "It deserves one back."

"No it doesn't," Steve retorted. "There's too much talk around here. It deserves a blow-job. Come, my dear. You can't say no. We can talk in bed. You can tell me why you're here, and what you want. I'll do my best for you. I always give fair value for a fuck. Ask anyone."

Starfire said firmly, "I'm obliged. But I don't fuck with humans."

Romano blinked. "How's that again?"

"Don't misunderstand, I'm not implying you're a lower life form—"

His dark eyes flashed with anger. His lips narrowed. Suddenly he didn't look so handsome. "Now, look, lady, who's calling who a lowlife?"

Starfire smiled. "I'm just following orders."

"What the fuck are you . . . ?" He gave an uneasy laugh. "Where *did* you escape from, anyway?"

"If I told you, you wouldn't believe me."

"Try me."

"The outer system of Rigel."

"You're right. On second thought, maybe I do believe you. You're weird enough. But if you're not here to see me, why did you come?"

"To meet someone else."

"Listen, lady, I don't like being used. Especially not in my own house."

Starfire pointed out, "But life's like that, about using and being used. And do you really mind? Nobody else knows except you and me, and you're not even bored anymore. Perhaps I've even made your evening, like you said."

And then, thankfully, the sparring was at an end. A bevy of brightly dressed people swirled around them. Voices chattered and chided.

"Stevo, darling, you look fabulous."

"Stevo, pet, don't hold out. Who's your friend?"

A woman with lots of hair and a very small dress told Starfire, "Great costume, dear. Who are you supposed to be?"

Romano said with a strangled snort, "Princess Leia with a new hairdo."

There was a muted trill of laughter. A man asked, "Is that your very own UFO in the driveway?"

Starfire shook her silver head. "Goodness, no, just a rental."

The trill rose to a mild shriek. Apparently she was being quite a hit.

A waiter appeared and filled glasses.

Where was Diamond? Perhaps he wasn't coming. Five more minutes, Starfire thought, and I'm out of here.

Then a woman with strident red hair threaded with seed pearls suddenly hissed at the man at her side, "There, Mort, look who's here. Didn't I *tell* you he'd come?"

And a brief total silence fell as the group all turned to watch the man coming down the steps.

Starfire turned with them. Steve Romano was saying something to her about how she owed him now, all right, she was going to meet Victor Diamond, which was certainly worth a fuck or two or three, but she didn't even hear him.

She stood quite still in the middle of the patio, convulsively gripping her champagne glass with both hands, no longer Starfire but just J.B. again, who was scared out of her wits. She prayed for a miracle, like Diamond not noticing her. She urged herself: I'm Starfire. I'm invisible. I'm Starfire. I'm invisible.

But of course the mantra didn't work. Her power had drained away.

Victor Diamond saw her at once and stopped dead for a split second on the bottom step, his dark eyes boring into hers. She felt about ten years old. He looked huge. He looked magnificent. He was the embodiment of every authority figure she had ever known.

"Vic," Romano was saying, "glad you could join us."

Behind J.B. the red-haired woman muttered, "Go on, Mort, you'll never have a chance like this . . ."

Diamond acknowledged Romano's greeting with a slight inclination of the head. He passed through the cluster of guests as though they didn't exist and stopped immediately in front of J.B. "Who are you, and why are you trying to be Vangie?"

Vangie? Who was *that?* She stared up at him and tried to speak, but her mouth and jaw felt as stiff as though recently injected with novocaine. After a long moment she managed, "I'm J.B."

"Oh, yes. Of course." Diamond's eyelids drooped tiredly. "I should have know. Arnold Blaize sent you. I wondered what stunt he'd try to pull next."

No point denying it. "Yes."

"He's going to regret it," Diamond said.

She believed him.

"And so are you."

J.B. drew a sharp breath. *Damn* Arnie for forcing her into this. It wasn't fair. She felt a fierce bright anger toward Arnie—and toward Saint too for being the unwitting cause of this humiliation.

She set her lips in a thin line. "I'm sorry. For what it's worth, I said it wouldn't work."

"Oh, but you're wrong. For an instant up there on the steps I really did think I was seeing a ghost. I didn't know what I was seeing." Diamond took a step forward until he was looming theateningly over her. J.B. backed behind a small glass-and-wrought-iron table. She stared at him. "A ghost?"

"Oh, come now," Diamond said with an unpleasant smile, "give me credit for a little sense. I've been around a very long time, my dear, and I've seen every ploy ever hatched, every game in the book. Or I thought I had. This does deserve a category for itself, however, and congratulations, you just won the award. The starlet who will go to the most despicable lengths to get attention. Now make your acceptance speech and get out of here."

With a shaking hand J.B. set her glass down on the table. This was worse, much worse than she had dreamed. "I don't know what you mean, talking about ghosts. Listen, I agree with you, it was a dumb thing to do. I'm sorry. I'm leaving right now."

She turned away. Diamond caught her by the arm. "Wait. One more thing."

The table lantern reflected in his black eyes like burning coals. His hand moved smoothly and unhurriedly down her arm until he held her hand tightly in his. "I want you to take a message back to Arnie Blaize. Tell him no way will I help his sleazeball friend out of jail; I hope he stays there till he rots." His fingers tightened on hers. "Also tell him that if he tries to take this *Starfire* project anyplace else, I'll ruin him so fast he won't know what hit him. I won't allow Vangie to be degraded like this."

He tightened his grip. He held her so hard she could feel the bones scrape together. She tried to flex her fingers; his grip tightened again, and she thought: Jesus Christ, he's going to break my hand.

"I'll tell him," J.B. said, trying not to flinch. "Let me go now."

"As for you," Diamond said, "you better go back to whatever pockmark in the prairie you came from and forget all about being a movie star."

He squeezed her hand again.

J.B. drew a ragged breath. Suddenly she was no longer afraid of him. He was just a man, after all, a cruel son of a bitch with a power complex, like so many of them. Was it that bad, what she'd done? Of course it wasn't. Her eyes flashed. "Cut that out." Her lips whitened against her teeth as she dragged her hand away from him. "*Nobody* pulls that kind of shit on me."

He gave her a nasty smile. "Spare the dramatics, dear," and flicked her derisively across the cheek. "They're wasted. Your promising career just ended."

J.B. massaged her hurt hand. She didn't know when she'd ever felt so angry. "If I've already killed my career," she said in a tight voice, "then I might as well bury it." And with her entire weight behind her arm, she smacked him hard across the face. His head snapped backward. He dropped his glass, which shattered on the marble floor.

All pretense at conversation died around them, then rose in a sibilant chorus of hushed avid voices in which the words "sue" . . . "assault" . . . "sue" . . . "suit" hissed like venomous snakes, Steve Romano's rising above the rest, insisting, "I'm sorry, Vic. Jesus, I don't even know the bitch. She crashed the party, she's insane, I'll call the doctor right now, and the cops."

J.B. ignored him. She faced Victor Diamond, eyes blazing. "Good-bye, Mr. Diamond. I'll be sure to give Arnie your message."

Then she turned on her heel and marched up the steps without looking back, all the way to the top, through the vermilion doors and into the driveway, where her car was already waiting, as if summoned by magic.

She didn't begin to shake, or to cry, until the long ride home was over and she was safely inside her own front door. Then she didn't think she would ever be able to stop.

"I did my best," she told Arnie on the phone next morning. The night before, she hadn't trusted herself to speak. "It didn't work. Because of something we didn't know. . . ." In faltering tones she told him about Vangie; how she, J.B., looked just like Vangie Sellors. "And it was horrible.

Just horrible. I thought I'd never hated anybody so much in my whole life, the things he did, the things he said. Then, when I got home, I just felt so ashamed. That poor man. I'm sorry, Arnie. I can't do it again. Please don't tell me to do it again."

It was Saturday, a model's day off. A day for sleeping late, shopping, or lunching with friends.

J.B. did none of those things. She put her answering machine on—she couldn't stand the idea of talking to Arnie again or, even worse, to Vera—and spent the morning restlessly pacing her apartment, listening to the phone ring twice and then stop, imagining her own voice saying: "Hello, this is J.B., I can't come to the phone right now . . ."

In midafternoon she drove to the beach and spent the next two hours walking aimlessly.

It was a hot, airless day, the sun a colorless disk barely visible behind a thin white overcast. J.B. wore cut-off jeans, an oversize striped shirt, her silver hair tied up in a bandanna. She had removed all her Starfire makeup, scrubbing vigorously at her face as if it burned her. As she walked, last night's events circled through her head in a wretchedly endless loop. She realized she had failed everybody. She had failed Saint, Arnie, and Vera, and she'd actually hit Victor Diamond in the face, which would have unspeakable repercussions. If only she could have that time back, perhaps she could have played it differently. As it was, she would never have a second chance. Diamond had said he would block any attempt Arnie made to take *Starfire* anywhere else, and she believed him. She felt terrible. Just terrible. Although, how *could* she have known she looked just like Vangie Sellors?

She returned to her car with listless steps, too absorbed in her own misery to notice the black Jaguar which had pulled in beside her own silver BMW, or the man with the thick white hair who sat in the driver's seat, chin resting pensively on his arms, which were linked over the wheel, until he opened the door and got out and said, "That was a long walk," to which she replied mechanically, "Why are you following me, Mr. Diamond?"

J.B. smelled the salt air from the ocean. The overcast had rolled back at sunset. Sitting on the chaise Diamond indicated and tilting her head back, she saw a black velvet sky in which the stars were huge and blurred and densely packed. She stared into the deep bright reaches of space and wondered which was Rigel.

Hamura appeared with champagne and two crystal flute glasses. He poured, bowed, silently disappeared.

Diamond raised his glass to hers. "I owe you an apology. I thought at first, you see, that you were intended to impersonate my wife."

J.B. still couldn't quite take it in, this miraculous second chance. She shook her head in the darkness and said in a low voice, "I didn't know . . . I've never seen any of her films . . . or a picture. Afterward I was so sorry . . ."

"Vangie made just three films, and I have all the prints. I found it very hard, you know, thinking of strangers watching her as she'd been then. I wanted to keep her for myself. Selfish, I know, maybe kind of warped, but I couldn't help it."

J.B. said, "You must have loved her very much."

"Even after all this time, my feelings are amazingly strong. I prefer not to talk about her." Diamond was silent for a long time. J.B. didn't dare break into his reverie. Finally, "It didn't take me long to realize it was a misunderstanding and that I'd done you quite an injustice. I thought we should talk. Perhaps I can make it up to you. Although," he said, a hint of a smile in his voice, "I'm not so sure you don't have more to make up to me." He rubbed his face in the dark. "You're strong. You pack quite a punch."

She murmured guiltily, "I know. But I was so angry . . ."

"But under the circumstances, justified. So now, J.B., you finally have all my attention. Tell me exactly what you think I can do for you."

After that it was easy.

J.B. explained everything, about Saint, Fletcher, Arnie, Vera, and herself. Against all expectation, Victor Diamond seemed incredibly easy to talk to, and he very seldom interrupted. She found herself feeling more and more at ease and secure; she had seldom felt more comfortable in her life.

At one point he said, "You all seem to have touching faith in me. Do you seriously imagine I can have your friend released? Just like that?"

"Arnie says you have connections. That you know people in the Mexican government. Police and drug-enforcement people."

Diamond nodded. "That's true."

"And that they'd release him if you asked."

"Perhaps. I could try."

"Thank you," said J.B.

"My pleasure. I think," Diamond said dryly. "And now, let's talk about you. And *Starfire*. . . ."

Sometime later, he led her through a glass door into a wide tiled hallway, under an arch, and up a narrow staircase of stone that zigzagged back and forth up the side of the house.

The bedroom occupied the whole third floor. It was a very simple room, plain white walls, tile floor, the west-facing wall entirely of glass. The only furniture was a high-backed wormwood bench which looked as though it had come from a Spanish cathedral, and in the absolute middle of the room a huge bed, raised on a platform, covered with an oversize spread in violent colors: rust, scarlet, magenta, and black.

J.B. said, "It looks rather like an altar."

Diamond agreed. "Yes, doesn't it?" He touched a panel on the wall beside the arched entryway and the light level sank to spectral dimness. Another touch and the roof rolled soundlessly back. "Undress," he ordered softly.

J.B. raised her hands to the zipper at the back of her neck. The metallic dress slithered down her hips and puddled luminously at her feet. She stepped out of it and unlaced the sandals. Walking barefoot on the cool tiles, she folded her clothes and piled them carefully on the bench.

Diamond told her. "Stand over there, by the window."

J.B. obeyed. The floor-to-ceiling glass panel slid soundlessly open onto humid air and she could hear the hiss of the waves again. She turned to look out at the ocean, not wanting to watch him undress, though she could sense his movements as he took off his own clothes. Then he was moving toward her across the room and J.B. stiffened, hands clenched. He was old and maybe had a heart condition, but seemed gentle enough now, and she liked him very much and felt intensely grateful, but suddenly she thought of that vicious grip on her hand, which still ached, and remembered she was alone in this weird house with just him and an invisible servant who, she was sure, would never come if she screamed.

Goddammit, she demanded of herself, why am I doing this? Why am I letting this happen?

And answered herself: Because this man is Victor Diamond, he's influential and powerful, and he's promised he'll get Saint out of jail. . . . But that wasn't the whole answer. I'm not just doing this for Saint, J.B. realized, I'm doing it for me too, because I want to, because he's the most extraordinary man I've ever met . . . and—a sudden jolt of her heart—because he's going to let me be Starfire. And when I'm Starfire, I'll be powerful too. I'll have all the power in the world. . . .

Diamond reached out his hands for her, held her by the shoulders, and drew her against him. He raised his hand and touched her forehead, his fingers lightly traveling over her face, throat, tracing the curve of her breasts, back over her shoulders, both hands resting for a moment flat against her shoulder blades before moving down her back, his fingers searching for and finding the twin dimpled recesses above her buttocks, where the downy hairs grew in soft little whorls on each side of the base of her spine.

He murmured, "On the bed now."

What followed was a long, drawn-out ballet of calculated motion, response, and delicate frictions, performed with monumental patience.

He demanded nothing of her at all, save to whisper, "Raise your knees now, turn, stretch," as though directing her in a film. He barely touched her.

She knew he was watching the play of light and shadow on her body, and noting each texture of skin, hair, and sliding inner flesh with his hands and tongue, and all the time he was watching her, watching her face, his hands touching and stroking, one hand on her forehead pressing her back into the pillows, the other between her legs, thumb pressed firmly against her pubis while she writhed against him.

Afterward he lay beside her, not touching her, his breath soft and even.

J.B. wondered whether he knew she hadn't really come, and if he did know, whether he cared.

Diamond spoke suddenly, surprising her because she thought he was asleep. "It's very seldom complete, the first time. It'll get better."

J.B. murmured, "I'm sure it will," and thought: He can't be fooled. I should have known better.

Long minutes later, when she was absolutely certain he had fallen asleep, he said, "I can get Saint out of jail. And I will. Tell Arnie and Vera Brown."

She sighed with relief. "Thank you. We'll all be so grateful——"

"Naturally. But there's a condition."

"Of course."

"I want the full rights to the character. Vera must sign over the rights. Do you understand, J.B.? I want *Starfire*."

Chapter
18

He was recognized at once:

"Look, Ma! Ain't that . . . ?

"Over there! The guy in the green shirt with the fat woman. It's . . ."

"Waddya know! Ten minutes in L.A. and a movie star already!"

Oblivious, Arnie Blaize scanned the arrivals screen for news of the Western Airlines flight from Mexico City. "Goddammit, Vera, it's an hour late. What're we going to do for two hours?"

"I told you not to leave so early."

The voices clamored:

"I love you, Arnie!"

"Sign your autograph, willya? Here, on my arm, to Billi, with an I!"

"I wanna marry you, Arnie. I want your babies . . ."

Arnie signed his name on cocktail napkins, the backs of envelopes, on rosy teenage flesh, and bestowed mechanical smiles upon which fantasies would be built, although Vera knew that the immediate scene didn't exist for him; that though his body was here in the international terminal at LAX, his mind and heart were with Saint in that plane still somewhere over the Sonoran Desert.

Vera wasn't surprised. She felt unreal herself. She couldn't quite believe that anything could happen so fast. After two years of rage and delay and frustration, things had turned around just like that.

Provided she agreed to sell her *Starfire* rights to Victor Diamond.

Arnie had protested angrily, "He can't expect Vera to do that."

"He'll be very generous with the terms."

"If it's the only way," Vera said, "what choice do I have?"

Now, a shrill scream: "*Arneee!*" Then more screams, rising in pitch to a sustained keening.

A well-built fourteen-year-old tore open her blouse to expose trembling white breasts. "I want you, Arnie!"

Vera grabbed his arm. "We can't wait here."

"Okay," Arnie said, "We'll go wait for him at the gate."

Vera glanced at the growing horde of clamoring teenagers with their clutching hands, greedy for a strand of Arnie's hair or a shred of his clothing. "Are you crazy? We have to get out of here."

But before the worst happened, a harassed official arrived flanked by a brace of muscular airport police. Arnie and Vera were rushed to the VIP lounge. Arnie's fans were dispersed. Vera wondered whether Arnie had even noticed the disturbance.

She sank gratefully into a seat. Arnie did not sit, but paced back and forth, glowering through the windows at the jets trundling down taxiways to and from the runway, rising into the air or ponderously setting down, so many planes, none of them with Saint on board. He ordered mineral water from a smiling hostess, drank it quickly, then spent the next ten minutes rapping the glass against his teeth or rattling the melting ice cubes, until Vera thought she'd scream.

Time passed very slowly. Minute by long minute stretched into half an hour.

Vera tried to decide how she felt, selling *Starfire*. Surely she ought to feel devastated with loss but ... No, Vera thought, I *already* lost her. Twice over, in fact, for in reality *Starfire* hadn't been hers since she first saw J.B. so long ago at Arnie's party. . . .

At her side Arnie muttered, "It's only been an hour. God, when's that plane coming in?"

Victor Diamond had taken J.B. to Mexico with him. When they came back, they were all to meet. He would have documents drawn up, claiming the cartoon character of Starfire as his and his alone. How would it feel, signing *Starfire* away?

But it was impossible to worry about it. Not now, when any moment she'd be seeing Saint again, free . . .

And then: "Vera!" Arnie was pointing at the board. "Vera! It's down. He's landed." He looked, she realized, absolutely terrified.

*   *   *

Arnie pressed close to the gate, eyes searching each passenger emerging from customs and immigration.

There were tourists with sunburns and bright clothes, businessmen, large Mexican families, and a bevy of priests wearing flat-crowned black hats. Everyone pushed a cart loaded with luggage, boxes, briefcases, souvenirs, and sometimes a small child. Not one of them was Saint. Finally, when Arnie was shifting his weight from foot to foot and Vera growing anxious—had Saint missed the plane or, much worse, had there been a mistake, had he not been released after all?—a lone man, almost the last passenger, stepped through the doors. He was pale, hair too long, wearing badly fitting clothes. He had no cart, no suitcase, just a brown paper package which he held protectively to his chest. He walked with the exaggerated concentration of a sailor on dry land for the first time in years.

Saint had come home.

A difficult week followed, Saint in turn bewildered, truculent, suspicious, or eerily docile, as when he allowed Arnie to take him to the dentist to have his broken teeth capped, then to a men's store on Melrose Avenue to choose new clothes. He had allowed Arnie to make all the decisions there, obediently moving his body around and lifting his arms for measurements, gazing blankly into mirrors as though he didn't recognize the person wearing all the new shirts, jackets, sweaters, and slacks.

Arnie said anxiously, "You probably have post-stress syndrome, like hostages and combat veterans."

"So?"

"So maybe you should see a counselor. Round Mountain is not just a rehab center for addicts anymore, they counsel veterans and kidnap victims. If you spent a month or so there . . ."

Saint said flatly, "Forget it. I'm not exchanging one jail for another one."

"You've got to give him time," Vera said. "He hasn't caught up with himself yet. It's a shock."

By the third day Saint grew compulsively voluble. He talked and talked, the words tumbling over themselves in an endless, aimless stream, his voice harsher and more husky than Arnie remembered.

When Arnie asked about the new voice, Saint was evasive. "I had trouble with my throat."

"What kind of trouble? You were sick?"

Saint shrugged and walked out onto the terrace.

"Don't ask him about it," Vera advised. "They tortured him to get the confession. His throat was damaged."

"They *what?*" Arnie's voice rose in a thin scream of distress. "They——"

Vera glanced at the open door. "Hush."

"But . . . Oh, God, Vera. That's the worst . . . *Jesus!* I can't stand it. I . . ." And then in an almost hostile voice: "How do you know? How come he talks to you and not to me?"

Vera shrugged. "I just happened to be there. Torture's a fact of life in Santa Paula. One of those things."

Arnie parodied, "Just one of those things . . . God, Vera, that makes me sick, that Saint . . ."

"Arnie, believe me, it's better to leave it alone."

Arnie said vehemently, "He needs to share it, to get it all out. It'll help him."

"He will when he's ready," Vera said sharply. "Don't press him."

Saint disliked low ceilings, closed doors, and crowds.

He insisted on sleeping on a futon on the terrrace, although he actually slept very little, spending much of the night padding barefoot around the apartment staring at the different views from each window.

He became anxious in the street amid rushing traffic and all the people, all hurrying from somewhere to somewhere else, and after the shopping trip to Melrose he refused to go anywhere with Arnie again, even in the limo with the tinted windows. Arnie attracted too much unwelcome attention.

To the obvious disappointment of Arnie, who had so looked forward to watching Saint enjoy the tempting menu of the Italian restaurant downstairs, he far preferred to go to McDonald's with Vera, where they would eat Big Macs and fries and slather everything with mustard and catsup.

Saint, who had eaten very well in prison, thanks to Gallegos, had in fact developed a yearning for junk food. "I'd dream about pizza," he announced on his third day in his new, gravelly voice, "and hot dogs, and hamburgers with everything on 'em . . . and there's no way *you* can go to McDonald's," Saint told Arnie patiently. "You'd cause a riot." Although that wasn't all of it. He found it more comfortable to be with Vera, who talked to him like a normal person and not a fragile convalescent just returned from a sanatorium, and he also felt pleasantly invisible in her company, realizing for the first time how few people actually look at a fat woman.

Arnie grumbled, "McDonald's, for God's sake."

"I like it. You can sit outside. And you can get away quickly too, if you want."

"But you're *safe*. You're in California now."

"Sure," Saint would reply, "I know that." But he didn't sound convinced.

By the end of the week, "What he really needs," Vera said pragmatically, "is some peace and quiet. Out of the city."

Which was when Arnie thought of his new house at Lake Tahoe.

Ever since that summer of recovery, alone with Saint, Lake Tahoe had seemed like a refuge to him, and he had bought the house a year ago, a haven to which he was able to escape all too seldom, a place of wind and sky and water and solitude. Saint would mend quickly there.

He chided himself: Why in the world didn't I think of it before?

They took the boat out on the first day.

Saint drove. He cut the engine two miles from shore and announced, "I'm going for a swim."

Arnie looked dubious. "It's awful cold."

"I don't care. I haven't been able to swim for over two years." Saint stripped off his shirt and jeans and poised, toes clenched for balance, over the side of the boat. He sprang, cut the water cleanly, then struck out and away.

However, after such long incarceration in the tropics, his blood was thin and his body untuned and humiliatingly weak. He foundered within a hundred yards. Arnie nosed the boat carefully toward him while Vera put out the swim ladder. "You must take care," she chided as Arnie dragged him bodily out of the water and Saint collapsed panting and shivering in the bottom of the boat. "You're in terrible shape. You have to work up to this stuff."

Saint hunched on the seat, wearing the oiled wool fisherman's sweater Arnie had bought him on Melrose. He defiantly pulled the sleeves up to his elbows. His wrists and forearms looked very white. "Vera," he said between the chattering of his teeth, "don't be such a goddamn mother hen."

The days passed uneventfully.

Saint spent most of the time walking the trails or driving the boat at full speed up and down the lake.

On the seventh afternoon he lay in the boat out on the water and watched the thunderheads piling up around him. They had swelling blue-black bellies and soared thousands of feet into anvil-shaped towers.

Arnie hadn't wanted him to take the boat out by himself, but Saint had been determined. "I'll be fine."

"Promise me you won't swim. Not alone. And the weather doesn't look good."

Arnie and Vera had stood on the dock watching after him as though he were about to circumnavigate the globe single-handed.

Saint had waved a cheery good-bye, cast off the line, and puttered gently away, then, further out, had opened up the throttle and roared across the water through curtains of spray. He drove in a wide loop past Tahoe City, Homewood, then right across the lake to the Nevada shore, where he cut the engine and floated idly a mile off Sand Harbor Cove.

Here, staring up at the boiling sky, feeling the rising wind on his skin, listening to the sullen mutterings of the thunder rolling around him and to the energetic slap-slap of the waves against the hull of the boat, now at last was the moment he had waited for for so long; he was free to think about J.B. Back in Los Angeles, Arnie had no sooner suggested coming up here than clearly he had remembered Saint had met Fletcher at Lake Tahoe. Both embarrassed and contrite, he had mumbled, "Well, maybe it's not such a good idea after all."

"Why not?"

"It might be kind of painful for you. It was dumb of me not to think . . ."

Saint had been genuinely surprised. "That's okay, Arn." For Fletcher was over for him. And Tahoe had always, in his mind, been J.B.'s lake anyway, to which one day he would bring her again. That long-ago scene in San Francisco seemed so trivial now, and the very intensity of her rage and her desire to hurt surely indicated that she still cared.

Now, painstakingly, Saint recreated their long-ago picnic at Sand Harbor Cove. A brown-and-white-striped blanket barred with shadows from the tree branches above. Beside the blanket a magazine, sandwich wrappings, and their Playmate cooler, white with a red lid. Saint closed his eyes tightly and once again he was running across the burning sand toward J.B., who should have been there, sitting under the pine trees waiting for him.

J.B. in her blue bathing suit, drinking a Coke.

But to his frustration, the blanket remained obstinately empty. There was no one there.

The boat rocked crazily beneath him in the sudden steep chop.

The rain was coming now, moving fast up the lake in a solid wall of dark water. Saint lay on his back across the white plastic seats and dangled his bare feet over the side. Immediately overhead, thunder made a long tearing sound that hurt his ears; then the rain swept over him in a solid, cold gush. Saint paid no attention, preoccupied with the unfairness of it, that despite all his efforts he still couldn't summon up J.B.'s face.

In jail, he had told himself it was all for the best. J.B. didn't belong in such a place, not even in dreams.

Now he couldn't bring her back at all.

He felt himself being lifted, then abruptly dropped.

He opened his eyes in involuntary fright. He had actually been asleep, then—had he? He was still afraid to sleep, not trusting this sudden freedom, sure each time he would wake up back in his cell after all.

But now, looking up, he could see rain and clouds and, I'm free, Saint told himself, recalling for the thousandth time that last confused day, Gallegos congratulating him on his powerful friends, "the very best kind," and promising a warm welcome whenever he chose to dine at his restaurant; the prison commandant shaking his hand and pumping his arm with unctuous warmth, as though saying farewell to a very important guest; the admiring glances of the young police officer who escorted him to the waiting helicopter . . .

I'm free, Saint reminded himself. Really and truly free.

He was free because of Victor Diamond. He was under an obligation for the remainder of his life to the unknown man who had saved him— and taken J.B. away from him.

No wonder he couldn't bring her back; she was no longer his even to dream about.

Arnie's house was designed to make full use of the mountainous, rocky terrain. It was cheerful and sunny, of natural woods, slate floors, skylights, and terraces which had been built around half a dozen large Monterey pines; it was like living in a tree house, Arnie said.

The hot tub was on the lowest level, carved directly out of the mountainside and commanding, in front, a dazzling panoramic view of the lake. It was Arnie's pride and joy, bigger than many a swimming pool, with islands formed by rocks too huge to excavate, its tile border a tropical garden of dwarf palms, ferns, and orchids.

Now, past midnight, the air outside was very cold and the tall windows wept with moisture.

Vera had gone to bed long ago.

Saint perched naked on the tiles, wet hair plastered to his scalp, and absently doodled on the glass with his fingertip. Arnie sat quietly on the steps, his legs in the hot water, drinking Seven-Up from a green glass goblet.

Saint sneezed abruptly. I knew it, Arnie thought, he caught a cold, fooling around out there on the lake in the storm. While Saint stared at the dripping black glass and at his trickling pictures, Arnie found himself counting every vertebra on Saint's spine, and each rib, starkly shadowed despite the bounty of Señor Gallegos, then anxiously searching his body for evidence of torture. They had damaged his throat, Vera had said; what else might they have done? Arnie dreaded to think but hated not to know. However, he could see nothing. Saint's body appeared unblemished.

With an impatient movement Saint erased his drawing with his palm and splashed back into the pool. He swam around the rocks and disappeared underwater. Then he was returning, still underwater, his body a rippling pale shape, his long black hair fanning behind him like seaweed.

He pulled himself onto the steps beside Arnie and tossed his hair back with a flurry of droplets.

It was immensely hot and humid now, the windows once again solidly steamed over. They were encased together, thought Arnie, in a bubble of steam.

Saint gave a heavy sigh, propped one elbow on his knee, and sank his chin into his hand.

Arnie watched him cautiously. What was he thinking? How was he feeling? If only he would talk about it all, get things off his chest, allow him, Arnie, to share his trouble and torment. And now, in this hot, almost womblike place, perhaps it was the perfect time.

Arnie moved closer and sat beside Saint hip to hip. He laid a tentative hand on his friend's wet shoulder.

"Saint," Arnie murmured through the steam, "now might be a good time to . . ." He paused, not quite daring to continue.

Saint turned his head. His eyes looked blurred and distant. "To do what?"

"I thought perhaps you might want to . . . Oh," Arnie said, losing his nerve, "forget it."

"Leave him alone," Vera had said. *"He'll tell you when he's ready."* And perhaps she was right after all.

In the meantime, at last he had his friend back, alive and as well as could be expected. That was a lot to be thankful for.

Arnie hugged him close and for a moment or two Saint blindly turned into his arms. Arnie held him with quiet joy and stroked his soaking hair. "It's okay," he murmured, "it's okay. Everything's all right." And then . . .

He lost himself. It was the lateness, his tiredness, the dark and the steam, the heat, the closeness, and the wet slick feel of Saint's skin against his own flesh.

In a daze, Arnie touched Saint's cheek, tucked his fingers under his chin, and raised his face. He kissed Saint gently on the mouth, and before he could stop, not so gently.

It took Saint a moment or two to understand what had happened, to orient himself; perhaps, lost in some inner personal dream, he even thought he was kissing J.B. But the moment passed and then came the recognition and the immediate, inevitable withdrawal.

Saint moved away from Arnie and sat staring at him, wide-eyed with surprise.

Arnie trembled in horror. Oh, Jesus, what had he done? What would

Saint say? What would he do? He waited in helpless dread for the revulsion and the sneers. He knew he couldn't stand it, hearing what Saint would say.

But Saint said nothing. He looked at Arnie very seriously, and for the first time since his release, his face was completely focused and aware. The silence stretched, unbroken and, for Arnie, increasingly unbearable. "Oh, Arnie," Saint said finally, "have I ever been a selfish son of a bitch."

Arnie, wretched, stared between his knees at his barely visible feet. He thought: I blew it. Forever. What we had going between us is lost, broken, it'll never be the same again, and it's all my fault.

He clasped his hands in his lap so Saint couldn't see that shameful burgeoning erection. He thought he would be sick.

Beside him, he heard Saint sneeze again.

Then, in the now familiar rasping voice, "Oh, Arnie," Saint said, "I'm so godawful sorry."

Chapter

19

J.B. woke in the dark beside a strange man.

Panic. Her heart hammered in her chest.

Who am I?

Where am I?

Who is *that*?

Then the terror subsided and her pulse slowed to near-normal as she began to remember.

I'm Starfire.

I'm at the Casa Los Suspiros in Puerto Vallarta, Mexico.

I'm with Victor Diamond. He's a powerful man with powerful friends—but I'm more powerful still because *I* was the one to make it all happen.

Starfire reviewed the past week, in which everything had worked out so well, with satisfaction.

First, the flight to Mexico City in Diamond's jet, a gleaming white bird, so graceful, everything white inside, attendants in white uniforms with navy-blue insignia supplying her with cocktails, glossy magazines, and a gourmet lunch, while Diamond had supplied her with a fire-opal pendant on a gold chain and hung it around her neck. "This is your stone. Never take it off."

Next a limousine ride—herself and Diamond in the backseat, an armed bodyguard beside the driver—to the penthouse suite at El Presidente Chapultepec, where the very air, she thought fancifully, reverberated with power.

The next day, wearing her opal and the new silver-blue dress Diamond had bought for her that morning at a designer boutique in the Zona Rosa, they lunched at the San Angel Inn with a group of well-dressed middle-aged men who all spoke good English and wore a lot of gold jewelry. One was a government minister, another a state governor, the third the chief of federal police, and at the end of lunch Starfire learned she had been totally successful in her mission: a helicopter had been sent that very afternoon to fly Saint to the capital, from where he would at once connect with a plane for Los Angeles. "He'll be there in an hour or two," Diamond said. "I hope you are pleased."

The following day they left for Puerto Vallarta. It was combined business and pleasure, for there was a village somewhere down the coast which Diamond wanted to check out as a possible location. Perhaps, he suggested, for *Starfire: The Movie.*

In the meantime they were staying at the Casa Los Suspiros, house of sighs, high on a hill above the yellow-silted waters of the Rio Cuale. It was a magical house of irregular spaces where arches opened unexpectedly onto hidden courtyards filled with flowers; where water gushed into a pool on the lowest patio through the mouth of a stone gargoyle; where tiny caged birds sang in cascades of sweet jagged notes like breaking glass.

It had rained this afternoon and evening, ending with a spectacular thunderstorm. As they climbed the front steps in the rain, white lightning playing around them and the thunder crashing over their heads, music, even louder than the storm, had rolled majestically from the house next door.

Diamond had laughed. "*The Ride of the Valkyries,* how appropriate. I can see you flying through space."

Then she woke up completely and remembered she wasn't Starfire. She was only J.B., who had said, "I thought it was from *Apocalypse Now,*" and listened to Diamond explaining with a patient smile, "It was used in *Apocalypse Now* for the helicopter scene. The music was written over a hundred years ago in Germany by Richard Wagner. It's from an opera called *Die Walküre.*"

She had at once felt very ignorant and vulnerable. She had the oddest feeling that Starfire would have known about Richard Wagner—then reminded herself impatiently: Come on, knock it off, you're Jo-Beth Feeney from Corsica, Texas, who never made it through twelfth grade, and don't you forget it. . . .

Tonight, still raining, the narrow cobbled street outside the house a raging torrent of muddy water, they stayed home rather than go out. Diamond said, "Let's talk about you now. Tell me about yourself. It's time."

So, drinking tequila in the mellow light of a hurricane lantern, J.B. told him the story of her life, but an edited version, instinctively omitting that six-month nightmare in New York.

Starfire would never have allowed Angelo to lie to her, trick her, and use her. She would never have posed for a sleazy calendar or passed a humiliating half-hour of nude cheerleading for Coach.

Now the bus ride from Amarillo to New York blended almost seamlessly into the cross-country ride with Saint, and if Diamond suspected there might be more, he didn't ask.

Later, eating the salad and the dish of chicken and rice which the maid had prepared and left for them hot in the oven, Diamond asked, "And you never dreamed of being a movie star?"

J.B. shook her head. "Not me. That was Melody's dream, she was much prettier; she won beauty contests."

"Why did you become a model?"

"I didn't know what else to do to make a lot of money fast."

"You want to be rich?" He was gently amused.

Under that quizzical gaze she found it impossible not to spill her guts, to tell him all about Momma and Melody Rose and their difficulties. "Not just for me. For them."

Diamond asked, "Are you supporting them now?"

"Sure. Who else is there?"

"Well," Diamond suggested tentatively, "there's Floyd."

J.B.'s lips thinned in hatred and for a microsecond saw that empurpled face, the blood, the nametag on the blue overalls reading "FLOYD" and rejected the image at once. "No way. He's out of our lives forever. Thank God."

Diamond smiled wryly. "Don't count on it. People have a way of coming back into your life when you least expect it."

* * *

Around nine o'clock the electricity went off; shortly afterward the wind gusted so violently through the house the hurricane lamp blew off the table and smashed on the tile floor.

"We might as well go to bed," Diamond said.

He made love to her again in their wide bed shrouded in mosquito netting so it was like a cave, while the lightning flickered over the hills beyond the river.

He took her by the shoulders and gently turned her onto her face. She felt the pressure of his knees against her hips, the motion of his hands as they twisted her long hair and drew it away from her neck. Then his lips on the nape of her neck and the delicate tracery of his tongue down her spine. He shifted his body, slid his hand between her legs, and raised her. His fingers were expert and deliberate and he already knew her body so well. "Exquisite," Diamond whispered. "Like satin."

He had never yet penetrated her body. "You can't see what happens," Diamond would explain in a whisper. "I want to see it all, I want to watch us both come . . ."

He liked her to lick the shaft of his penis in small fluttery movements of her tongue. He would watch her watch the long, rhythmic motions of his final ejaculation, and then, drowsily sated, he would twine her long hair around her nipples.

But those times were for the hours of late afternoon and early evening, the light changing from storm dark to the lemon and purple of sunset, with Diamond exclaiming at the colors, the lights, and the shadows. Now it was dark and, between dreams, they were locked together in their small private world under mesh and, "Like satin," Diamond repeated, his fingertips reading the textures of her body in the dark.

Afterward J.B. lay very still, feeling the wetness on her thighs. Diamond's arm lay across her body, his hand loosely cupped over her hip. In her mind she watched herself, a dazzling sight, visiting expensive boutiques with Diamond in Mexico City and now in Puerto Vallarta, buying jewelry, designer clothes, hand-tooled leather purses and shoes. She thought of private planes, luxury hotels, and servants waiting on her hand and foot. What am I doing? she wondered uneasily. What am I? The obvious reply was uncomfortable, she chided herself scornfully: Just an upscale version of Melody Rose, that's what.

But that wasn't true. She wouldn't let it be true.

She was Starfire now, and to Starfire came the satisfying thought: Victor Diamond is mine now, he'll do what I say, and soon I'll have all the independence and power I can use.

She ignored J.B.'s voice, which warned: Get out now, while you still can.

But perhaps she knew that it was already too late.

Vera lay in the bathtub in her apartment on Telegraph Hill, shaving her legs.

Saint was just the other side of the door, in the room where he had once worked for so many hours, pacing as restlessly as a caged panther. "There's too much goddamn stuff in this room. Can't you get a bigger place? How can you live like this? I'll never be able to work in here again. It'll drive me crazy." He had carried his beer over to the window where at least he could watch the action at the biker bar.

It seemed particularly noisy out there tonight; riders roared in and out, the engine sounds magnified by the close-set walls. People yelled and shrieked; amplified music boomed. "How can you stand the racket?" Saint asked irritably.

Vera shrugged. "I don't care. It's company."

Methodically she soaped her right leg and began to shave the fuzz from knee to ankle, and wondered yet again what had happened last night between Saint and Arnie.

It had been such an ordinary, homey evening. They had eaten a pizza for dinner, then played Scrabble on the rug in front of the fireplace. Saint had won easily, of course, and been childishly pleased.

Vera had then gone to bed. She had dimly heard Arnie and Saint's voices for a while in the kitchen; there had been the soft thunk of the refrigerator door closing. Then silence. She slept, to wake suddenly sometime later, she had no idea how much later, knowing someone was in her room standing beside her bed. A voice whispered through the darkness, "Vera? Are you awake?"

She struggled up onto one elbow and reached for the light switch. "What is it, what's the matter?"

"I've done something . . ." Saint sounded confused and distressed. "I've done a terrible thing." He caught her by the arm. "Please don't turn the light on."

Vera whispered back, "*What* have you done?"

"It happened so fast. I'd never guessed. I didn't think."

She waited for him to explain. She prompted, "Saint?" but he didn't respond, just a small sound like a sigh. Then he said, "It's no good. Sorry I woke you. Go back to sleep." And he had put a hand on her head and pushed her down into bed again. She heard the click of her closing door and he was gone.

In the morning she wondered whether she had dreamed it.

But something had happened, all right. Saint and Arnie avoided each other's eyes and were curiously polite and formal with each other.

Saint said, "Arn, I need to talk with you."

Arnie replied, "There's no need. There's nothing to say."

"But—"

"Drop it. Okay?"

A long silence. "I think I'd better leave, then," Saint said.

And Arnie: "Where will you go?"

Vera had glanced from one tense face to the other. "You'd better come to San Francisco with me."

Arnie drove them to Reno to catch the plane. He dropped them off outside the terminal, where he hugged Vera and kissed her on the cheek. He didn't touch Saint, not even to shake his hand. Saint, looking wretched, tucked his hand back in his pocket.

That had been this morning. This afternoon Saint had determinedly begun to pick up the torn threads of his life. He talked with a real-estate agent; he had to have a place of his own to live in. He had called his lawyer, his business manager, Aunt Gloria, and a travel agent. He was going to New York, he said. He barely spoke a word to Vera all day. Apart from mailing the finished screenplay to Diamond's office at Omega, he hadn't mentioned *Starfire*. He was drinking too much.

"What the bloody hell's going on?" Vera said aloud, and climbed heavily out of the tub. She toweled herself dry and marched into the living room, a solid, resolute shape in navy terry cloth. "You can't go on like this. You're going to have to talk."

Saint was a dark silhouette against the flashing pink neon outside the window. He asked without turning, "Do you think there's a curse on me, Vera?"

"No," Vera said flatly. "You've had some bad things happen to you. But it's all over now."

"That's not what I meant." Saint's head tipped back as he drank. She saw a pink neon flash on metal. "Listen, can you tell me why I love the wrong people and the wrong people love me?"

Vera said firmly, "Love's never wrong. How can it be?"

Saint crunched the empty beer can in his fist. "It is when it hurts." He muttered, "I hurt people, Vera. I don't mean to, but I can't seem to help it. I hurt Arnie. I hurt J.B. And Fletcher . . ."

Vera stood in front of him, hands on her solid hips. "You're being morbid. Come on, Saint. You did *not* hurt Fletcher. What that girl did to you . . ."

"You don't know the whole story, and I'm not about to tell you. Not tonight. The thing is, I never loved her. I married her to do damage. If she hadn't been there at the wrong time, maybe things would've been different, but she was, and I hurt her and never loved her and she knew it. She isn't dumb. She's pathetic, Vera. She's a terrible mess. She likes to play games—"

"Stop it, Saint—"

"They were fairly harmless games to start with, but now she likes to fool around with knives and guns, she gets involved with dangerous people, she's destructive as hell, and she'll probably kill herself or get killed, and I could have stopped it once. I could have got help for her. I didn't. I—"

"Saint, please!"

"—made her worse by not caring. And now it's Arnie. Jesus, Vera, I feel like such a shit. He's so vulnerable. He—"

"Hush. Listen, Arnie will be okay. He's much stronger than you think."

"You don't know what happened."

"I can guess. I know how he feels about you, he told me."

"I don't know what to do."

"There's nothing you can do, not the way Arnie wants, except be his friend. He needs friends." Vera held her arms out for him. "So do you."

Saint half-fell against her, so that she staggered; then she held him very tightly. "It's all right," Vera said. "It'll be okay."

"When I was in jail," Saint said suddenly, "I'd think of you. I never dreamed about J.B., but I'd dream about you. You were always my friend. You'd be wearing my mother's wig, telling me it'd all work out, it'd be all right."

"Well, then"—Vera stroked his hair, feeling very old and very motherly—"let me make it happen." She took his hand. "Come to bed. You're exhausted. You'll feel better in the morning."

Vera woke very late. By the position of the sunlight on the wall, it was past noon.

She turned and stretched luxuriously. She was alone in the bed. Well, that was to be expected, wasn't it?

She closed her eyes. She wasn't yet ready for the day. She wanted to hold on to her waking dream, in which she relived her night with Saint all over again, every minute, every second.

It had not happened the way she supposed a first sexual experience should; she had not exactly been swept off her feet and driven to distraction with ardent lovemaking.

Saint had staggered to her room on unsteady feet, had collapsed heavily across the bed, and passed out.

After a while, one arm numb, she had struggled to shove his body to one side so there'd be room for her as well. Saint had woken up, and then . . . Vera couldn't help it—she giggled. It had been the least romantic act she could have imagined, the two of them struggling together in the narrow little bed, Saint complaining and sliding around and swearing, and then the locked, awkward positioning, sharp plunging, brief pain, quickly over. Afterward he lay in her arms, head pillowed on her breasts, and slept, exhaustedly inert. Later, long past two o'clock—because the flashing neon was extinguished and the alley was silent save for the gruesome sounds of marauding cats in the backyard—she had felt him stir, then wake. She opened her eyes and found him gazing at her, although it was too dark to read his expression.

He said nothing, but stroked the soft hair back from her forehead and kissed her eyes, then her lips. He still didn't speak while kissing her breasts and then gently entering her body for the second time, and throughout, his hands never stopped touching and caressing and loving her. This time it was easy and their bodies moved as though dancing together. In the darkness, with Saint, Vera felt slim and graceful and beautiful.

Afterward he kissed her again, kissed her closed eyelids, whispered, "Thank you, Vera," and fell asleep like a stone. This time he didn't move until long after dawn, when she had vaguely felt him leave the bed. A little later she had heard a door closing, but was too exhausted to stir.

Now, reluctantly, she opened her eyes.

He would be gone. She knew that.

Still, she dared to hope—for all of fifty seconds, which was the time it took to get out of bed, check the empty living room, kitchen, and bathroom.

In the middle of her drawing board lay a note.

As she picked it up, the phone rang.

Vera said, "Hello?"

The note began, *"Darling Vera . . ."*

A male voice asked, "Is Ms. Brown there, please? This is Victor Diamond."

"There aren't the right words which can thank you for last night, so I'm not even going to try except tell you I don't know what I'd have done without you. You're a real friend, in the best sense of the word."

"Oh." For a moment she absolutely could not recall who Victor Diamond was. Then: "Oh! Yes."

"Forgive me for running out on you, but I'm not the greatest company right now and obviously must get myself together before I burden you or anybody else. I'll call you as soon as I have some plans. Or sooner."

"I'm sorry I haven't been in touch before now, but I've been in Mexico."

"Yes . . . yes, I know."

"My lawyer will be mailing you the necessary documents regarding *Starfire*. You'll want to have your own lawyer look them over. I'm sure you'll find the terms more than satisfactory . . ."

Goodness, he came right down to business, didn't he? Vera said coolly, "I'm sure I will, Mr. Diamond."

"I'm looking forward to meeting you. We need to get together as soon as possible, you, John Saint, and I. Incidentally, I'm trying to reach him. I was told he's with you."

"He was, but . . . he left. . . ."

"You mean an awful lot to me, Vera . . ."

"I'll tell him you called. I'm sure he'll be in touch soon."

She hung up and sat staring at the private phone numbers Diamond had given her, to reach him directly either at the studio or at his home in Malibu. "Time is of the essence," Diamond had said.

Well, she thought weakly. Well! She had just spoken with the great Victor Diamond himself, back from Mexico with J.B.

"There aren't the right words which can thank you . . ."

Dreamily she opened her sketchbook, wondering when Saint would call.

She drew for half an hour, astounded at her new liberation, being able to draw something like this. Then she put her pen down and touched herself happily between the legs, from whence came, every so often, a pleasurable pang of discomfort, pleasurable because it was a reminder that, yes, it had really happened, she had a lover, she was a real woman at last.

She couldn't wait for them to do it all over again. She wondered if she was a nymphomaniac, wanting it so much.

Saint, she told the drawing, I love you. Please call soon.

She didn't leave the apartment all day, waiting.

The doorbell finally rang at nine o'clock in the evening, when Vera had just given up hope.

She was washing her hair. In case he came back after all, she wanted to have clean, sweet-smelling hair.

The bell rang again.

It was him; it had to be him. Who else would show up so late? "Thank you, thank you, God," Vera gasped, "but I wish you'd had him come before I got all lathered up."

Then she thought: What the hell? Who cares? She leapt out of the tub and threw her robe over her wet, soapy body, heart pounding inside her ribs like a hammer.

She threw open the door.

The man waiting impatiently outside wasn't Saint after all.

"Oh." Vera stared at him blankly and clutched her damp robe across her breasts. "Oh. It's you."

"Take care you don't overdo the welcome," said Dr. Donald Wheeler.

*   *   *

He was looking quite handsome in a well-cut pair of beige twill slacks, a navy blazer, a paisley ascot around his neck. His face was sunburned and his freckles stood out across his face. His terra-cotta eyes were cautiously amused.

Vera said weakly, "What a surprise."

"Obviously."

"Do come in." She led him into her cluttered living room. "I'm afraid it's a terrible mess. I've been away, you see. If I'd known you were coming, I'd have——"

"Gone out," said Donald, "which was why I didn't call. You've been avoiding me." He moved purposefully toward her and for an instant touched her cheek. His fingers felt cool on her hot skin.

"No! Of course not. I mean . . ." Vera clutched at her robe again and took an involuntary step backward. She managed, "I . . . uh . . . would you like some coffee? I'll just go and . . . Excuse me a sec . . . Or a drink? I think I have some wine . . ." She couldn't bear him to touch her, not now, not after Saint. She thought with feverish guilt: This is Donald Wheeler, my best friend in the whole world, who's done everything for me, who made me see myself as I really am, and I can't stand it if he touches me.

She rushed into the kitchen. Behind her Donald said, "No wine. I've been at a sales dinner in town and I'm driving back to Saint Helena tonight. Just coffee. Who did you think I was, anyway?"

She pretended she didn't hear him and took rather a long time with the coffee, making ostentatious clatter with cups and spoons.

When she came back, she found him leaning over her worktable peering at the new *Starfire* strips. "You're getting better and better. In fact, pretty damn good."

He made no attempt to touch her again. The relief was intense. She sighed, "Thank you." And, "Sugar?"

"Sure. Two spoons." He looked up at her and his eyes crinkled with laughter. "You look like Madame de Pompadour after a bad day at the beauty shop. Shouldn't you go and rinse your hair?"

Returning from the bathroom, hair clean and damp and slicked back, she found him sitting at her drafting table examining her sketchbook.

"It's been a long time. We have a lot to catch up with. I thought I'd get a head start, reading your diary."

Vera said, "I told you most things in my letters." She offered the pot. "More coffee?"

"But I'm not exactly up-to-date with recent developments. A lot's been going on. And now Saint's out of jail."

"Yes. Safe and sound."

"The master plan worked."

"Victor Diamond pulled strings. He's a movie producer."

"And wheeler-dealer." Donald said dryly, "I've heard of him. So have most people, I'd guess. But I doubt he does anything for nothing."

"No. Well . . ." Vera explained about Arnie's idea for a *Starfire* movie, and how he'd sold the idea to Diamond. How Saint had written the screenplay while in jail.

Donald prompted, "And . . . ?"

"And what?"

"What's the catch?"

"There's no catch. Except Victor Diamond is now the senior partner of Starfire Productions, and I sold him the rights to the Starfire character. But there was no way around that, really, if we wanted Saint freed . . . and he's paying me a lot of money."

"That's quite a hefty 'except.' "

"We had to get Saint out of jail."

He gave her a shrewd glance from under thick red brows. "Of course. Well, congratulations. I guess."

"Thank you." And Vera urged, before he could say anything else about Saint, Diamond, and *Starfire*, "Now tell me about you. How does it feel, being home for good?"

He followed her lead, to her great relief. "Even better than I expected. I'll be practicing family medicine at a clinic in Saint Helena, and am I ever grateful to be out from under the British National Health system, though the experience was useful. Yes, it feels just fine being home, especially this time of year. I even made it in time for the fall crush."

"The . . ."

"When we crush the grapes. Saturday after next is our annual cere-monial grape stomp."

At Vera's blank expression: "A big bash to celebrate the harvest.

Everyone gets to tread the grapes with their bare feet and pretend they're Italian peasants. That's one reason I stopped by, to ask you to come. To *demand* that you come."

"I should be useful. I can stomp enough for ten."

Donald nodded. "That's an unexpected bonus."

Vera asked shyly, "Are you shocked at how I look?"

"I'm never shocked."

"Not even surprised?"

"Not really. You've been unhappy. Perhaps I can do something about that."

She didn't answer. Donald glanced at her flushed cheeks, set his coffee cup down, and picked up her sketchbook again. He began to turn pages. "It's all right, Vera. I'm not totally stupid. Now, tell me about these people. Who's this?"

"Arnie Blaize"—leaning on his parapet in Beverly Hills, gazing into the murky sunset—

"Of course, I should have known." He turned a page. "And Starfire."

"Well," Vera said, "no. It's J.B., actually"—her eyes, widened in shock, staring out of a mirror lined with light bulbs.

"You don't say!" Donald peered at the picture. "But she really *is* Starfire. He flipped the page. "And this, of course, is Saint."

"Yes." There was Saint, wearing two days' growth of beard and a baseball cap, hunched over his Big Mac.

Next, Arnie up at Tahoe. He stood behind a seated figure, holding a towel. The figure was Saint, of course, but all that was visible was a line of naked shoulder and arm.

Then Saint again, head bent in concentration, cross-legged on the floor, surrounded by scattered manuscript pages and three-by-five index cards. "Working on the script," Vera explained.

"Well, I guess you didn't need to tell me who they are after all," Donald said.

He turned to the last page, and Vera caught her breath in dismay and grabbed for the book, but it was too late.

There was Saint yet again, as she had drawn him just this morning.

She had seen him only as a pale blurred shape in the darkness, but her hands had read his body faultlessly. Now, recalled in absolute detail, he knelt, sinewy thighs braced as though ready to spring, leaning his weight on his hands. He gazed out of the picture vibrantly alive, his eyes intent, mouth a determined line, his penis rigidly erect, just as it had been then, about to plunge into the body.

"Well," Donald said in neutral voice, "you certainly have a way with anatomy, Vera."

She snatched at the book. She wanted to die. Why hadn't she torn that picture out? Why had she even drawn it in the first place? What had she been thinking of? It was a shockingly revealing drawing, intensely personal. Nobody should see it, particularly not Donald.

Thankfully, at that moment, there was a commotion in the alley and a sudden squall of sound; of running feet, curses, and high-pitched screams.

Donald turned away and peered through the window. A moment later he announced in a perfectly normal voice, "A girl wearing a bra made of feathers has just poured her beer over another girl's head. You don't see that kind of thing in Orpington. I've been away much too long."

He stood watching at the window for several minutes. She couldn't see his face. When the furor had died down, he turned to face her. "Listen, Vera. You don't have to tell me anything. It's always been Saint, hasn't it? Don't forget, I've known you since you were fifteen."

"I . . . I'm sorry . . ."

"Well, don't be. I'm a grown-up, you know. Now, pay attention. I've been thinking. I've got a proposition."

And then, to her utmost surprise, he suggested she call Victor Diamond and offer the Wheeler property as the location for their first informal get-together. "It's not a bad idea, when you think about it. It's bound to be a difficult meeting, and it might help, being on neutral ground. Tell him to come to the grape stomp."

She stared at him. "But why? Why are you doing this?"

"It'll get us some good publicity. Why not?" Then, more seriously: "I feel I have to see this thing through." Finally, with a rueful grin: "And to be honest, I'm consumed with curiosity. I want to meet Starfire in the flesh."

Chapter

20

The air trembled with heat above the barbecue pit, where a gang of sweating cooks basted the carcasses of two lambs turning slowly on spits, but it was cooler in the shade of the oak trees, where most of the guests had gathered and where Vera sat at a picnic table, sketchbook open on her lap, compulsively drawing.

At a nearby table upon which rows of glasses and bottles were arrayed, two men poured wine. Their identical purple T-shirts bore the entwined vine and oak leaf of the Oak Crest Winery logo. One man, in his mid-thirties, black-haired, was John Bardelucci, wine master of Oak Crest. He poured sparingly, with dedication: "This is our eighty-six chardonnay . . . our eighty-two cabernet—a fine, velvety flavor, we're very proud of it." The other man, whose red hair glowed in the shafts of sunlight, poured more generously with less ceremony. "This is our eighty-three zinfandel—bloody good stuff." This was John's first cousin, Donald, the doctor, just returned from England.

On the graveled driveway which led to the winery a large metal tank, one of the gondolas used for the transportation of the fruit, had been loaded with fresh-picked ruby-colored zinfandel grapes and surrounded with straw bales. Close to twenty people had climbed onto the bales and into the gondola, where they now crushed the grapes with their bare feet to the lively tunes of the Bill Sharp Country Trio, three whiskery old men in overalls and plaid shirts playing two fiddles and a banjo.

From where she sat, Vera could see the dancers only from the chest up, and the children, offspring of the Mexican winery workers, as mere bobbing black heads. She had already taken a turn and found, even though she bragged she could stomp for ten, that it was unexpectedly hard work lifting the knees up so high, then stomping down into the thick morass of fruit, where the bees buzzed and the huge bunches of grapes slid with rubbery smoothness up to her thighs.

She had waited resignedly for Donald to make some rude remark about her bulk and her lack of staying power, but when she returned sweating to the picnic area he just laughed—"Tougher than you thought, huh?"—and went on pouring. He was probably being kind because he felt sorry for her. He would be remembering that revealing drawing of Saint and would of course be noticing that Saint was avoiding her. She felt humiliated and miserable. She didn't understand what had gone wrong. But still, Vera reminded herself, there was always the drive home. Perhaps then, on the road alone driving through the dusk together, then perhaps Saint would tell her that, after all, he'd meant every word he'd said in his note.

"You mean an awful lot to me, Vera. I'll call you as soon as I have some plans. Or sooner."

She had believed him; but he never did call, and each successive morning had arrived with diminishing hope and a sinking heart.

She had reminded herself he was in New York.

That he was incredibly busy.

But it wasn't good enough, and when he finally called, she learned he'd been back in the Bay Area for two days already.

His first words were an accusation. "You sold *Starfire*." He had already talked with Diamond, then. "Why didn't you tell me?"

"I wanted to wait until I thought you—"

"How could you do something like that?"

Vera couldn't believe her ears. She'd done it all for *him*. She said stiffly, "I'm entitled to sell if I want to."

"I don't like it, Vera."

"Then you'd better. If I hadn't sold, you'd still be in Santa Paula."

"So where does that leave *us*?"

"Nothing has to change."

"You shouldn't have done it. *Starfire's* yours. Ours."

237

She wanted to say: No, it isn't. Not anymore. But she didn't know how she'd make him understand. He'd been gone two long years.

During the whole conversation, he never mentioned their night together. He was all business and indignation.

He didn't even come over to see her. There wasn't a whole lot to discuss, he said, that they couldn't talk about on the ride up to Napa for the grape stomp. Well, at least he'd be giving her a ride. That was something.

They talked business until they turned off the highway onto the Silverado Trail. Then Saint told Vera about the house he was thinking of leasing at Seadrift, an ocean community twenty miles up the coast off Route 1. "You'll have to come and see it, Vera." The casualness of the invitation hurt almost more than anything, as though she were merely some distant acquaintance.

Say something, Vera begged mentally; please say something about that night, even if I don't want to hear it . . . don't act like it never happened at all.

Toward the end of the journey, on the winding road beside a dry creek through the hills, he grew preoccupied and progressively more silent, and suddenly Vera understood everything. *"You're a real friend, in the best sense of the word."* He'd said that in his letter too. I'm no more than his fat old pal, she guessed, a convenient shoulder to cry on, who probably no longer even exists for him, because in an hour, maybe less, he'll see J.B. again for the first time in two years . . . he'll fall in love all over again, how could he possibly not, someone as . . . as *obscenely* beautiful as that, and after all, it was J.B. really who got him out of jail; it was J.B. who fascinated Victor Diamond. . . .

Arriving, already emotionally distraught, she wasn't ready for her confrontation with Diamond. However, as if sensing her distress, he was low-keyed and pleasant and full of praise for her work. "It's a pleasure to be associated with someone with such talent. And a project like this is quite a new experience for me, Ms. Brown."

They sat together on a bench while he led her through the sales agreement clause by clause. Vera nodded and smiled, the legal boilerplate swimming in front of her eyes, while behind her she could hear J.B.

saying, "I want to talk with you, Saint—there's something I have to tell you. Can you walk with me a minute?" And then, a moment later, there they went, Saint and J.B., their bodies moving in step with unconsciously remembered ease, until they stopped under the oak trees, out of hearing range but not out of sight. Vera saw J.B. rest her hands on Saint's shoulders and Saint lean forward and kiss her on the forehead. She knew Diamond was watching too, although apparently his eyes never left the document or her own face.

She answered his questions mechanically, for the agreement itself seemed a mere formality now. In any case, it appeared to be perfectly fine and aboveboard, the terms were generous, and by almost anybody else's standards, Vera supposed, she had pulled off quite a coup. But she didn't care anymore. She just didn't care.

She had to force her attention back to Victor Diamond and the document. His face was close to hers, such a striking face, and so sincere of expression. She knew she should feel grateful for his intervention, flattered by his praise, and fascinated by his personality—so how was it that she felt none of these things?

Vera shifted in her seat, instinctively putting space between them, which was when she realized she found him physically repellent and that she neither liked nor trusted him.

Well, was it surprising? How could she like someone who demanded *Starfire* as a condition of Saint's freedom? She also guessed that his praise was too calculated and glib, mere flattery to woo an easy mark, and that he used his fine looks and body as an adjunct to his brain, to captivate, then manipulate.

When Saint returned with J.B. and Diamond led her away to stomp grapes, Vera watched after them for some time before thoughtfully taking out her sketchbook.

She drew the aquiline features, the trademark head of thick silver hair, the black eyebrows and brooding, deep-set eyes, but the result, although strikingly handsome, was strangely flawed. It was a reptilian face that stared up at her, the thin lips cruel and mocking, the eyes onyx hard, predatory, and not quite human.

No, she didn't like him. And she knew he knew it.

Despite the heat, she shivered.

*   *   *

All the way up in the car, Saint wished Vera would say something about their night, anything, because he didn't know what to say himself, or how even to begin.

Since his release he'd ridden an emotional roller coaster. There seemed nothing stable to hang on to. While he'd been away, events and lives had moved on without him. Now his own life had shifted gears and changed beyond his control. For a moment he even felt a pang of nostalgia for Santa Paula, which at least had been predictable.

He thought: Vera must think I'm a real shit, just running out like that.

And she'd be right. But the truth was, he'd felt confused, embarrassed, ashamed of himself for taking advantage and imposing, and actually scared to call. He'd hurt J.B., Fletcher, Arnie—now he was afraid he'd hurt Vera too.

What a mess. He knew he must apologize, make sure she understood how crazy and confused he'd felt, and tell her how great she'd been. Which was the truth anyway, wasn't it? It *had* been great. Actually, to his astonishment, another turnaround, it had been wonderful. Who would have believed it? But not knowing how to begin, he said nothing. I'll talk to her on the way home, Saint promised himself; we'll stop somewhere quiet, some nice little inn, have a glass of wine and something to eat. I'll tell her then.

They arrived at the winery. He parked beside a big silver car which would turn out to be Diamond's

There were greetings from the Wheeler mother and son. Handshakes for him, kisses for Vera. He went through it all with mechanical courtesy, because the moment had now arrived about which he'd fantasized for two long years.

Here was J.B.

He couldn't stop staring at her.

She looked . . . otherworldly. There was no other word for it. She wore a brief white linen shift, white sandals, and a silver headband. A fire-opal pendant burned at her breastbone.

"Thank you," he told her rather formally, "for everything," realizing to his shame that he had never thanked Vera for her own sacrifice in selling *Starfire*, only raged at her.

"I'm just glad you're back," J.B. was saying, and kissed his cheek. Then: "Listen, I want to talk to you. Can you walk with me a minute?"

They walked along the path under the trees and he listened to her tell him she was sorry, that he'd taken her by surprise arriving at the apartment like that, she hadn't known what she was saying and she hadn't meant it, any of it; she'd been so mad and felt so threatened, she had said the first thing to come into her head. Words he had dreamed of hearing. He kissed her cool brow and thought of J.B. on the beach at Sand Harbor Cove; on Jake Plank's boat throwing bread crusts to the sea gulls; in the dress he had bought her at I. Magnin, dancing in the house up on the hill—but that had been a different girl entirely, a long time ago. He took her hand and held her slender fingers in his, waiting for the old resonance to strike him, but to his shock, he felt nothing. Nothing at all, and not because she was with Victor Diamond and would never again go to Lake Tahoe with him. Now it didn't seem to matter. He didn't understand. Nothing's the same, Saint thought with dismay. Nothing's the way I expected.

When J.B. and Diamond walked off toward the gondola, he drifted to the tasting table and Donald Wheeler poured him a glass of eighty-six zinfandel. "So tell me, what's your take on the Hollywood big shot?"

"I don't know. He seems okay," Saint said guardedly. At least Diamond wasn't wearing the silk suit, pinkie rings, and gold chains in which he had mentally arrayed him. He went on, "I guess I'm surprised he agreed to come here. I wouldn't have thought it was his scene."

"No," Donald agreed equably, "but I told Vera to insist. She's giving up a lot. The first meeting should be someplace she feels comfortable. And he went for it. Showed at least some class, I thought."

Saint suspected that was a loaded speech, but gave Donald the benefit of the doubt. "It's real good of you to do this."

"My pleasure." Donald gave an oddly twisted smile. "After all, I feel I've known you all for years."

In the gondola, J.B. was prancing happily in an oversize Oak Crest T-shirt and a much-too-big pair of khaki shorts belted tightly around her slender waist.

Saint asked, "Where the hell did she get those clothes?"

Donald answered at once; he was watching J.B. too. "Mother must've

241

found them for her. She couldn't exactly tread grapes in what she had on, could she?"

Diamond returned to the tasting table. He had rinsed the purple stains from his feet and wore Top-Siders without socks. He had stayed miraculously clean.

He nodded pleasantly to Donald, refused more wine for now, and told Saint, "It's time we had a talk, you and I."

They walked together up a trail into the hills among a thick growth of oak and madrona. The festive noises diminished, to fall away altogether as they turned a bend in the road.

Diamond walked like an Indian, taking long limber strides, his feet falling softly in the dust.

It grew very quiet save for insects and the dried oak leaves crackling underfoot; Saint thought it was the very sound of heat.

A quarter-mile further on they came upon a scattering of large moss-grown rocks bordering a ravine half-filled with rusted car bodies and abandoned farm machinery. "It always amazes me how country people are so untidy," Diamond observed distantly. He sat down on a rock and beckoned Saint to join him.

Saint said, "I suppose they have to put it somewhere."

They both stared at the wreckage until, "Yes," Diamond agreed, "you have a point. But we're not here to talk about the Wheelers' disposal problems. We're here to become acquainted. You and I are in business together. I've taken a risk with you. You're going to have to satisfy me it was worth it."

Saint was silent for a moment. "You want me to convince you I'm not a drug dealer?"

"I've heard it from everyone else. I'd like to hear it from you. So take it from the top. Tell me exactly what did happen in Mexico."

And, much to Saint's surprise, he found himself telling Diamond everything, the entire disaster of his marriage to Fletcher, the planted cocaine, his arrest, confession, the parody of his trial, his sojourn in Santa Paula, the relief and the escape in writing the *Starfire* screenplay.

Diamond listened attentively; Saint thought his very silence drew forth more than he'd ever planned to tell.

Finally: "I believe you." And after a moment: "Where's your wife now? What is she doing?"

"I don't know."

"She's unlikely to be happy about your release."

"I suppose not."

"She appears to be a vindictive, unbalanced woman. A very loose cannon."

Saint said, "I'll check up."

"No you won't. You will do nothing. Leave that to me."

Saint turned with surprise. Diamond was watching a lizard crossing a rusty fender below him. It paused in profile, throat pulsing in the heat. He tossed a small pebble; a flick of its tail, and the lizard was gone.

"You'll stay away from her, whatever happens. Keep as low a profile as possible, for your own safety."

Saint shifted uneasily on his rock. It hadn't occurred to him that Fletcher might be angry enough at his release to seek reprisals. He also pitched a pebble down the ravine. It hit metal with a small clang and bounced away. "Do you seriously think she's dangerous?"

"I most seriously do."

"Well . . . okay, then, you're the boss."

"Yes," Diamond agreed. "And you'll let me handle Fletcher."

Then, as if they were working their way down an agenda and the Fletcher item had now been checked off, Diamond said. "Next, Arnie's project. *Right Exit Closed*. It's in preproduction, but I understand there've been setbacks."

Saint nodded. "Major photography should have started by now."

"Financing and distribution problems, I hear."

"You heard right. A backer pulled out unexpectedly, and the distributor didn't like it. The way things are going now, the whole thing might fall through."

"Too bad. It's a good property." Diamond mused, "I'm recommending that Omega take it over. What would you and Arnie Blaize say to that?"

Saint shrugged. "I'd have to talk with Arnie."

"I'd strongly advise you to accept."

"You mean, we don't have much choice?"

"Not really," Diamond said easily, "if you want it in the theaters."

"Then I guess," Saint said, "that we'd say thank you."

So much for *Right Exit Closed.*

Next Diamond said, "I think you should move to Los Angeles as soon as you can."

Saint shook his head. "No, thanks. I don't want to live in L.A. I'm planning to buy a house up the coast."

"I didn't say you couldn't buy it. You can use it on weekends or when I don't need you at Omega."

Saint felt a flash of antagonism. He thought: This man has taken over *Starfire*, and now he's taking over my life too. Who the hell does he think he is?

He sat there listening to the faint crackle of metal expanding in the heat while Diamond, who had apparently taken his silence for consent, was saying, "I've always had a dream, you know, of building the perfect creative team. A group of talented people who work together, know one another's minds, are completely loyal. With a committed group like that, with suitable properties and the right direction, one could work miracles." Then, on an apparent tangent: "I understand Spring Kentfield's your mother."

Saint nodded.

"And your parents are divorced."

"Since six months after I was born."

"I knew Spring Kentfield once. A long time ago. Twenty-five years, I suppose. Then she met your father. If you'll pardon me for saying so, your mother always saw a personal relationship in terms of a career move."

"I suppose so," Saint agreed. Then: *"Oh."* He stared into a tracery of oak leaves, the sunlight bright behind them. Against other trees and another bright sky he saw himself at his own wedding, walking with his mother in her Scarlett O'Hara crinoline.

He had demanded she tell him about his father. "Don't pretend you don't know," he had said—and she had hesitated just half a beat too long. His mouth went dry.

Diamond gave him a measured look, appeared about to say something, then changed his mind except to venture mildly, "We'd best be getting back. That's enough for one day."

*   *   *

J.B. had been dreading this day when she would see Saint again. On the flight up: "I never even wrote to him in jail." She stared broodingly through the window onto the wrinkled brown-and-gray mountain chain below them. "I should have."

"Perhaps. But you didn't. And another page has turned, as they say."

However, meeting Saint again was surprisingly easy. He had clearly forgiven her, and although he was very glad to see her, the elements of tension and unrequited longing were missing. She almost felt comfortable with him.

In her relief, she felt freer than usual to enjoy the day, which, largely free from Diamond's supervision, she did enormously. Just for today she decided to pretend that she wasn't Starfire after all, that she lived at Oak Crest and grew grapes, like the Wheelers.

She loved all of it. The house was just as it should be, rambling and cool, surrounded by wide verandas. Across the well-tended lawns and gardens was the winery itself, also perfect, an eighty-year-old stone building swathed in Virginia creeper, just now turning a mellow range of rust and red, beyond which the vines marched in diminishing geometry off into the distance. "Zinfandel," Donald's mother had told her, "cabernet, pinot noir, and chardonnay," and the lush names of the varietals resonated inside her head like poetry.

J.B. would have loved a tour of the winery to see how it all worked, and to walk out there among the vines. Anna Bardelucci Wheeler would have been delighted to abandon her guests and oblige, but as hostess she had responsibilities. "What a bore," she sighed. "Donald must take you later. Now, take off that silly dress, put on these shorts, and earn your lunch."

J.B. splashed down into the grapes with a shriek of pleasure, to join the group churning slowly clockwise through the fruit and the buzzing yellow jackets. The toe-tapping country music called to her very soul. She danced through the sticky mass as though treading on air. The Mexican children were purple from head to foot, screaming with laughter and flinging handfuls of mashed grapes at each other. A San Francisco society matron in trailing chiffon was stung by a bee and yelled oaths that would have awed a construction crew. A very fat man slipped and fell and was dragged to his feet by a wiry crone in a battered felt hat.

J.B. heard the Oak Crest P.R. woman telling the television cameraman, "Make sure you get good footage of the kids and the celebrities. We could go national with this!"

The sun beat down. The temperature climbed well above ninety. A hot wind was rising, flapping the tablecloths, sending small avalanches of paper napkins and Styrofoam cups rolling across the picnic area. The group in the gondola began to thin out. Diamond left for his meeting with Saint. Donald Wheeler climbed into the gondola in his place. He was wearing an Australian digger hat, the brim pinned up at one side, which he removed now and then to fan himself or swat the bees. His red hair clung to his head, darkened with sweat. He grinned at J.B. "Enjoying yourself?"

She looked up at him, her face smeared, and grinned back. "I never thought people still stamped grapes with their feet."

"Only on special occasions. The rest goes in the crusher."

J.B. said wistfully, "Too bad."

Donald laughed. "You wouldn't think that after the first ten tons."

The Bill Sharp Country Trio was playing "Turkey in the Straw." J.B. hummed along. "This is my kind of music too." She thought: Screw Richard Wagner anyway.

"Are you excited," Donald asked curiously, "getting your first big part in a movie?"

J.B. shrugged her shoulders as she danced. She had almost forgotten *Starfire*. "I suppose so."

Donald raised his brows. "You *suppose* so? Listen, lady, you're going to be rich and famous."

It didn't seem very important anymore, not here. "It's not real," J.B. said with sudden intensity and a wide gesture to include the whole green-and-gold landscape. "This, now, *this* is real."

They were almost alone, dancing on in the blazing sun. She could see Diamond and Saint, two small figures, one white head, one black, climbing up a dusty trail into the hills.

The air was so hot and dry it seared her lungs.

Donald stripped off his T-shirt and flung it over the metal side of the gondola. J.B. grinned at him. She liked him very much. It was hard to believe he was a doctor; he seemed just like an ordinary person. It was hard to believe he was so old, too, because his body looked young and so did his smile. She liked his body and his smile, she liked the red-gold hair on his chest, and his tawny eyes that gleamed at her with approval under the rakish Aussie hat. She knew he liked her too, and she thought with sudden clarity: He likes me just for me, as I really am, not as a fantasy.

Donald reached out his hands for her, and she took them. He said, "I've about had it with the heat. Come and see the winery before lunch."

And J.B. said happily, "Oh, yes, I'd just love that."

Mrs. Wheeler sat at the head of the long trestle table, Diamond on her left, her nephew John on her right, then J.B. and Donald; Vera sat on the other side of Diamond. The dowager sat at the end, flanked by Saint and the fat man, apparently a state senator, who was now glassy-eyed and almost comatose.

J.B. was flushed with excitement. She had climbed up to a gallery to overlook the fermentation tanks, where the swollen purple skins of the grapes had thrust to the surface to form a glossy, solid-looking dome.

"The cap," Donald said. "We call it the cap."

"It looked so solid. It made me want to throw myself into it and roll."

There was a momentary silence, every man at the table clearly relishing the image of J.B. rolling in fermenting grapes.

A waiter passed a heaped plate of lamb. Vera accepted a second piece, then helped herself to sourdough bread and a large slice of Brie.

J.B. unself-consciously picked up her chop bone in her hands and chewed hungrily. "God, I'm starved. This looks fantastic."

Donald Wheeler chuckled. "You took a lot of exercise, one way and another."

"I like to see a hearty appetite." Mrs. Wheeler regarded J.B. with approval. "I hope he was a good guide on your tour."

J.B. confided, "He's not too bad, but there's a lot he doesn't know." She added, "I'm sure you could have told me."

Donald begged J.B., "Don't get Mother started. She'll bore you to death."

J.B. retorted, "She will not."

"Shut up, Donald. When do I ever have a genuinely interested audience?" And without ado, Mrs. Wheeler launched into a highly technical lecture on winemaking, covering the chemical balance of soils, ground water, frost protection, and micro climates, to which J.B. listened with rapt attention. "My deepest regret is that my only son had to run off and be a doctor," her tone implying that compared with the growing of grapes the medical profession was absurdly frivolous.

Diamond watched J.B. with a quizzical expression in his dark eyes, then glanced at Donald Wheeler's dazzled face.

Donald didn't notice. He reached among the pile of grapes in the center of the table, broke off several leaves, and twined them into J.B.'s disheveled hair. "There. The nymph of Bacchus."

"Who?"

"The god of wine. Our patron."

She turned to him and laughed. Her eyes were shining. Diamond's eyes, in contrast, grew as cold and empty as infinite space.

With sunset it cooled down fast, and the party began to break up.

Saint sat down alone at the table under the oak trees and opened Vera's sketchbook.

There was J.B. at the table, impish and messy and slightly tipsy, the grape leaves threaded raffishly through her hair, the sunlight striking long fiery rays from the huge opal on her breast. It was Victor Diamond's opal, but Diamond had not caused the glow in her eyes. Saint knew her eyes had never worn that same glow for him either.

Now, Donald Wheeler, shirtless in his Aussie hat, Crocodile Dundee dancing on grapes. His face was in shadow but his eyes glittered from under his hat brim with a message as easy to read as if it was written in mile-high letters.

Saint thought dizzily: Everything's turning around again. He loves her. And she loves him. And Diamond has her. Now what?

Next, Diamond. All elongated line, an impression of coiled strength held in check, heavy lidded eyes bearing a suggestion of menace. A snake, Saint thought, waiting to strike. And the diamondback is deadly....

Finally, himself. Saint stared down at his own image, and his eyes burned back from his thin face. His cheekbones looked sharp as knives. He thought he didn't look like someone anyone would want to know.

He turned the page to Diamond again, and back.

Was there a resemblance?

He couldn't be sure.

Inside the house, the phone rang.

Mrs. Wheeler called, "Saint? It's for you."

When he picked up the receiver, the line seemed dead. Then he heard a faint hiss of breath and a voice said, shockingly loud, "You son of a bitch. You thought you'd got away from me, didn't you? Well, think again. I'm coming after you. You won't get away again."

A click, and the empty hum of the dial tone.

Saint stared at the receiver in his hand.

A voice said, "Mrs. Treadwell, I presume."

He looked up. Diamond stood in the doorway, an enigmatic smile on his mouth. Behind him stood J.B., once again wearing her silver headband and remote Starfire persona, the only incongruous note a spray of vine leaves she held clutched in her hand.

"Yes," Saint said. "That was Fletcher."

PART FOUR

Chapter
21

Twenty months later, in June 1988, the double-page spread in *Variety* showed her face superimposed upon a night sky, her eyes wide, each pupil replaced by a glittering star.

The caption read, "J.B. IS STARFIRE."

Slashing across the page, in acid yellow: "$9,931,026—first five days."

And tonight, in celebration of a record-breaking week whose magnitude astounded everyone but Diamond, Soundstage One at Omega Studios was transformed into a moonscape of craters filled with silver sand.

Everybody who counted in the industry was here, including the top executives from the parent corporation in New York.

Victor Diamond had pulled it off; with a ridiculously low budget and mostly unknown talent, he had unleashed a real blockbuster.

Now he stood center stage receiving his due homage, distinguished in a tuxedo, Starfire at his side wearing an extraordinary dress of holographic design so that from some angles she seemed disembodied, just a beautiful face and floating silver hair above a swirl of unimaginable colors.

Who was Starfire? Where had she come from? True, she had once been J.B. the model, but who was J.B.? She didn't even really have a name. She might have sprung from nowhere, and although tantalizing rumors were spread—Starfire was the orphaned heir to a Southern plantation . . . descended from Eastern European royalty . . . the granddaughter of an infamous Nazi war criminal living in seclusion in Argentina—no one knew for sure except her closest friends, and they weren't talking.

"We're selling mystery," Diamond explained to J.B. "Starfire's a total enigma. People must think of you as alien, someone very different, untouchable. Starfire has no past on Earth, no family."

J.B. had said obstinately, "But I don't want to be alien and untouchable. And I do have a family. What about Momma? And Melody Rose? If I get to be famous, you'll *never* stop Mel saying she's my sister. No way."

Diamond said confidently, "She'll see reason."

Wanna bet? J.B. might have said. But that was a long time ago now, and so far Mel, against all her expectations, had cooperated.

Initially Melody had fought hard against coming to California; she wanted to stay in New York—"and continue to spend your money," Diamond said dryly.

However, sullen and abusive, she had finally allowed herself to be sent to a drug clinic in Pasadena and after six months of rehabilitation she seemed a new woman and duly grateful to Diamond for snatching her back from the very edge. Now for the first time she had her own share of the good life, albeit a relatively small slice.

Diamond had found her a job as hostess at La Pergola, a well-known restaurant in Westwood Village, where, known now as Melrose, she seated guests with a charming smile and was even building a following. She drove a dashing litle orange BMW and lived in a pretty one-bedroom apartment in Santa Monica.

"Funny how things turned out, isn't it?" Melody said to J.B. in a rare meeting of the sisters. "Look at us now. You a big star, and me with a nice car and clothes, working in a class place like La Pergola. . . . Diamond's quite something, isn't he?"

"Yes," J.B. agreed. "He's something, all right."

For a while she had regarded Diamond with near-reverence, almost as the father she had never really known, someone who made things happen, a man—perhaps—at last to trust. "Of course you're not like Melody Rose," Diamond assured her once during another midnight of self-doubt when she had at last confided her dread that after all she was only just another whore; "what a ridiculous idea! You have talent and an exploding career and you only receive your just due."

And what a relief to know that Melody was safe at last, off drugs, off booze, and off the streets, and seemed to have a chance for a real life.

"He told me, 'Stay clean and we'll do well together,' " Melody confided. " 'You let me down just once, and you'll regret it.' "

"And he means it, Mel."

"Yeah. And he said I'd keep my job, my looks, and my goodies so long as I keep my mouth shut. I'll do that too. I'm not dumb. He never talks loud, but he don't have to." Melody confessed with a small, delicious shiver, "With those eyes, and that voice . . . He frightens me a hell of a lot more'n Angelo ever did."

J.B. hadn't paid much attention at the time; Melody Rose always responded joyfully to ruthless men, and everything was going so well.

Now, months later, with all she had ever wanted either in her hands or within close reach, J.B. wasn't sure of anything anymore. She had made it beyond her wildest dreams—but not on her own terms. She had thought wealth and success would bring independence, but they hadn't at all, and odd phrases, innocuous at the time, returned to haunt her in the dark of night: *"My job, my looks, and my goodies . . ."* My *looks*— what did that *really* mean?

J.B. stopped sleeping well. She began to use Valium to go to sleep, something she'd never done in her life.

Wakeful at three A.M., she would see how Diamond had manipulated her from the very beginning for his own ends—whatever those were— as he had used and manipulated all of them in ways in which they didn't yet comprehend, although in the bright day that seemed nonsense. They all had so much to be thankful for.

J.B. studied Arnie Blaize, standing beside Vera, talking with a television news reporter.

Arnie's success had been phenomenal since he had taken up with Diamond. He had had two hits back to back, *Right Exit Closed* and now *Starfire*. He was very hot, the nation's number-one sex symbol after his steamy scenes with Starfire in the black lava dust on the island of Lanzarote off the coast of Africa. He was also a role model for the nation's youth. From a ruined reputation, surely untouchable, he had fought back to the top again, and now, a crusader against drugs, gave talks on college and high-school campuses, and made antidrug commercials: "You *can* say no," Arnie would insist. "I didn't say no once, and someone died. I do now, believe me."

He was fast becoming a national icon, offering something to everyone, admired by kids, revered by parents, idolized by every female over the age of eight.

The interviewer, a young Asian woman wearing a stylish crimson dress with huge shoulders, was saying, "Thank you so much, Arnie, and good luck." The camera turned toward Vera, away from Arnie, and for a split second his bright, smiling face looked old and haunted.

"For viewers who have just joined us," the interviewer continued, "this is Wendy Morita of *Peoplewatch*, and I'm talking with Arnie Blaize and Vera Brown at the launch party for *Starfire*, Omega's latest blockbuster. Vera Brown is the creator of Starfire, the comic-book character who has captured the imagination of the nation. This must be a wonderful moment for you, Vera."

Vera nodded and agreed that, yes, it was wonderful.

"Vera not only oversees the animation sequences for the movie but still continues to turn out the comic book each month from her studio in San Francisco, even though her writing partner, John Saint, lives in Los Angeles. How do you manage that, Vera?"

"It's all done by computers. Saint faxes me the scripts, then I do the art and graphics on a modem which hooks into the mainframe computer at Omega Studios."

"So although you are partners, you hardly ever meet?"

"We don't need to, not with a fax and computer."

"So high-tech. Animation and cartoons have certainly come a long way since the classic Disney days. One last question while I have you, Vera: can you tell our viewers how it all started? How was Starfire born?"

Vera, slender as a wand in a gown of mushroom satin, her hair cut in a gamine Louise Brooks style which suited her perfectly, shrugged and gave a half-smile. "In those days Starfire was my alter ego. I saw myself as so plain and dull, and my life seemed very narrow. Starfire was beautiful and had thrilling adventures. She was everything I wasn't, did all the things I knew I'd never do."

"Well, things have certainly turned around. What a success story, a fantasy come true. Thank you for sharing that, Vera, it's an inspiration."

J.B. nodded. That was true enough: life had certainly turned around for Vera.

She had lost weight again, and Arnie had overseen her hairstyling and cosmetics and found just the right designer to create her individual look.

Newly chic and beautiful, she was also rich.

Diamond had paid her a great deal of money for the *Starfire* rights; he had now put her in touch with a Japanese movie company producing a new series of quality animated cartoons. She was considering their offer. If she accepted, she would be based in Tokyo.

Vera's life was hardly dull and narrow anymore . . . but she had lost *Starfire* and Diamond didn't want her around. She had been bought off, and she knew it.

And then there was Saint, also a phenomenal success story. J.B. could see him now—dramatically handsome in a midnight-blue tuxedo, black shirt, and wide silver tie—pinned against a Styrofoam crater wall by a creamy-bosomed sitcom star.

In taking over production of *Right Exit Closed,* Diamond had placed Saint's feet firmly on the fast track to the top. He was treated by everyone at Omega as Diamond's heir apparent and now enjoyed almost as much power as David Zimmerman himself.

In the same time frame, Saint's personal problems had melted away like snow at high noon.

"Mrs. Treadwell, I presume?" J.B. had followed Diamond into the room that evening at the Wheelers' grape stomp, which now seemed a million years ago.

"Yes, that was Fletcher."

"What did she want?"

Saint's expression clearly read "none of your business." When pressed, however, he admitted Fletcher had made threats, "but nothing to take seriously."

However, Diamond had taken Fletcher very seriously indeed, and against Saint's strenuous objections, demanded he return to Los Angeles with them at once.

"I can't do that. I'm driving Vera home."

"Someone else can give her a ride." Nor had he allowed Saint to explain to her the reason. "The fewer people know about this, the better. And you don't want to frighten her, do you?"

Diamond had moved Saint into a suite at the Beverly Hills Hotel and assigned him a baby-sitter, a young man called Jeff, who looked like a Bible student from a Midwestern seminary but was actually an ex-Green

Beret and a trained assassin. Saint had been outraged. "I don't need this guy. I can handle Fletcher. For God's sake, what can she do to me here?"

And then, suddenly, Fletcher was no longer a threat, killed in a freakish accident with a horse, kicked to death by her father's famous stallion, Trumpet Call. Harlan McGraw, poor man, clearly driven mad by the death of his idolized daughter, had shot the horse with the pearl-handled Mauser he had once given her, and then blown out his own brains.

There was some speculation, of course, but not for long. It seemed so clear what had happened. The stallion had a reputation as a savage bastard, the autopsy showed Fletcher McGraw Treadwell's blood alcohol way above the limit, and she was known to be eccentric if not downright crazy.

Although stunned by Fletcher's death, Saint was kept so busy handling his new success and responsibilities that he had little time to wonder or to grieve. "Now the Fletcher situation's been neutralized"—that had been Diamond's own word for it: "neutralized"—"you can put the whole thing behind you and get back to business." As if it were easy to "put behind" him such a devastatingly traumatic chunk of his life.

It was small wonder that sometimes he wore the expression of a man at war with himself, that sometimes J.B. caught an expression of angry speculation in his eyes as he looked at Diamond, his mentor. Saint struggled with the slavery of gratitude . . . and Saint was nobody's slave.

Although what do I really know, J.B. wondered, about anyone? These days she was so out of touch, her every moment filled from dawn to dark.

There was no chance to confide her creeping sense of unease to anybody, for she hardly ever saw her friends anymore. There was no opportunity to talk with Vera alone, or Saint, or even Arnie, and Donald Wheeler and his mother had vanished from her life as if they'd never been. She had written to thank them for the lovely day at the winery, but neither had written back or called her.

Now she was realizing that that day of the grape stomp had been the happiest day of her life. She missed Donald sadly. She missed everyone. She felt very lonely sometimes. She didn't quite understand how it had happened, how everyone important in her life had somehow managed to melt away.

Her family too. True, Melody Rose was relatively close by, but J.B. saw her so seldom, and with her life in perpetual motion, she forgot about Melody for increasing periods of time. Memories of Momma, and of Floyd, were fading like images in old sepia photographs.

A long time ago a misspelled note had arrived for J.B., in care of Omega Studios, signed "Dad." The tone of the note was whining and vaguely threatening. Now that Jo-Beth was hitting the big time, Floyd didn't see why he shouldn't be cut in for a share, "else things might get said you mightn't want."

"Just what I expected," Diamond had said flatly. "Don't worry; I'll take care of him." He added, "Your mother too." He had called for the plane. They flew to Amarillo, where Diamond rented a black Lincoln Continental for the drive to Corsica.

J.B. hadn't been to Corsica in seven years and was astonished to find it so small and insignificant, just a flyspeck on the road map. It was thoroughly depressing, and she dreaded seeing Momma and Floyd again. The only bright spot was looking forward to a reunion with Charlene.

Phil's Sandwich Shop was just the same, she supposed, only she didn't remember it being so seedy. Charlene, over thirty now, looked forty at least, with pale, puffy face and thickened body.

"Jo-Beth? Jeez. That really you?" Charlene took an involuntary step backward against the Mr. Coffee machine. She gazed from J.B. to Diamond and back to J.B. and the long black car outside and smiled uncertainly.

"I called you, Char. I said I was coming."

"Well, yeah," Charlene stammered, "but I wasn't . . . I guess . . . well, you kinda took me by surprise, hon . . ."

Her voice drifted away. J.B. ordered a cup of coffee and sat drinking it, a radiant vision on a bar stool of cracked orange plastic. She asked awkwardly, "So. How's Leroy?"

Charlene's husband, Leroy, was working in construction in Amarillo. He'd brought a new pickup. The kids were fine.

After that the conversation floundered.

J.B. asked, "How's Momma?"

"Doin' okay, I guess," Charlene said. "I been taking her groceries, like you asked, but I dunno. You'll have to go see for yourself."

"It was like I wasn't me anymore," J.B. sadly told Diamond in the car. "Like she doesn't know me anymore."

"You're not," Diamond said gently, closing them once more inside the frigid air inside the car. "And she doesn't."

"But she's my friend."

"She was. But that's all over now and she knows it."

That's terrible, J.B. thought wretchedly. Terrible that a friendship can just die . . . although the mean little thought crept into her mind that it really wasn't so terrible because Charlene was tacky and getting fat and would be a real embarrassment if she ever came to Los Angeles . . . until she pulled herself up in astonished self-disgust. My *God!* thought J.B. What's happening to me? I'm not *like* this.

But wondered moments later: Or am I? Have I changed that much?

Momma's hair was unkempt. She wore a soiled housedress and broken-down espadrilles. Her toes were dirty. She peered at them through the broken screen door and shouted, "Don't you come near me. You're a damned soul."

"Momma, I've come with a friend to—"

"Josephine-Elizabeth, it ain't no good. Get away now, you hear? You're living in the pit of sin. Go away and take your wanton shame . . ." And then she noticed Diamond. He smiled at her through the screen and said gently, "May we come in, ma'am, and visit for just a minute?"

She blinked at him, flustered, and opened the screen door at once. The flat light from the bright gray sky backlit Diamond's silver head like a halo. She said falteringly, "Josephine-Elizabeth, who's this man?"

Inside, the trailer was a mess and smelled bad. The living and kitchen area was cluttered with empty cans of Dr. Pepper, cracker boxes, and religious tracts: "You, Too, Can Be Chosen;" "Inherit the Universe;" "After Armageddon with Jesus."

Slapping dust from a chair, Momma said apologetically, "Guess I'm kina late gettin' on with my chores." Then, with defiance: "But doin' the Lord's work takes an awful lot of time."

Diamond said, "Of course it does. And I'm proud of you. We all are."

"Huh?" Momma gazed into his eyes, which gleamed like polished black stones, and whispered, "Are you from Them?"

Diamond nodded.

Overwhelmed, Momma clasped her hands together, her smile luminous. "I thought . . . seeing you, it sure looked like you'd be one of the Chosen."

Diamond said, "And so, Mrs. Feeney, are you. I'm here to reward you for all your good work and to help you begin your new life of bliss. My emissaries will be calling on you later in the day. Pack a suitcase, then go with them and rejoice."

Floyd still worked at the Texaco station. He seemed much smaller than J.B. remembered.

"Fill it up," Diamond ordered.

"Sure enough, sir." Floyd made a great show of washing windows, checking under the hood.

In quite a different voice from the gentle tone he had just used with Momma, Diamond asked, "You Floyd Feeney?"

"Yessir, that's me." He touched the tag on his breast pocket.

"You have a stepdaughter called Jo-Beth. That right?"

Floyd looked wary. "So what?"

Diamond's voice was quiet and carried a deadly chill. J.B. thought of how Floyd must see him, the silver hair, black glasses, expensive clothes and car, how theatrical a symbol of power he must seem. "You tried to rape her." As if it were yesterday.

Floyd stepped back from the car, face flushed, eyes bulging. "That's a lousy lie. I never touched her. I—"

"Afterward you told people she'd made advances to you."

Floyd sidled, shifted, and the dark color rose higher in his face. "She's a lying little bitch. If I ever lay my hands on her again I'll—"

"You will never lay your hands on her again. Nor will you demand money from her or threaten her. If you ever try to contact her again, I shall have you killed."

It was said with such flat certainty that J.B. shivered. Floyd hadn't once looked at her, sitting there in the passenger seat. She wondered whether he would have recognized her if he had.

Now his face turned a dreadful lumpy gray and his lips trembled. Diamond asked, "Do you understand?"

Floyd stammered, "Y-Yes, sir."

"Good. Don't forget it." Diamond nodded curtly. He pressed his foot down and the big car glided smoothly away. "Well," he said to J.B., "that's taken care of."

Well, yes, it certainly had been. Floyd was neutralized too, and Momma was now living in a very nice establishment in Dallas. She understood that, as one of the Chosen, she was no longer Lurline Feeney. Nor did she have any daughters, which, under the circumstances, was fine with her. The grounds were beautiful, and there was a high wall with broken glass on the top to keep out the ugliness of the world. The attendants all wore white, just as angels should, and she was free to do the Lord's work morning, noon, and night.

J.B. had felt relieved and thankful to Diamond at the time; it wasn't until weeks later that the resentment had crept in, and the sudden realization of fear.

Diamond had been kind and gracious with Momma, he had smiled at her and talked to her like a princess, but he hadn't meant it; J.B. guessed he felt nothing but contempt for Momma underneath, as he felt contempt for anyone who didn't measure up to his own strength. He hadn't even seen her as a person, much less felt sorry for her or wanted her to be happy, just bundled her into the funny farm and declared her finished business, and that wasn't right. Momma had had it tough, J.B. thought; it didn't come much tougher.

Even Floyd—seeing him threatened and humiliated hadn't made her feel jubilant, as she had once been sure it would; she now knew she had felt sorry and ashamed. He was only a small, bitter man who drank too much so that, briefly, he could forget all the failed dreams.

Now Momma and Floyd were out of her life. Corsica was over. J.B.'s past was rolled up behind her like a rug—and the rug had been thrown away.

Standing there beside Diamond, smiling and drinking champagne, she knew she had no past—and what the future would bring, she could not begin to guess.

She had gained the whole world, and was just now beginning to understand how much she had lost.

Chapter

22

Starfire crouched, knees drawn up to her chin, alone in the darkness and silence of infinity.

She was a speck of dust, floating somewhere in the universe. She had no substance, no body, no self.

She scratched at her knee with the tip of one long silver fingernail for the reassurance of sound and touch, reminded herself that she did in fact have a body, that that body belonged to J.B. Feeney and was squatting on a black carpet in a pyramid-shaped, windowless room in a weird house in Malibu in September 1989.

She had been studying yoga and meditation, and Diamond was encouraging her to spend longer and longer periods in the dark room, venturing to the furthest inner reaches of her mind. "It's the closest you'll come," he said, "to being lost in outer space."

It had been over a year now since the climactic release of *Starfire: The Movie.* Following upon its astonishing success, they had swung immediately into production of the sequel, although, Diamond had pointed out, it was in fact more of a prequel, both telling the story of what had gone before and setting up the stories still to come.

Starfire II, riding the success of the original, had a much bigger budget and, from the start, tearaway publicity.

J.B. saw her face and her star-studded eyes across full-page print ads, on thirty-foot highway billboards, and one time, in a television showroom, on fifty screens at once: "J.B. *IS* STARFIRE."

An avant-garde designer had brought out a line of Starfire fashion, featuring a great deal of silver lamé, metallic mesh, and leather; there was a Starfire line of cosmetics; and licensing negotiations were almost complete with a major toy company for the manufacture of a nine-inch Starfire doll plus wardrobe and accessories.

J.B. went nowhere anymore without her phalanx of bodyguard, driver, publicist, and secretary. The days were long gone when she could go into a store to make a casual purchase, take a walk, or go to the beach by herself. She seldom drove her own car, for she was invariably recognized, followed, and harassed on the highway, so now, reluctantly, she rode in a limousine behind tinted glass.

Her mail was carefully vetted, "for your own protection," Diamond said, so she read neither the passionate, adoring letters from her fans nor the maunderings of the crazies. Nor did she know until long afterward about the death threat from a fundamentalist religious group in Oklahoma, for she was so cushioned by security that the extra precautions and guards had passed her by unnoticed.

She made carefully staged public appearances at charity events, and was guest of honor at an international science-fiction convention, but was never allowed to give interviews or mingle, for her image as an enigmatic, mysterious, otherworldly creature must be preserved at all costs.

On the very few occasions Diamond took her out to dinner, it was for a specific purpose. In Spago's one night: "That man across the room"—Diamond had leaned his head to hers confidentially—"the man in the gray jacket? With his back to you?"

J.B. studied the man. "Yes?"

"He's vice-president, development, of Calco Oil. He's corrupt and evil. you must reach inside his mind, Starfire, and find out his plans for drilling on the Alaska Shelf."

"I . . . Wh . . . ?"

"You watch him, and concentrate. Empty your mind of everything else but him. Look inside his brain and learn the truth." She half-smiled, but Diamond was serious. "You must get used to doing this. You can do it perfectly well. It's in your power."

"Oh. Yeah. Okay." As Starfire, she stared fixedly at the back of the man's head. He had thick, neatly combed gray hair. She imagined herself parting the hair just above his collar, then sliding between the cells of blood, bone, and tissue into the soft, pulsing grayness inside. She rested her chin on her hand, eyes narrowed, directing a concentrated shaft of intent.

After a few moments, to her satisfaction, the man began to fidget in his seat—"It's working," Diamond said softly—then twist his body, minutely raise his shoulders, put down his fork, and finally turn to look at her, puzzled and slightly annoyed.

"Well done, Starfire," Diamond murmured quietly. "I knew you could do it."

J.B. *IS* STARFIRE.

Now she could almost believe that, yes, she truly could see into people's brains; control their thoughts; even, in the black pyramid, project herself through space. More and more she was learning to lose herself in her role.

Diamond was very pleased with her.

It all showed in her work, he said.

Her studio scenes had been completed; very soon now, in just two weeks, they would be going on location to tropical Mexico to shoot the primeval jungle and swamp scenes. Diamond was down there right now with the second unit, which for the past six weeks had been gathering background shots of palm trees lashing in the wind and muddy torrents cataracting down mountains, although the rains should be mostly over by now.

Somewhere far away a red light was pulsing on-off, on-off. A pulsar, Starfire thought, in a distant galaxy.

Then in some dim part of her mind she remembered that that was Hamura's half-hour signal before he served dinner.

She climbed to her feet. The door was somewhere below the blinking lamp.

Disoriented, feeling as though she walked at a steep tilt, she found the panel that, when pressed, moved the door silently aside onto a dimly lit anteroom that served her as a mental and sensual decompression chamber. She stood there for a full five minutes readjusting, then drifted into her dressing room, where she chose a shimmering robe made of Mylar.

Hamura had set a place for one on the terrace. He bowed, smiled, poured her wine from a frosted bottle, presented a plate upon which scallops and vegetables had been arranged like a work of art. From the hidden speakers tumbled the liquid cadences of Debussy's "Clair de Lune."

Suffering the inevitable letdown of being herself again, J.B. sipped her wine, absently fingered her opal, and stared at the ocean. She didn't feel very hungry. She didn't feel much of anything. She wondered how she would pass the time before going to bed. If Diamond were here, they'd watch a movie, but she wasn't allowed in the projection room without him—the equipment was too delicate and he always kept the place locked when he wasn't here.

She wished there was somebody, anybody, to talk to her, to remind her she was human.

Up at seven the next morning, J.B. had donned her silver leotard and was in the middle of her routine workout when Hamura called her to the phone. "Mr. Braize," he announced with a bow.

But it wasn't Arnie Blaize at all. "It's Donald Wheeler. Remember me?"

She was astonished. "Don—"

He interrupted, "Hush. Don't say my name out loud."

"But . . . What do you want? Why are you . . . ? I mean, it's been so *long* . . ."

"I know. What are you doing today?"

"I . . . I guess I'm working."

"Then take a break. I've rented a boat. You said once you'd never been sailing."

"But you're . . . How . . . ? Where are you?"

"At a gas station at Highway One. I'll pick you up in ten minutes."

"I can't."

"Why not?"

"Diamond wouldn't want me to."

"He won't know. He's in Mexico. He won't be back till tomorrow at the earliest."

"How do you know that?"

"Vera told me."

"You talked to Vera?"

"Is there a law against talking to your friends? Yes, she told me. She also said she's worried about you. She's not the only one. So go get your things."

She had shaken her head before she realized that he couldn't see her. She said, "I really can't, Donald. Suppose he calls?"

266

"Then you'll be out, won't you?"

"But what'll I tell Hamura?"

"Why tell him anything? It's none of his business. He's only an employee."

"He's more than that." A spy, thought J.B.

"Then say you're going to the studio to meet Arnie Blaize to discuss
a scene. Now, are you coming or not?"

"No . . . yes!" she cried with an indrawn breath and a sudden soaring
joy: *"Yes."*

She ran downstairs just as she was and waited breathlessly. The moment
the black Corvette pulled up outside, she slid into the passenger seat and
quickly slammed the door. The powerful car roared through the security
gate, carrying Starfire out into the world, although, an uneasy imprint
on the tail of her eye, was the image of Hamura staring after her.

But she didn't care anymore. She was away and free.

Donald Wheeler was wearing jeans, a faded Stanford sweatshirt, and
scuffed Top-Siders. He had driven more than five hundred miles through
the night and looked tired.

J.B. said, "I don't understand. Why are you doing this?"

"I missed you."

"But it's so sudden. You never called me or anything."

"Sure I called. And wrote you letters. And sent you wine. The wine
from the grapes you personally stomped on. You never answered. I
thought: Now she's a big movie star, she's forgotten the little people."

She stared at him. "You *did*? I never got anything."

His mouth tightened. "I guess not."

Shocked: "Are you saying Diamond censors my mail?"

"What do you think?"

"Well, yes, of course . . . he protects me. I get letters from weirdos
and nuts, and he makes sure I don't see those—he says actors can't
handle that stuff without it affecting their work. But surely my personal
mail . . ." Her voice drifted away in dismay.

"Listen," Donald said, "don't think about it now. Not today. Today's
just for fun."

Fun. She had almost forgotten the word. She was Starfire, and Starfire
worked constantly to save the Earth, the forests, the oceans, and the
animals; she didn't have time for fun.

Then, in mild panic, J.B. slid down in the seat and cried, "People will see me."

"There's an answer for that too." Donald pulled over, stripped off his sweatshirt, and thrust it at her. "Put that on, and pull the hood over your hair. There're some dark glasses in the glove compartment."

She obediently put on the sweatshirt, which was warm from his body and which smelled very faintly of sweat and horses. She felt breathless with her own daring. Whatever would Diamond do when he found out?

Donald asked, "Must he find out?"

J.B. said, "He always knows everything," half-expecting Diamond suddenly to appear, even though he was far away, and stop her. She was Starfire, capable of throwing her mind around the universe. She was thinking of him, perhaps involuntarily summoning him to her side this very moment through telekinesis.

Donald said, "There's nothing he can do. You're with me."

Briefly she felt very safe, hearing him say that.

"And anyway," he told her, turning the car onto a frontage road, "where we're going, there'll only be sea gulls and fish. They've never heard of Starfire. Or of Victor Diamond."

The manager of the marina in the small beach community was a middle-aged woman wearing an oil-stained orange sweater. She was thick-set and tanned, her graying hair tied back in a ponytail. "Hi, there, I'm Marge. You folks sure picked a great day for a sail."

She eyed J.B.'s long bare legs and the silver leotard. "Pretty snappy bathing suit, hon, but looks kinda fragile for sailing. Bring some pants?"

J.B. shook her head. "I came in kind of a hurry."

They followed Marge down the wooden dock onto a finger pier that swayed and dipped under their weight, to where a line of white boats was tied up. "You folks're my only customers today. You get first pick."

Donald said, "Your call, J.B."

She looked at the boats, one of which would be theirs for the day, and pointed at random. "That one."

Marge grinned and applauded. "Good choice!"

They climbed aboard, and she showed them around the boat, where the sails were stowed and how to pump out the head, which was located behind a plastic curtain up forward.

There were two bunks and a locker containing extra lines and some tools. The tour took about three minutes. Then Marge started the outboard motor with one hefty tug, left it sputtering in neutral, and climbed ashore to cast off the lines.

Donald put the engine in forward gear. They pulled away from the dock and headed for the harbor mouth and the open sea.

J.B. said shyly, "Can we go far enough out so we can't see land?"

"Of course."

"I'd like that, not being able to see land." It was too late to worry about Diamond anymore. J.B. sighed with contentment and leaned back on the blue plastic seat cushion, wondering what it would be like to be Marge, who didn't dress in silver Mylar, exercise to workout tapes, knew nothing about inner space and could care less. Who just rented boats and sold bait and didn't have to be—

Donald asked suddenly, "What are you thinking about?"

"—Starfire."

"Then don't. It's ten o'clock and the sun's shining and it's time for a beer."

A beer. "Hey," J.B. cried, "you bet! Coming right up."

She burrowed in the paper sack he had brought, dragged out a can of Coors for Donald and one for herself, then explored the white wax-paper package he had bought at a local grocery store, finding four bologna-and-Swiss sandwiches with yellow mustard on white bread, and two fat dill pickles.

He grinned. "Not exactly movie-star food, but it's all they had."

J.B. said very sincerely, "Just what I wanted. Can I eat one right now?"

"You can do anything you want."

They were coming out of the calm water into the breeze; J.B. could see the dark line of wind on water not more than a few hundred yards ahead. Donald eased back the throttle of the outboard. "Time to get sails up. Know how?"

She shook her head.

"It's pretty easy." He left the engine idling in neutral, climbed on deck, and clipped the main halyard to the head of the sail. "I'm going to pull on this now," he told her from his position at the mast, "and the sail's going up. Watch."

Up it went, flapping gently back and forth.

He raised the foresail, returned to the cockpit, trimmed both sails, and cleated them down.

As he turned the bow away from the wind, the small boat heeled slightly.

"Great," Donald said. "Now we're sailing." He cut the engine and at once it was immensely quiet, blissfully peaceful save for the slosh of water at the bows and the hum of the wind.

J.B. spent the next hour lying flat on her stomach on the foredeck, leaning down, staring at the bow slice through the water.

She leaned over further until she could stick her hand into the ocean, and watched the water surging through her fingers in silver-green ribbons.

They were almost alone on the face of the ocean and the water stretched to the horizon like a pleated quilt of indigo satin. Behind her the shore was receding into a smoky mist. She was no longer Starfire. She was J.B. again, on a sailboat at last, traveling nowhere or anywhere. Best of all, nobody knew where she was, she thought suddenly with a thrill, not even Diamond.

The sun was high overhead now, and it was getting hot. She took off the sweatshirt.

The silver leotard dazzled in the sun. The opal flashed fire. Donald smiled. "I need dark glasses just to look at you."

J.B. said, "It's kind of dumb, dressing like this, I guess."

"You could always take it off. It's not as though anyone would see."

"Except you."

"That's different."

"And anyway," J.B. surmised, "you're a doctor, right?" She laughed because he was still so unlike her image of a doctor, someone gray-haired and dignified wearing a white coat and stethoscope. She also laughed because it was a beautiful day and she was having fun, and what the hell—but she kept the leotard on.

They drank more beer and finished the sandwiches. J.B. savored every mouthful, crunching happily on a dill pickle and licking her fingers.

Donald mused, "It must get tough after a while, living on champagne and caviar."

J.B. nodded seriously. "Sure can."

"But I guess you'd get just as bored with a diet of pickles and bologna sandwiches."

It was hard to imagine that, but she agreed peacefully. "I suppose."

Donald had taken off his T-shirt and his shoes, and was guiding the boat with one bare foot on the tiller. He raised his head and took a long swallow of beer. J.B. could see his throat muscles slide convulsively as he swallowed. He stood up, stretched, flexed his shoulder muscles, and yawned with repletion. "What we're going to do now is teach you to sail a boat so I can take a nap."

It was easy, so easy, as natural as breathing. J.B. held the tiller, kept one eye on the plump curve of the sails, the other on the compass, which she held steady on 265 degrees, southwest, just as Donald had told her to do, "so we can find our way home again." Although she would have been happy just to sail on and on over the curve of the earth.

Donald Wheeler lay quietly on the narrow seat. He must be so tired, she was glad he was sleeping; he had come so far—*just to see her*.

She leaned forward, scrutinizing his face now that it was relaxed in sleep, noting the networks of pale laugh lines around his eyes and mouth. His upper lip and jaw were rough with ginger stubble. She peered at his bright, springing hair, suddenly wanting to touch it, knowing already how it would feel in her fingers, strong and crisp and exuberant.

She wondered what it would be like, going to bed with him, and was taken aback by a rush of heat through her body.

She caught her breath, stunned by her sudden arousal. The rush was *so* strong. She eyed him warily. After all, she was Starfire and projected her thoughts into other people's minds.

But he didn't stir, and her wariness shifted into speculation. *What would it be like to go to bed with him?* She couldn't begin to guess, although sex with Donald Wheeler, she knew, would be different from anything else she had known. Not that she had had many lovers for comparison. Just two, in fact.

Saint, for whom she had been a fair maiden to be rescued and worshiped; and Diamond, with whom she performed an elaborate and soulless ballet in the darkness.

Now, rather like the bologna-and-Swiss sandwich and the pickle and beer, she imagined sex as a rough-and-tumble, down-and-dirty, no-holds-barred frolic with an equal partner. What fun it would be, she thought wistfully, to wrestle with somebody in bed, get sweaty and tumbled, and not have to think, not calculate, just scream and maybe bite and claw and just goddamn well *fuck*. She would—

Oh. She put her hands to her mouth as though she had cried the words out loud, and once more glanced anxiously down at Donald. That thought had slipped out so violently that *surely* he must have felt it.

But no, his eyes were still closed. What color were his eyes? She couldn't remember. She laid her head to one side, considering. Brown? Green? Hazel? But no, they were reddish gold, a warm terra-cotta, and they were wide open and watching her stare at him.

"You look beautiful upside down," Donald said lazily, reached out a hand, caught her by the hair, pulled her face down to his, and kissed her lightly on the lips. He was grinning. She had a sudden suspicion he had been awake for some time. Also that, after all, he could read her mind. "Where are we?"

"I don't know. Somewhere."

"That's good. Are you still on course?"

"More or less."

"Good for you. You're a natural sailor. So what's wrong with the sails?"

J.B. glanced up at the mainsail, which hung limply above her head. "I guess the wind died."

Donald struggled up onto one elbow and peered at the flat, calm ocean, which stretched to the horizon like polished glass. "You're right. Terrific. Feel like a swim?"

J.B. had had to learn to swim properly for her Starfire role. She had trained with the best. She was glad of that now.

Donald tied a flotation pillow to the end of a line and flung it into the water. He loosened the main and jib sheets so the sails flapped free. "We don't want the boat to take off without us." He caught J.B. by the chin and kissed her again, then with one lithe movement shucked off his jeans and underwear and dived in.

He called up to her, "Come on in. It's great."

It did look good. Well, thought J.B. recklessly, why not?

She peeled her leotard off and, naked but for her opal pendant, plunged into the water after him.

She surfaced, hair streaming across her face, to feel cold wet arms around her and Donald kissing her again. They sank in a stream of bubbles, surfaced, chased one another around the boat. J.B. grasped Donald by the shoulders and pushed him underwater. He grabbed her ankles and pulled her down with him. She felt a slight tug at her neck and a sudden slackness, but she didn't think about it then.

She floated gently, hugging the pillow under her chest, her long hair streaming out behind her in the calm water. She wished the day would go on forever.

"Hey! J.B.! Look at me!" She peered upward, shielding her eyes. Donald was back on the boat again, a black silhouette against the bright sun. She heard the click and whir of a camera and reflexively flung her hands over her face.

"Too late," Donald said with satisfaction. "I got you."

"Hey. No. You can't *do* that."

She swung on board and, quite disregarding her nudity, reached frantically for the camera. "I don't let people take my picture."

"Do you seriously think of me only as 'people'?" He handed her the camera at once, his face suddenly grave. "What do you think I'd do with it? Blackmail you? Sell it to the tabloids?"

She shook her head. "No. Of course I don't . . . I don't know."

"I'm sorry, J.B. You're right. Take it. Expose it."

She held the camera in both hands, staring at him.

He went on, "I just wanted it for myself. A memory of a beautiful day. Of the girl I . . ."

J.B. watched him, her face closed and cautious. "The girl you what?"

"The girl I love."

She said in a small voice, "Oh." And handed the camera back.

He nodded thanks. "I promise you nobody's going to see that except me." He carefully placed the camera on the bunk below, and held out his arms. She went to him.

He twisted her hair into a long pale rope and wrung the water from it, then wrapped it around her throat like a halter.

They stood facing each other while the boat rocked under them and the boom swung to and fro above their heads. Donald said slowly, "I've dreamed about you for a long time. Two years. Ever since I saw you up at the ranch. There you were, a beautiful thing, perfect, all silver and glitter, everything about you shining except your eyes."

J.B. waited, the breath catching in her throat.

"And then," Donald went on slowly, "that girl had purple feet and stomped grapes, got a bit drunk, wore vine leaves in her hair, and laughed, and her eyes were shining. I've dreamed ever since of making them shine again." He bent over her, still holding her tightly by the hair. "Kiss me."

She couldn't have imagined such a kiss. It was not so much a kiss as a fusion of teeth, lips, and tongues, a fierce shared hunger.

They fell together onto the seat. She felt his hands on her breasts, which now felt hot and hard as stones; she locked her legs around his hips, and it was no carefully choreographed ballet, this, but urgent, ungraceful, violent. She had never known it could be like this, such abandon, such confidence, such pleasure, such relief; there was no need to lie or pretend she was coming when she was not. She didn't know how she could hold on, she wanted him as much as he wanted her, and they would do what they wanted to each other again and again, until one last time, when he burst inside her and howled and she felt herself spinning away somewhere dark and alone and secret.

Afterward he held her tightly and kissed her closed eyes.

J.B. whispered, "They were shining."

He said gently, "I want to sleep with you in my arms."

"There isn't time."

"Not now. But there will be. Someday. Someday soon."

She wished she could believe him.

On the way back to Malibu Donald asked, "When am I going to see you again?"

"I don't know."

"You have to leave him, you know that."

"It's not that simple."

"People leave people all the time."

"But not Diamond."

"What's to keep you? *Starfire?*"

She shook her head. "No." And at that moment, it was true. *Starfire* didn't matter to her anymore.

"What, then? You don't love him."

"No. But I can't leave him. Please, don't make me say any more."

"He doesn't own you."

But he does, you see—only she didn't say it. I'm in a trap, and I didn't know it for such a long time. He owns me, my mother, and my sister too. . . . J.B. knew Donald was watching her closely, and stared down at her hands in silence.

He asked softly, "Are you afraid of him?" And didn't wait for a reply. "You don't have to be afraid. What could he do?"

In her mind, J.B. saw Fletcher McGraw lying dead in the grass; she saw a black horse with bloodstained hooves sidling uneasily and whickering with distress. She suddenly knew as surely as she'd ever known anything that Fletcher's death had not been an accident.

If she left him . . . She thought of Momma alone in Dallas at Diamond's mercy, and of Melody Rose—"*I can keep my job, my looks, and my goodies*"— without a face.

Now she knew just what Diamond had meant.

His arm was very long; it could easily stretch to Saint Helena and the Oak Crest Winery.

With sudden intensity she said, "Don't come down here again. Don't call me ever again. *Promise me.*"

"No. I love you."

"If you love me, then promise me. Goddammit." J.B. clenched her teeth. "You have to."

They passed the guard station. At Diamond's driveway the security gate slid soundlessly back. Someone was watching for her.

"I'll wait until you're back from Mexico. But no longer. Not a minute longer. You might be afraid of Diamond; I'm not."

"We'll see. But now go. Please . . . just *go.*"

She watched the black car pull away, then squared her shoulders and turned toward the house, where the front door was now open wide. A tall figure stood silhouetted by pale light.

She wasn't the least surprised to see him.

The first thing Diamond demanded was, "Where have you been?" And the next, studying her sunburned face and bare shoulders, "And where's the opal?"

For a long time she would see it in her nightmares, falling from the broken chain and sinking away into the dark depths below her, twisting and turning, its colors flashing ever fainter as it fell.

Chapter

23

⟡

Diamond and Starfire arrived in La Playita by floatplane the first week of October. The plane taxied up to the brand-new dock, where a reception committee waited for them. The heads of the most important local families, who owned the cantina, grocery, and liquor store, stood out front, flanked by farmers, fishermen, and the decrepit and somewhat senile Father Ignacio. The women clustered behind the men, and behind them small boys chattered and played in the dust. Somewhat apart from the group, a wiry figure crouched on bony yellow heels, fingered the blade at his hip, and watched the strangers from under his dirty hat brim.

Diamond stepped out onto the dock. The old priest made an enigmatic gesture that might or might not have been a blessing. Diamond responded with a salute, then turned and held out his hand for Starfire.

She emerged, a vision of gold and silver, so tall, so radiant, so pale that there was a moment of absolute silence. Cutting into the silence, seeming unnaturally loud, one of the women hissed. Father Ignacio reached for the small bag of herbs that hung on a string around his neck, along with the cross, and which warded off the evil eye.

It was Salvador Ochoa, owner of the cantina, who bridged the awkward moment, for he was too sophisticated a businessman to concern himself with superstition, and this exotic couple would be renting, at vast expense, a house he owned. A beautiful house, he had assured them; simple, but such a fine setting, such a wonderful view, and cool—being high on the hillside, they would catch the ocean breezes.

Indeed, six people had worked all day making it fit for its celebrity occupants (although he didn't go into details), the women scrubbing the tile floor and beating the scorpions and tarantulas out of the matting while the men repaired the toilet, pulled the luxuriant growth of weeds from the little graveled patio out front and raked it, whitewashed the walls and posts, and removed the noxious pile of ancient refuse that had collected out back.

Ochoa pressed his battered straw hat against his chest and bowed to Diamond, and then, deeper, to Starfire. He beckoned, and two young boys led up a pair of swaybacked ponies.

Diamond and Starfire, accompanied by an entourage of villagers, all jostling for a closer look or even a touch, proceeded at a jarring walk into the village, past the cantina, the church, the liquor store, the grocery store, and a clutter of shacks; across the Río Verde, the ponies' hooves rattling on the timbers of the new bridge; up a steep pathway and through a sagging wooden gate, until, suddenly, there was the house. White and shining, bright Indian rugs on the gleaming tile floor, flowers overflowing from hand-painted vases. "It's beautiful," Starfire told Ochoa, and smiled at him warmly, thinking that it wasn't too bad—for a prison.

Saint and Vera, the assistant director, the unit publicist, and other key staff were berthed in the *Desperado*, a 110-foot motor yacht with communications and computer center, projection room in which to view the dailies, office space, and ten compact but comfortable sleeping cabins.

Arnie Blaize, the only principal not staying on board, occupied an air-conditioned trailer in a clearing beyond the village, his trailer one of an encampment housing the camera crew, technicians, supporting actors, wardrobe, props department, commissary, and medical clinic.

Victor Diamond, however, did not intend to stay with the rest of the principals and crew on the boat down in the bay, or in the trailers, but to keep his distance and make sure Starfire kept hers.

Except for her time on the set, she was under house arrest. The village, knowing nothing of this, merely accepted the sequestration as being entirely suitable for a goddess.

The third evening in La Playita, J.B. sat on the step outside the house watching the darkness rush in and listening to the rising chorus of insects. Bats skittered through the trees; a small lizard paused in front of her and inflated its throat into a bright red balloon to produce an astonishing sound like a resonant gong.

Now, waiting for Diamond to return from a meeting with the camera crew, she had a rare window of time for herself, time to remember her day in the sun—remembering as J.B., for in her Starfire persona, thinking could bring dangerous results.

She would regularly tell herself this was nonsense, that of course she couldn't really project her thoughts for Diamond to intercept—but she felt increasingly uncertain. At Diamond's decree she'd spent most of the past two weeks alone in the dark of the meditation room. Not as a punishment, he insisted, but to help her free her mind of Dr. Wheeler's dangerous intrusion. As a result, she was further into the role of Starfire than ever before.

He had said little more about her act of defiance. Nor had he mentioned the opal again, which at one level she found alarming; one didn't carelessly toss away Diamond's gifts without suffering the consequences one way or another.

So she smiled and apologized and made light of the whole adventure; trying to blank Donald Wheeler out of her mind for his own protection in case Diamond could somehow guess what they had done together, while every night, in her dreams, the stallion reared and screamed and trampled a broken body into the grass—only this time it wasn't Fletcher McGraw.

However, even though Diamond had said little, she was clearly not trusted anymore. She wasn't allowed into the communications room alone, and was never given an opportunity to talk privately with Vera, Saint, or even Arnie. During times when, perforce, Diamond was occupied without her, she was watched over by a guard he had employed from the village. "For your own protection," Diamond told her, but she knew better. At this moment the guard sat patiently on duty down by the rotting gate, although Starfire, her senses preternaturally sharp, sensed other shadowy figures moving through the humming, whispering darkness, and was sure she had actually seen one dark shape, very close, flitting soundlessly into the thorny trees behind the house.

She rested her chin in her hands, emptied her mind as she had learned to do, and reached out with her thoughts.

For a split second it seemed she connected out there, as though she touched another mind, which instantly recoiled and fled.

There were a lot of people out there watching her; by now she was used to the stares and the silences wherever she went, and the silent hostility of the women. She should expect that, Diamond said; to all of them she was extraordinary, and to the women, looking the way she did, she was clearly a threat. So she was accustomed, although not reconciled, to being stared at and followed all the time; but who was that one in particular from whom she was receiving different emanations than mere curiosity? Was he another servant of Diamond's? A second watcher, to watch the guard?

Who? And what did he want?

While J.B. brooded on the steps of her house, Saint made his way surefootedly between the boulders and potholes toward the cantina.

It was a utilitarian structure with a concrete floor and corrugated iron roof that reverberated deafeningly during rainstorms. There were eight metal tables and a number of randomly placed, mismatched chairs. Lines of colored light bulbs were strung across the ceiling, although these were turned on only on Saturday for disco night, when the generator was cranked up and the entire village gathered to drink and dance until long after midnight.

Tonight the place was almost deserted save for Tomás Ochoa, sixteen, who sat on a stool behind the bar and leafed through a *Batman* comic book; Borracho Pete, an American expatriate who had lived in La Playita since 1968 and had over the years become an expert moocher of drinks; and a scrawny hen that scratched desultorily under one of the chairs.

Saint ordered a can of Tecate beer, a shot glass of tequila, and a small saucer of limes, laid a twenty-thousand-peso bill on the bar, and was informed by Tomás, with a charming smile, that he had no change.

"Fine," Saint replied in Spanish. "I'll run a tab."

He sat down at a corner table, facing the harbor. There was a persistent smell of mud tinged with sewage and the occasional waft from the fish dock. In the middle of the bay the *Desperado* bobbed gently at anchor.

Saint gazed at the line of lighted portholes, trying to work out which was Vera's cabin. Watching the lights, knowing she was in there somewhere, brought him some comfort—a great deal more than his thoughts did.

"He's trying to turn J.B. into some kind of robot," Donald Wheeler had told him during a long, impassioned phone call. "He thinks he owns her, body and soul."

Saint had asked, "Why doesn't she leave him?" With an edge of remembered bitterness: "She's left people before."

"She's afraid of him. He has some kind of hold over her."

"What?"

"If I knew, I could do something about it. Listen, Saint," Donald said urgently, "you're going to be there, right on the spot. You and Vera. Watch over her. Call me as often as you can, but don't do it from this place La Playita. Go to Puerto Vallarta and call from one of the big hotels. For all I know, this phone we're talking on now is bugged. Jesus, am I paranoid, or what?"

So Saint watched and waited and asked himself questions he couldn't answer.

Was Donald indeed paranoid, or was he right to be afraid? Answering himself that, yes, Donald was probably right. Saint hadn't liked hearing what Donald had to say, that J.B.'s mail was censored, that she was forced to sit in the dark for hours at a time in Diamond's meditation room; and thinking back, he couldn't remember, nor could Vera or even Arnie, when they'd last been able to talk with her without Diamond being there too. Now, to all intents and purposes, she was a prisoner.

There was a dark rumor building around Diamond, which, after Donald's call, crystallized some of the elements in Saint's mind that had so far been ominous but vague. Now, for instance, he admitted he had never quite bought the official version of Fletcher's death. Fletcher was crazy, but not that crazy; she would never have fooled around with Trumpet Call, even if drunk out of her mind. Now he knew in his gut that Diamond had somehow had her killed. Perhaps by Jeff, the boyish ex-Green Beret.

Vera had never bought the story either. "It's just too neat." Saint knew she had never liked or trusted Diamond. "He's absolutely ruthless, but he hides it well. He seems to do the right things, but they're for the wrong reasons, and the only person to benefit in the long run is Diamond himself."

Saint thought: If Diamond is afraid of anyone, he's afraid of Vera; she sees too clearly; she sees into people's hearts . . . And she was the only one of them never to be deceived. Saint suspected Diamond hated her for that, although he was far too clever to show it; behind a smiling mask he simply maneuvered her out of his way, far away, across the Pacific.

Now Saint stared longingly at the bright porthole that might be hers and wished he could go there and be held in her arms and be comforted and strengthened. He wanted to lay his head on her breast and cry: This is a bad man, Vera, he's dangerous and cruel and evil, I'm totally indebted to him—and I think he might be my father. What am I going to do?

But he'd never go to her, not again; she had always given, and he had always taken. This time he'd give her a break.

Vera's cabin was small but quite adequate, with a comfortable bunk; a compact bathroom area with sink, mirror, shower, and toilet; a hanging closet with built-in drawers for clothes and a Formica tabletop that let down from the wall to provide useful desk space.

It shouldn't have been hers, because Diamond hadn't wanted her here. Of course, she had guessed for a long time that she was being systematically cut off from the pack. It was done in the nicest way, with smiles, rewards, and a job in Japan that no one but she would see as anything but a fantastic opportunity.

In fact, thinking of spending at least a month in close quarters with Saint, she hadn't planned or wanted to come anyway.

But then Donald Wheeler had arrived at her door, a new Donald, tense, haggard, afraid. "Vera, I need help. He keeps her in dark rooms . . . he censors her mail . . . He's sick, Vera. She's in danger."

So Vera had appeared in Diamond's sanctum, ignoring Jason Brill, who sat Cerberus-like in the outer office, and told him, "I changed my mind. Of course I need to see the location personally."

Diamond prevaricated. "You can work from the film itself."

"It won't be good enough. I'd like to pick up the atmosphere; my work will be much better if I can sketch during the actual shoot."

Arnie had backed her up. "I need Vera. I want her to come."

Diamond had capitulated with an apparent good grace that Vera completely mistrusted.

She vowed to give him not the smallest excuse to send her away. She would be quiet, retiring, unobtrusive—but she would act as J.B.'s second guardian. She might have sold Starfire, but she refused to abandon her.

Vera gazed through her open porthole at the lamplight gleaming from the little shacks across the harbor, the slightly brighter illumination from the cantina, and the spiraling greasy smoke from the garbage fires. Under other circumstances she would have enjoyed this place. She loved the casual extravagance of scenery, the contrasts of beauty and squalor, the faces of the people, especially the children, and of course the ordered chaos of the shoot itself.

Keeping in the background, avoiding Diamond's brooding gaze, she had plenty of time to draw.

She leafed through her newest book, which recorded the last few days.

First, the arrival. There they all were, the merchants, the priest, the women and kids, staring goggle-eyed at J.B., as if she were a goddess. She had drawn them all, her pencil flying in her own kind of shorthand.

Now, to her surprise, she found that the only clearly delineated figure was a small man sitting apart from the group, his hat brim shadowing his face.

She sat there for a few moments staring at the drawing and wondering: Why him?

Next, Diamond and J.B., their long legs almost reaching the ground astride those dirty little ponies, the villagers following in a straggling line up the hill. In this picture the small man with the hat trailed at the end of the procession.

Who was he?

Well, she thought, La Playita was a small place, and after a few days she'd doubtless find out.

In the next drawing, Saint leaned against one of the wooden canoes pulled up on the beach, talking to some local fishermen. At first she had had to look at him twice to realize it was indeed Saint. He wore a blue-and-white-striped cotton shirt and cut-off jeans and looked quite relaxed and normal, but at the same time strikingly different. He looks as though he was born here, was Vera's first thought; and eventually she understood why. Saint was speaking Spanish, but not the way a foreigner would speak; he was talking with colloquial fluency, like a native, and was using different muscles, which transformed his face.

She knew he had not wanted to come to Mexico, afraid he'd feel too vulnerable, fearing the associations. However, it hadn't been like that at all. "There's actually a freedom," Saint said, "knowing you've seen the worst and come through it."

She stared down at the portrait of this new, foreign Saint, sighed, ripped the page slowly from the book, turned it over, and began to write on the back:

Dear Saint:
Here we all are in Mexico with God knows what terrible things brewing up around us, and all I'm really thinking about is you.

I love you. I tell myself not to be dumb, that you don't love me, that you will never think of me as anything but a friend, but I just can't help it. I remember the time we went to bed together, and then think of you now sleeping just a few yards away from me. I want you so badly and I miss you so much.

I can't tell you how terrible it's been these last couple of years, trying to hide how I feel so I don't embarrass you and lose you completely. Anything, I thought, was better than not seeing you at all.

Now I've changed my mind. It's too painful. I've finally made a decision to accept the offer from the Onishi Corporation, and am sure it's the right one.

From now on I'm going to behave like a real grown-up, I'm just going to remember the good times we had, how wonderful it was to work with you, how we could almost read each other's thoughts and minds.

Our partnership will be over and Starfire Productions is all yours and Diamond's. Actually, it's a relief; I not only don't need Starfire but also don't feel she's a part of me anymore. She belongs to J.B. now.

I'm going to remind myself how successful I am on my own; how I don't need you anymore either.

But I can't fool myself or lie to myself; I loved you the moment I first saw you. I still love you and I always will.

But enough's enough, now. It's over.

What a good thing you'll never see this letter. . . .

Back in Westwood Village, while Starfire sought the mind of her unknown intruder, Saint finished his first glass of tequila, and Vera leaned over her letter and began to cry, Melody Rose Feeney, aka Melrose, was showing an attractive young man to a good table at La Pergola.

He ordered a house special (the grilled mahimahi steak), and a half-bottle of Chablis. She noticed all of this because he was not only handsome but also well-dressed, didn't wear a wedding ring, and was alone.

Halfway through his meal she approached his table and asked whether everything was all right. He said it was fine and would be even better if he could take her somewhere for a drink when she was off-duty.

She smiled a wide but demure smile and said she'd like that a lot and she was off at eleven.

His name was Whitney Davidson, which she thought aristocratic, but sadly he was from out of town. He actually came from Florida and would be returning tomorrow; just my luck, Melrose thought glumly, for in addition to his other attributes he said the nicest things. "How come you work in a restaurant? A girl like you, I'd have thought you'd be a model. Or an actress."

This kind of thing was music to Melrose's ears. She ordered a brandy alexander, which arrived stiff with cream with a cherry in it. She loved sweet drinks. She stirred it with the lime-green swizzle stick with the plastic pineapple on top and gave a rueful shake of the head. "That was my big ambition, to be a model . . . but I didn't get anyplace. Not tall enough. That's what they all said at the agencies."

"That's too bad," Whitney said. "Though I personally think petite women are more attractive and feminine."

"I won some beauty contests, though."

"I bet."

"I was Rodeo Queen, and Miss Tumbleweed at the county fair. And I did a little modeling, actually, in New York, but not real high fashion." Another drink materialized before her. She stirred and sipped and nibbled daintily on the cherry. "Lingerie"—Melrose dimpled—"and art calendars. Like that."

However, Whitney didn't seem curious about her New York days, although perhaps, thought Melrose, that wasn't altogether bad. Instead he asked, "Are there more like you at home?"

"Just one sister."

"And does she look like you?"

She tightened her lips. "Uh-uh. Not at *all*."

"That's good. One knockout in the family's quite enough." He reached out his hand and gently twirled a strand of her hair in his fingers. "I'll bet she doesn't have gorgeous hair like this either."

That was better. Melrose preened at the compliment. Yes, her hair was a much more becoming shade of bronze, thanks to the expensive salon Diamond was paying for.

"You see much of your sister?"

She wished he would take the hint, that she wanted to talk about herself, not Jo-Beth. "No. We're not close."

Whitney Davidson ordered another round of drinks. He said easily, "She's probably jealous of you. Getting all the looks, I mean."

He was certainly understanding.

Melrose sucked on her straw and found that, after all, she *did* want to talk about Jo-Beth. She wasn't supposed to, she knew that all right, but after three brandy alexanders she wasn't so afraid of Vic Diamond anymore, his threats seemed a long time ago, and he was far away in Mexico. After all, *someone* ought to know what a raw deal she'd had.

"Jealous?" With a short bark of laughter which caught her by surprise: "Not her!"

Her handsome companion raised an eyebrow. "How d'you mean?"

"She's one of those people just born lucky, is why. Everything works out for her without her even trying." In her indignation and growing fuzziness, Melrose's careful enunciation began to slip. She caught at it halfheartedly. "It ain't . . . isn't fair. She was the one got to be a famous model, and now she's a movie star and her picture's in the papers all the time. Me, I just get to wait tables."

Whitney murmured soothingly, "That must be real tough."

"Yeah. I tellya, it's the shits." Her glass was full again; she wasn't sure how it had happened. Melrose would have decided she'd had enough long ago—but ladylike Melrose had by now completely turned over the floor to Melody Rose Feeney, who stirred the cream with her finger, licked it, and announced, "What the fuck, I guess some people get the breaks and some don't."

Whitney Davidson nodded sagely.

"You see her now, she looks so pure you'd think she'd shit ice cream. But boy, the things I could tell if I wanted."

Whitney leaned back casually in his seat and said, "You don't want to tell me anything too personal. Or painful."

"Painful! Hell, I'll tell you from painful." Melody Rose jabbed her swizzle stick in emphasis and now the words poured out in a torrent like floodwater over a broken dam. "Guess what. She's Starfire. Saving the eco-enviro-whatzit. Kinda like Wonder Woman from outer space saving baby seals an' that shit. Jesus Christ, give me a break. And after all I did for her, taking her in and all after she tried to kill Floyd."

Whitney began, "Who—?"

"Stepfather. He tried to rape her 'n she slugged him. Thought she'd killed him. So she ran away to me, in New York, and I took her in, just like that, though it sure was inconvenient at the time and Angelo didn't like it, not right at first . . ."

"Angelo?"

"Yeah. He ran the model agency I worked for. He was my boyfriend. I shoulda just left her there on that bench," Melody Rose snarled, "back there at the bus station. She walks into my life, the bitch, and just takes it all away from me. Even Angelo, and he loved *me*." She drained her drink with an unrestrained gurgle. " 'N *she* got the trick with the movie star because she was a goddamn virgin."

Whitney asked carefully, "Trick? Instead of you?"

" 'Steada me?" Melody set her glass down with a belligerent crash. "Waddya saying? You calling me a hooker?"

Whitney looked pained. "Absolutely not. You've got class, Melrose. Anyone can see that."

"Yeah. Well." She looked slightly mollified, then leaned forward confidentially. "Let me *tell* you . . ."

Whitney Davidson drove Melody Rose home, carried her into her apartment, and saw her safely stretched out and snoring on her bed.

Back at his hotel, he called his office in Florida. It was four A.M. there, but his call was answered at once.

"You were right," Whitney said. "That little dirtbag pimp's worth his weight in solid gold. You better be sitting down, because you're just not going to believe this. . . ." Whitney kept his voice calm with enormous effort, but despite himself, it shook a little in his excitement, for Melody Rose's last speech had been too good to be true:

"Shit, *ever'*body knows she seduced Floyd, then lied 'n said he tried to rape her. I tellya, that girl's bad news. And cruel. After all I did for her. 'N then she gets to be a star with a big house at Malibu 'n a Mercedes 'n I get to be a fucking waitress and"—a breathless pause for effect—*"she's the one who was the hooker!"*

Chapter

24

Starfire stood in the center of the littered mosaic floor of the once-glamorous bathroom where the expensive marble sink hung at a drunken angle, the chrome fixtures glistened green with corrosion, a cluster of beer cans rusted in one corner, and mice nested in the Aztec-gold bathtub.

For today's scene, Starfire's first encounter with Arnie, she wore a complicated leather harness, a loincloth of metallic mesh, and a wide studded belt from which thrust the handle of some nameless futuristic weapon. She held a crossbow in her hands.

It was early afternoon, very hot, the humidity climbing. The light wouldn't last for much longer; the clouds were already swelling into fulminating cathedral shapes behind the hills. The afternoon storm was coming, and the rain again.

The sweat trickled down Starfire's naked spine and the makeup artist carefully dabbed at her with a sponge.

"Ready," Diamond murmured.

It was absolutely silent. Even the insects had crawled into their webs and burrows to pass the heat of the day.

"And rolling."

The clapper boy held up his board for the ninth take.

"And action. . . ."

Starfire held her head to one side, an intent expression on her face, listening, then slowly crossed the room toward the gaping window aperture.

For the ninth time she raised her bow in a slow upward sweep, sighted down the shaft of her arrow, and pulled the bowstring back and back, taut; she was getting tired now; her gauntleted arms were tense, the muscles standing out on her back.

The bushes down the slope quivered, then parted, and Arnie Blaize stepped out, wearing Levi cut-offs, a khaki tank top, and hiking boots, a twentieth-century vagabond lost in time. It was a long and critical scene—Starfire preparing to fire upon Arnie, and Arnie's reaction—and Diamond wanted it all in one long take.

Arnie stares up at her, his expression one of shock, fear as he realizes she's going to kill him, then resignation as he prepares to die. He says nothing, just raises his empty hands and spreads his arms wide.

CLOSE-UP: Starfire. Her eyes narrow in appraisal. Is he friend or enemy? Can she afford to take the chance that he's an ally, or should she play it safe and kill him anyway?

Starfire's body quivered with the strain of holding back the bowstring. It was a functioning bow with a fifty-pound draw with a real steel-tipped arrow.

Somewhere off to the left there was a faint rustle as some creature moved among dry leaves. For a second, distracted, she almost—but not quite—let the arrow go.

Then slowly, very slowly, she lowers her weapon.

Arnie stands in front of her, face pale and wet with sweat. He passes a hand across his forehead. It trembles.

"Cut," ordered Diamond with a sigh. "Print." And, looking up at the swelling clouds: "Okay, that's it for today."

There were several palapa restaurants on the beach, casual constructions offering fresh fish, homemade salsa, and tortillas, and Vera much preferred to eat her lunch there than in the commissary.

Her fair English skin protected by a wide-brimmed straw sombrero, she would sit pensively with her beer and limes, eat garlic shrimp or baked red snapper, then spend an hour sketching.

Today, as always, she attracted an admiring audience of children. They ranged in age from three to fifteen. She asked one of the older boys, "What's your name?"

He replied solemnly, "Raúl."

She drew his portrait with quick, decisive strokes. The other children clustered about her, exclaiming with shrill cries of excitement. Afterward she handed the drawing to Raúl. "Here, it's for you, if you like." He stared at it, at her, smiled brilliantly, and held out his hand. The other children set up an immediate clamor to be drawn as well. She drew Susana, Martín, and was putting the finishing touches to Paco, six, a beautiful child all shy smiles and huge velvety eyes. She had drawn him with Bambi ears sprouting from his head.

Lightning flickered behind the mountain. Vera, who spoke no Spanish, announced slowly and clearly in English that the session was over now; it would rain soon and she was going back to the boat. The children seemed to understand perfectly well. There were sighs, groans, and pleas for just one more. She shook her head. "But tomorrow," she promised; "mañana."

As the children scampered off, she found herself wishing she was just here on vacation, drawing for her own pleasure, for although Diamond was not openly hostile, she was not welcome and felt increasingly uncomfortable.

Diamond certainly didn't want her on the set. This morning she had made some quick sketches of Starfire in her warrior outfit and left before noon and . . .

There, she was doing it herself. Just like the makeup artists and wardrobe people and the rest of the crew, she was thinking of J.B. as Starfire.

But it was harder and harder not to.

In today's sketches, J.B.'s eyes looked strange and fierce. Vera closed her book firmly. Oh, yes, she thought, she so much preferred to draw Raúl and the kids.

Saint sat down on a rickety folding metal chair in the cantina and stretched out his legs. The heat enfolded him like a soggy blanket and, as was normal in the afternoons, he had the place almost to himself except for Borracho Pete, a leathery woman who sold Indian folk art to a gallery in La Jolla, and today a marijuana grower from upriver come to town on business.

Through a doorway behind the bar Tomás' parents lay snoring together in a hammock, Señor Ochoa shirtless and hairy; the señora stripped to her underwear, her breasts bulging over an elaborate bra of whalebone, foam rubber, and mauve lace.

Tomás brought Saint a can of Tecate and a shot glass of tequila without being asked. Saint tossed the tequila straight down; he needed it after this morning.

Arnie had been anxious. "Something doesn't feel right," he'd said after the first take. "Something weird's going on. Almost as if"—he glanced over his shoulder at Starfire—"she doesn't know who I am."

Saint had suggested to Diamond, "Break the scene up. Shoot them separately," but Diamond hadn't wanted it that way. He wanted the realism of the encounter, just as he had wanted Starfire to use a proper weapon.

Arnie would get rave reviews for his acting, undeserved really, because he hadn't been acting at all. He'd been more than anxious by the end; he'd been terrified.

"There's no danger," Diamond had reassured him. "She's more afraid of you than you are of her. She doesn't know who or what you are. Yes, she draws on you—but she doesn't shoot."

Perhaps not this time, was Saint's immediate thought, but what about the future? "Suppose J.B. gets so far into the role of Starfire that she ignores you?"

But Diamond only scoffed. "I told her not to shoot. I'm in control, and I'll stay in control."

Now one of the grips, a straw-haired youth called William, sidled into the cantina and sat down beside the marijuana grower. Saint watched as a transaction took place.

Leaving, William gave him a half-wave. "Hey, man . . ."

Saint raised his hand in acknowledgment. He reflected with irony that the news he had been in prison for alleged drug dealing had seeped by osmosis into the collective intelligence of both village and crew. That, plus the fact he spoke the language with the gutter patois he had learned in the cells, raised him to the level of folk hero. Everyone was a potential friend and admirer.

Just as Saint was wondering whether he should find a boat, go into Puerto Vallarta, and call Donald Wheeler—*"I'm scared shitless: he's turning her into some kind of robot"*—the mountains upriver lost their definition and vanished behind a dark cloak of rain. He'd never make it now, not till evening.

He decided to discuss the episode with Vera tonight and get her reaction. He needed her perspective and good sense. Thank God for Vera.

The folk-art woman was leaving.

Moments later Borracho Pete, as Saint had guessed he would, wandered erratically toward him.

"Hey, man. How you doing?" He sat down without waiting for a response and leaned much too close. Saint recoiled from the waft of goatish body odor. "You want some good grass?"

"Not today."

The American jerked his head in the direction of the man with the machete. "That's Real Gutiérrez. Means 'Royal' in English."

"I know."

"Grows the best weed in the valley."

"Yeah. I heard already."

"Crazy as a bedbug. People're scared shitless of him." Borracho Pete nodded wisely and scratched under his rank armpit. "C'd tell you something real far-out, if you wanted." He glanced significantly at Saint's empty glass. "Ready f'rnother one o' them?"

Saint sighed and signaled for Tomás, who refilled Borracho Pete's glass from an unmarked bottle of dingy liquid. "What's that?"

"Ricea." The American took a swift hit and leaned groggily back in his chair. "Great stuff, once you get used to it. Cheaper'n beer 'n kicks like a mule. Fucking firewater, man. Royal Gutiérrez was drinking ricea that time . . ." and he launched into a long, blurred tale which he plainly considered fair recompense for a drink, maybe two.

Royal Gutiérrez had come into town on one of his monthly selling trips. "He was sitting right there, always does, that's like his personal seat, you know? And this dog comes up and barks at him. . . ."

One of the sound men came in. He leaned behind the bar and took a beer from a cooler and left a small pile of bills on the counter. Above the wheezing voice of Borracho Pete, Saint could clearly hear both the Ochoas snoring in duet in their hammock. The sound man sat down beside Gutiérrez and leaned his head forward. There was a murmured negotiation. Gutiérrez' hat inclined negatively.

". . . he kicks it, but it goes right on barking. So he whips out his machete and . . ."

Borracho Pete was watching Saint's face with expectation. When Saint said nothing: "Bet you think I'll say he chopped its head off. Right?"

Saint agreed absently, "Guess so."

"Uh-*uh*." Now an emphatic headshake, and slowly, relishing the impact of his words: "No, *man*. Not his *head*. His legs, man. And tosses them one by one over the wall into the water."

Saint allowed the disquieting image a moment or two to penetrate. "That true?"

Borracho Pete looked offended. "Sure it's true. I was sitting right here. In this chair, you want to know."

"That's gross."

The sound man was wrapping something in plastic, Gutiérrez stuffing something inside his stained shirt. As if sensing the attention, he raised his head and caught Saint's eye. From below his hat brim glittered baleful yellow eyes.

Saint looked away with an involuntary shudder.

Borracho Pete leaned close again and whispered, "He comes into town once a month, at full moon. People say he stays up in the ruins. They say all kinds of things—how he's a werewolf, a demon, all kinds of stuff—but they don't dare do anything. Sometimes people go upriver and never come back. People say he's a cannibal too . . ." He nodded toward Saint's beer can. "You ready f'r nother one o' them?"

Diamond pulled on the ropes to make the bed swing, and reached for his bottle of body oil.

Suppose he had murmured, "He's an enemy, Starfire." He decided she would have killed Arnie, just like that. He sighed with satisfaction.

He turned his head to where she stood, wearing a tiny silver bikini, staring out into the rain and eating a banana. Her beautiful head was cocked slightly to one side, as though still alert for potential enemies.

He watched her finish her banana and toss the skin into the bushes, where he knew it would be segmented and carried away within minutes by carter ants.

Diamond climbed out of the hammock and crossed the room to stand behind her. He looked over her shoulder, down into the bay, where the *Desperado* bobbed like a bathroom toy.

Soon it would be time to go down. They would all squeeze into the projection room for the screening of the dailies and watch Starfire, time after time, sighting on Arnie's chest with her metal-tipped arrow, while the very real terror on Arnie's face would be endlessly repeated from different camera angles.

The rain stopped and suddenly the sun glared redly through swaths of low charcoal cloud. The valley looked impossibly lush, glistening emerald in the evening light.

A dinghy appeared from behind the rocks and moved soundlessly across the water. Diamond recognized Saint's lithe movements as he tied up to the stern rail of the *Desperado*, then swung himself on deck. He nodded to himself. He must talk with Saint seriously, very soon now, about the future.

Starfire sat in the dark, listening. Above the boom and hum of insects, frogs, and lizards, she heard the sound of Diamond's footsteps approaching up the stony path, and saw the occasional gleam from his flashlight.

There had been other sounds too during the past hour, underscored by an occasional lessening in pitch of the night creatures as, momentarily, they sensed the intruder.

"You should be asleep," Diamond said. "You have makeup at 4 A.M."

Tomorrow, at first light, they would be shooting upriver, on shoals of sandbanks where the sluggish yellow-green water was choked with giant ferns and grasses and wild iris, embellished with astonishing prehistoric flora of latex and plastic.

Here Starfire would land on earth for the first time, lost, alien, naked.

"I won't do it," J.B. had said flatly. "I won't do a nude scene."

"Don't be ridiculous." Diamond had smiled indulgently. "You can't travel through space as a mere shaft of energy, and materialize wearing clothes."

"Why can't I have a body double?"

"Because that's impossible for Starfire, and you know it."

Now: "It'll be morning soon enough," Diamond said.

She shrugged. "It's too hot to sleep."

He went behind the house to their open-air bathroom. She heard the sound of water running.

Returning, he pulled the mosquito net down around them and tucked it in, said, "As you're awake anyway . . ." Then arranged her body across the bed, raised her thighs, and lowered his head.

"Somebody's out there," she said as the bed swung under his weight. "Somebody's watching us."

"There's nobody," Diamond whispered. "Nothing at all. Come, now."

It was late.

Arnie Blaize sat in one of the folding chairs on the beach. He sat at a slant, for one chair leg had sunk into the sand.

Any minute now he would go to his trailer, turn the music on, the air conditioning up, and the light out, although he knew he wouldn't be able to sleep. He still trembled. This morning on the steps he had thought: She's going to kill me. Hell, he had *known* it.

He shivered, and stared at the white shape of the *Desperado* out there on the greasy swell, at its black windows like empty eyes, and wondered which was Saint's.

He thought of Saint lying on his bunk in there alone, not sleeping either, and felt very sad. He needed somebody so badly. A friend. A human contact. Somebody to hold.

A figure approached over the sand and sat down near him, but not close enough to intrude. One of the boys from the village. He turned his head; the boy was watching him. Arnie saw him smile, his teeth a flash of white in the darkness.

Arnie smiled back. He remembered the boy well now; he was taller than average, his hair a sun-bleached golden brown. He had stood diffidently in front of Arnie, holding an old evelope and a ball-point pen with a Mickey Mouse head on it for Arnie, the famous Hollywood star, to sign his autograph. His high-arched feet had been powdered with white grains of sand.

Arnie thought about the texture of the boy's skin again, the velvety smoothness of his dark cheek, and inescapably wondered how that cheek would feel to touch.

The boy ventured, "*Buenas noches, señor.*"

Arnie replied, "*Buenas noches.*" And in one of the careful phrases he had rehearsed, "*Cómo se llama?*" What is your name? Wondering again how old the boy was, whether he should use the third person or the familiar "*tu*," used for children and family and intimate friends, and if he got it wrong, whether the boy would be offended.

The boy replied, "Raúl."

"How old are you?"

"*Que?*"

"*Cuántos años tiene?*"

"*Catorze.*"

Fourteen. . . . For a moment Arnie felt overwhelmed by a rush of fantasy. Of gathering Raúl in his arms, of the feel of his young body, of the beating of his heart and his smile and his sandy feet; of crying out his desperation and being comforted and loved by somebody who not only admired him but also understood him, for Raúl was lonely too, Arnie could tell, and then, in the sand, they would . . .

He rose precipitately to his feet, thrusting the chair awkwardly away. He said curtly, "Good night." And strode away to his trailer, hearing the echo of the polite "*Adiós, señor,*" knowing that the boy stared after him through the darkness in hurt surprise.

Chapter

25

It was damp and chilly in the pre-dawn dark, and the bay was filled with sea mist.

Starfire rode with Diamond in the first of a series of jeeps, jolting across the river onto the rugged stones of the newly built road, winding three miles into the mountains, then veering sharply down and to the left onto an access road newly hacked out of the jungle, down to the river, to that elbow of shoals and rippling green water and lush artificial vegetation.

There had been strong security for this scene; none but Diamond and key personnel knew Starfire would be nude, in case of a leak in intelligence to the village; an entirely unnecessary precaution, since the village always knew everything.

For herself, although J.B. might worry about nudity, it was irrelevant to Starfire, who had submitted patiently to the complete shaving of her body hair and the lengthy application of silvery green body makeup. She now rode with closed eyes, hurtling through space, closing on the great blue-and-white planet with its water and air and resources, which would offer her her only chance of survival.

The jeep pulled off the road onto the steep track, and with the jolt of the vehicle Starfire entered the first thin outer layer of the Earth's atmosphere.

She senses at once the drastic differences from her previous journey, but is not yet aware that, through a warp in time, she has returned into the very distant past, at a time when a mighty civilization is over but the next age, that of man, is yet to come. Nor can she be aware that an alien force is at work plundering the Earth's resources at will.

The air screams with the force of her passage; the jungle rushes up at violent speed, towering ruins are glimpsed to either side: her shock wave produces spreading concentric circles of flailing vegetation like ripples in a vast pool of leaves.

The tops of the mountains were now outlined in gray light, which grew first rosy and then scarlet. It was a perfect dawn. In the foliage and undergrowth, waking birds and insects began a noisy chorus of whistle, hum, or croak. In contrast, the humans were tense and almost completely silent.

Diamond murmured, "Places."

Starfire slipped the wrap from her shoulders and climbed down the riverbank. She lay prone in the soft mud. She could hear murmured voices, the trickling of water, the soft scrape as someone erased her footprints. Then:

"Lights."

A sudden shaft of heat fell across her silvery shoulder blades.

"And rolling."

New sounds, far-off, manmade. She ignored them.

A final crescendo of sound, a whirling kaleidoscope of color, then stillness in which labored breathing can be heard, and a heartbeat, growing steadily stronger and louder. Against a background of soft greens, Starfire's human arms appear as in a developing photograph, flesh forming on bone, at first transparent, then increasingly opaque, until, in a pull back shot, we see her lying prone in the viscous slime of the shoals, staring in perplexity at her muddy hands. Dazed, she struggles to rise. The planet has a stronger gravitational pull than she remembers; she forces herself slowly to her knees, pushing herself into a sitting position and squatting back onto her heels. Bewildered, she looks up into the tangle of lush flowers and the dense leaves glossy with dew. She raises her hands in front of her face and studies her fingers; she touches her knees, her thighs, wipes at the greenish slime coating her breasts. The scene holds overtones of a painful birth.

Saint had wondered how he would feel, seeing J.B. naked. He had anticipated this morning's shoot with very mixed feelings, but now felt no longing for J.B. whatsoever, only distress for Starfire. Poor thing, he thought with a pang, so dazed, so lost . . . Then he shook his head with impatience. That's J.B., he reminded himself. You're watching J.B. *acting*.

From the jungle a dozen pairs of hidden eyes watched, and Spanish voices whispered, one to the other, in uneasy bravado.

"See? She is a real girl. I told you so."

"She has no hair down *there*."

"And she's green."

"Asshole. She shaved it off. And the green's makeup."

"El Loco says she's Chirihuatetl."

"El Loco's crazy. You *know* that."

"But just suppose she——"

"You wanna try it, then? You wanna fuck her?"

"You fuck her, man, you'll grow a cock like a horse. You got it made for the rest of your life."

Of course she wasn't Chirihuatetl, they knew better than that, they weren't dumb—but just the same . . . just perhaps . . .

So the boys and young men of the village watched and whispered, eleven pairs of dark eyes and—of this, even the secret watchers were unaware—one pair of yellow ones.

There was a leech attached to her calf, three inches long, writhing languidly as it sucked. This was not in the script. Starfire was curious about the leech. She tried to brush it away, but its mouth was firmly locked on her flesh. She pulled at it; it tore in half; she looked astonished. The cameras rolled. But within Starfire was J.B., who knew all about leeches and gave a sudden yelp of disgust. "Somebody get this thing off me."

"Cut!"

She twisted awkwardly to her feet, as though trying to escape her own body. "Get it *off*!"

A technician lit a cigarette and held the smoldering end to the squirming remains, which flopped back into the water.

J.B.'s face was the color of putty. She said, "I *hate* the fucking things." She fell to her knees, turned her head, and vomited dryly onto the mud.

Behind the screen of leaves the voices pondered:

"How d'you know witches don't throw up?"

"I just know."

"Well, shit. I wanted to fuck a witch."

"I'll bet she'd feel pretty good anyway." Eleven pairs of black eyes stared at J.B.'s mud-streaked breasts.

So did the pair of yellow ones.

J.B. felt bad the remainder of the day, and the next day felt worse, complaining of nausea and stomach cramps.

In fact, Starfire was supposed to fall sick, prey to a virus for which her body had no defense; it was written into the script, but she was not supposed to be really sick and miss several days' shooting.

Diamond worried initially about the budget. Then, as Starfire didn't improve, about her health. He thought of the murky waters of the Río Verde, in which she had been immersed over and over again.

Dr. Schiffrin, at the clinic, kept busy by a constant stream of patients suffering from fever, minor injuries, diarrhea, and cuts that festered in the dank humidity and refused to heal, examined her carefully and asked, "She had all her immunization shots before she came?"

"Of course," Diamond replied. "We all did. You know that."

"That water's contaminated," Dr. Schiffrin allowed gloomily. "And there's hepatitis in the village."

Starfire insisted, "I don't have hepatitis. My system can't adjust to Earth. That's all."

Samples of her blood and fluids were expressed to a San Diego lab, but although the test results were all negative, Starfire was still sick.

Saint rented a fast boat from Señor Ochoa and roared off to Puerto Vallarta, where he called Donald Wheeler from the lobby of the El Camino Real. "She's got some kind of stomach bug, but all the tests were negative and nobody knows what it is. It's not an amoeba. Thing is, and this may seem off-the-wall, she was actually *supposed* to get sick in the film. Things are getting a bit weird here."

Donald Wheeler said, "I'd sure like to get down there—but I want to hold off a bit if possible. I've been digging around, and this Diamond is not a nice person. Another week or so and I should have enough on him to deal with him once and for all."

"What about J.B.?"

"If she gets any worse, let me know and I'll come at once."

However, the following morning Starfire felt much better. She explained she had been on Earth long enough now for her system to adjust. Diamond took advantage of her weight loss and newly hollowed cheeks to shoot her sick scenes next, out of sequence.

At the end of the following week, almost back on schedule, with only a few days left before the wrap, they returned to the shallows of the Río Verde at dawn for the pivotal scene between Starfire and Arnie.

In the final print, this scene would be preceded by an underwater sequence of Starfire swimming, already shot in a tank in Hollywood. It was a joyous scene, her body dappled with filtered light, breasts and hips and long scissoring legs stippled with zebra stripes of gold and emerald. She somersaulted, plunged, twisted, and turned, clearly ecstatic, her weightlessness a remembered joy.

By now the silvery sheen of her limbs had been muted by exposure to Earth's sunlight; with golden-tinged makeup she looked more substantial, less eerie.

She wades knee-deep through the river to where the man is waiting. They touch. For an instant the man recoils as though hit by an electrical charge. He reaches for her again and she cautiously allows him to touch her shoulders, her breasts, her face, and then finally to kiss her. The camera closes slowly on their faces. Starfire has never been kissed before. Her eyes widen in curiosity, then cloud with emotion. She portrays a complicated range of feelings: compassion for this human and his vulnerability, for the emotional need of the whole human race, and a tentative delight in her own sharing of it. His mouth closes on hers. His hands clench on her shoulders. She tilts her head back; his fingers twist into her hair; he kisses her throat and her breasts; they fall together into a soft bed of slime; the water laps at their feet and ankles; they roll together, playing like young animals, their bodies now plastered with the warm mud, until the man's movements grow more urgent and he pins her to the ground. Their final convulsions are half-concealed by rising steam; the sky darkens, rain begins to fall, and Starfire gives a sudden wild cry. . . .

That night, Arnie and Vera ate dinner together by candlelight in the garden of the Joya Escondida. True to its name, it was indeed a jewel of a hotel hidden in a fold of the cliff an hour up the coast by boat on the way to Puerto Vallarta. It was carved partly out of the living rock, each room set at an angle and at a slightly different level to ensure absolute privacy, each with its own terrace overlooking the ocean.

After Diamond had called it a day, Arnie seemed to collapse. "I have to get away." His face alarmed Vera. "I can't take it one more minute."

"But, Arnie, you can't just walk out."

"I don't care. I'm going. Just for a night."

"But the insurance——"

"Screw the insurance. Screw Diamond. If I stay here one minute longer, I'll go crazy."

Now, however, he seemed to be recovered, sitting in the garden under the palm trees, where the air smelled of flowers and the sea.

"I'm sorry, Vera. Don't know what happened to me back there. Thanks a million for coming with me. You're a real friend. You're looking fantastic, too."

Vera was wearing her best dress. She had bought it three months earlier at the Giorgio Armani boutique on Rodeo Drive. It was a shapeless tube of black silk which, alone, she would have passed without a second glance. When Arnie insisted she try it on, she had been astonished by its unexpected elegance. She had almost not brought it with her to La Playita, not expecting an opportunity to wear it; what a good thing she'd changed her mind. She thought wryly: I'm wearing a fabulous dress and staying at one of the most romantic places on earth with the sexiest man alive. Me, Vera Brown. Millions of women would kill to be me right now . . . and all it means to me is a dinner out with an old friend.

Arnie ordered a bottle of Perrier for himself and half a bottle of Dom Perignon for her. While they drank, he consulted with the maître d' on their choice of food and wine, which resulted in wild-mushroom pâté, endive salad with garlic dressing, followed by rack of baby lamb seasoned with rosemary.

By the time the coffee was served, the color had returned to Arnie's face, the smile was back in his eyes.

Vera ventured, "It's Paris with palm trees."

Arnie nodded. "The best of all possible worlds. This is a famous place, you know. It's a hideaway for world-class lovers."

She asked sardonically, "Does Publicity know we're here? They could get some mileage out of it. Too bad we don't have a photographer handy."

"I'm sure that could be arranged."

Vera offered a toast. "To the best meal of my life. I hope I haven't put back too many pounds. And to you."

"To us. You're beautiful, Vera. I like your dress."

"You chose it for me. Don't you remember?"

"So I did," Arnie mused. "I did, didn't I?"

Afterward they walked on the beach. It was almost full moon and the stars were huge. The sand was cool and soft under their bare feet, and the waves washed soothingly on the shore. Arnie took Vera's hand. "Thank you for coming with me. I'd have gone crazy without you. . . ."

Back at the hotel he said, "I want to ask you something, Vera. A favor. If you say no, I'll understand."

She laughed. "Of course I won't say no."

"Will you come to bed with me? I need somebody. Just to hold on to."

After a second's hesitation she said, "All right. Just to hold . . ." It was the least she could do for a friend.

Arnie didn't turn the light on. Vera climbed into bed beside him, wearing a white nightgown of *broderie anglaise*, which J.B. had once given her for her birthday. Outside, the cicadas sang a thrumming song and a rising onshore wind rattled the palm fronds.

Arnie turned toward Vera, took her in his arms, and kissed her lips. His arms tightened around her, so tight she felt the breath squeezed from her chest. He whispered, "Kiss me properly, Vera."

She was too surprised to resist. Arnie's mouth closed on hers, his tongue probing inside almost before she could draw breath.

She forced her head to one side. "Arnie. What are you doing? Don't."

"Please, Vera. Let me make love to you."

"Arnie, no, I—"

But his mouth covered hers again; his fingers teased her nipples. For an instant, in reflexive impulse, she felt heat flood her body; then it dissipated with the sure knowledge that this wasn't real, Arnie was acting the role of a lover.

"Touch me." He guided her hand to his groin. His penis was flaccid. "*Please*, Vera," Arnie begged, "make me hard. *Do* something."

She began to stroke him gently until she felt the soft flesh stir under her fingers. Arnie gave a soft moan and buried his face in her neck. His voice muffled in her hair, "Please, now—in your mouth . . ."

"Arnie, I don't—"

"Please."

"All right." Reluctantly she bent her head, circled the limp organ with her lips, and ran her tongue over its smoothness, feeling it stir and grow stiff. Arnie was lying on his back now, arms outstretched, head thrown back, wide eyes watching the ceiling fan as it silently turned in the darkness. He was a million miles away, and whomever he was with in his mind and heart, it wasn't her. Vera gazed over the ridge of his hip to the sky, where the stars were burning bright.

A while later she lay full length on top of him, holding him in her arms while he cried. "I'm sorry, Vera. I was so sure I——"

"It's all right. Stop now, Arnie. It doesn't matter."

When the pounding of his heart had slowed and his breathing deepened, when Vera actually thought he might be asleep and drew her arms from around his neck, ready to ease away from him, Arnie said in a perfectly composed voice, "It was the stress. It'll be better tomorrow."

"Don't worry about it, Arnie."

"I love you, Vera."

"I love you too."

"I guess I've always loved you." He sat up and looked at her, his face a pale blur in the darkness. After a long, quiet moment, his voice almost too soft to hear, he asked, "Will you marry me?"

She didn't even pause for thought. "No, Arnie."

Like a frustrated child he demanded, "Why not? We love each other. We'd have a good life. And we'd have fun too."

"I know we would, but . . . no."

"I'd give you whatever you wanted." He began to list all the things he would give her. All the houses and the clothes and the cars and jewels and vacations and toys.

She cut him short. "I don't want that stuff, Arnie. It's not important."

"Other women would find it important."

She shook her head very slowly in the dark. "I'm not other women"— despite herself, imagining telling Mum: By the way, a film star just asked me to marry him. What d'you think of *that*?

"But I need you. I can talk to you. I have to have somebody to talk to." She felt his body begin to shake. "This afternoon did it for me. People will see that scene, me making love to J.B., and they'll think I'm really *like* that. That that's *me*. You don't understand. You can't."

She held him tight while he poured out a litany of despair. "It goes on and on and on. The gossip: who's my latest girl friend?...who was my date for the Academy Awards?...and if I have no date, then there're the rumors—*why* didn't I have a date, what's wrong with me, do I have herpes or even AIDS? So the studio fixes me up with someone and makes sure there's a photo opportunity, I get to kiss her in a public place, some kid gets her picture in the paper, and bingo—another new romance! Which comes to nothing next week or sooner. And it happens over and over and over again. Please, Vera. I need you."

"You'd be marrying me just for camouflage. It would be a lie. That's not what either of us wants."

He abruptly swung his legs off the bed and walked to the window. He stood there looking out, a naked silhouette against the bright stars. "No, of course not. Sorry, Vera. Sorry for dumping on you."

"Don't be. It's what friends are for."

After a moment: "Do you know, I'm a virgin," Arnie said with a hollow laugh. "I'm a sex symbol who's never had sex. Pathetic, isn't it? I felt sure with someone I cared for, I'd be able to do it. But I can't even do it with you. I'm sorry for that too."

"But you will. Somewhere, there's the right person." Vera drew a deep breath. "And you'll find him. One of these days."

There was a dense pause. Arnie turned slowly. "*What* did you say just then?"

"I said 'him.' You're tearing yourself up. Please don't pretend any longer."

"What do you mean, pretend?"

"Arnie," Vera said with resolution, "you're not the first person in the world who's had to face the fact he's gay."

There. She'd said it. She sensed Arnie's body go rigid. He asked in a remote voice, "Did Saint tell you?"

"Not really. I kind of put it together for myself. It wasn't difficult."

"Oh." He sighed and looked out at the stars again. "I couldn't look at him, after. I've hardly been able to speak to him since."

Vera said firmly, "Give him a break. Saint cares for people as people, you know that, you told me so yourself. He doesn't care what they look like, whether they're rich and famous, or what sex they are."

From the window she thought she heard Arnie's whisper of agreement.

"He's tried ever since to tell you you're still his friend."

"I can't—"

"You don't have to make a big deal out of it, just show him he's still yours."

Diamond asked, "What do you do on these trips to Puerto Vallarta?"

Saint had been expecting the question, and replied easily, "Testing the water. Seeing how I feel, walking around in a Mexican town on my own."

"You can't do that here?"

"This isn't a town and there're no cops with uniforms and guns."

Diamond seemed satisfied. "True." He cut the engine of the *Zodiac.* They bobbed in the water off a rocky point at the entrance to the bay. It was bright moonlight. "So, how is it?"

"Okay. Better than I expected."

"I'm glad to hear it." Diamond looked up at the sky. "It'll be full moon pretty soon now."

Saint asked, "Did you want me to come out here with you to ask me about Puerto Vallarta?"

"No," Diamond said. "I wanted to talk with you."

"About what?" Saint leaned over the side and plunged his hand into the water up to the elbow. He withdrew it luminous with phosphorescence. "Hey, look at that."

"Yes," Diamond observed. "Pretty." Then: "I wanted to talk about plans. Mine for you. But first, I thought the time had come to tell you something about myself. I wanted things to be straight between us."

Saint agreed guardedly. "Yes?"

"I'll start from the beginning. I never knew my parents, you know. I'm told I was found in an alley in Brooklyn, wrapped in a sack. I was raised in a Catholic orphanage."

Saint made a small sound of sympathy.

"The nuns didn't like me; I was always a proud child; they didn't care for pride. Pride was to be brought down, to be humbled; they weren't surprised I'd been thrown out like garbage, they said, no one would have wanted a mean, troublesome child like me. They provided endless petty torments I won't go into. I escaped onto the streets when I was six, but I was picked up right away. There was juvenile hall, then the foster homes. A lot of them. I was angry and still proud; not an easy child to love. They took me in for the money, of course; they'd usually tell me that. I'd run away, end up back in juvie hall, get sent someplace else, and run away again. Meantime, I developed certain survival skills, as one has to do."

Saint sat quietly in the boat, stirring the water and watching the phosphorescence. He said nothing, knowing Diamond would detest and reject pity, just as he would himself.

"One of those skills, of course, was lying. I developed it into an art form. By fourteen I decided it was pointless fighting the system anymore, because by now, one way or the other, I could usually make people do what I wanted. By sixteen I was tall for my age and reasonably good-looking; I changed my name from Joe Smith to Victor Diamond and became an actor." He gave a short laugh. "I'm sure I could have had a great career. But soon enough I realized an actor is little more than a paid hand. He has no control, no power, and by now I knew power was everything. I had to have control over my own life—and over other people's."

Saint shifted in his seat and watched the blazing girdle of Orion over Diamond's head. "What did you do then?"

"I moved to Hollywood and became a player in the game. I was very good at it. . . . Then I met Vangie Sellors."

"Your wife."

"Not just my wife. My creation. Before she knew me, she was *nothing*, just a pretty girl from Texas who'd won a beauty contest."

"She was supposed to be the most beautiful woman in the world."

"Perhaps. And she thought I was God. With me to guide her career, she would have become a big star; perhaps the greatest ever. I had a dream then, and it grew into an obsession—that Joe Smith, who had once been discarded like garbage, would establish a ruling dynasty over the world of film and that Vangie and I, the most powerful man with the most beautiful woman, would create gifted, beautiful children to inherit it.

"But the dream died," Diamond said tiredly, "and I lost her. You know the story. The dynasty was over before it began, and I set the dream aside because I knew I'd never find another Vangie. In any case, I convinced myself I didn't need a child. I was young then, and when you're young you're sure you'll live forever. But as it turned out," he said with a wry smile, "I was wrong on all counts."

Saint asked very quietly, "What does this have to do with me?"

"I'm getting old, and surprisingly, I find I'm not immortal after all. Nor am I able to father children anymore, for they tell me I'm sterile." Diamond gazed at him from his position in the bow of the boat, his eyes black holes in the darkness, and in an even voice, as though working through tomorrow's scenes, explained, "This is where you come in, Saint. You're the only child I'll ever have. You must father my children for me."

The rocks were much closer. Saint automatically pulled the oars from the oarlocks and paddled the *Zodiac* further out to sea. He had never asked. Diamond had never brought it up. "You're telling me I really am your son?"

With impatience: "Why else would I have had you released from Santa Paula? And hasn't it gotten through to you how I've been grooming your career every step of the way? Of course you're my son."

Saint heard himself ask in conversational tones, "Did Mother tell you herself?"

"She told me I was the only person who could possibly have fathered you; under the circumstances, I believed her. Now, listen to me." Diamond's voice grew very cool, very measured, and the apparent lack of emotion made the outrageous speech which followed appear at first quite reasonable. "I want you to father a son for me. Afterward I'll make my move to take over Omega. It won't take much; I'm the de facto chief already. Zimmerman and his pen-pushing drones will be history. Then just imagine what we can do, you and I together. We'll have all the money in the world and an elite core of dedicated talent turning out superior product, answerable only to me—and eventually to you, to pass on in time to your own son, my grandson. I'm offering you the world on a plate, and immortality to go with it."

Holy God, thought Saint with a sensation of sheer unreality. After a while, into Diamond's expectant silence: "I'm not sure I could handle all that power. And I'm not actually planning on marrying anyone right now."

"That's quite irrelevant. And in any case, she will already be married."

Saint drew a breath. "*She?*"

"My new Vangie. Yes, Saint, I have found Vangie again. I told you I'd been wrong on all counts." And with disbelief, against the gentle slap of waves against the rubber sides of the boat, Saint listened to him say, "You and she will make a child for me, and in the eyes of the world I'll be his father. No one will know otherwise."

"You mean—"

"That Starfire and I will marry as soon as we return to the United States. Then *you* must make sure she becomes pregnant as soon as possible."

The next morning, Starfire was sick again. Diamond studied her drawn face with dismay.

He told Dr. Schiffrin the lab must have made a mistake. Some critical factor had been overlooked. "I need a second opinion. Someone who knows what he's doing. Something's wrong."

In the early evening Dr. Reinaldo Suárez, from the University of California Medical Center in San Francisco, arrived in the Omega jet. Dr. Suárez was an internationally renowned specialist in tropical diseases, particularly those endemic to western Mexico, where he had been born.

He was small and delicate-boned and looked very young to be such an important doctor. Starfire gazed up at him with resignation. "Don't forget I'm an alien. My system can't deal with human diseases."

"We'll see, shall we?" Dr. Suárez smiled at her where she lay in the bed at the clinic, her blanched face almost as white as the pillow. He told Diamond, "I need to make an examination. If you would be so good, please wait for me outside."

When Diamond, with reluctance, had left the room, Dr. Suárez asked Starfire routine questions relating to her recent state of health, which she answered with impatience. Then he examined her eyes, ears and throat, breasts and chest, tapped her back and listened to her lungs, took her blood pressure, and finally, with judicious arrangement of the sheet, carried out a swift abdominal and pelvic examination.

Afterward he pulled up a chair beside her and took her hand in his.

"I've ordered more tests," Dr. Suárez told her, "but I'm sure they'll continue to be negative."

Starfire nodded in weary agreement.

"All except for one," the doctor continued. "People are foolish sometimes and don't see the wood for the trees. They overlook the most obvious answers."

Starfire looked puzzled. "What answers?"

"Why, that you're young and beautiful, and have a man who is in love with you."

"What does that have to do with what's wrong with me?"

"Everything—except there's nothing wrong. You are merely showing the normal symptoms of early pregnancy. And pregnancy's not a disease." He patted her hand and rose. "Congratulations, my dear. I recommend rest, good food, that you remain in this comfortable trailer with the air conditioning, and that you get home as soon as possible. A baby's more important than any movie that's ever been made or ever will be."

She sat up abruptly and stared at him in astonishment. *"Pregnant?"* It was impossible. Starfire could never be pregnant.

"Why not?"

"Because I . . . My God!" J.B. said, "I never thought . . ." She flung out a restraining hand. "Please, Dr. Suárez, wait!"

He paused at the door.

"Do something for me—promise not to tell Diamond."

He nodded with understanding. "Of course I promise. I'm sure you'd like to surprise him yourself with the good news."

Then he was gone. J.B. stared at the closed door and thought grimly: It'll be a surprise, all right.

Chapter

26

Vera wiped the sweat from her forehead and wished Saint would slow down. The air hung motionless; the sky glared and far out to the west merged with the sea in a shimmering white line. The ride back in the launch from the Joya Escondida had been been marginally refreshing, but the moment the boat stopped, the heat struck her like an open oven door.

It was early afternoon now, the beach, the huts, and the jungle beyond rippling in mirage, but Saint didn't appear to notice or be affected by the heat, striding along the low water line through a swirl of debris while Vera trotted, panting, at his side.

"He's got some master-race fixation; his dynasty's going to rule Hollywood like royalty. He's appointed me his surrogate. He's sterile, so I'm supposed to get J.B. pregnant and produce an heir for him." Saint kicked aside a discarded plastic cup with unnecessary violence. "I'm his son, you see, so the succession will be in order. He went on and on about how great it was all going to be, the power, position, and fame we'd have, all in such a matter-of-fact voice, like it was the most reasonable thing in the world."

Vera tried to sound calm. "And what did you say?"

"What do you think I said? I said 'No way.' But he didn't pay any attention. I'd come around, he said."

"But how about J.B.? Surely she'd never—"

"He said he hadn't discussed it with her yet, but he didn't imagine she'd object. It was to everybody's advantage, after all."

"My God. Then what?"

"Then we went back. I dropped him off at the dock and he said, still in this same calm voice, that I really had no choice because a lot of people's futures depended on my decision. That I was the touchstone. At least I'm not supposed to . . . do anything till we get back and they get married . . . but then, Jesus, Vera!" He jammed his fists into the pockets of his shorts and glared out into the bay where the *Desperado* rode sluggishly on the long, oily swells. "He expects me to service her, like a fucking stallion. It's crazy."

"It's more than crazy," Vera said; "it's absolutely insane. And outrageous and ridiculous. And what did he mean about other people's futures?"

"I don't know."

"I don't like that; it sounds as if he's threatening you. Or . . . somebody."

They reached the burned-out restaurant, their feet kicking up powdery spurts of sand and ash. Saint said slowly, "I get the worst feeling about him, Vera. Like he's sitting there like a huge spider with eight eyes, spinning his webs, and then I think of Fletcher . . ." He began restlessly to stride back toward the village, his bare feet apparently impervious to the scorching sand. He drew a breath. "I think of Fletcher. I should tell Diamond to go fuck himself, that no way will I do what he says, but I haven't done it because I'm afraid to. Not for me; for J.B. And then I think: Christ, he's my *father*! And no matter who he is, I still owe him— I mean, look what he did for me. And I respect his talent and his intelligence and I even feel sorry for him too. I don't really know what I think except . . . Oh, Vera"—Saint passed a weary hand over his face— "I don't think I want to be his son."

Vera made a short sprint to catch him again, her feet burning, her shirt sticking to her back, black spots swimming dizzily in front of her eyes. She grabbed him by the elbow and tugged him into the water, which lapped around their ankles in a tepid froth. She demanded, "But is Diamond *absolutely* sure?"

"He said he checked it all out after he first met with Arnie. He called Spring himself."

"Is there any chance Spring was lying again? If she was, this whole dynasty thing's pointless."

"According to Diamond, it was impossible for anyone else to be my father, and I believed him. Mother doesn't throw herself away, you know. She never screws around without good reason."

"But perhaps she *did* have a reason. Perhaps there *was* somebody else that no one knew about, not even Diamond. Saint, you have to ask her. For your own peace of mind."

"And do you think for one minute she'll tell me?"

Vera replied stoutly, "She certainly won't if you don't ask her."

In a travesty of his "anyone-for-tennis?" voice, Arnie asked, "Is this seat taken?"

When Arnie had settled, poured beer into a clouded glass, and squeezed lime into it: "I want to talk with you, Saint. Vera said . . ." He sounded horribly self-conscious. "Vera said it would be all right."

Saint made an encouraging sound. As Arnie didn't seem ready to go on, he prompted, "Sure it's all right."

Arnie sighed and hunched his shoulders. "We went to the Escondida last night. You know that place?"

Saint nodded.

"I just had to get away from here. I couldn't handle it one more minute."

"I know the feeling."

"No you don't," Arnie said tightly. "You couldn't." His hands were white-knuckled on his glass. He looked very fragile.

"I'm sorry." Saint wrenched his mind from Diamond, Spring, and J.B. "I didn't mean to be flip."

"I always used to be able to talk to you."

"You still can."

"Can I?"

"Get off it, Arnie. Of course you can. If you're still worrying about that night in Tahoe, then don't."

"I didn't know what to say to you."

"You didn't trust me. It pissed me off."

"I'm sorry."

"Forget it. Apology accepted. Don't not trust me again. Now, for Christ's sake, drink your beer and tell me what's on your mind."

Arnie laid his hands flat on the grimy table and stared at his fingers.

After a while he said in a determined voice, "Last night, Vera and I went to bed together. I thought that with Vera, of all people, I'd be all right and I'd be able to . . . to make love with a woman. She's beautiful. I'm fond of her. Shit. I *love* her. But I couldn't. Couldn't do anything unless I . . . pretended."

"That she was someone else?"

"Yes. And I felt so bad, Saint. Like I was . . . violating her, you know? It was lousy, awful, and I felt even worse because she was so understanding about it."

"Yes," Saint agreed, "she would be."

"I was lying to her. And lying to myself." His voice sheered to a cutting edge of tension. "My whole life's a lie. It's harder every day to pretend to be somebody I'm not and that I never can be."

After a pause Saint said, "Well, you're going to have to make some decisions, aren't you?"

"It's easy for you to say that——"

"Hey, guys!"

Their heads jerked up in unison. Tomás stood beside their table, grinning in triumph. "Look, Santo. Inocencio rented it in Puerto Vallarta!" The boy thrust a lurid-jacketed videocassette under Saint's nose, his whole body trembling with suppressed excitement. "Michael Jackson video. 'Thriller——' "

"Well, cool," Saint said, "or it would be if you had TV."

Arnie muttered, "And a VCR."

"Claro." Tomás pulled out a chair and flung himself into it. "Santo, I need a *big* favor." He explained the favor in a torrent of Spanish, almost incoherent with his urgency. The movie would wrap at the end of the week, he knew that, everyone knew that, and Saturday was disco night. Tomás knew all about the television equipment in the trailers; he had seen inside; couldn't one of the technical guys fix up a projection system in the cantina? "You got the juice to do it too." Tomás exclaimed, "We never had the juice to do nothing like this before. This is a real lousy, cheapo setup, not like a real disco in PV. I seen it there, man, lights flashing under the floor, and this movie on the wall, real big"—he spread his arms like wings to show how big—"two guys fighting on horses in a church . . ."

If all needs could be so simple, all problems so easily solved. "Sure," said Saint easily. "Why not? I'll bet they could run some cable in, move a unit around . . . I'll check on it."

"Oh, man," Tomás cried, slamming back his chair, which grated on the concrete with a shriek, "with a projector and enough juice and Michael Jackson, we'll fix you one hell of a fucking wrap party!"

As Tomás vaulted over the top of the bar, babbling his excitement to his younger brother, Inocencio, Arnie asked, "What was that all about? I lost him almost right off."

Saint explained.

Arnie gave a wry smile. "A wrap party. With a Michael Jackson video." He traced small patterns in the moisture on the table. "We seem to have been here forever, and now suddenly it's almost over." In a stifled voice: "And then it'll start all over again."

Saint said patiently, "Like I said, Arnie, it's your call."

"I know."

"If it's that tough being Arnold Blaize, then you have to stop it."

"I can't."

"Sure you can." In his mind's eye Saint saw Arnie back in school so long ago, a lonely fat boy grimly fighting on against losing odds. "You've got guts."

"When it got tough before, I'd do a few lines and everything would be all right."

"I was thinking further back. To St. Regius. You didn't do any lines then."

Arnie stared at the grimy tabletop. "If I admitted what I am, my career would be over. Finished. Down the tubes."

"You don't *admit*," Saint admonished sternly, "you goddamn well tell them. And let them take it or leave it. Anyhow, the way you're feeling right now, would it matter so much if your career did go down the tubes?"

Arnie closed his eyes. "Can you *imagine* the headlines? The dirt? The gossip? People'd hate me."

"Some would, sure. But they'd forget about it pretty quick. And think of all the people who'd admire you and wish they had the guts to do the same thing. The people whose lives would be changed. By you."

"I'd be letting him down."

"Who?"

"Diamond. I'm committed to two films a year for three years."

"Walk away. It'll only cost you money. Not your soul."

"I can't do that. I owe him."

"For what?"

"For all of it. For listening. For the *Starfire* project. And then, you see, I think he suspects about me and makes sure I'm protected. Like having Publicity bust themselves puffing up my little 'romances.' He doesn't have to do that."

"He's protecting his investment, not you."

"Once he asked me if there was anything else he should know that I hadn't told him; anything that, if it came out, could be trouble. He hates surprises. 'Tell me now,' he said, 'and we can fix it.' I said no, there's nothing, you know it all. . . . God knows, that's true enough." Arnie's face tightened in despair. "And now Omega's planning to license an Arnie doll to go with the Starfire doll." He gave a slightly wild laugh. "Can't you just see it? A *gay* Arnie doll? . . . Omega has a lot tied up in it, and Diamond personally."

"They can afford it."

"It's easy for you to say. You can stand up to him. I can't."

"You did it before, when you went to see him at the Polo Lounge."

"Yes," Arnie agreed simply, "but you see, that wasn't for me, it was for you."

Saint berthed the boat in the marina and this time took a taxi to an airport hotel. Through instinct he used a different hotel each time for his calls. Just in case.

It took a long while to trace Spring Kentfield and a great deal of money, during which a thought that had nagged in the back of his mind for a long time suddenly meshed with an almost audible click. When he eventually heard her voice, somewhat annoyed, against a background of clinking glass, muted laughter, and music, he demanded bluntly, "Mother, why did you tell Vic Diamond I'm his son when you know it's a lie?"

He heard her gasp, then splutter with shock and anger.

"Sloane, is this some kind of ridiculous game?"

"No game, Mother. Why did you tell him?"

"I can't possibly talk now. I'm having dinner with some very important people."

"For all I care, you could be having a foursome with Steven Spielberg, George Lucas, and Francis Ford Coppola. Listen to me. And if you dare hang up, you're going to be sorry."

Another gasp of outrage. Then Spring Kentfield said coldly, "I don't care for threats, Sloane. I'll talk to you for five minutes. But it'll have to be on another line."

He heard a muffled exchange of voices, then continued clinking, laughter, and music. Finally another receiver was lifted; the phone in the dining room or wherever was replaced and the party sounds cut off. "Now, then," Saint said, "talk to me."

Spring said in tones of arctic chill, "I suppose you've forgotten that if it hadn't been for me, you'd still be in that place. You should be eternally grateful, not flinging accusations in my face. And believe *me*, Sloane, only Diamond could have got you out of the mess you'd gotten yourself into."

"What I want to know is, why did you wait so long?"

"I don't understand you, Sloane."

"Sure you do. I'd been in Santa Paula for almost two years before you told Arnie to see Diamond and mention your name. If you knew he was my father and he was supposed to be so all-fired powerful, why didn't you go to him at once?"

"I didn't want to approach him except as a last resort."

"You didn't approach him because you didn't think of it."

"Sloane, that's not true. I was waiting for the right moment."

Saint persisted, "You didn't think of it because he's not my father. But perhaps, you thought, maybe it was possible, it was worth a try. You knew Diamond well enough to know he'd always wanted a son, and you thought that after all these years you'd provide him with one, ready-made and in Santa Paula."

"Well, so what if I did? I only did what any mother would. I had your welfare at heart. If that was what it took, that was what I did."

"That's a beautiful thought, but I can't buy into it a hundred percent. I know you too well, Mother. Your career isn't so hot right now, is it, and it sure wouldn't hurt to get close to Victor Diamond by giving him something he wants."

"Sloane, that insinuation's disgusting."

"Mother, listen to me. In return, you'd get nothing. He has a plan for the future, and I don't think it includes you.

"This is ridiculous goddamn non——"

"Don't you realize he's crazy? He's a megalomaniac. And now he has Vangie back."

A pause; then, hushed: "Sloane, *what* was that you said?"

"He thinks of J.B. as his own creation, just as he did with Vangie."

"Oh, my God." Spring's voice cracked in rage. She whispered harshly, "It should have been me. Oh, that bastard; it should have been me."

"What do you mean, Mother?"

"It was me. *Me*. He and I were *together*. If I'd only stayed with him . . ."

"But you didn't. You traded up. At least, that's what he said."

"Oh, Sloane. That's not true. He'd seen Vangie, you see, and that was the end. For me."

"Did you tell him you were pregnant?"

"Of course."

"What did he do?"

"He gave me money for an abortion."

Saint observed sardonically, "I'm lucky to be alive, you know that? That's two fathers tried to get rid of me."

"Sloane, this is no time for jokes."

"That wasn't really a joke, Mother." Saint sighed. "But then when I was in jail, you told him you hadn't had that abortion after all."

"Yes."

"And he believed you when you said I was his son."

"Of course he did. He always knew I hadn't been seeing anyone else. Otherwise he wouldn't have been prepared to pay for it in the first place."

Saint said carefully, "They have DNA tests now, completely reliable. It could be proved beyond doubt. Or not."

Spring didn't reply. The silence strung out until Saint pressed, "You *were* seeing someone else. Come on, Mother. Tell me."

"No. For God's sake, no. If he found out now . . ."

Saint said formally, "This is for me, Mother. I promise I'll never tell Victor Diamond if you had another lover."

"All right, then." Spring drew a deep breath. "But I don't think you'll like what you hear."

"Let me decide that."

"Yes . . ." Her voice sank almost to a whisper. "It's actually *very* unlikely Victor Diamond is your father—there were physical reasons I won't go into—but there was a time, just once, when it would have been possible; I had to work like a slave, you won't imagine what I had to do, but it would have been possible . . . and when I told him I was pregnant, he believed me at once when I said he was the father. He needs to be more than a man in every sense of the word. He *wanted* to believe me, Sloane. He wanted a child very badly."

"Who was it?"

"I've never told anyone this in my whole life. Nobody knew. Your father was a stunt driver for Paramount. It was the only time in my life I ever did anything like that. I never went to bed with a man just for sex." Her voice flattened, as though she was still in shock that she should so forget herself. "They said he drove like the devil; I wouldn't know. I never saw any of his footage. I don't like that kind of thing, violence, noise, dirt. He was an arrogant bastard, a Mexican from a barrio in Tijuana, with eyes that could scorch you. That's one reason I never wanted you near me. You brought back too many humiliating memories."

Saint stoically ignored that last statement. "But how *could* you keep it a secret? Especially from Diamond?"

"I was never seen with him; we never went anywhere together; I never spoke to him in public. I barely spoke to him at *all*."

"Then when?"

In a raw voice: "He'd come to my trailer between scenes, odd moments, five minutes here, two minutes there; we'd do it on the floor, over the table . . . God"—she sounded nauseated—"it was disgusting."

"Where is he now?"

"He's dead. Killed in one of those dumb cop chases with wrecks and flames. Thank God, was all I thought of at the time, now Diamond need never know." She gave a short, bitter laugh. "But then he saw Vangie. He didn't want me or my child anymore. Now, of course, he wants you badly. And I thought: Maybe he'll make it up to me for everything he's taken away."

"Oh, Mother. It won't work." Saint pointed out gently. "It's too late.

You've already given him what he wants. You've no trumps left in your hand. None at all. . . ."

At seven o'clock, having watched Diamond's lean figure climb aboard the *Desperado* and disappear below to watch the dailies, Saint and Vera slid surreptitiously into J.B.'s room in the clinic. They found her propped up in bed drinking a glass of iced soda water, pale but looking much better.

Vera asked, "How do you feel?"

"I feel fine. I told Diamond I'm working again tomorrow. I only have one more scene."

Saint said, "We have to talk with you. It's been impossible to get to you without him knowing . . ."

Vera began, "Has he said . . . has he told you about . . . ?"

J.B. nodded calmly. "Sure. He and I will get married as soon as we get back to California. Then Saint and I will make a baby."

Vera gasped. "And you can talk about it just like that. J.B., he's mad, just like Hitler with his selective-breeding programs." She couldn't help it: in her mind the dreadfulness of it all was threaded through with light. Saint had been ordered to bed with J.B.—and on every level he was appalled.

J.B. shrugged her slender shoulders. "It won't happen."

Saint affirmed, "Of course it won't. I'd never do that. But anyway, it'd be pointless. I'm not even Diamond's son. Listen, I talked with my mother last night." He began to tell her about it. "I'm not sure yet how I feel, being the son of a Mexican stuntman. Not much, really. I don't think it makes a whole lot of difference now . . ."

He stopped because J.B. began to laugh. She laughed and laughed on a note of rising hysteria until Vera begged, "Don't! Don't do that. It'll be all right. You can leave Diamond just as soon as we get home. . . . Stop now, J.B. Please."

"I can't . . . can't help it." J.B. spluttered, drank some more water, half-choked, and said in a smothered voice, "It's so goddamn funny."

"*Funny?*" Saint and Vera both stared at her.

"I mean, the timing, You see, he's too late."

Vera frowned. "What do you mean?"

"Because I'm pregnant already. Dr. Suárez told me yesterday. There's nothing wrong with me at all except for"—she quoted—"normal symptoms of early pregnancy."

Vera's eyes widened. "Why haven't you told Diamond?"

"Because it's not his baby."

"Not . . . Are you sure?"

"It's impossible." J.B. choked again over her water and put the glass down on her night table with a shaking hand. "We've never done anything that could make me pregnant. He can't. He's not just sterile, he's impotent. Do you understand me? Impotent. He can't get it up. He never has."

Saint's immediate feeling was one of deep sadness for Diamond. It was a tragedy, really; or rather, a black tragicomedy.

After a strained silence Vera asked: "Whose is it then?" As if she didn't know.

"Donald Wheeler's." For an instant J.B.'s eyes glowed, then turned as cold as the ice water in her glass. "You know, it was the strangest feeling, having Dr. Suárez sitting there right where you are now, telling me. It was like I just woke up after a long dream. Or nightmare, maybe. It jerked me back into myself so damn quick I can't tell you. This is *real*, not some dumb fantasy. *I'm* real." She patted herself on her flat stomach. "There's a baby in here, my baby, a *real* baby."

Vera asked numbly, "What d'you think Diamond will do when he finds out?"

Saint said, "You have to get away. Right now."

J.B. laughed grimly. "Running away won't solve anything. Nobody hits Diamond in his ego and gets away with it. Nobody. But this is my baby and I'll do whatever I can to protect it. Anything." She added, "It's funny; I thought women got all soft and sweet and gentle when they were pregnant. Well, they don't. They get hard and strong, and I think they could get real cruel if they had to."

Saint returned from Puerto Vallarta long after midnight.

"She's having a baby," he'd told Donald Wheeler. "Yours."

Donald hadn't sounded surprised. He said crisply, "I'll be down there tomorrow. Until I come, don't do *anything* that might make him suspicious. Act as normal as you can. Do as I say, Saint. Do *nothing*." And then: "It's going to be all right, you know. I promise you."

Saint wished he could believe him.

*   *   *

A line of light showed below Vera's cabin door. Saint tapped gently, then opened it. "I reached him. He's coming."

He was met by silence.

He opened the door. The room was empty. The bunk was neatly made up; she hadn't been to bed.

Saint was stunned with surprise; he had expected to find her waiting impatiently for news. But then he remembered. Vera was going to the cantina tonight to help the Ochoas and the *Starfire* production crew set up for the Michael Jackson video: "I'll go crazy if I just sit around and wait for you."

He turned to leave. Lying on her table was a drawing of Diamond, and on impulse he stopped to look. Diamond had fully metamorphosed into a snake now, with scales and darting forked tongue. Saint smiled grimly. Beneath the drawing was one of himself leaning against a boat pulled up on the beach. He looked different somehow, even to his own eyes. He picked it up and examined it, suddenly understanding the difference. He looked Mexican, like an arrogant stunt driver from Tijuana.

Then he noticed the writing on the other side: "Dear Saint: Here we all are in Mexico with God knows what terrible things brewing up around us, and all I'm really thinking about is you."

He read it through very carefully to the end: "I loved you from the first time I saw you, I still love you, and I always will. But enough's enough. This is the end. What a good thing you'll never see this letter."

Saint didn't go to find Vera in the cantina after all.

He went on deck and sat down in the bow of the boat, alone in the dark.

The moonlight struggled wanly through thickening overcast. The surge was coming from an unusual angle, snubbing the boat uncomfortably against its anchor chain. At a different season of the year one would imagine some serious weather to be coming.

Ashore he could see a loom of yellow light above the cantina and hear snatches of music with a heavy bass rhythm. He sank his chin in his hands and thought.

For a moment his mind was absolutely blank, as though this final shock had paralyzed his brain and thrown him into emotional overload.

Then a warmth began to spread through his body, starting in his heart and moving through to his fingers and toes.

Vera loved him.

And he'd never guessed. Then, he realized: of course he'd known inside, but there had always been J.B. in between, casting such a dazzle that he was blinded, unable to see that it was Vera who always picked him up when he fell and to whom time after time he'd fled in despair and been taken in without question, even into her bed and her person; that it was in fact Vera for whom he had instinctively headed after that dreadful dinner in New York; Vera who had visited him in jail with peanut butter and a tape recorder; Vera whose mind worked so well with his that they could communicate even without speech.

Oh, Vera.

And now, unless he did something very quickly, she would be leaving him for good, to go and work in Japan, and she mustn't do that, she mustn't leave him, he absolutely couldn't bear it.

No, Saint decided, he and Vera must start over—and this time he'd play it right.

Chapter

27

The afternoon was hot and still, a darkness slowly spreading like a stain from the southwest.

Tomás Ochoa had been watching the sky all day, praying for a miracle, that there would be no rain, or if there was, it would not be the torrential rain the ominous sky portended, which would drum like thunder on the galvanized roof, cascade through holes and crevices, short-circuit the electronics, and generally ruin his wonderful evening. "*Por favor, Dios,*" Tomás prayed, "don't let it rain."

Saint had left a message on Vera's bunk: Donald was on his way; she should continue to play it cool with Diamond. He almost added: We have to talk ASAP. But didn't, finding himself, now that the moment had come, strangely reluctant and almost afraid to confront Vera. Suppose, despite everything, she refused him. She had every right.

In any case, he didn't see her until afternoon. She didn't come to the set in the morning, when a reenergized Starfire raced time after time down the steps from the ruins, until Diamond was satisfied with the shot. It wasn't until after the final wrap that Saint found Vera on the beach surrounded by children who waited with dogged persistence for portraits to be drawn. She asked anxiously, "Is Donald coming? It's after two o'clock."

"He said he had some final fish to fry, then he'd be down today even if he had to charter."

"What did he mean by 'final fish'?"

"I guess we'll find out. How many more kids are you going to draw?"

"As many as I can. It passes the time."

"Vera . . ."

Vera carefully shaded the folds of Celestina's blindingly white First Communion dress, which the child had worn especially to have her portrait drawn. "Yes?"

"I wanted . . . Oh, never mind. I'll tell you later."

At the same time that Saint left Vera sketching on the beach, almost relieved it was so hard to talk with her alone, Dr. Donald Wheeler nosed his rental car between a Mercedes SDL 320 and a black Buick sedan in the crowded driveway of David Zimmerman's home in Bel Air.

The very correct English butler who met him at the door told him, "Terribly sorry, sir, but Mr. Zimmerman can't possibly see you today." Inside, telephones shrilled, raised voices argued, doors slammed. The very texture of the air vibrated with disturbance.

Donald assumed his most pompous British voice. "I have an appointment. He's expecting me. And he'll want to see me." As he had expected it might, the accent helped.

"You see, there's a bit of a flap on, actually," the butler confided. "He told me nobody, absolutely nobody . . . It would be much better if you called next week."

"No it wouldn't," Donald contradicted. "It would be much too late. Tell him I want to talk about Victor Diamond, Fletcher McGraw, and Vangie Sellors." Donald wrote the names on the back of his business card.

The butler's right eye twitched in paroxysm. A chord had been touched. He said in a strained voice, "I can't promise anything. This is *not* a good day." But he took the card and disappeared with it.

Within a very few minutes Donald was shown into a wide room overlooking lawns and sculptured shrubbery, where two men argued violently across a desk. One man was tall, his tanned bald head surrounded by a crown of wiry dark hair; the other was small and pear-shaped, wearing a black silk suit and brandishing a tabloid newspaper. There was a photograph of a naked girl on the cover, and four-inch black headlines that Donald was able to read from the doorway: "STARFIRE WAS A HOOKER."

"Goddamn right," the bald man yelled to the pear-shaped man, "you're going down there. And you're going *now*."

At Donald's entrance he said, "All right, Dr. Wheeler, whatever this is about, it had better be good."

And Donald promised, head to one side to make sure the photo was indeed J.B., "It will be."

Tomás had created a screen from a bedsheet suspended from the cantina roof, its lower corners secured tautly to pegs on the floor. A generator truck rumbled gently behind the building to power the newly assembled television projector, sound equipment, and the spots, which, at the touch of a switch, would flash in sequence to form a blinding, multicolored light show. It would be much better, Tomás bragged to all and sundry, than the best disco in Puerto Vallarta. In skintight jeans and scarlet shirt, his hair oiled to patent-leather gloss, he darted like some brilliant piping bird between the bar and the makeshift booth where a burly technician in earphones manned the improvised sound and light panel.

People had been pouring into the cantina from six o'clock onward, villagers, Indians, resident Americans, and all the technicians and crew from Omega who hadn't left on the late-afternoon shuttle plane or ridden one of the trucks over the mountain. Even Father Ignacio wandered in and perched on a bar stool, looking like a very old vulture with disheveled, dusty feathers. He had left his empty church; it was much too hot and no one was coming to confession anyway. There was a low rumble of thunder. Tomás darted up to him and seized his arm. "Pray, Father. Pray there won't be rain."

The Omega hierarchy occupied a table between the sound booth and the bar, where they were the object of a great deal of attention, gossip, and speculation. They were an impressive-looking group.

Victor Diamond sat in the center, all in white—white knife-edged slacks and stiffly starched white shirt that had, incredibly, not yet gone limp in the stifling heat—only lacking, in several minds, a crown and the diagonal slash of a watered-silk ribbon across his chest emblazoned with some glittering order to look every inch the emperor. Saint sat on his left, darkly tanned, in black jeans and black tank top with a red-and-white bandanna wrapped around his forehead, offering the vaguely menacing aura of a homeboy from a Los Angeles barrio. Across the table, Vera wore a crimson blouse and a short black skirt that swirled above her knees, defiantly bright lipstick, and a spray of scarlet bougainvillea behind one ear. Arnie, at her side, wore a blue-and-white checkered shirt and blue jeans, a navy-and-white bandanna loosely knotted around his throat. Although dressed in somewhat similar fashion to Saint, he managed to project an entirely different image, as innocently wholesome as Curly, the handsome cowboy from *Oklahoma!*

And then, of course, there was Starfire, who gleamed on Diamond's right, her short dress made from fabric like silver foil, her eyes elongated and very dark, her long hair twisted on top of her head and secured with a silver filigree barrette. She looked remote and eerily beautiful, an incarnation of Chirihuatetl herself, if one believed the malicious gossip of the old women and the maunderings of El Loco.

Tomás slammed onto the table a pitcher of beer, another of margaritas, and a glass of grapefruit juice for J.B., who had refused alcohol. He accepted a fifty-thousand-peso bill and forced it, with effort, into the pocket of his jeans.

Borracho Pete loomed hopefully at Saint's elbow, but catching Diamond's discouraging glare, muttered, grinned, and melted away.

In the sound booth the technician was running through Tomás' well-worn tape selection, which sounded truly terrible on the superior speakers.

The Mexican boys drank and stared at J.B.

"You gonna dance with her, man?"

"You kidding? Dance with a goddess? Or a witch?"

"You afraid she'll put a spell on you?"

"I wouldn't mind a spell of hers."

"Come on, man, she's no witch. You're not *that* dumb."

"So, you ask her."

They drank and whispered and plotted. There she was, available for the first time. She could be touched, talked to, danced with, without fear of retribution, for this was a fiesta, this was disco night.

This was also their last chance. The movie people were leaving tomorrow.

"Why should she dance with us? She may not be a witch or a goddess, but she's a movie star."

"And *he's* with her." They all fell silent, staring balefully at Diamond, of whom they were all unaccountably afraid.

"Ah, don't be chickenshit, ask her. She's just waiting for you to ask her."

"Come on, man."

"Who needs it? Ever see her smile? She's cold as ice."

"That's all you know." The leader grinned and preened. "I'm telling you, she'll be real hot."

"How come you know so much?"

" 'Cause Inocencio's spiking her juice with ricea, man. I fixed it."

"No kidding!" With bated breath they turned as one to stare at Inocencio, fourteen years old, behind the bar. "Couple or three of those," the leader promised, "and the ice'll melt in your hands!"

Diamond stood and raised a hand for silence. His presence was so commanding that an instant hush fell upon the room.

Entirely appropriately, thunder growled in a long drumroll. He now looked not so much an emperor as a sorcerer commanding the elements. At the bar, Father Ignacio fumbled at his belt for his protective little bag of herbs.

"We're leaving here tomorrow," Diamond opened, "and I want to say a few words." His dark gaze rested first on Starfire, then upon Saint and Arnie. "We have magic going here, people. We are creating magic with our talent and our chemistry. We're a great team and we have a great film. Together we can do just about anything. We've created a new world together, and all of you"—he made a wide gesture of inclusion—"are now part of it. A part of us, of Omega and *Starfire*. Part of history in the making."

The crowd applauded itself. Diamond waited until the noise subsided, his eyes raking the room in triumph. "I got the word a while back, but I wanted to wait for the right moment, and this seems to be it." He drew a deep breath and announced, "Well, we got the green light from the money people. We're going ahead, with no holds barred and a bigger budget than ever. We start rolling in the new year." He raised his glass. "A toast. To *Starfire III!*"

He seized J.B.'s hand and raised it high in the air.

Few but the Americans understood much, but the import of the words was clear enough. The room roared with approval and thudded beer bottles and fists on the tables.

"And now," Diamond cried with the air of a grand lord officially opening the annual servants' ball, "let's dance."

At the sound panel the technician pushed Tomás' tapes aside with a sigh of relief and plugged in "La Bamba." People surged onto the dance floor; colored spots swooped and thrust in brilliant parabolas and La Playita's most memorable disco night in living memory began at last.

Saint held out his hand. "Come on, Vera." On the dance floor, regardless of the jostling bodies, he held her close in his arms. He could put it off no longer. It was now or never. He had rehearsed what to say to her for hours. For the whole day.

Vera objected in a breathless voice: "You can't dance like this to 'La Bamba.' "

"Why not?" Saint was oblivious of the music, conscious only of Vera's waist, warm under her thin silk blouse, and the touch of her fingers twisting restlessly in his. Even the nonarrival of Donald Wheeler had faded to the back of his mind. He pressed her closer. She was so slender now, so delicate. He had known her fat, thin, and in between. What the hell? What did it matter? Now he forgot the clever words he had planned to say and yelled against the deafening music, "Vera, I don't want you to go to Japan. I want you to stay here. I want you to marry me because we're terrific working partners, I don't want to lose you, and"—God, he'd almost not said it, it was so obvious—"I *love* you, goddammit."

He breathed a sigh of relief, looked down at her expectantly, and waited.

She said nothing. For an instant her body felt limp. She didn't look at him. "Vera? Can't you say something?" He thought: Perhaps she didn't hear me. Then, with a twist of panic: Perhaps she's going to say no. My God, thought Saint, what do I really know of what's going on in her life or in her head? I've taken her for granted again, assumed that all I had to say was "Marry me" and she'd come running. He blurted, "I was a monumental blind fool not to know it years ago. I realized that last night when I went into your cabin and saw that letter."

Vera tripped over his feet. She said in a strangled voice, "You read my letter?"

"I know I shouldn't have. But I did anyway. Vera, I love you. You'd better believe me. It's true. I've always loved you, but I guess I didn't realize it. It's taken me too long to understand. I'm a fool. You'd be marrying a fool. And an ex-con. Please, Vera, say yes."

He thought she answered, but the words were muffled against his chest and drowned by the deafening noise. "*What* did you say?"

He crushed her against him, desperate for her answer, but all she said was, "Please, Saint, can we sit down now?"

When Saint and Vera had gone to dance, "Vic," Arnie said, "there's something I have to say to you."

"Sure, Arnie," Diamond cried expansively, "I'm all ears."

"I know this isn't the time, but I have to tell you now. It won't wait. Listen, about us being a team and all. Well, I can't be part of it any longer. I want out."

There was a second's pause; Diamond's smile faded a touch, then flicked back on again. "You're right, this is no time to talk. You're burned out, Arnie, and exhausted like we all are. I know that. That's why I didn't hit the roof when you took off for the night with Vera. We'll talk about it back in L.A."

"I can't wait that long. I know how dumb that sounds—I've waited this long, you'd think I could wait a little longer."

"You're right. It's dumb. I'm not listening, Arnie."

"You have to, because I'm serious. This is the end. I won't be around for *Starfire III*."

Diamond still smiled. "Don't be crazy, Arnie. You're going to be making more money than you've ever dreamed of. Or did someone make you a better offer?"

"It's not the goddamn money. It's never been the money."

"What, then?"

"I'm just not a good enough actor . . ."

"What do you want to do? Shakespeare? Listen, Arnie, you may not be Laurence Olivier but you're still a major star. We'll work something out you'll like."

"You're not getting it. If I was a real actor, I could fake it. But I can't live with being the nation's sex symbol. I just can't do it anymore."

Diamond gazed at him thoughtfully. "I believe you are serious."

Arnie nodded.

Diamond's expression shifted. It was a minute but profound change, as if the cells of his skin realigned to reveal an entirely new creature underneath.

"I see," Diamond said. And after a moment: "You're going to tell me you're coming out of the closet."

Arnie blinked at him in surprise. "You knew?"

"Of course I knew."

"But how?"

"Since you first talked to me about Saint with your heart and your soul in your eyes. Beware of that, Arnie. You're much too revealing."

Arnie gulped in confusion, then rallied. "Well, then, yes, I'm glad you understand. Yes, I'm gay, and I'm not ashamed of it. Not anymore." With resolution: "I'm going public," and Arnie smiled in pure relief that it had been so easy after all, until he realized Diamond was gazing at him as though he were some naked and repellent specimen trapped in formaldehyde.

As if Arnie hadn't spoken, Diamond went on, "You lust after him, don't you? Perhaps you dream at night that you're fucking him. Yes, it must be tough, being a faggot and having to make love to women on screen and look like you're enjoying it."

Arnie's face drew into gaunt lines. He heard a tinny roaring noise inside his head.

"No," Diamond was telling him, "I need you, Arnie. You can't just walk. Sorry, kiddo, you signed on for the duration. You leave me, you'll never work again. Your career will be deader than yesterday's news."

Against the roaring in his head Arnie muttered, "I don't care." His voice sounded artificial in his ears, as though it didn't belong to him.

"Then do you care about all those kids out there, and their parents, who think you're a hero because you're tough enough to give up drugs and say so?"

"I . . ."

Diamond smiled. It was the kind of smile, Arnie thought, that a spider smiles, watching the fly suddenly realize it can't get out of the web.

"How'd you like them to read in their morning papers how you were canned by Omega for fucking little Mexican boys on the beach? I saw you the other night, you know."

Arnie's face was the color of ash. "There was nothing to see. We were only talking. Jesus Christ, Diamond——"

"These people are poor, Arnie. Give the boy a hundred bucks and he'd say anything. What's his name? Raúl?"

"You couldn't do that. Nobody could——"

"Suppose it was spread around how you had AIDS, Arnie? How you'd infected a whole innocent village?"

Arnie stared at him, speechless, and Diamond returned his gaze with eyes like dark, burned holes. "People don't screw me over and thrive, Arnie. And they never leave me unless I'm ready for them to go. Never."

J.B. drank thirstily. Her juice tasted rather strange, but it was cold and refreshing and she was so hot. If I can only make it through today and tomorrow, she thought blurrily, and Dr. Suárez doesn't tell Diamond about me, if I can only get back to California, everything will be all right.

The light bulbs swung dizzily in the rising wind that buffeted through the cantina, and the spots swirled with the pulse of the music. She finished her drink and immediately there was Tomás with another. She drank again, laced her fingers across her stomach, and thought about the baby inside there, so small but growing steadily, minute by minute, cell by cell.

She knew she must leave Diamond at whatever cost. She had no illusions about him anymore, not like Arnie. When he knew about the baby, he'd try to kill it, and she would do anything to protect it (she didn't dare yet think of the baby as "him" or "her"), even if it meant sacrificing Melody Rose or Momma.

She drank more juice and tried yet again to think coherently, but the thoughts felt loose inside her head and wouldn't come together. And now a young man stood in front of her, not really a young man, more like a boy, he couldn't have been more than seventeen, grinning and holding out his hand.

She glanced at Diamond, but he was talking intently with Arnie and didn't notice.

She knew he wouldn't want her to dance. So I will, thought J.B. It was a small token rebellion which pleased her. Then she thought of dancing away into the crowd, through the door, and not stopping, but dancing across the beach, through the ocean and sky, safe forever and ever with Donald Wheeler and the baby. She took the boy's hand and stood up. She smiled at him and followed him into the crowd and an illusion of safety. She closed her eyes, and for a glorious, glittering moment he actually *was* Donald Wheeler, come for her, to carry her away. . . .

The lights flashed in brilliant swaths of color across her short silver dress. The boy held her hand and spun her; she must have lost her barrette, for her hair suddenly tumbled down around her shoulders.

She opened her eyes again and laughed a little wildly, for he looked nothing like Donald Wheeler at all; he was thin and brown, with heavily oiled hair, wearing a shirt of cheap electric-blue satin. However, he was a very good dancer.

Nearly everyone was dancing now, bodies jammed against bodies. Some Indians stood by the wall, wearing beautifully embroidered white cotton shirts and trousers, watching the party with a gently remote curiosity. Beside them a small man in a sombrero leaned in the doorway, a big sickle-shaped knife at his belt. His somber eyes tracked her progress around the room. For a moment she thought she recognized him.

The boy was holding her tightly in his arms; too tight; she smelled the cloying odor of his hair oil and felt nauseated. The lights reeled around her, the music throbbed unpleasantly, and the back of her neck prickled.

"Let's go," the boy was saying. "Let's go outside."

She couldn't feel the floor under her feet, actually she couldn't even feel her feet at all, and must have stumbled, because he tightened his grip on her. If she hadn't known for sure she'd had nothing but fruit juice, she would have said she was drunk. She felt herself being guided through a gusty aperture into darkness where the wind whined through the sand, the surf pounded with a peculiar leaden rhythm, and a ball of lightning sizzled horizontally across the bay. Blinded, she felt rather than saw two figures stumble past her toward the cantina, then clapped her hands to her ears as a peal of thunder crashed right overhead.

In the cantina all the lights went out.

When they came back on, a small figure in a drenched black suit was clawing his way around the taut belly of the billowing sheet, followed by a second figure, taller, his red hair flattened and dark with rain.

Jason Brill and Donald Wheeler.

Brill was stunned with fright and drenched to the bone. "I should have been here hours ago," he told Diamond with clattering teeth, "but the weather's god-awful. Some freaking tropical storm. The airport's closed now; we were the last plane they let down."

Diamond snapped, "What're you talking about? Why are you here? And why the hell"—casting a baleful glance at Donald Wheeler—"is he with you?"

"He's been very helpful," Brill moaned fussily. "I was very ill in the boat. Very ill indeed. For two hours. It was a dreadful ride, and I don't know when I've felt worse." He added, "Particularly when I have such unfortunate news."

Arnie, wearing a quenched expression, glanced incuriously from Brill to Donald.

Vera thrust her way through the crowd, Saint behind her, and gripped Donald by the hand. "Thank God you came."

Diamond fixed Brill with an inimical stare. "Whatever it is, did you have to deliver the news in person? There are phones, remember; you could have sent a fax. This makes no sense, especially when we're coming back tomorrow."

"It couldn't wait. Dave told us to take the plane. Told us himself."

"David *Zimmerman*? Told *us*?" Diamond regarded Donald Wheeler with a cold eye. "You had better have some very good reason for being here."

"I do," Donald said politely. "Believe me."

The music pounded; the spots flung lurid patches of color. Diamond's face flashed acid yellow, crimson, and blue. He caught Brill's arm in an ungentle grip. "Perhaps you'd better give me this news outside, Jason." He herded him away like a warden strong-arming a prisoner.

The generator truck shielded them from most of the wind and some of the noise. With a trembling hand Brill reached inside his suit jacket and produced a sodden newspaper.

Diamond demanded, "What's that?"

Brill smoothed it out against his damp black-silk thigh. "Today's *National Enquirer*." He half whispered, "It seems there's a lot you didn't know about Starfire."

"That's a lie," Diamond said softly. "I know everything."

"No," Brill said, more courageous now, "not everything."

And so, indeed, it appeared.

"STARFIRE WAS A HOOKER," screamed the huge headline.

Below, in grainy black and white, a very young nude girl, unmistakably J.B., flung a pale-eyed, challenging glare over her bare shoulder.

Diamond stared at it for a moment in silence; then: "Where in God's name did they get this shit?"

A subhead offered in slightly smaller type, "Had Her Regular Johns," Says Sister.

"Says *sister*," Diamond enunciated with a hiss. He stabbed his finger at that revealing word. "Sister. That coke-head bitch gave them this stuff . . ." He smiled grimly. "She's going to regret the day she was born."

Jason Brill went on in a colorless voice, "I understand there are over a million of these photographs now being marketed by a poster company."

Diamond rubbed at the back of his neck. Despite the heat, he had broken out in a cold sweat. "They must be recalled. They're my property."

"No they're not. She posed for this ten years ago. She signed a release. And the Macklin Corporation—the toy company," he said, as Diamond stared at him without recognition, "is suing both Omega and you personally for misrepresentation and fraud. They 'cannot allow such an unwholesome association for their product.' " Their words, not mine."

Diamond snatched the newspaper from Brill's hand and violently ripped it across and across again. "They can't do this. Sue the shit out of—"

"Inadvisable. We have no position. A lawsuit against the newspaper would not only be useless but also extremely costly, both for Omega and yourself. Regarding the Macklin Corporation, Dave plans to settle at once and attempt to downplay the whole sorry business."

Diamond repeated slowly, "The whole sorry business. Somebody's certainly going to be very sorry indeed." He reentered the teeming room, Brill a step behind. In a very quiet voice he asked, "Where is she? Where *is* Starfire?"

"All right," Saint demanded, "what's the news?"

"That can wait."

"Then tell me why, for God's sake, you went to see Zimmerman."

"Because he's top banana. Nominally, at least, he's Diamond's boss.

Nominally he has the corporate ear, and Diamond for once was offstage."
Donald's eyes darted. "Where is she?"

"She's here somewhere."

Arnie was drinking straight from an unlabeled brown bottle. He said
tonelessly, "Dancing."

"In fact," Donald said, "I walked in on one hell of a situation. Zimmerman was glad to see me and *very* happy to talk. He hates Diamond's
guts, you know. He's scared shitless for his job and wants him out in
the worst way, even if *Starfire III* has to be dumped. Believe me, the
knives are out at Omega. There's a power play going on that makes the
Mafia look like nursery school." Donald paused. "I need a drink. I didn't
think I was going to survive that boat ride, and that miserable little shit
threw up all over my pants."

He reached for a half-full glass from the table and drank the contents
straight down. Some color crept back into his face and he rubbed at his
wet, salty cheek. "That's better. Whatever the hell it is. Tastes like paint
remover." He glared through the swooping lights. "These things're making
me feel seasick again. Where the hell *is* J.B.? She should be back by now."

It was very dark out here; no stars. She tripped on the uneven ground
and the boy swung her off her feet altogether and was suddenly holding
her tightly against his chest. She had a moment of nauseous disorientation,
not knowing whether she was standing or lying down. He felt incredibly
hot, radiantly hot, and wet with sweat, and he had an erection—it was
jabbing into her with persistence, no matter how she twisted away. He
was grinning at her and now had cupped her ass and was pulling her
against him very hard, and she could feel his hand under her skirt.
"Chirihuatetl . . ." He grinned, all fingers and penis and silver teeth.

With a monumental effort she gathered her foggy wits. "Hey!" snapped
J.B. Feeney, "you knock that off or I'll kick you in the nuts."

Insinuatingly: "Chirihuatetl . . ."

"I'll give you Chirihuatetl!" She flung herself backward and slammed
upward with her knee. He doubled over with a wail and she chopped
him a backhanded blow across the face as he folded, hands clasped between
his legs.

The world spun dizzily around her. She staggered to regain her balance.

Thunder boomed and a gust of wind splattered her with rain. As she tried to push the hair from her eyes, the rain suddenly rushed upon her in a solid wall. It was so heavy she could barely see the lights of the cantina, and so loud that the music was drowned. She turned blindly, tripped over the body at her feet, then felt her hand taken in a bone-hard grip. "Sokay," a voice whispered close beside her ear. "Sokay. Come."

Donald, she thought with relief; Donald was here after all. She had somehow managed to summon him, perhaps calling upon Starfire's residual strength. Now she would hold his hand and he would lead her away from Diamond, away from the cantina, far away to safety.

The rain pounded on the galvanized roof, louder than the thunder, louder than the music. "The video!" Tomás screamed. "Start the video!" The wind howled in from the ocean and the sheet ballooned into the room, humming on its ropes like a close-hauled mainsail.

Donald Wheeler emptied the glass and set it back on the table. "This is powerful stuff. What is it?"

Vera said, "Nothing. It's just J.B.'s grapefruit juice."

"Bullshit." Donald thrust the glass at Saint.

He sniffed cautiously. "Ricea." At Donald's blank expression, "Distilled cactus juice. The local brew. It's not too bad mixed with . . ." His face paled. "Oh, my God. She thought she was drinking just juice. She had at least six of those."

Donald said, "We'd better go after her," just as the lights went out for the second time, but now with a purpose.

From the speakers, amplified at top volume above the rain and the thunder, roared the opening bars of "Thriller," and on the screen Michael Jackson flirted with a pretty girl outside a movie theater. The crowd screamed with excitement.

Diamond's voice grated into Saint's ear. "Where is she? Where's Starfire?" his face ghastly in the necrotic light.

Saint ignored him. He began to force his way toward the entrance, aware of Diamond at his heels.

Images came and went. A churchyard filled with mist. Dreadful shapes crawling from broken graves.

Father Ignacio watched with fixed attention and fingered his cross.

A line of ragged ghouls danced with frenzied abandon, faces frozen in decaying grins.

The rain pounded on the roof and jetted through the holes, although no one either noticed or cared. Tomás watched and waited, holding his breath. Perhaps it would be all right after all.

Then a crash, as though the heavens themselves had split in half over their heads. A boom—and the ropes gave way, the sheet exploded inward, carrying its writhing cargo of ghouls forward onto the shrieking audience. There was a searing flash of blue light. A sharp smell of ozone. Then the images were gone and so was the music.

"Well, fuck," came the technician's Kentucky drawl through total darkness. "Guess the show's over, folks."

Donald and Saint, immediately followed by Diamond, then by Arnie and Vera, climbed through the tattered screen and out into the rain, where a figure stumbled toward them, hair plastered to his scalp, hands clutching his groin. "She's gone," the boy told Saint. "And good riddance. She's a fucking bitch, man."

"Gone where?"

With a shaking hand he pointed down the beach toward the ruined hotel, where a flicker of purple-white lightning showed, for a split second, two figures a long way off across the sand.

"She's gone with Real Gutiérrez. You better get after them, you want her back in one piece, not sixteen." Calling after them, almost with satisfaction: "Don't forget it's full moon. He gets rabid at full moon."

The man was dragging her down the beach. She stumbled awkwardly, her feet plowing through the wet sand. As the driving rain revived her and she realized that of course he wasn't Donald Wheeler, she stopped dead. "No," she yelled, "I'm not coming with you. Let me go."

"Sokay," he said, and again "sokay."

J.B. cursed whatever it was she had drunk that made her so fuzzy, so dull and stupid. If she had had a problem before, she was in serious trouble now. This was the man in the hat, the marijuana grower with the metal teeth, the crazy man they called El Loco. He was small and old but astonishingly strong for his size, and he had a machete.

She gasped for breath and her heart hammered sickeningly inside her ribs. What am I going to do? J.B. agonized. What in hell am I going to do?

What could she do but wait for a chance to break loose and run for it—suspecting with a feeling of doom that this wiry little man could not only run faster than she but also see in the dark.

The lightning flashed; she saw they were almost at the end of the beach. She stumbled deliberately and sank to her knees. He pulled her to her feet far too easily and dragged her after him, past the pool, the restaurant, and onto the steep steps leading into the ruined hotel.

Don't panic, she ordered herself. Don't struggle. Go along with him, let him think you're not trying to escape, and when he eases up a bit, then tear away. He's got to ease up sometime.

The jungle loomed over them. In the intervals between lightning flashes it was blacker on the steps than she'd believed possible. If only there was some light, a moon . . . tonight was full moon . . . She was moving by feel alone, blinded by rain, flailed by invisible branches, half-strangled by vines. She slipped on the slimy stones and almost fell except for that hand, tough as horn, which jerked her upright as though she weighed nothing at all.

Risking a backward glance, she found she could no longer see the lights of the village. She wondered whether she'd be able to find her way back even if she did escape. She didn't think so, not in time. She'd lose herself and he'd catch her easily; she'd *never* get away from this man. With despair she knew nobody had seen her leave the cantina. No one would miss her until too late. They'd never find her, she would have vanished into the storm without a trace, dragged away to his lair, wherever that was, where he'd do God knew what and then chop her into pieces. . . .

Then her mind clicked back into coldness. She remembered reading in one of Momma's psychic healing magazines how ordinary people, at times of great need, could occasionally summon up supernatural strength. There had been a pregnant woman who had somehow lifted the back of a truck off her two-year-old child.

A pregnant woman.

Like her. Remember the baby.

The steps were gushing cataracts of water. She fell forward, grazing her knees on the step above. Then gathered herself, made herself lift one leg, then the other, climbing faster and faster, until she drew almost level with Royal Gutiérrez.

She knew exactly where she was after all. She had worked here on and off for weeks. This was the precise place she had leapt this morning, step by step . . . and now she remembered one more thing.

Another lightning flash momentarily showed a dark opening to the right, where a swath of ropelike vine had been hooked back to make way for the film crew. As Gutiérrez turned into the path, which would gradually descend and lead upriver, she flung herself forward, reaching over his shoulder, tearing the vine free so it tumbled around him in fibrous coils. For a second, distracted, he loosened his grip on her arm. It was enough.

She tore from his grip and hurled herself down the steps in the pitch dark, praying she wouldn't miss her footing, knowing he was somewhere right there behind her, compact and deadly, swinging his machete. Her breath shredded into sobs. She tried to concentrate. This was how it went: right foot, one bounding step at a time, body loose, legs flexed, left foot, thinking herself back into this morning's shoot, praying at each stone ledge that she wouldn't misjudge the height, the depth, her timing.

Gutiérrez grunted, not six feet behind her. She thought she felt his hand clutch at her flying hair. She screamed. She took a corner too fast, her foot slid out from under her, she gathered herself in mid-flight, and leapt blindly toward the golden specks of light she could see gleaming weakly through the long silver spears of rain. Lights . . . It took her a full second to make the connection. That the lights were carried by people.

She mistimed her leap and hit the next step too fast and too soon, her knees driving up into her chest. Her body jarred achingly and she almost fell. But she dared not fall.

Gutiérrez grunted once more. He was right behind her now. She could see him imprinted in her mind's eye, the sodden hat low over his face, the blade ready in his hand.

Forget him. Blank him out. Right foot. Leap. Left . . .

The flashlights were much closer. She screamed a tearing, anguished scream. A beam stabbed up toward her, caught and held her—and the next lightning flash seared the scene forever into her brain:

Saint leaping up toward her, eyes fixed on what was behind her,

Diamond at his heels, white hair almost incandescent in the glare, his mouth a black square opened on a scream, and then, behind Diamond, Donald Wheeler—although that was impossible. Now she knew she was hallucinating. With dread she wondered whether there was anybody there at all. Whether she might be already dead and still moving convulsively like a chicken with its head cut off.

Darkness again. Her eyes dazzled, J.B. slipped on the broken stones. She thought she heard Saint yell, "Out of the way, get out of the fucking way, get *down*."

As she fell, she felt a rush of air across the top of her head. Something snatched at her hair. Saint was moving very fast, coming up on Gutiérrez as he once again raised his arm. She saw the blade, a sickle of deadly light in the flashlight beam, and Diamond's arm reaching out, catching Saint across the throat and hurling him aside. She heard Diamond's voice scream, "Vangieeeee . . ."

Then a metallic hiss, a thump, and a receding patter of bare feet.

She closed her eyes. She dug her fingers into mud and wet leaves for support as the ground heaved sickeningly underneath her. When the vertigo passed, she crouched on her hands and knees and threw up the entire contents of her stomach. Afterward, cold and shivering, she crawled toward the steps where Diamond lay sprawled on his stomach, one hand hanging limply over the edge, the fingers curled gently, as if he was asleep.

On the step below, Donald Wheeler and Saint leaned speechless over a pale, humped object.

Saint said, "Don't look, J.B. Don't look."

But it was too late, she had looked, and in the second before he jerked the flashlight aside, she saw Victor Diamond's severed head, the eyes washed by rain, wearing an expression of fixed surprise.

Chapter

28

Vera stumbled up the steps, trying to stay at Arnie's heels, breathless in the wind and teeming rain, her feet leaden with dread. She felt she had been climbing those tall steps for years and that it was all useless, for she knew they wouldn't be in time, that no one could stop Diamond from killing J.B.

Then, rounding a bend in the steps, Arnie's hand caught Vera's arm in a vise-like grip, bringing her up short.

There they stood, Donald and Saint, their flashlights aimed downward so that their faces, lighted from below, seemed only cheekbones and gaunt eye sockets.

And there was Victor Diamond.

Vera took one appalled look and turned away, her stomach convulsing.

Nobody paid any attention to her distress, however, because J.B. needed help much more than she did. It was Arnie who led Vera away, holding her tightly in support, for her legs trembled so much she could barely walk. "It's all right; it's all over. Let's go."

He walked her down the steps, back along the beach through a mob of villagers rushing toward them, then up the path to the village and at last to the Omega clinic, where he made her lie down while from somewhere he conjured up a cup of hot tea. "Arnie. His head . . . how did . . . ? Arnie, he didn't have a *head*!"

"I know. Hush, now."

Arnie's calm voice soothed her; the tea helped too, and she was feeling slightly recovered by the time Donald and Saint arrived, carrying J.B. between them on a makeshift stretcher.

Vera helped Donald wash the mud off J.B. and get her to bed. "There's not much we can do," he told J.B., "except keep you warm, patch you up, and keep you quiet." She lay holding Donald tightly by the hand, staring up at him with an expression of trust and comfort. Now it was difficult even to imagine J.B. as Starfire, for with her face washed clean of makeup she looked about sixteen years old.

Arnie brought another cup of hot, sweet tea. "Drink this. It'll help."

Then the nurse arrived, disheveled and smelling of beer, but, confronting a patient, immediately all business. She wanted J.B. to take ten milligrams of Valium "and sleep the clock round."

J.B. refused strenuously. "I'm not taking any drugs."

"But you've had a dreadful shock, dear. What you've been through—"

"Leave me alone! I'm not giving my baby any drugs. I'm fine."

The nurse echoed, "Baby?"

"Sure you're fine," Donald reassured her. "You're tough. There aren't many people who could have done what you did tonight. Especially when they'd drunk all that ricea shit."

"I didn't *know*. I could kill that dumb kid." J.B. pleaded, "Will the baby be all right?"

"Of course it'll be all right. That stuff didn't have a chance to get past your stomach."

"But I fell."

"Babies are well packaged and well insulated. More than you think."

"Don't lie to me. Please."

"Have I ever?"

Tearful and childishly fretful: "Donald, make the baby be all right."

"Sure I will. But you have to help me. Keep quiet and go to sleep. Rest."

"Don't leave me alone."

"Of course I'll never leave you." Vera watched him smooth the hair off her forehead, lean over her, and kiss her while her fingers closed convulsively on his. She knew he would sit beside her for the rest of the night, holding her hand.

Saint said quietly, "Let's go."

*　　*　　*

Arnie waited for them outside. It was still raining hard, but he didn't seem to notice. His checkered shirt clung limply to his chest; his bandanna hung about his neck like a wet rag. "Is she okay?"

"So far."

He nodded. "Then I'll see you in the morning." He turned away toward the village.

Saint asked, "Where are you going?"

"Up to the church. They've taken him there, you know. I'm going to pray for his soul." Arnie's face was pale and set and strangely determined. "Of all the people I've ever known, that man's soul is the most damned. He needs all the prayers he can get."

"But Arnie," Vera blurted, "you're not a Catholic."

"Does it matter?"

Arnie set his shoulders resolutely under his sodden shirt and turned off up the rough track toward the church, where the candlelight trembled through the window apertures and Father Ignacio's ancient voice quavered through a mass for the dead.

"Well," Saint said, closing Vera's cabin door behind him, "here we are."

Vera nodded. "Here we are." She could think of nothing more to say. Reaction had set in; her body ached with exhaustion, but she knew she would never be able to rest, for a huge hot pressure had built up inside her and her eyes burned with unshed tears.

"I feel the same way you do," Saint said. He moved toward her and held out his arms. She leaned against him, resting her hot face into the warmth of his shoulder. He turned her face up to his and kissed her, at first gently, then with increasing violence, and she felt her own confusion and desperation flow through that kiss to merge with his own. "Oh, God, Vera," Saint muttered, "I need you." She barely felt the hardness of his fingers or the sharp pain as his teeth grazed her lip. Nor did she remember how, naked, they came together in her narrow bunk, where they fought and tore at each other like ferocious animals, the physical violence the only possible expression of emotion beyond pain. She abandoned herself to it all, her mind dark, until they fell unconscious in each other's arms to a background of rain and wind, their inert bodies pitching gently to the rhythm of the ocean swells.

She woke in the morning to a clear, washed dawn, and turning, found Saint's dark blue eyes fixed on hers. She felt astonishingly refreshed, renewed, and hopeful, as though something fearful inside her had been purged. Saint seemed to feel the same. He smiled. "What I told you last night in the cantina, Vera, I meant it, every word. I love you." He wriggled in the bunk until they were lying face-to-face. He traced the line of her lips. "I've always loved you. I was a terrible fool not to know it. Will you marry me?"

"Yes," Vera said.

Dreamily she felt the warmth of his breath on her skin as he kissed the hollow of her throat. She sighed.

"I want to make love to you in the light," Saint whispered. "We've never done that. We've got so much making up to do . . ."

Her body fitted his so well. She twined her legs around his hips, and despite the narrow bunk, it was easy and their movements flowed like dancing, just as they had done so long ago in her room in San Francisco. She held him tightly in her arms and studied him as though she had never seen him before, pore by pore, the veins on his closed eyelids, the tilt of his eyebrows, the almost blue sheen of his hair, the careful sculpture of his ears and the neat way they fitted to the side of his head. "I love you," Vera whispered. "I've always loved you. You know that."

He rolled her over and molded his body onto hers, his hands underneath her, cupping her breasts. "They fit my hands like they were made for them."

"They're so small now that I've lost weight."

"They're perfect."

She felt him enter her again. She whispered, "Don't ever stop."

Saint murmured against her ear, "How can I?" He moved his hands to her waist and drew her tightly back against him. She felt his warm belly against her bottom and knit her fingers into his. They rocked together with increasing violence. She heard his breathing grow ragged and heard his hoarse gasp: "Oh, Jesus, Vera . . ." He felt huge inside her as he gripped her by the shoulders and they fell forward onto the bunk and the world darkened and they spiraled away, fused together, somewhere far and still, and for a very long time.

Much later, floating on the edge of warm drowsiness, clasped in Saint's arms, Vera suddenly found herself thinking with pity of Royal Gutiérrez, forlorn without his goddess, padding lone and feral along the dripping jungle paths. She asked, "Will they catch him, d'you think?"

Saint seemed to know at once whom she meant. She felt him shake his head.

"No," he said. "They'll never catch him."

The following day Jason Brill was once again an efficient machine, his embarrassing lapse into humanity quite forgotten. He placed top-level calls to officials in Mexico City, proving that Victor Diamond's name had power even in death, for the formalities, inquiries, and reports that normally would occupy weeks were compressed into days and carried out with almost supernatural speed, until, wearing his now-so-appropriate black suit, Brill supervised the loading of Diamond's coffin into the Omega executive jet outside the terminal at Puerto Vallarta, his face registering as much emotion as if he were supervising the loading of a crate of oranges.

Vera herself, with Saint, Donald Wheeler, and J.B., declined the invitation to ride with him. Instead they traveled to Los Angeles by private charter plane, to be met at LAX by a driver with a nondescript station wagon, who trundled them around the terminal in evasive loops, finally dropping them unobserved by even the most alert news photographers at the National Car Rental parking lot.

Donald handed J.B. into the passenger seat of a mud-colored Toyota. She was wearing a green-and-white-striped cotton shirt from the Benetton shop in Puerto Vallarta, a blue denim skirt, a black-and-white bandanna over her hair, and a pair of huge sunglasses. She imagined she looked insignificant, a typical tourist. She was wrong. "Get in," Donald said, "quick, before someone sees you."

J.B. had seemingly made a miraculous recovery. As J.B. once again, Starfire was out of her life, never to return, and with Starfire gone, so was the aura of Victor Diamond. She had discarded another section of her past with the ease of a snake shedding its skin. "After all, I've had practice," she reminded Saint, leaning out the window to kiss him good-bye, "but I swear that this is the very last time. Now I'm going to Napa to grow grapes and have a baby." She looked radiant, the corners of her mouth curving into an irrepressible grin. Vera had never seen her look that way. "We're driving up Route One," she said, "taking it real easy, and staying in Big Sur for the night. Then we're going to Oak Crest and I'm never, never leaving again."

She didn't attend Diamond's repellently awesome funeral, although Saint and Vera did, for Saint found himself in the uneasy position of succeeding monarch.

The king is dead; long live the king.

He and Vera rode with David Zimmerman in a black limousine immediately following the hearse, leading a seemingly endless procession of other black limousines whose headlights cast parallel beams of jaundiced light through the midday murk.

Afterward Saint was presented with the casket containing Diamond's ashes, to be disposed of, at Diamond's instructions, upon the sands of Malibu outside his house, which now, according to his will, belonged to J.B., together with a very large sum of money.

J.B. had cried violently, "I don't want it. Do what you like with it. I'm never going there again."

She refused even to pick up her personal possessions. "I hate that house, and I don't want anything that's in it. It's all Starfire's stuff and she has nothing to do with me anymore—and I don't want Diamond's money either. It's tainted."

Saint pointed out, "Money's just money. It's only people that make it bad. If you don't want it, then let it do some good, like support your mother for the rest of her life in luxury. Start a foundation for orphans. You'll think of something."

A silence; then: "Well, there's Vangie," J.B. said slowly. "I think about her a lot. I'll start with her. At least I can make sure she'll always be comfortable. One day, I'd like to go and see her, even if she doesn't know who I am or if I'm even there."

Hamura had kept the Malibu house clean and ventilated, but, as though it were a sentient creature, it bore an unmistakable air of abandonment, as though it knew Victor Diamond would never return and now passed the days in limbo awaiting the imprint of a new occupant.

Vera, with Saint, David Zimmerman, and a lawyer whose name she would never remember, explored the house from top to bottom, from the immense bedroom to the blankness of the meditation room to the businesslike projection room below it. "There must be prints of Vangie Sellors' films," Saint said. "I'd like to run one, just to see."

David Zimmerman asked, "To see what?"

"Whether she really does look like J.B."

Zimmerman opened his eyes wide. "*Vangie?*"

Saint explained, "One reason why J.B. agreed to stay with Diamond in the first place was that she felt guilty. Vera and Arnie hadn't realized she looked so much like Vangie."

"How could we?" Vera asked. "We'd never even seen a photograph of her, let alone a film."

The lawyer looked restless and checked his watch.

Saint pursued, "Diamond accused J.B. of pulling a rotten, cheap trick to attract his attention."

"But that doesn't make any sense." Zimmerman was loading *Terry's Image* into the waiting projector and doused the lights. They sat in a row in their wide comfortable seats in darkness, their faces gray and grainy in the flickering light from the screen.

The film was terrible. The lawyer sighed impatiently and began, "You don't need to pay me to go to the movies, especially one like——"

But then, "There she is! That's her," Zimmerman said softly; "that's Vangie Sellors," and as they watched the girl's approach, swinging her body with lithe grace between the handholds of a subway car, they all forgot how bad the film was; they forgot everything.

Zimmerman froze the frame and Vangie Sellors stared at them from the screen in close-up, extraordinarily beautiful, but so much more than beautiful that she seemed to glow with inner light.

After a hushed moment Vera pointed out, "But she doesn't look anything *like* J.B."

"So why did he do it? Why did he pretend she did?"

It was a misty, gray day of seeping chill, but nobody wanted to stay in the house. The four of them sat around the table on the outside patio, where Hamura served tea in delicate little porcelain cups.

"He was lying from the beginning," Zimmerman explained, "when he told Arnie he wouldn't take on the *Starfire* project because Saint was in jail for drugs. The moment he heard about Spring Kentfield, he was intrigued; when he heard about the drugs, it gave him a great excuse to buy time while he found out more about Saint."

"What do you mean, a great excuse? Diamond hated drugs; everyone knew that."

Zimmerman said tonelessly, "Diamond didn't give a shit. It was all a pose, his war against drugs."

"Why?"

"We'll get to that in a minute."

Saint asked, "Couldn't he just have told Arnie he was interested and he'd let him know?"

"Sure he could. But that's not—wasn't—Diamond's style. It was a piece of fancy manipulation, what he did. Diamond's mind was Byzantine. He appeared to refuse the project on moral grounds, which automatically put you on the defensive. When he decided after all to take the project, you were all doubly grateful; you'd refuse him nothing. He had you just where he wanted you."

"But suppose Arnie *had* taken the project to somebody else?"

"It would have got nowhere. He'd have been forced to come back to Diamond in the end. Which was what happened when he decided he wanted *Right Exit Closed*."

Saint drew a long breath. "I wondered about that."

Zimmerman went on, "He pulled the same kind of play with J.B. He lied to her at Steven Romano's party; of course she looked nothing like Vangie, but he wanted her feeling guilty, intimidated, and defensive so he could crowd her into a corner she couldn't get out of. Even more so after he had her mother and sister in his pocket."

Vera objected, "She would have found out the minute she saw a picture of Vangie."

"But the chances are she wouldn't. Diamond would have made sure she never did. If she'd asked, he only had to say he had none because the memories were too painful. There were no prints of her films available because he'd acquired all of them. And remember, J.B. said he kept the projection room locked and she was never allowed there alone."

Vera fixed him with an accusing gray stare. "If you knew all this, I'd have thought you'd have done something."

"But I didn't know. Not all of it, not then. It wasn't until Donald

Wheeler came to see me, with all the stuff he'd put together—he'd compiled quite a dossier on Diamond, you know, going way back: separately, meaning nothing; together, quite damning. There were so many people who crossed Diamond and who died or disappeared or had terrible things happen to them. Like Fletcher McGraw—"

Vera said softly, "But Vangie O.D.'d. She did it to herself."

Zimmerman set down his little cup and gazed sightlessly at the steel woman holding her lamp. "Diamond did it to her. He put the acid into something she was drinking. She'd left him, you see; she'd run off with a young director, Lester Marshall, and he'd never forgive her for that. Diamond went after them to New Mexico, apparently to try to persuade her to come back to him. Instead, when she was tripped out of her skull, he drove her into the desert and told her if she looked at the sun long enough she'd see God. Then he drove away and left her there standing in the sand. Staring at the sun."

The languid waves sounded very loud in the utter silence.

"Afterward," Zimmerman added tiredly, "he declared his one-man drug crusade. It was just a cover-up."

Vera whispered, "That's truly bad. That's evil."

Saint asked, "How do you know all this?"

"Because Lester Marshall was my friend. He told me. He saw them drive away. He told me not to tell a living soul; he was dreadfully afraid of Diamond."

"I never heard of Lester Marshall."

"You wouldn't. He's dead. He's been dead for years. He walked over a cliff when he was stoned. He was always stoned. Nobody thought much about it. It was Donald Wheeler who fitted it into the pattern, although I always suspected . . ."

"That Diamond—"

"Arranged it. Probably." Then Zimmerman, head lowered, told the lamp, "I loved her, you know. I loved Vangie Sellors. But I didn't love her enough, I guess. I hadn't the guts to go after Diamond because I knew I'd be next. I was actually glad when Marshall died, because he was the only other person who knew. I lived through hell after that— which is where I hope Diamond is right now." In a voice suddenly harsh and utterly damning: "And I hope he rots there forever."

*　　*　　*

Vera and Saint stayed on after Zimmerman and the lawyer left.

Saint stood in the sand staring at the ocean, holding the urn containing Diamond's ashes. "I was ahead of him on the steps, you know. Gutiérrez would have hacked *my* head off if Diamond hadn't pushed me out of the way. He saved my life."

Behind him, Vera nodded in agreement. Whatever the motive, that fact was unquestionable—although she couldn't help but remember that howling cry echoing down the steps on the wind. *"Vangieee . . ."* She almost said: *Diamond was mad. He wanted you out of the way so he could kill her . . . his Vangie had betrayed him again, don't you see?* But instead she stood silently in the cool sand and watched Saint carry the urn down to the water line and stand there alone looking out to sea. She watched him dig a very deep hole, empty the ashes into it, and fill it in.

He squatted beside it a moment, his back turned to her, and from the rigid stillness of his body Vera suspected he might be crying.

On his return, "He loved the beach," Saint said shortly. "He's part of it, now." They looked at the spot where he had buried the ashes; it was already almost covered by the first swirling eddies of the floodtide.

And now they were living on another beach far to the north. They were spending time together alone, which was very precious.

Vera lay sprawled across a pillow on the floor of Saint's living room at Seadrift, not far north of San Francisco, alternately leafing through a pile of sketchbooks and staring out at the windswept gray ocean. She lay on the floor because they had no furniture except for two large pillows in a vivid blue-and-orange-paisley print, her drawing board, drafting table, the computer, and a bed. There either seemed to be no time to shop for furniture or, when there was time, so many better things to do.

The house was cleverly designed so that it looked much bigger than it really was. It was built of redwood, concrete, and glass, its ceiling contained skylights through which sunbeams angled in surprising directions, and its rooms surrounded a sheltered patio in which there was a small swimming pool. When the weather was warmer, they would spend a lot of time out there. Now, in early January, they spent lazy hours curled up beside the potbellied stove or took long windy hikes on the beach. Often, returning, Saint would grab Vera by the hand or sweep her up in his arms and carry her off to the bedroom, where they would roll together like puppies—or they might not make it to the bedroom, they might lie right here on the pillows in full view of anyone walking dogs or jogging on the beach. Not, Vera thought, that they would have noticed or cared if the whole world stood outside their windows.

Sometimes they didn't speak to each other for hours at a time, merely content with each other's company; other times they talked far into the night, making plans and changing them and making more plans.

Some would be realized and some wouldn't, but it didn't matter because they were together and had all the time in the world.

They didn't talk much about that last night in La Playita, and the case was closed now in any case. The decomposing body of Royal Gutiérrez had been discovered deep in one of the *barrancas*. It was impossible to make a definite identification, for the body had been badly mauled by animals and there wasn't a great deal left but bones.

Saint had said with conviction, "It wasn't him, of course."

"How do you know?"

"He knew that country like the back of his hand. The man they found was someone else, some traveling Indian, maybe, unlucky enough to be at the wrong place at a very wrong time."

"Should you say something?"

"Why? I can't prove a thing. And even if I could, I doubt anyone would do anything. The Mexicans are practical people, Vera; they needed a body; they found one. Everybody's happy."

"Good," Vera said. "Let's leave it that way."

"And let's talk about something else. Or not talk. Which do you want to do?"

"Not talk."

"I hoped you'd say that; come here." And, his mouth against her hair: "I love you, Vera Brown. . . ."

Vera smiled and adjusted the pillow under her chest, straining her eyes through the gathering murk, trying to see Saint, who had run off into the rain toward the Bolinas lagoon. The ocean was kicking up this afternoon, the surf was high, the crests blowing spume in the rising wind.

Saint loved this wild weather; he would return tousled and bright-eyed and his face would feel at once cold and fiery against her skin. For the moment he was nowhere in sight.

Vera turned to the last page of her final sketchbook from La Playita, to a drawing she had never shown anyone, especially Saint, and never would. A drawing she had had to make because the image was seared into her mind with a fierce white light, and only by releasing it onto paper could she come to terms with what she had seen and gain peace.

There. Victor Diamond's head lying on the steps, his wide, rain-soaked eyes staring upward in fading shock, surprise—and perhaps a touch of glad acceptance that it was all over.

It was the only portrait she had made of him in which he was not portrayed as monstrous. In this last drawing, dead, he looked human at last.

If circumstances had been different, what would Victor Diamond have been?

They would never know.

On impulse, she picked up another book and opened it at a marked page showing Saint, absorbed, working at the computer.

Glancing from face to face: Yes, Vera thought; oh yes.

The similarity was not obvious but if you knew *how* to look it was there all right, spelled out in body type and facial structure.

Appearances apart it was revealed in unconsciously similar movement and gesture, in parallels of talent, imagination, and taste, even in their mutual need for wide spaces, beaches, the ocean—and they both, Vera thought with a small inner smile, drove Jaguars.

Did Saint, deep in his bones, know?

She decided: Yes, he did, recalling the telltale tremors of his body while digging in the sand at Malibu. Then she wondered: Shall I give Diamond the benefit of the doubt? That last night on the steps, *was* he trying to murder Vangie—or was he in fact determined to save his only child?

She would never know.

She tore her last drawing of Victor Diamond from her book, ripped it into shreds, and dropped them into the potbellied stove, where they blackened and curled, flared brightly, then fell softly into ash.

Epilogue

1990

Saint and Vera were married the following September at the Oak Crest Winery in the Napa Valley. It was a small ceremony for close friends and family, with J.B. as the matron of honor and Arnie as Saint's best man for the second time.

Vera was three months pregnant. It was so far a joyful secret between them. Traditionally, Vera's mother ought to be the first to be told, "but it would just kill her if she thought we'd jumped the gun," Vera said. "I'll tell her in a month or so."

Saint had said dryly, "Then when it's born early, she'll think it's premature."

"Yes," Vera nodded in agreement, "exactly."

Saint had flown Mum, her sister Cynthia, and her new friend, Albert, a bookkeeper for the Harrogate County Council, out to California for the wedding.

Mum, still antagonistic in attitude toward Vera's adopted country, had mixed feelings about the trip and found the wedding itself downright outlandish. It wasn't in a church, they were married out-of-doors by a judge instead of a proper vicar, and nobody wore the right clothes. Instead of white lace, Vera wore a yellow-and-white dress with a fringed shawl and frills around the hips like a Gypsy, while Sloane (she refused to call him Saint), who could obviously afford better, wore a pair of baggy linen slacks and a jacket that looked too big for him, and it was no good Vera telling her it was supposed to look like that and it was designed by Giorgio Armani—whoever he was. The matron of honor, right after the service, spoiled the effect of her pretty pink cotton frock by strapping a husky blond-haired baby onto her front in a little sling. The only person who, in Mum's opinion, was dressed suitably for a wedding, apart from herself, Cynthia, and dear Albert, of course, was the fat Mexican gentleman in the gray suit—although here again the effect was ruined by his lady friend, who didn't speak English, wore too much makeup, and whose magenta satin dress was too tight and showed too much bosom.

"It's not my idea of a wedding," Mum complained, missing the dainty little cucumber or salmon-paste sandwiches, confronted instead by a whole barbecued sheep, hams, huge platters of salads, breads, and fruit. With hazy logic she told herself she might have expected something of the sort from Donald Wheeler—although you had to hand it to him: he was certainly a generous host.

"Oh, I shouldn't," Mum protested as he approached her yet again with the champagne bottle, but she was too late putting her hand over her glass. If she didn't watch out, especially with this heat, she would be a bit tiddly before she knew it, and poor Albert wasn't supposed to drink—"He has a *liver*," Mum had told Vera proudly. "I have to watch him every second."

"That poor man," Donald had said. "She'll nuture him to death."

"Of course," Vera said, "but won't they have fun while she does it."

"It's wonderful," observed Aunt Cynthia, in hot-pink linen that exactly matched her streaming face. "She met him on the chronic medical ward when she was doing her hospital visiting. He has a council house with a nice bit of garden and grows prize dahlias. You know, dear, it's a mercy on all of us, you getting married. Soon as she knew she could never really be a mum to you again, she turned right around and took up with Albert. They might even make a match of it one of these days."

Arnie had driven up from San Francisco with his new friend, Sean Kelly. Sean was a lawyer with the Catholic Archdiocese, a thin-faced academic with a gentle voice and obviously failing health. He looked pale, exhausted, and dazzled in the hard gold afternoon light, rubbing his eyes as if they hurt. Arnie was protective of him, made sure he sat in the shade, and brought him tempting things to eat and drink, although Sean could manage only a few grapes. Arnie's days of stardom were over. He was once again Arnie Blessing, now studying for the lay priesthood. He had created a mild sensation by proclaiming his homosexuality on Gay Freedom Day, but the outcry hadn't been nearly as negative as he had feared, and just as Saint had predicted, he had gained a million new supporters in place of the few he might have lost. He looked very happy, "and I feel I'm really being put to use," he confided to Vera, "on every level. If only I'd done this long ago. It makes me so mad, thinking about the wasted time."

The support of the brotherhood he had entered had bolstered his self-esteem much as Round Mountain had done; the AIDS counseling he was doing made him feel needed; loving and taking care of Sean had given his life new focus. "I'm lucky," Arnie said with sincerity. "God, I'm lucky." Then, to Vera's amazement: "The ironic thing is, if it hadn't been for Victor Diamond, I might never have done it."

Vera echoed, "For *Diamond?*"

Arnie smiled ruefully. "He said some things to me that last night in La Playita which made me so angry and so disgusted and humiliated, I didn't know what to do. I didn't think anyone could say something like that to another human being. I literally thought I'd die of it. Or go mad. But I didn't. And when the anger had cooled, all I felt was just terribly sorry for Diamond, though thank God he never knew—he'd have killed me."

"Did you pray for him?"

"Of course. And you know, watching Father Ignacio, even though he was old and doddering and a bit drunk, it seemed to me he was doing his very best in the only way he could, and really, what else matters? Anyway, I decided it was idiotic to go on being Arnie Blaize. So here I am." He gave a wry shrug. "Say hello to Brother Arnold. By the way, Vera," with a shy smile, "is the baby a secret?"

Vera looked up, startled. Then nodded with a faint blush. "I didn't think Saint had told anybody."

"He didn't have to."

"You mean—"

"I mean, you look different, Vera. I've never seen you look quite so radiant. And then," blushing faintly, "your dress kind of gives it away too."

Vera touched herself at the waistline. "But the dress is supposed to be—concealing. The frill's supposed to lead the eye away from the stomach. At least," she declared defensively, "that's what the girl said in the store."

Eyeing Vera's solid middle, "She was obviously on commission." Arnie shook his head. "You need me, Vera. You don't know diddly-squat about clothes. But why keep it a secret? Why not tell everyone? I would."

Vera sighed. "Because we thought it would be a bit much for Mum, you know, on top of everything else."

"I'd tell her. She might surprise you. Anyway," Arnie raised his glass of iced tea, "congratulations to you both. When's it due?"

"They said March 21."

Arnie looked sad. "Sean may be gone by then. The AZT has helped, but he only has a few more months." He added wistfully, "It would be wonderful if Sean were still here to see the baby."

Javier Gallegos cried, "Congratulations, Santo. You took my advice after all, and you look a happy man. I was right, yes? You mated with the lioness, and soon you'll see your first cub."

Glad they were speaking in Spanish, Saint demanded, "How do you *know*? Did Vera tell you?"

"She didn't have to. I have eyes in my head."

"It's not official yet."

"Don't be ridiculous. It exists. How can it not be official . . . ?" But Gallegos' attention had wandered. "Santo!" he cried urgently, gripping Saint by the arm. "Who is *that*? Introduce me!" Turning, Saint watched a gaudy redhead approaching on the arm of a stout elderly man.

"So glad you could make it, Mel." J.B. greeted the couple with mild coolness. She told Saint and Gallegos, "I'd like you to meet my sister and brother-in-law, Melrose and Herman Schwartz."

Gallegos grabbed Melrose by both hands. "*Mucho gusto!*" he cried with enthusiasm. "What a great pleasure."

Melrose never knew just how close she came to losing it all, and by now had almost forgotten about her indiscretion with Whitney Davidson and the ensuing uproar. By now she regarded the whole *National Enquirer* venture as completely justified. Under the circumstances, she had been unfairly treated, "and after all, one has to take care of oneself." She had spent the large sum of money she was paid on a new resort wardrobe and a Caribbean cruise, during which she had landed Herman. It had been so easy, she now suspected she could have done much better if only she had waited. Still, she cautioned herself, one shouldn't look a gift horse in the mouth.

Herman Schwartz, founder of a chain of ladies' shoe stores throughout the eleven Western states and Hawaii, had not only made an honest woman of Melrose but also provided her with a mansion, furs, and the longed-for Mercedes. He had also written a will granting her upon his death an estate of four million dollars, thereby enraging his other two ex-wives and their sundry offspring. All Melrose had to do now was wait it out. It was her turn in the sun . . . and just look at poor Jo-Beth now!

J.B. observed dryly, "I guess you landed on your feet after all, Mel."

"Yeah. Some people are born survivors." Melrose sighed with satisfaction at her own cleverness and smoothed the ruched green silk over her rounded hips. She offered generously, "Anything I can do for you, sugar, you just let me know. I don't like to see you stuck out here on a farm with a kid and all. You need a lawyer, I got a real good one. A real flesh ripper."

"Thanks."

"I mean, you must be missing it all. This sure isn't L.A."

Vera asked, "Do you miss Starfire?"

"Starfire?" J.B. stood with squarely planted feet, fingers linked under her baby's rounded bottom, looking as though she almost didn't remember who Starfire had been. Then she shook her head. "She seems a very long time ago. And I don't need her anymore."

Vera nodded. "And you're certainly busy."

"Oh, yes. We added some acreage, and we're experimenting with some new varietal grafts. The Bardeluccis are making me a partner, you know." J.B. smiled, looking very contented and very sure of who she was. "I'm studying like crazy. There's so much to learn. I'm going to U.C. Davis to do a crash viticulture and enology course as soon as Anna's weaned."

"Enology?"

"The science of wine making. So you see, with Donald and Anna and everything else, I don't have much time to think about Starfire at all." She extricated the baby, a rounded parcel with plump, busily waving hands, and passed her to Vera. "Want to hold her?"

Vera took Anna with stiff-armed awkwardness. The baby gave a small squawk of protest. "I guess I'm doing something wrong."

"Then you'd better practice a bit," J.B. advised matter-of-factly. Adding, "Did you and Saint choose a name yet?"

Aunt Gloria was wearing the identical suit in which she had attended Saint's previous wedding, "but I must say, dear," she congratulated him, "I like this one so much better."

"Thank you, Aunt Glo. I like it a lot better myself."

"You're looking well. I'm so glad you're happy. And you're busy too, I hear."

"Real busy." Saint was commuting regularly to Omega, and recently he and Vera had entered the computer software business, designing a game called "The Sorcerer's Curse." It looked as if this new venture would be even more successful than the comic books.

"She's so clever, isn't she? What a pretty dress. Pregnancy certainly suits her." And at Saint's look of surprise: "Why, yes, dear. Of course I know. So does everybody else, I should think."

Relentlessly youthful in a cornflower-blue dress in much the same style as Vera's, Spring Kentfield kissed the air in the vicinity of her co-mother-in-law's cheek, then announced with satisfaction, "I do think Vera might have chosen a more becoming gown. I told her yellow would make her look sallow . . ."

Mum had finished her fourth glass of champagne. "Nonsense," she responded with spirit. "She looks simply blooming."

". . . and particularly," Spring added, "now that she's putting on weight again."

"Well, so she should, she's eating for two. I'm sure," Mum riposted with deadly aim, "you can't *wait* to see your first grandchild!"

Saint said, "Vera, you'd better give that baby back. We have to cut the cake before the frosting melts."

As they crossed the lawn toward the oak grove where a massive four-tier cake loomed with sugar bride-and-groom figures on top, "J.B. knows," Vera said. "She asked me what we were going to call the baby."

Saint said, "Everybody knows. Even Aunt Gloria."

"At least Mum doesn't."

They took up their position, hands linked over the long knife with its ornate handle of antique Italian silver.

Flashbulbs exploded around them as they brought the blade down with slow ceremony.

Saint muttered, "Sure she does."

"Smile!" cried Donald, crouching with the camera. "Hold it!"

They smiled.

Vera hissed through her teeth, "What do you mean? How could she?"

"I heard her tell my mother that you're eating for two."

"Oh, Saint! Did she really? That's awful."

"What's more, she told Mother"—Saint began to shake with uncontrollable laughter—"that she was sure she couldn't wait to see her first grandchild. You should have seen Spring's face."

Vera let out a strangled whoop of glee. Her hand clenched on the knife and she bore down much too hard.

"You know, your mum's a tougher old bird than you think. I . . . Hey watch it! You don't want to chop right through the base."

But it was too late.

The towering cake listed forward, off balance.

Vera bit back her laughter and gazed at it in horror. "Well, don't just stand there," she cried, "do something!" She leapt forward as Saint lunged for the cake with outstretched arms. His foot caught the table leg, he and Vera collided, the little bride and groom toppled from the top tier, and to a mingled background of applause and shrieks of dismay, the edifice began an inexorable slide to the ground.

Donald Wheeler recorded the whole disaster on film.

Click! Flash!

Vera sat on the grass, most of the largest tier in her lap. "Well," she exclaimed, "well, bloody hell!" Then started to laugh again. She couldn't help it.

"Accidents happen." Saint sat down beside her, scooped a handful of frosting from her forehead, and licked it. "Don't worry. It tastes just fine."

"Of course it does," Anna Bardelucci Wheeler stated pragmatically, "and we can save quite a lot, you know. The bottom layer didn't even touch the ground."

As she hurried off to find paper plates, Vera observed, "They shouldn't have called the baby Anna. It's too confusing."

"You're right. If it's a girl, let's not call her Vera. Or Louise, after your mother."

Vera added, "Or Spring."

"God forbid. And if it's a boy," Saint said with a chuckle, "we won't call him Sloane St. John."

"Well," Vera said cheerfully, "that's a start, isn't it?"

"And you know the best thing of all?" Saint soaked a napkin in champagne, leaned forward, and wiped more frosting from Vera's nose. He announced with heartfelt satisfaction, "Nobody will *ever* call the kid Junior!"

Acknowledgments

I would like to thank the following people most sincerely for all their support, generosity and expert advice during the writing of this book: Gustavo Bravo; Stuart Dodds, Editor/General Manager, Chronicle Features, San Francisco; Walter and Jo Landor; Jeremy Larner and Frank Pierson for sharing Hollywood insights; Lucille Meyer of Rustridge Ranch and Winery; Chuck Wood, Assistant District Attorney, San Francisco, for legal background material; and especially Adrian Ruyle, creator of the cartoon cult classic "Rat."

My warmest thanks also to my co-members of the Saturday Group: Lucy Diggs, Caroline Fairless, Cary James, Patrick Jamieson, Kermit Sheets, Elizabeth Stewart, Katie Supinski, Marilyn Wallace and most particularly to Joan Cupples, expert creator of titles.